P9-AFF-288

THE PRINCE
&
THE COYOTE

THE PRINCE

&

THE COYOTE

DAVID BOWLES

ILLUSTRATED BY
AMANDA MIJANGOS

LQ

MONTCLAIR | AMSTERDAM | HOBOKEN

This is an Arthur A. Levine book

Published by Levine Querido

LEVINE QUERIDO

www.levinequerido.com · info@levinequerido.com

Levine Querido is distributed by Chronicle Books, LLC

Library of Congress Control Number: 2022931605

ISBN 978-1-64614-177-7

Printed and bound in China

Published in September 2023

First Printing

For my grandson, Daibhidh Nicancoyotl "Coyo" Navarro.
Nimitztlazohtla, noxhuiuhtziné.

HOUSE OF ACAMAPICHTLI
ROYAL FAMILY OF TENOCHTITLAN

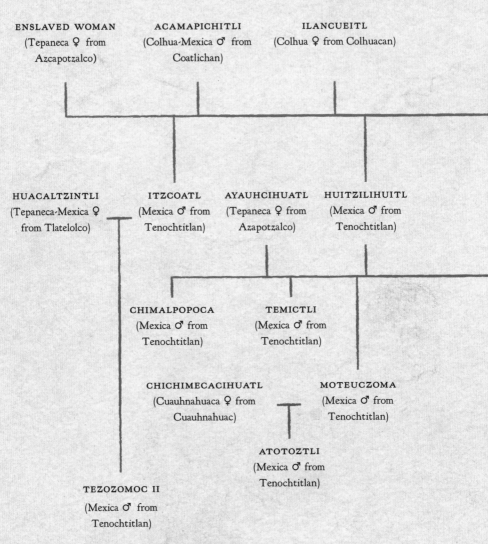

ENSLAVED WOMAN
(Tepaneca ♀ from
Azcapotzalco)

ACAMAPICHITLI
(Colhua-Mexica ♂ from
Coatlichan)

ILANCUEITL
(Colhua ♀ from Colhuacan)

HUACALTZINTLI
(Tepaneca-Mexica ♀
from Tlatelolco)

ITZCOATL
(Mexica ♂ from
Tenochtitlan)

AYAUHCIHUATL
(Tepaneca ♀ from
Azapotzalco)

HUITZILIHUITL
(Mexica ♂ from
Tenochtitlan)

CHIMALPOPOCA
(Mexica ♂ from
Tenochtitlan)

TEMICTLI
(Mexica ♂ from
Tenochtitlan)

CHICHIMECACIHUATL
(Cuauhnahuaca ♀ from
Cuauhnahuac)

MOTEUCZOMA
(Mexica ♂ from
Tenochtitlan)

ATOTOZTLI
(Mexica ♂ from
Tenochtitlan)

TEZOZOMOC II
(Mexica ♂ from
Tenochtitlan)

KEY

♂ - Man

♀ - Woman

⚥ - Xochihuah or Patlacheh (Two-spirit/Non-binary/Trans)

Italics - Fictional or Fictionalized character

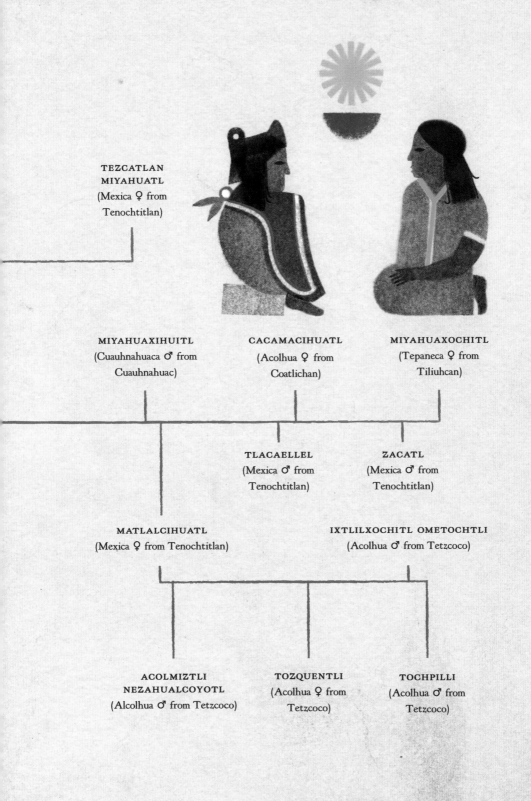

TEZCATLAN
MIYAHUATL
(Mexica ♀ from
Tenochtitlan)

MIYAHUAXIHUITL
(Cuauhnahuaca ♂ from
Cuauhnahuac)

CACAMACIHUATL
(Acolhua ♀ from
Coatlichan)

MIYAHUAXOCHITL
(Tepaneca ♀ from
Tiliuhcan)

TLACAELLEL
(Mexica ♂ from
Tenochtitlan)

ZACATL
(Mexica ♂ from
Tenochtitlan)

MATLALCIHUATL
(Mexica ♀ from Tenochtitlan)

IXTLILXOCHITL OMETOCHTLI
(Acolhua ♂ from Tetzcoco)

ACOLMIZTLI
NEZAHUALCOYOTL
(Alcolhua ♂ from Tetzcoco)

TOZQUENTLI
(Acolhua ♀ from
Tetzcoco)

TOCHPILLI
(Acolhua ♂ from
Tetzcoco)

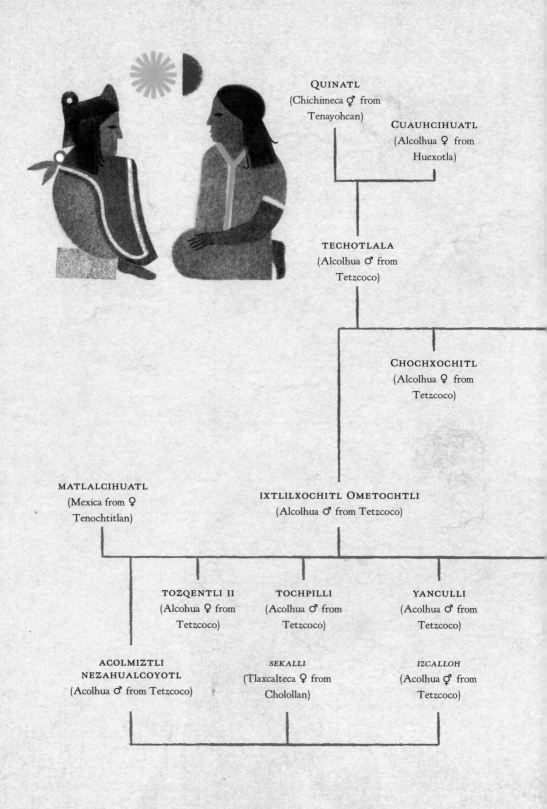

QUINATL
(Chichimeca ♂ from
Tenayohcan)

CUAUHCIHUATL
(Alcolhua ♀ from
Huexotla)

TECHOTLALA
(Alcolhua ♂ from
Tetzcoco)

CHOCHXOCHITL
(Alcolhua ♀ from
Tetzcoco)

MATLALCIHUATL
(Mexica from ♀
Tenochtitlan)

IXTLILXOCHITL OMETOCHTLI
(Alcolhua ♂ from Tetzcoco)

TOZQENTLI II
(Alcohua ♀ from
Tetzcoco)

TOCHPILLI
(Acolhua ♂ from
Tetzcoco)

YANCULLI
(Acolhua ♂ from
Tetzcoco)

ACOLMIZTLI
NEZAHUALCOYOTL
(Acolhua ♂ from Tetzcoco)

SEKALLI
(Tlaxcalteca ♀ from
Cholollan)

IZCALLOH
(Acolhua ⚥ from
Tetzcoco)

HOUSE OF QUINATZIN
ROYAL FAMILY OF TETZCOCO

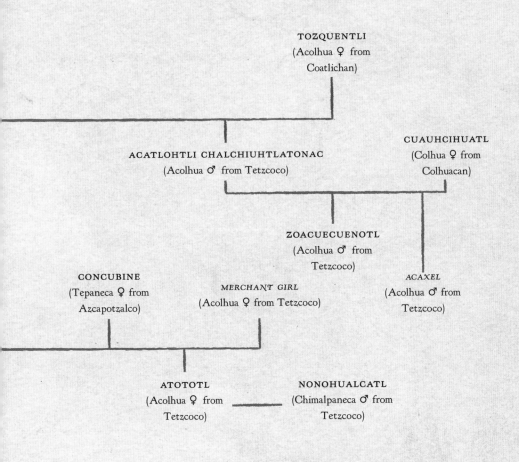

TOZQUENTLI
(Acolhua ♀ from
Coatlichan)

ACATLOHTLI CHALCHIUHTLATONAC
(Acolhua ♂ from Tetzcoco)

CUAUHCIHUATL
(Colhua ♀ from
Colhuacan)

ZOACUECUENOTL
(Acolhua ♂ from
Tetzcoco)

CONCUBINE
(Tepaneca ♀ from
Azcapotzalco)

MERCHANT GIRL
(Acolhua ♀ from Tetzcoco)

ACAXEL
(Acolhua ♂ from
Tetzcoco)

ATOTOTL
(Acolhua ♀ from
Tetzcoco)

NONOHUALCATL
(Chimalpaneca ♂ from
Tetzcoco)

KEY

♂ - Man

♀ - Woman

⚥ - Xochihuah or Patlacheh (Two-spirit/Non-binary/Trans)

Italics - Fictional or Fictionalized character

TEPANECAPAN

LAKE TZOMPANCO

LAKE XALTOCAN

Tepotzotlan

Teotihuacan

Tenayohcan

MOON LAKE

Azcapotzalco

Tetzcoco

Tlacopan

Huexotla

Tlatelolco

Coatlichan

Tenochtitlan

Chimalhuacan

Chapoltepec

Mixcoac

Coyoacan

IZTAPAYOCAN HILL

Colhuacan

LAKE XOCHIMILCO

LAKE CHALCO

Xochimilco

Chalco City

Tlalmanalco

CHALCA
CONFEDERATION

ANAHUAC

& THE
EASTERN HIGHLANDS

ACOLHUACAN

TLAXCALLAN

Tlaloc

Tlaxcallan City

Iztaccihuatl

Huexotzinco

Amaquemehcan

Cholollan

Polok's Farm

Popocatepetl

NOTE ON NAMES
OF PEOPLE AND PLACES

Most of the unfamiliar names you will encounter in this book are from the Nahuatl language. Here is a guide to help you pronounce them.

Vowels
a—as in "father"
e—as in "bet"
i—as in "police"
o—as in Spanish "no" (without the lip-rounding of English "o" sounds)

Diphthongs (vowel blends)
hua—like the "wa" in "water"
hue—like the "whe" in "where"
hui—like "wei" in "weird"

Consonants
c—like "k" before "a," "o" and "u"; like "s" before "e" and "i."
h—silent before vowels; a glottal stop like the middle sound of "kitten" after vowels.
l—as in "like"
m—as in "moon"
n—as in "now"
p—as in "pet"
t—as in "ten"
x—like "sh" in "shoe"
y—as in "yes"
z—like "s" in "see"

Digraphs (two letters always written together)
ch—as in "check"
cu/uc—"kw" as in "queen"
hu/uh—like "w" in "we"
qu—like "k" in "key"
tl—a sound that doesn't exist in English, a blend of "t" and "l." It's
  okay just to pronounce this like a "t" at the end of words (or even
  like the "ttle" in "bottle").
tz—like the "ts" in "cats"

Note also that all Nahuatl words are stressed on the next-to-the-last syllable:
Nezahualcoyotl—ne/sa/hual/CO/yotl
Tetzcoco—tetz/CO/co
Tezcatlipoca—tez/ca/tli/PO/ca
Sekalli—se/KAL/li
Quetzalcoatl—que/tzal/CO/atl
Yancuilli—yan/CUIL/li

At the back of this book, we've also included a "Guide to Unfamiliar
Concepts" that you can use as a reference to help clarify many of the
Nahuatl terms.

PROLOGUE

T HE PROCESSION BEGINS at the palace, wending its colorful way through the streets of Tetzcoco like the tail of the Feathered Serpent himself, elite troops arrayed behind the vanguard of musicians and ministers. Mother sits straight and regal beside me on our litter, smiling with benevolence at her adoptive city. The widening spiral of our journey takes us through all six of the boroughs, each with its particular variation on the typical architecture of our region:

Public steam baths and shrines, brick cubes teeming with people, steam, incense. Working-class houses, clustered around shared patios, echoing with the shouts of children, the yips of dogs, the cackling of turkeys. Merchant estates, guarded warehouses burgeoning with precious goods. Aristocrat mansions, white stone walls sprawling silent in the shade of cypress trees.

The streets are packed with citizens, joyful at the prospect of peace after so many years of battle and loss. Some shout praise for the Queen Consort, but the majority chant my name.

A-col-miz-tli! A-col-miz-tli!

It's hard to describe the humble love that fills my chest at the sound. I am the Crown Prince; one day I will rule over this happy throng. Though I can never be one of them—though luxury and privilege are my birthright—I have learned from my father the king that my job will be to protect them, to work to make their lives better, and to provide culture and stability.

And most of all, to defend the hybrid heritage of our people: the Acolhua Way.

It is a huge responsibility, but one I look forward to with relish. To spend my days defending and sharing knowledge, learning and creating beautiful things, improving the lot of my fellow human beings—what else could I possibly desire? Heaven's blessings shower down on me like flower petals.

Two faces appear amid a cluster of aristocrats in the Chimalpaneca borough to shake my joy for a moment: Atototl, my half-sister, and her husband, Lord Nonohualcatl. Though they nod in deference, I see their smiles shift as I turn away.

Their sneers snag at my thoughts, like a sour note in the midst of a lovely melody.

We make our way past the municipal gardens and zoo, over the river, and into the sacred precinct. My gaze sweeps up the steps of the Pyramid of Duality, towering over the city like a symbolic mountain that brings us closer to heaven.

I think of my public dedication upon its summit two years ago, my solemn consecration as Crown Prince of Tetzcoco. As I knelt there, my father—sturdy as a ceiba, tall and imposing—placed the coronet upon my brow.

"Acolmiztli," he said, "My forelock and fingernail, my flesh and blood. In time you will sit upon my throne."

Not until today, however, has the reality of royal succession truly sunken in.

I will be these people's king.

Thankfully, that day lies far in the future. My father is healthy and strong. Undefeated. So why this uneasiness in my heart?

It's my half-sister's wry smile. I doubt her loyalty.

I try to dispel my worry with my favorite pastime: imagining all that I will build around me when I am king. New temples soaring up from the earth, a center for music and literature, better drainage systems for the commoners, a royal financing of repairs to older homes so that commoners can more comfortably fulfill their duty to gods and king.

As we turn to make our final approach to the southern gate, the litter dips unexpectedly at one corner. I reach out to steady my star-tled mother, who recovers with her usual elegance and straightens the coronet upon my brow in turn.

I cast my eyes at the guards escorting our litter. Father has entrusted that role to the youth captains of the calmecac, . . . includ-ing my bastard older half-brother Yancuilli. He returns my look with a defiant smirk.

My chest tightens. I can't help but be suspicious of my rivals' grins. My conniving half-sister or cruel half-brother may decide to arrange my death. They resent my title. They despise being at the margins of power. And there are factions in this city that—dissatisfied with the war my father triggered fourteen years ago—might use them to legitimize a coup, . . . which would begin with my assassination.

It's the sort of possibility that all princes face, everywhere. The palace is often more dangerous than the battlefield. Alliances shift. Jealousies grow. Only one prince can become king at a time, after all.

Being so close to that ultimate power is intoxicating. It's no surprise royal families disintegrate into factions bent on betrayal and assassination attempts.

"Ignore him," Mother whispers.

I realize that I have been staring at Yancuilli. I turn to face the Queen Consort, who continues waving without dropping the veneer of her smile.

"I would if he were the only one. However—"

My words are cut off by the sound of conch trumpets to announce our arrival at the gate of the city. We are greeted with bows and salutes from my uncles Acatlohtli and Coyohuah, as well as other leaders of our army and community, gathered there to usher in a new era of peace.

The porters set the litter down, gently this time. Attendants rush forward to help Mother and me descend.

Through the arch of the gate we see two clusters of men approaching along the southern road, flanked to the east by fields of maize, glittering gold in the morning light. On the right strides my father, the king of Tetzcoco, accompanied by his prime minister, his brother General Acatlohtzin, and his personal guard. To his left comes a similar group led by my maternal grandfather, the king of Tenochtitlan, vassal of the Tepaneca Empire that has waged war on us for fifteen years.

The two kings exchange friendly looks as they walk, laughing at each other's jests. They have just signed one of the most important treaties of our times. I should rejoice to see them so relaxed.

Instead, my stomach feels tightened into knots.

Beside me, Mother sighs, content. Her eyes glitter with happy tears. "Long have I prayed for this moment. Reunited with my father. Watching three generations of my family's men standing together in harmony."

I reach out and take her hand in mine. She squeezes it in return.

"You deserve this happiness and peace, Mother."

As if prompted by my words, the corn shudders with movement.

Hundreds of Mexica warriors explode from their hiding place amid the stalks, weapons held high as they descend upon my father's party. His brother and personal guard find themselves engaged in a vicious fight, trying to keep the enemy from the king of Tetzcoco.

But my father is one of the greatest warriors in Acolhuacan. He spins away from the attackers and seizes his father-in-law, his ceremonial sword at the man's neck.

"No!" Mother cries, bolting toward the gate, swept along with the battalion of elite warriors that have accompanied our procession and who now rush to help protect king and city. But her attendants stop her, clinging and pleading.

Our soldiers enter the fray alongside the king's guard, clashing with the traitorous Mexica as Father continues to force Grandfather forward, toward the city. But the king of Mexico-Tenochtitlan manages to slip free, seizing an obsidian sword from a fallen warrior. It is a big two-handed weapon, its wooden body the length and shape of an oar, with black razors along the edges of the paddle that glint deadly in the sunlight.

The two men square off, circling each other, ignoring the battle around them as they prepare to duel.

My heart is thundering wildly. I would hurry to Father's side, but I would be dead in moments if I stepped beyond these walls.

I'm no fighter. My martial arts are mediocre at best.

Movement to my right. I flick my eyes over to see Yancuilli, inching toward me, sword in hand. I realize I'm unsafe even inside the city.

My half-brother advances, a grin splitting his blunt features. The muscles of his bare chest and abdomen tighten as if preparing for attack. The topknot that crowns his head reminds me that he has actually been in battle, and captured an enemy soldier or two.

A screech pierces the din. Overhead, a owl wings its way over the city.

Harbinger of death.

But before Yancuilli can attempt anything, Uncle Coyohuah throws an arm around his shoulder and pulls him to me faster. My father's brother-in-law is unarmed, but his bright regalia and authoritative voice are as good as any shield or weapon.

"Good thinking, Yancuilli," Coyohuah says, giving me a sidelong glance of warning. "We must protect the Crown Prince from the Mexica, no matter the cost. Guard his left flank. Hand me your dagger, and I shall cover his right."

The bastard mutters a curse as he complies.

My gaze returns to the patch of road right outside the gate. Father and Grandfather are slamming their weapons into each other's shields, each attempting to wear the other down. But the weight of the weapon Grandfather has chosen wears *him* down. I can see his muscles straining with every blow.

Then, Grandfather's shield cracks. He falls to his knees.

"Yield!" howls Father, lifting his sword to strike.

"Never!" spits the king of Mexico-Tenochtitlan. "Long live Emperor Tezozomoc!"

Pulling a dagger from his belt, he buries it in Father's thigh.

The sword swings in a downward arc, the obsidian razors at its edges sliding along Grandfather's defiant throat.

A spray of blood spatters Acolhua soil and the king who protects it.

And Grandfather's body goes sprawling lifeless in the dust.

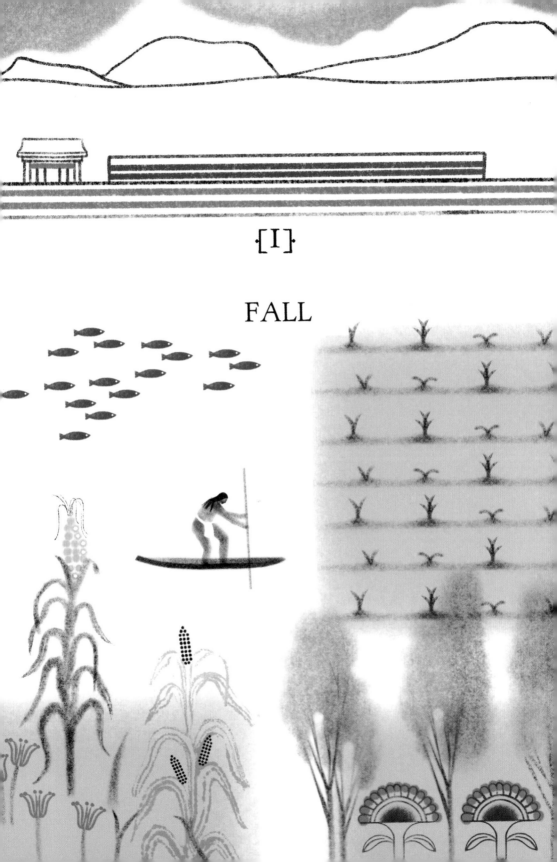

·{I}·

FALL

{1} TRUCE

SIX MONTHS LATER, I find myself overwhelmed by exams.

    I am just weeks from my sixteenth birthday, when I will be admitted at last to the calmecac. Of all the schools in Tetzcoco, it is the most elite, open only to noble teens and those few commoners who excel in skill or knowledge well above others of their social class.

As crown prince, I *must* attend. But I still have to take the exams—and each of my private tutors has to give me a pass. If I am unsuccessful, and the king approves my entrance to the calmecac nonetheless, my name will be stained ... as will that of the entire House of Quinatzin, royal family of Tetzcoco.

I have no trouble admitting that I am ... brilliant. In almost everything I choose to attempt. These last few days I have been cloistered away with Huitzilihuitl, my father's chief counselor and my principal tutor. Eyes impassive beneath his bushy white eyebrows, he has tested me in math, engineering, and large-scale military strategy. I assumed I would be questioned by lovely Izcalloh when it came to history, philosophy, and courtly etiquette. But no, the king's chief counselor even took it upon himself to quiz me in *those* areas, too.

Begrudgingly, he then informed me of my perfect scores in every field.

Today, however, I stand before Itzcuani, commander of the royal guard. The humorless, stony man has been my instructor of martial arts and weaponry since I was twelve. Now he puts me through my paces as I demonstrate my fighting form.

"You are like a young boy," he scoffs as I wipe sweat from my brow. "You simply mimic the moves of men. There is no power, no *will* behind your attacks. Here."

He tosses a wooden sword at me. I catch it deftly. That much I can do.

"Strike me, Acolmiztli. If you can."

Tightening my grip on the pommel, I look his solid form up and down before moving toward him and swinging.

He steps aside and slaps me in the back of my head, which begins to throb painfully.

"Again."

I fail once more to land a blow. This time Itzcuani punches me in the shoulder. My whole arm goes numb.

"Again. You will not enter the calmecac until your weapon strikes my flesh."

"Crown Prince Acomiztli?"

Huitzilihuitl has entered the sparring chamber. I have never been happier in my life to see his old white head and pious features.

"Yes, Chief Counselor?" I respond.

"The king requests your presence."

As I return the wooden sword to the weapons rack, Itzcuani rasps, "We will resume your testing soon. Get yourself ready. Your future depends upon it."

Soon I am standing beside my father in the palace strategy room. A large map has been painted onto the floor. It is Anahuac, the vast highland plateau—ringed by mountains, with a chain of broad lakes at its heart—where we Acolhua people live alongside enemies and allies.

Fourteen cities spread in a crescent to the east of the water, each with a population of between ten and fifty thousand residents, counting rural settlements and farms. A quarter of those individuals are able-bodied men trained for combat. The king of each community has primary authority over his troops, but as part of the confederation, they have each agreed to call them to arms in times of war and place them under the command of the Acolhua Overlord.

In short, my father can deploy one hundred and fifty *thousand* warriors when the need arises. And the need has arisen—for at least six months of every year for more than a decade.

Right now, the Acolhua Overlord is moving stone representations of troops and ships with a long pole, explaining the most recent developments.

"The irony, Acolmiztli," he says, stroking his graying goatee, "is that the Mexica's betrayal brought a sort of forced peace. After your grandfather's death, they retreated for mourning and then began debating who would succeed their king. Meanwhile . . . well, tell me what you see."

I consider the map. The biggest body of water, right at the center, is Moon Lake. Tetzcoco stands near the marshes of its eastern shore. Close to its southwestern extreme, the island of Mexico, where the Mexica live in their twin cities of Tenochtitlan and Tlatelolco. Beyond them, from the western shore to the slopes of the western mountains, lies Tepanecapan.

The Empire.

Our mortal enemies.

Taking stock of the troops that father has ranged around the imperial capital of Apotzalco, I clear my throat.

"You have taken advantage of the Mexica's absence. Sent troops over Moon Lake to lay siege to the capital."

"Correct. Eighty-thousand men, more than half the warriors in Acholhuacan. Yet it was not easy. Many citizens here and throughout the fourteen cities were quite upset at the failure of the peace talks."

I narrow my eyes. "That was hardly your fault, sire. My *grandfather* betrayed you. Neither the Mexica nor their puppetmaster the Emperor had any intention of actually ending this war peacefully."

"Indeed. But many commoners can't appreciate those niceties. Others simply allow themselves to be swayed by rumors and lies, spread by my political rivals and the Emperor's spies. So that is why I had to shore up my support, especially in Coatlichan."

Coatlichan is ruled by Paintzin, my father's maternal uncle. Beyond culture and homeland, our cities are bound by family ties, albeit tenuous ones. Perhaps that king has been unable to resist the strain of imperial temptation. Realization dawns in my mind.

"Ah, that's why you put that city's crown prince in command of your invading force."

"In part, yes. Lord Tochinteuctli is also a formidable warrior who caught Emperor Tezozomoc unawares, distracted by his attempts to shape the outcome of the succession deliberations in Tenochtitlan. Now the crown prince's second-in-command—your cousin Zoacuecuenotl—has beaten back every attempt by other Tepaneca troops to provide food or aid to the imperial capital. So the Emperor, left with no choice . . ."

"Has yielded?" I can scarcely keep the excitement from my voice.

My father smiles as he taps the glyph representing Azcapotzalco on the map.

"Yes. Or rather, requested an armistice. A halt to hostilities while the coronation ceremony is held in Tenochtitlan. During the truce, our troops will remain outside the imperial capital, but members of Tepaneca nobility will be allowed to travel to the Isle of Mexico. Afterwards, the Emperor swears he will engage in peace talks."

I draw in an uneasy breath. "I don't trust him, Father."

"Neither do I. But this ceasefire applies to *all* vassal states of the Empire, including the Kingdom of Mexico. And that gives us an opportunity, Acolmiztli. To appeal to the new king of Tenochtitlan, in secret. To convince him to ally with us against the Tepaneca."

It's a tenuous hope, but it quickens my pulse. "Whom have they chosen for the throne?"

"One of your mother's younger brothers," the king replies, sliding his stick across Moon Lake to Mexico. "Your uncle Chimalpopoca."

Then he looks at me with deadly, earnest eyes.

"Get your attendants to pack enough clothing for a fortnight. I have postponed your remaining exams, Acolmiztli. You will be coming with us. We leave at first light."

My first diplomatic mission in hostile territory. I should feel elated, proud.

But how I truly feel is relieved.

I won't have to face the combat exam.

At least not for a while.

{2} CORONATION

ONCH TRUMPETS SOUND, trilling in the fading mist of morning.

Then comes the thundering of drums, a regal rhythm that signals the arrival of a king.

The sun crests the volcanoes in the east, and rays of light converge at the apex of the new pyramid. Stone and mortar have replaced the old timber and packed dirt. The gods of wind and rain sweep away the remaining fog, revealing five men standing before the double temple at the top.

The new rulers of the small kingdom of Mexico.

Three of them are my maternal uncles. Chimalpopoca, who will be king, flanked by his half-brothers Tlacaellel and Moteuczoma, new members of the governing council. They are almost unrecognizable in their poses of solemn dignity, nothing like the joking youths I remember.

From inside the temples come priests who drape the five Mexica nobles in ceremonial capes. It is woven from the same sort of cloth that bundles the bones of their chief god, Huitzilopochtli: born a man, made divine after death.

"Behold," declares one of the priests, "the future king and his council! Like the great Feathered Serpent and Our Lord the Sun, they must descend in order to rise. Pray for them, O Mexica, as they enter the sacred chamber beneath the temple to die a symbolic death. Then, no longer merely human, they will emerge to rule!"

Shouts erupt all around me. Some ten thousand souls have poured themselves into the ceremonial center of Tenochtitlan, not only standing shoulder to shoulder in the broad square before the pyramid, but also crowded on the steps of other minor temples nearby, and even—in the case of some daring youths my age—clinging to stone images of the gods. The upturned faces of this mass of Mexica fill the morning air with such a shared booming of approval that the flagstones beneath my feet vibrate with the sound.

The five men are guided into the temple of Huitzilopochtli, where I imagine some sort of staircase spirals down into the innards of the pyramid, to the cave it was built upon.

The joyous noise is replaced by loud cries and lamentations at the disappearance of the princes from view. A conch trumpet signals the beginning of a communal feast, and those in attendance head in clusters toward the three accessible gates.

Brow beetling, my father calls the guards to our side.

"We must leave the sacred precinct at once. Escort us to my brother-in-law's villa," he commands. "Before some overly patriotic fool decides to break the armistice by killing us right here and now."

The stares we get as we walk east along the broad road of packed earth suggest that my father's decision is well timed. Around us sprawls Tenochtitlan, the city where my mother was born. Capital of Mexico. This rocky island at the southwestern end of Moon Lake

●◖◉◗●

should by all rights be my second home, where uncles and aunts and cousins greet me with smiles and open arms. My heart should fill with joy at the sight of the Mexica nobles, merchants, and commoners crowding the street around me, excitedly discussing the future of their people under a new king.

But I'm a stranger. My mother, a traitor to the House of Acamapichtli.

My father, the enemy. The regicide.

I walk between them both, holding my head high, nonetheless. As we make our way through the dispersing crowd, I imagine what onlooking Mexica perceive.

To my left is Queen Matlalcihuatl, "green lady," named for the goddess of the sea, wearing lovely hues that echo her name. Her father was Huitzilihuitl, former sovereign of Mexico, whose recent death at the hand of my father has triggered these rites of succession.

To my right is King Ixtlilxochitl, "blackened flower," dark and deadly handsome like a battlefield scorched by fire. He has defied tradition and treaties, risking the wrath of the Tepaneca emperor to be with my mother.

I am their son, Prince Acolmiztli, "puma of the Acolhua people," heir to my father's throne. Singer. Poet. Fifteen years old.

Our names, whispered even now by gawking passersby, are curses in this place.

But my father wants to shift that dynamic. It's the only reason we're here, risking our lives.

Still, a truce can be broken in a heartbeat. Just like what happened six months ago. So I ready myself, body and mind, for whatever might come.

The villa sits on the shore, not far from the causeway that joins Tenochtitlan to Tlatelolco. We arrive to find my mother's older half-sister Azcatl overseeing the preparation of a large celebratory meal.

"Why didn't you attend the ceremony, Aunt Azcatzin?" I ask with honorifics as she directs servants to set out an additional low table.

She arches an eyebrow at me with quiet mischief. The grey frosting her double-horned hairstyle makes her look like an owl, patiently awaiting its prey.

"I helped change and wash my brothers' diapers, you handsome little puma. I don't trust myself to not burst out laughing in the midst of some dignified rite."

I smile. "It's strange indeed to think of them as men, as the leaders of the Mexica people. We've seen them at their worst."

Azcatl glances around. My parents still have not emerged from our quarters. "Still, it behooves neither you nor me to speak outside these walls of anything they might find shameful. You may be nephew to the new king, but his grandfather is still Emperor Tezozomoc. He may be decrepit, but he's also bent on destroying your family. As for me, I'm reluctant to give my brothers cause to rid themselves of an ornery older sister."

"Oh, I doubt that will ever happen," says my mother, being led by a servant to her place around the table. "The noblewomen of this city either respect or fear you, Azcatl. The extent of your knowledge inspires awe."

"Knowledge?" I ask.

"Of gossip and clan secrets," says my father, taking up his position at the head of the table, beside my mother. "Stretching back several generations. Princess Azcatzin is not a woman to be trifled with. Yet . . . she is wise not to risk angering this city's new rulers."

My uncle Zacatl's bright tenor pierces our conversation long before he enters the villa. He is singing a springtide ballad, "The Warrior's Bride," and clapping out a rhythm as he reaches the chorus.

> I swear this true,
> to return to you,

as victor or hummingbird,
as veteran or butterfly,
by love and the gods
bound to my bride.

As he comes into view, I see he has thrown his arm around his own bride, Nazohuatl, whose belly bulges with their first child. They are both young and beautiful, like images in a painted book brought to life. They are also the two most foolish, merriest Mexica I have ever met.

"Ah!" Zacatl shouts. "Elder Sisters! Little Puma! Were you routed from the sacred precinct by angry commoners or something? How did you get here so quickly?"

My father, a much more serious man than my uncle will ever be, looks at Zacatl with dispassionate eyes.

"Revered Brother-in-Law," my uncle murmurs, catching his eye and lowering his head. "I beg your pardon for delaying your meal, King Ixtlilxochitzin."

"Not at all, Prince Zacatzin." My father reaches out to gently stop Zacatl from bowing. "It is, after all, your home. We are grateful for your hospitality in these fractious times."

After the delicious midday meal and a conversation that favors family reminiscence over political speculation, Zacatl stands and gestures to me. Though he's feigning maturity and seriousness in front of the other adults, I can see mischief and fun sparkling in his eyes.

"Acolmiztli," he says, lowering his speech since I am younger, "shall we relax with a little music?"

I have been hoping he'd make this suggestion. I nod, excited.

"Yes, Uncle. That would be delightful!"

We head outside, to a raised platform between the villa and its canoe dock. Zacatl calls his manservant, an aging and scarred fellow from Huexotzinco, one of many enslaved by the Mexica when they conquered that city-state for Emperor Tezozomoc.

"Eyozomah, bring the drums out."

The older man bows his balding head. "Aye, milord."

I stare past the railing at the rectangular chinampa gardens lining the shore, dredged-up soil anchored by the roots of wispy willows. It is a feat of agricultural engineering the Mexica learned from the conquered Xochimilca, who have been gardening thus for many turns of the calendar round. But my grandfather and his family have adapted the technique for other marvels, pulling up sediment to build the stunning causeway here and its twin to the south, which connects Mexico-Tenochtitlan with the islet of Acachinanco.

"Your brow is quite wrinkled for a boy of fifteen," my uncle jokes as he sweeps the platform of leaves. "What notions are spinning behind those furrows?"

Zacatl himself is only nineteen, a year younger than his three brothers who will soon rule this city. It's bewildering how a handful of years can change everything. I wonder what transformations await me, just beyond tomorrow.

"The causeways," I say. "They're acting like dikes, aren't they? Keeping the brackish water of the eastern side of the lake from filtering in as easily. These gardens are greener and lusher than the rest of the city."

"Indeed. Do you see those workers in the distance, dredging up more soil?" It's hard to make out much about them from our vantage point, beyond the fact that they are covered head to foot in muck. "My father's plan, which my brothers will continue. If we can make bridges and gardens, why not make Mexico *bigger*?"

I understand in a flash. It is brilliant.

"Fill in the gaps between all the little isles with sediment. Expand Mexica territory without loosing a single arrow."

Eyozomah returns, his arms full of percussion instruments. The huehuetl, with its leather drumhead; ayacachtli rattles; and a tetzila-catl gong.

"Goodman," I say, addressing the manservant in the variety of Nahuatl spoken in his native Huexotzinco, with its broad vowels and clipped consonants, "could I bother ye for the tecomapilohua? I ken that it's unwieldy, yet I love its tones."

His face brightening to hear his own dialect, Eyozomah nods. "Aye, Your Royal Highness. With haste."

My uncle stares at me, mouth agape. "You really are a mockingbird, aren't you?"

I wink at him.

"I don't have four hundred voices yet," I say, "but I can speak six languages and switch between a dozen dialects of Nahuatl. Tetzcoco is a diverse city, and its crown prince would be remiss if he couldn't communicate with all of his subjects."

Zacatl pats me on the shoulder. "Wise. And when you become king, you'll have to speak with the voice of your city's patron god, so having a supple voice is vital."

In just minutes, Eyozomah has set up the tecomapilohua before me. From the bottom of the wooden two-tone drum are suspended three gourds, giving the instrument a soft resonance that is hard to describe.

"Okay, Little Puma, or Mockingbird, or whatever animal is ascen-dant in your soul today," Zacatl announces, taking up a position in front of the huehuetl. "Listen closely. Do you hear the chant of those workers on the far shore? That *heave-ho* they use to mark the pulse of their labor?"

I squint and tilt my head. Soft, but sure, their joined voices reach my ear, synchronized with their diligent movements to dredge up mud and pass it in a chain.

"Yes, Uncle. It's like a rowing rhythm."

"Then let us improvise upon it," he suggests, beginning to tap out the beat upon the tight head of his drum, "until we fashion our own special teponazcuicatl."

Playing percussion transports me. My mother tells me that as a little child, I would sit in the palace patio, listening to the muffled thudding from the House of Song where my father and his greatest soldiers would gather for chants and dance. As I swayed, entranced by the thrumming, I would pat my little hands upon the clay tiles, in perfect time.

Now, eyes shutting against the world, I feel Zacatl's ornate echo of the workers' chant, and my hands slip in and out of the beat, making incidentals ring out, spattering rapid notes amid the steady ebb and flow. I imagine the heartbeats of each worker and thread them in counterpoint, keeping the collective rhythm with my left hand and sounding out their individual pulses on the hanging gourds. My sandals scrape against the planks in mimesis of the winds slipping down mountain slopes, the ripples of water on Moon Lake.

They say that the Lord of Fire and Time, first god to emerge from the cosmic sea, spent four hundred thousand years floating above the waters, harkening unto its hushed waves and deep currents until he saw the pattern at last. Then, pounding out that eternal beat upon his own chest in a flurry of sparks, he set the cosmic wheels to turning.

Then did time at last begin.

Though it be blasphemy, I cannot help but feel myself a master of time when my hands dance like this across a surface that resounds at my touch.

Can one reshape the world through rhythm? What time signature might I employ? What meter? Stately and slow, notes few and heavy? Or galloping and bellic, a frenzy of staccatos?

"Dredge up the rich and dead," I start to sing, the words spontaneous, "from the unsoundable depths of the cosmic sea, and forge a new empire, an unforetold destiny."

Whatever holy fount I've tapped into, I let it continue flowing through me.

> Take up the multiple strands of our lives
> and weave on the loom of time a new tapestry,
> voices entwined in unforeseen harmony
> a symphony spiraling beyond the skies.

After a while, I realize my uncle isn't playing. My hands slow their mad dance, and I open my eyes to see him staring, tears on his cheeks.

"You are unparalleled, Crown Prince Acolmiztzin." He uses honorifics now, raising his speech as one does when addressing a superior or elder. "I can only listen in awe. The men who one day follow your beat onto the battlefield should count themselves lucky. Surely any enemy will fall when faced with warriors fighting to such rhythms."

I lower my eyes, feeling shame. "Uncle, what good does it do me to pound out such rhythms if I cannot fight? My father's life was in danger just yards from me, yet I did nothing. For there was nothing I could do. I am no warrior. Just a middling swordsman, at best. Who would follow me into battle?"

Zacatl embraces me. "You excel at so many things, Nephew. Perhaps your forte will be military strategy rather than battlefield prowess. But I suspect that you just need time. Practice. Willingness."

"I *am* willing," I mutter into his cloak.

"To kill? For that is what I mean, Acolmiztzin. I know you love to create, to learn, to preserve. But are you ready to destroy? To do so with the same level of devotion and glee?"

I swallow heavily. We both know the answer.

Four days of fasts and feasts and festivities later, I'm standing once again in the sacred precinct of Tenochtitlan. A more languid drumbeat

begins, marking the beginning of the closing ceremony without calling attention to itself. The mood it sets is undeniable. Like the teeming mass that crowds the plaza, I can't help but hold my breath as the
fifth day of the king-making ritual dawns.

The figures around me grow more distinct. Men, women, and
children, dressed in white cotton and fasting collars, each carrying a
single prickly pear fruit in their hands: bright red or purple with black
spots where the splintery hairs have been burnt off.

I'm reminded of an old folk song about the thorns that protect
sweetness—some Toltec metaphor about the balance in life between
pain and pleasure, grief and joy. What happiness lies on the other side
of this conflict, I wonder. Will we ever get past the poisonous barbs?

A procession of soldiers, the elite brotherhoods with their gaudy
uniforms and banners, makes its way to the pyramid, and marches up
the steps until they've lined each side.

I'm desperately trying *not* to imagine myself on a battlefield,
running like a coward from this impressive array of warriors, when a
giggle comes from nearby. Not far off, backs to the serpent wall that
separates the sacred precinct from the rest of Tenochtitlan, stand five
lovely girls from noble families.

The youngest and prettiest can't keep her eyes off me, though she
blushes when I return her stare with open attraction. I don't avert my
eyes. She covers her mouth and laughs again, soft and high.

Despite the solemnity, I find myself imagining what it would be
like to cover those lips with my own. To feel that giggle fluttering
against my tongue.

Then the girl beside her—an older sister, I imagine—notices our silent
exchange, gets a good look at me, and elbows the younger, whispering
angrily. The pretty one's eyes go wide. She bows her head, avoiding my
gaze, clutching at the folds of her colorful skirt. No more giggling.

Making an effort not to sigh, smirk, or outwardly flinch, I turn
my eyes back to the temple with slow disdain.

A flourish of trumpets, then my uncle Chimalpopoca emerges. The priests have bathed him and dressed him in finery: quetzal feathers, jade and silver, cape and sandals befitting a Mexica king, . . . especially one as pompous and self-important as Chimalpopoca, who even as a child ordered his siblings and cousins around because his mother was Tezozomoc's favorite daughter.

"I'm the Emperor's *grandson*, you fools," he would snap. "One day you'll *all* bend the knee to me."

His prophecy has come true, I suppose. Now some of his half-brothers and cousins step into the tenuous sunlight behind him, arrayed like princes, members of his royal council.

Tlacaellel stands out, his hair longer, his cape black as night—the new Fire Priest. Fitting. He has always been more interested in the power of ceremony than in military might. If anyone in Tenochtitlan might consider Father's proffered alliance, it would be him . . . if he thought the House of Acamapichtli could benefit as a result.

The past keeps bubbling up below the surface of the present. Like my aunt, I find it hard to keep the two separate as I watch. These young, resurrected men are just five years older than me, barely twenty solar years of age. And now they control Mexico. A vassal state, yes, but a kingdom nonetheless.

And right now, watching my uncle kneel before his fire priest, I feel time unravel.

Mother still loves Mexico. She is, after all, the older sister of this new Mexica king, of his captain of the armory, and of his fire priest. After I was born, during moments of armistice when warfare was stilled, she would bring me to visit her royal family in this city. Back then I looked up to my uncles, following them around as a child on toddling feet, imitating their bold ways. They never ran me off, even if they could be cruel.

Five years ago, they were admitted to their own calmecac. As now, the city was awash with joy: the king's three sons—born the same day from three different queens, a sign from the gods—were leaving their father's tutelage and coming into their own, the cusp of manhood.

I was almost ten, serious, my brain teeming with lore that my father was teaching me, dreaming of expanding the kingdom of Acolhuacan someday—obsidian sword in my royal hand, dispatching the cruel tyrant, Emperor Tezozomoc, who attacks every year.

At the feast, I was unprepared for all the muttered comments and wide-eyed stares from girls and women alike.

Unfortunately, my uncles noticed the attention.

"Ha!" Chimalpopoca laughed. "They find you handsome, Nephew! Won't be long till some girl takes you back to her room!"

Moteuczoma chimed in.

"It's not just his looks, brothers. Notice the way he struts, slinking back and forth like a real ladies' man!"

My composure cracked.

"It's a puma's prowl!" I snarled, glaring at them, fists curling.

But they just scoffed. Tlacaellel then clapped his hands with glee.

"No, Nephew. Here's your nickname: Yohyontzin—Lover Boy! You'll delight the eye of all Mexica girls, rich and poor."

"How many queens do you suppose he'll have when he ascends the throne?" Chimalpopoca asked, grinning.

"Easily five," Moteuczoma opined.

"With another fifteen concubines," Tlacaellel added. "One lover for each night of the month!"

On and on they went, ribbing me and winking as they so loved to do.

As if they wouldn't be marching into battle soon against my father and my Acolhua uncles; against the people I am destined to one day rule.

It was the last time we shared such jokes. The calmecac, strict and punishing, has beat that coarseness from them. As the noble sons of a vassal state, they have learned that while blood is thicker than water, tribute trumps everything.

Tlacaellel sets the turquoise crown on Chimalpopoca's brow, and I realize I hardly recognize in these hard, somber men the joking youths that I once worshipped.

The Fire Priest's voice, deeper and more elegant than I remember it, booms out across the plaza, addressing the Mexica and their allies.

Their enemies, too.

"Mexica, behold your new king, Chimalpopocatzin! Let us all eat of the fruit that burst through stone to signal the promised land to our weary ancestors one hundred years ago!"

Around me, in unison, the Mexica bite into their prickly pear fruit. And I remember the legend my mother told me of how the Mexica escaped bondage in Colhuacan and came to this isle. Their chief god had long before told them to look for a sign: a prickly pear growing from stony soil, and an eagle perched upon its spiny paddles. Here they found it, on the very spot where the pyramid was later built.

Everywhere, the Mexica give whoops of celebration, their chins dripping with the juice of the bright fruit—*nochtli*—that grew upon the rocks—*tetl*.

The origin of this city's name: Tenochtitlan, place of prickly pear fruit amid the stone.

A sad premonition strikes me, watching their mouths go red with metaphorical blood.

The Mexica will not accept Father's proposal.

They have too much pride.

{3} ROYAL AUDIENCE

THE NEW KING descends the south face of the newly rebuilt temple, his father's lifework—symbolic of Coatepec, Snake Mountain, birthplace of Huitzilopochtli, god of sun and battlefield.

At the foot of the temple await visiting dignitaries from many nearby city-states, including Tlacateotl, the recently crowned king of Tlatelolco, who is also a grandson of Emperor Tezozomoc. With his entourage complete, Chimalpopoca heads through the south gate to his palace near the island's carefully guarded freshwater spring.

It's one of Mexico's greatest weaknesses, this lack of plentiful water. My curious mind goes to work at once, reviewing engineering options that might help. The closest fresh water wells up from the springs atop Chapoltepec Hill, to the southwest. If this were Tetzcoco, our city, I would have crews dig a canal to redirect its flow. But here?

The fresh water needs to travel over the lake without co-mingling. A challenge.

"Escort the queen back to her brother's villa," my father orders his royal guard. "Prepare everything in case we are compelled to suddenly leave."

He's felt it too, I understand. The futility of this attempt. But the other cities of Acolhuacan expect a diplomatic solution from the Overlord. So he plans to do his best.

His hand alights on my shoulder. "Come, Acolmiztli. We have an audience."

The palace is bustling with attendants, judges, and heads of various merchant guilds. All of them want a chance to petition the new king. As royalty and relatives, my father and I are given greater priority, but we nevertheless find ourselves waiting most of the morning in a suite of rooms. I grow restless, tapping out quiet rhythms on the mat where I am sitting.

My father is still. So are the two guards that accompany us. I should be shamed by their discipline, but we are four enemies in the heart of Tenochtitlan. The tension is palpable.

Finally, a tall, wiry noble in his mid-thirties enters, wearing ceremonial military garb. Faint scars mark his cheeks and arms.

It's General Itzcoatl, commander-in-chief of the Mexica army, who has led troops against my father multiple times over the last decade.

But also my great uncle. Bastard half-brother of the late king.

Met by the obsidian black of his eyes, I can't help wondering if he resents being passed over. If he chafes at the ruling council's decision to crown his nephew, the younger if more legitimate heir. The hereditary traditions of rulership are a divine gift of Quetzalcoatl, the Feathered Serpent, who values order and continuity. Yet they are balanced by the need for expediency, for strength and wisdom, for the willingness to do whatever is needed to protect a kingdom. Such leadership is the domain of Tezcatlipoca, the Smoking Mirror, who shatters lineages and lifts men to power at his whim.

Does my uncle ever whisper prayers to that Lord of Chaos?

"General," my father says, rising to his feet. I do the same.

"Your Majesty," Itzcoatl rasps before his gaze flits to me. "Your Royal Highness. King Chimalpopocatzin will see you now."

As the general escorts us to the audience chamber, my father addresses him quietly.

"I should like your support, Itzcoatzin. The Mexica deserve better than Tepaneca tyranny."

Itzcoatl's jaw tightens till his mouth is like a gash.

"I shall obey my king," he says, "but first I shall give him counsel. Like Your Majesty, I tire of this protracted war."

Their exchange is cut short as we approach the crowd of dignitaries waiting in the great hall. A figure emerges from the audience chamber—all hollow eyes and crooked sneer.

It is the cruel and despotic Maxtla, King of Coyoacan, son of Emperor Tezozomoc and therefore my uncle Chimalpopoca's uncle. The only reason he can be in attendance is that the Acolhua troops that have been blockading his city and the imperial capital of Azcapotzalco are standing down, as part of the truce.

Still, Maxtla's face crinkles with unbridled yet somehow joyful hate as he sees us.

"The Usurper and his kitten," he remarks with a laugh. "Good luck trying to turn him against us, fools. I'll see you both on the battlefield soon enough."

Once again, I'm reminded that royal families are complicated. Alliances mean that marriages cross the boundaries of kingdoms. Chimalpopoca, for example, is Mexica, true. But also: Colhuacan, Chichimeca, and Tepaneca. Imperial blood, as he reiterates ad nauseum.

I am a blend as well. Dynasties identify with and serve the cities they rule—yet warfare sometimes feels like family squabbles are being decided on the battlefield.

As Maxtla departs, Itzcoatl pushes open the door to the audience chamber. A pair of Jaguar Knights fall in beside us, dressed head to toe in their spotted uniforms. They walk us to the dais where Chimalpopoca sits glorious and haughty upon a glassy black throne.

My father tips his head in a measured show of respect. I bow deeper.

"King Chimalpopocatzin," Father begins. "Kin of mine. Friend. I come to you requesting an alliance. Stand with family against a tyrant. Help the Acolhua, whom your sister my queen loves with all her heart."

"Revered, royal brother-in-law," Chimalpopoca replies, "you started down this path many years ago when you married my *half-sister* against the emperor's wishes, and you sealed your fate when you made her son the crown prince."

I swallow heavy, hands balling into fists that I quickly unclench.

My cousin continues. "Rumors have reached us. Your dominion is faltering. You've managed momentarily to stave off a schism in Acolhuacan. Maintaining unity by appointing as commander of your troops the Crown Prince of Coatlichan? It's a sound strategy, as that city is more powerful than yours, more respected."

Even as the young monarch seeks to school my father in politics, he forgets just how wide the web of family spreads. My father's mother was a princess of Coatlichan. While our ties are not unbreakable, perhaps, it has supported Tetzcoco's ascendancy for decades.

Nonetheless, a bitter laugh leaves Chimalpopoca's lips.

"But the Emperor—my *grandfather*, recall—has many allies in Acolhuacan, and even now they ply King Paintzin of Coatlichan with gifts and threats. How long can he withstand?"

My father, his jaw tight now, sneers a response.

"What would you have me do, newly minted king? Surrender?"

Chimalpopoca leans forward, tipping back his crown with a battle-scarred hand.

"Yes. The Emperor has promised me Tetzcoco once it falls. I'd rather it were still intact."

I take a step toward him, fury rising from heart to lips like magma ready to erupt. The *willingness* Zacatl spoke of seems to blossom in me like a poisonous flower.

It's the city, I realize. The thought of my beloved city in Chimapo-poca's graspy, greedy, ignorant hands. Enraging!

The Jaguar Knights grip their obsidian swords, but my father glances at me with cold eyes that quench my fire. But the epiphany remains. A moment ago, I would have twisted my hands around my uncle's throat if circumstances had permitted me.

With devotion. With glee.

The revelation startles—even sickens me. Still, such murderous rage may be useful . . . if I ever have the fighting skills to channel it.

"Why would I surrender," Father asks, "when Acolhua troops wait outside Azcapotzalco, ready to resume our siege of the imperial capital once this truce is over?"

My uncle makes a dismissive gesture.

"Because the absence of those troops in Acolhuacan leaves Tetzcoco open and vulnerable to attacks by allies of the Tepaneca."

"Like the one that left your father dead?"

Chimalpopoca recoils a bit, then smirks with disdain.

"I promise you that I won't make the same mistakes. And I will have Acolhua warriors marching under my banner when I come, dear brother-in-law. But let's avoid that bloodshed, yes? Step down. Bend the knee. Live your last years in quiet exile. Acolmiztli must relinquish his title as well. Then I swear I will protect him, as his Mexica nobility demands."

Enough. I have to speak. The ferocity uncoiling within me is almost unbearable. Any remaining shred of kinship I still felt for the House of Acamapichtli now boils away in the fire of my heart.

"I am no Mexica," I snarl, puma livid in my veins. "I am Acolhua. Toltec and Chichimec blood co-mingled, both wildness and wisdom."

My father does not rebuke me. Instead, he nods.

"We shall not yield," he tells my uncle. "Let him know. He must pry Tetzcoco from my dead fingers before he gives it to you."

Chimalpopoca lunges to his feet, fingers clawing at the air. For a moment, I'm certain he will order his guards to seize or slay us on the spot.

But my father has judged the situation well. The new king won't put the Emperor at risk by breaking the armistice.

"Get out of my throneroom," he hisses. "Get out of my city. I shall come for you fools soon enough."

We give the curtest of bows and leave the chamber in silence, stomachs made hollow by ominous possibilities.

Mother and Father shut themselves up in our quarters, conferring. Father has always called Mother his best adviser, though woman are usually excluded from such affairs of state and military maneuvers.

I take a moment to bid farewell to my uncle and aunts.

"Be well, Little Puma," says Aunt Azcatl. "Remember that this is your second home, when and if hostilities cease between your father and the Emperor. In the meantime, I shall continue to use every bit of influence I have over my younger brothers and other nobles. With time, their hearts may be made to change."

I kneel before Lady Nazohuatl, addressing my unborn cousin.

"When you at last arrive, whether sturdy boy or wily girl, I shall greet you warmly and protect you always."

Zacatl wipes at his eyes as he pulls me to my feet and embraces me.

"Your time on the battlefield is fast approaching," he says, voice thick with emotion. "Be sure, steady, and speedy, like your hands on the drum. That is how you'll survive and gain honor. I believe the gods have something truly special in store for you, Acolmiztli. Sing their praises, Mockingbird, and obey tradition. Pleased, they'll protect you. Angered, they'll abandon you."

My parents emerge and say their farewells as I help the porters and guards stow our belongings on the canoes docked just outside.

Then the rowers are plying the water with their oars as we head toward the gap in the causeway. I look up as we pass through, admiring the sturdy wooden bridge that can be pulled up to frustrate the plans of an army marching in either direction.

The canoes leave the islands behind as they head northeast. My parents turn their backs on Tenochtitlan and Tlatelolco, holding hands as they fix their eyes ahead, ready to return to the home they've build together.

"Together, then," my father says, cryptic if romantic.

My mother lifts his hand, kisses it.

"Until the end, my precious flower."

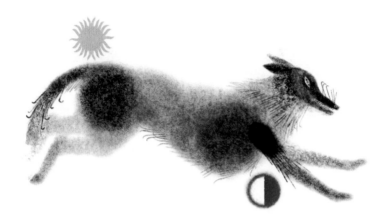

{4} TETZCOCO

L IKE CURLING LEAVES spilled upon jade tiles, our canoes skim the emerald waters of Moon Lake as we leave the Isle of Mexico and its floating, flowery gardens behind. Sunlight glints gold upon wind-driven ripples. For a moment, I imagine Anahuac itself—all the lands bordering these lakes—to be a jewel set amid the mountains: like a necklace whose central gem rests in the hollow of a lover's throat.

Though I keep a steady beat for them to follow, the rowers slow as we pass from sweet to brackish waters, stiff against their oars. I recall the causeway joining Tenochtitlan and Tlatelolco, how it helps keep the water fresh near the chinampas. What would it take to wall off all the brine in Moon Lake so that the water flowing north from Lake Xochimilco stays pure? I picture its contours—a massive dike, a wall of sediment, and stone and wood scores of rods long. Raised high enough above the surface, this imaginary dam could also protect Mexico from flooding during the rainy season.

What resources would be required for such an undertaking? What engineering knowledge? When I begin a deeper study of science at the calmecac, perhaps I'll find the answers—even if our war with the Tepaneca and the Mexica means I have little motivation to help create, in effect, an entirely new freshwater lake to the east of Tenochtitlan.

Still, the mental exercise keeps me distracted during our trip. It takes most of the morning to curve northeast toward the farther shore of Moon Lake, the salt marshes thick with reed and cane. The rowers switch to poles, making their careful way through a maze of channels that have kept Tetzcoco safe from invading fleets of canoes for centuries.

At last we come to the docks. The soldiers on watch bow to my parents and me.

"Welcome, Your Majesties," the commander says with reverential awe. "We will send word of your return ahead so that you be met with the proper pomp and circumstance."

My father lifts a hand. "Hold, Commander. We do not return with the glad tidings I had hoped. Better our reception be restrained and simple. We shall need our resources in the near future, I fear."

A swift messenger is dispatched with the king's instructions as we begin our escorted walk up toward Tetzcoco. The road of hard-packed earth takes us past the marshes and the scrubland until we find ourselves plunging into the familiar forests of Acolhuacan.

My father's homeland. Mine.

Beyond that sea of pine, peaks rise white. I have never seen the ocean, but I imagine it trembling above us in that looming range. Foam-topped breakers, frozen at the brink of falling upon the world. And mountains and volcanoes, both dormant and smoking—gods that watch impassive the lives of men.

It isn't far from the salt marshes to the city. Before long, the white temples and mansions of resplendent Tetzcoco rise above the treetops. Pride knots in my throat. I was not lying when I growled at my cousin. I am Acolhua, though my mother is Mexica. Our capital city, founded a century before the smaller and less beautiful Tenochtitlan, is the culmination of our culture.

I began learning lessons about our lineage, our legacy, before I could even walk. The son of a king must embody such heritage. And by my eighth summer I had been assigned a teenaged tutor and surrogate elder sibling—Izcalloh, scion of my father's best friend—who drilled me in the history of our royal family and gently corrected my courtly behavior.

Long ago, this forest was Toltec land. But when their empire fell into ruin, a fierce warlord swept in from the northwest—Xolotl, chieftain of the Chichimec nomads.

My ancestor.

He subjugated cities on the eastern and western banks of Moon Lake. Established new ones. Forged an empire. Began the fusion of Toltec and Chichimec.

In the aftermath of the chieftain's demise, two new peoples arose— Acolhua and Tepaneca, on either side of the lake, embers of Xolotl's fiery glory. His sons and grandsons ruled city-states throughout Anahuac. They abandoned their native tongue for Nahuatl, language of the Toltecs.

One of Xolotl's descendants was Quinatzin, my great grandfather, founder of Tetzcoco. In time, our city opened to Nahua immigrants of many nations: Chimalpaneca, Huitznahuaqueh, Tlailotlaqueh, Colhuahqueh, and even our rivals the Tepaneca and the deadly Mexihtin, cousins of the Mexica. Six new boroughs, each retaining the ethnicity of its residents, while also becoming part of a new and vibrant identity: Tetzcoca, the people of Tetzcoco.

We Acolhua, heirs to great traditions, became Tetzcoca, too. Cradled by forests and hills, we rise generation after generation, music and art and engineering lifting us toward the snowy summits that ring Anahuac, this region of lakes, eagles gliding sunward on dream-like currents.

Now Tetzcoca voices ring out in greeting as we enter the city through the eastern gate. A throng of our diverse populace crowds the streets, vying for a glimpse of the royal family, clamoring for news.

"What did the queen's brother say?"

"Has the war ended?"

"Did you bend the knee, Our Lord King?"

Soldiers keep the most zealous citizens at bay. I know Father will address his people tonight, from atop the Pyramid of Duality, before the temple of the Feathered Serpent. He will speak hard truths to them, while also working them into a patriotic fervor. Few can move a crowd the way Ixtlilxochitl does. Most Tetzcoca will come away sobered but sure.

But not all. Even now, as we move past the side roads that lead to the Tepaneca and Mexica boroughs, I notice that few of their inhabitants have come out to greet us. Those present glance about nervously, as if afraid their loyalty to their king will have unwanted consequences.

Something deep in my gut twists. I sense dark possibilities at the edges of things.

Then comes divine surcease: we pass the serpent wall, entering the sacred precinct, where the Pyramid of Duality rises before us. Its ornate steps glow at this golden hour, easing my worries with its splendor. The moon is a transparent sliver of white between the two temples at its summit: Chaos and Order, Destruction and Creation, Tezcatlipoca and Quetzalcoatl.

Beside it sprawls the royal residence, surrounded by an artificial lake that we use wooden bridges to cross. Father named it

Cillan—Place of Shells—for the spiral patterns Mother loves: bas reliefs and encrusted snails.

Once we're within the castle walls, Mother sighs, content.

"At last. Our home."

Father smiles and brushes a strand of hair from her face.

"Has Tenochtitlan finally lost its charm? You now see my city as your home?"

"Home," she says, eyes bright with happiness, "is at your side, my Lord."

Wanting to give them some privacy, I walk toward the gardens, running my fingers over white stone quarried from distant hills, transported block after block and lifted skillfully into place to create a sprawling space full of elegance and light.

The canals, carved into the stony soil, sparkle with the light of the setting sun as vivid flowers float upon water channeled from streams that flow down the face of looming Mount Tlaloc. A miracle of engineering made all the more breathtaking by the love that wrought it.

My mother's home may be at my father's side, but he remade this palace to look like her own, to ease her homesickness all those years ago.

I believe in love. How can I not? I have seen it every day of my life, glinting in the eyes of my parents as they exchange smiles.

They didn't get engaged for love. Royalty never does. My Mexica grandfather pledged his daughter's hand to the Crown Prince of Tetzcoco before she could talk. So, my mother and father were bound by custom and fate, despite the decade difference in their age.

Ah, but everyone in this city knows the true story, from dewy-eyed youths longing for romance to aging crones reminiscing about lost beauty. The tale is sung in taverns, kitchens, fields. "The Lay of Black Flower and Green Lady," it is called.

I know it by heart.

The prince became a knight,
a general, a king.
The princess grew more lovely
than he had ever dreamed.

Black Flower's heart would race
like a hundred prancing deer
when affairs of state
brought his Green Lady near.

In public, their words
were formal and pure,
but everyone watching
could feel that allure.

Alone, the princess
extolled him in verse,
while weaving a gown
that she wore to rehearse.

But word came from the east,
an imperial decree—
Tezozomoc's divorced daughter
was the new bride-to-be!

Black Flower rowed
like the wind o'er the lake;
he had to reach Mexico
before it was too late.

Tenochtitlan was happy then
to see the wedding done

so Mexica and Acolhua
would be bound as one.

But no sooner had Green Lady
settled into her new home
than word came from Azcapotzalco
to the Isle of Mexico—

In exchange for Black Flower's head,
the Emperor explained,
I'll share power with the Mexica—
As partners we shall reign.

If you refuse, Mexica king,
you and all your kin
will be wiped from this earth
as if you'd never been.

One child against a kingdom,
power against romance—
the new Queen of Tetzcoco
never stood a chance.

But Green Lady is blessed,
the gods have shown her favor
The man she married loves her,
will burn the world to keep her.

And that is how I know what love is—I have spent my entire life,
all fifteen years, in the midst of a war my father is waging against an
empire, for the woman he loves.

The nation of Acolhuacan follows him because of national pride. We are the heirs to the Toltec Way—not the barbarous Tepaneca, despite their claims. And he is our Overlord, the Chichimeca Chieftain, ruling the fourteen allied cities by dint of his wisdom and skill.

But though we believe it an honor to die in battle, unrelenting years of sacrifice, and the loss of thousands of sons. . . .

It tests the patriotism of even the most pious.

{5} THE WAY OF SONG

Master of Song

The morning after our return,
I arise with the sun.
My attendants help me bathe,
dress me in soft cotton breechcloth,
hipcloth and sleeveless xicolli,
dyed green with puma patterning.

Stepping into white sandals,
I hurry to the House of Flowers,
our temple dedicated
to music and poetry.

The Master of Song is waiting
at the entrance. He greets me
with a curt nod. Of all the priests
in Tetzcoco, he gets to decide
what songs are sung,
what dances performed,
at all our major festivals.

He also teaches my father's sons,
bastards and princes alike,
to play the flute and drum,
and to intone the ancient songs.

"You have been absent a week,"
he scolds, his voice soft and low.
"Now that my lessons have ended
and you are bound for school,

you have failed to present
your final hymn."

"I am ready now, Master of Song,"
I reply, pressing my fist to my heart.

His silver hair—loose
upon the shoulders
of his deep blue,
star-bangled robe—
snakes up and down as he nods
and enters. I follow close.

"Recite the musical truths," he commands,
"then approach the flower drum."

The House of Flowers is spacious,
room for many dozen men and boys.
At the far end stands a wooden cylinder,
carved with intricate vines and blooms
by some ancestor of mine
whose name now escapes me.

"All song is an echo," I begin,
"of the celestial chorus.
The bravest of our ancestors,
transformed into birds
to accompany the sun,
learn those holy hymns.
When they flit through our lives,
warbling and chattering,

the most open of hearts
can perceive their meaning
and craft songs for human ears.
Composers are rare—
most men must content themselves
with performing what their betters
have spun into song."

The Master of Song, hands behind
his back, bows a little lower.

"Well recited. And you,
Prince Acolmiztli?
Are you merely a singer?
Or have you heard
the whistling of your forefathers,
learned to twine those notes
into novel melodies?"

I take a deep breath.
I feel my destiny quivering
in the air all around me.
More than king, I wish to be
a poet, a composer of song,
my words wending down the ages,
sung by many voices.

"I have heard them, Master of Song.
I have fashioned a new hymn,
rhythm and rhyme,
melody and meaning."

He gestures toward the drum.
"Then make me weep, boy."

Trembling, I approach
that holy space,
lay my fingers
on the rim,
close my
eyes.

Then my hands
beat out the rhythm,
ti co co to qui qui qui,
and I tilt my head back,
let the song flow free,
call heaven down
to sing through me.

The Hymn I Sing

There where we are headed,
the place we go when dead,
will we still somehow live?
Is it a realm of joy?
Is it a land of mirth?

Alas, we cannot know—
For no one has returned.

Are these sweet flowers
just for the here and now,
only for this earth?
These songs we love to sing,
will they also one day fade?

Ah, yes, it is true—
We simply go away.

Yet be of good cheer,
dear Chichimeca lords!
We are all of us bound
for that Unknowable Realm
to be shorn of worldly cares!

None becomes a mountain—
Not a soul is left on earth.

Still, like a fleeting dream
we cling to friends and fame,
we laugh and love and weep

because we are alive
and that's what humans do.

So lift your voices with me now—
Let us sing while there is time!

His Tears

I open my eyes.
The Master of Song
is kneeling.
His face is wet
with tears.

"Your Royal Highness,"
he whispers,
the first time
he has ever addressed
those words to me.

"Twenty-five years
have I taught boys
to sing. Never has a pupil
so moved my heart.
I have no more
learning for you, sire.
Now you must teach us all,
for you hear more clearly
than any man I know."

Then
he lowers
his head
till it touches
the ground.

I rush to lift him to his feet.

"Holy One," I rasp,
"if I hear the voice of god
it's because you opened
my ears and my heart.
You will never lack anything,
Master of Song,
not while I live."

{6} THE LAST EXAMINATION

T HE NEXT MORNING, I find Chief Counselor Huitzilihuitl waiting outside my chambers.

"Come with me," he commands, and I obey. I may no longer be his student now that I have passed his examinations, but his authority is unquestionable.

I follow him to a quiet spot, my father's meditation room, whose broad windows and archways open onto a grove of cypress.

The king sits on the floor, dressed in a simple white cape and breechcloth. In his hands he holds two nezahualli: collars made of thick paper twisted together, ribbons dangling. You wear one as a symbol that you are fasting, so that others will not offer you food or otherwise disturb your ritual.

"Sit before me, my son," my father says. "Let me affix the fasting collar to your neck. Fast with me. These are difficult times, but your schooling cannot wait."

I do as he asks. The paper is uncomfortable, scratchy. It is meant to be.

"In just three days you will be leaving this palace for the calmecac. You will not be pampered or respected there. You go to learn, not just how to be a warrior and statesman, but how to endure. How to be sad. How to live with humility and austerity. You must be moderate even with food. Never gorge yourself. Learn to love the feeling of an empty stomach."

I nod. They are lessons I have heard before. Battle is unpredictable, as is life. Huitzilihuitl is fond of saying that we live and fight on slippery terrain, as if walking along the highest ridge of a mountain. To either side are sheer drops into bottomless chasms.

Any misstep could be fatal.

The thought makes me shudder. I don't think I'm well enough prepared. My mind grasps the concepts, but violence still feels foreign to my heart and body.

"Hear me well, Acolmiztli," the king continues. "You go to pluck secrets from the heart of the Sovereign of the Near and the Nigh, the source of all, who unfolds many-faced into all the gods we worship. Fasting and penance are the keys to such wisdom. Mortify your flesh."

Lowering my head, I make my reply:

"Yes, sire. I place your words in my heart of hearts."

Then I sit by his side. Hour slides into hour. Hunger claws at my stomach, but I ignore it. The feeling fades, then comes again.

I listen for the celestial chorus, contemplate my family tree, review rituals and formulas, keep my mind focused.

Then, after some unknown length of time, my father rasps, "You must learn to empty your mind, rupture thought and self, and let teotl—vital divine energy—flood you through and through. A king must protect and command his people, speaking with the voice of the gods. To be such a speaker, you must cease to be Acolmiztli. You must become a conduit for holiness."

Though his face is expressionless, his hand trembles slightly as he places a maguey thorn in my hand. Long, sharp, hungry for blood.

I do not hesitate. With a flick of my wrist, I pierce the flesh of my thigh, watch the dark red welling, and feel the sharp pain and then the bitter ache.

Hunger. Pain. Thirst. Sorrow. Humiliation.

If I am to sit upon his throne—to lead our people, and teach them to hear—I must endure it all.

It takes several shakes for my father to pull me from the depths of meditation.

"Son," he says. "Accompany me outside."

As I stand, hunger resurfaces, making my legs wobble for a moment. But I grit my teeth and get my muscles under control, following the king into the courtyard.

The sun is low on the horizon. It will be dusk soon. I'll be able to eat.

Any joy I feel at the notion dissolves as I catch sight of Itzcuani. The cold eyes of the royal guard commander regard me with what he probably intends as dispassion, but which feels to me like utter disappointment. My empty stomach knots up painfully as he salutes my father and assumes the initial stance.

"Commander Itzcuani has spoken to me, Acolmiztli," Father says softly, "of some reluctance, some hesitancy, in your fighting. It is not unusual for a young man as sensitive and intellectual as you to quail before another's fists—to falter in battle. Yet you are the crown prince of Tetzcoco. My heir. Show me that you understand the fullness of the role the gods have ordained for you."

After the lightest of sighs, King Ixtlilxochitl pulls back his shoulders, changing his bearing completely. The man before me sloughs off all traces of my father. Only our brave commander-in-chief remains, the brutal warrior who earned the titles of Acolhua Overlord and Chichimeca Chieftain on the battlefield, long before I was born.

"Defend yourself. Now."

Itzcuani comes at me like a giant of legend. Implacable. Fierce. Fast.

I manage to block many of his blows and kicks. But they keep raining upon me, unpredictable and never-ending. And he isn't holding back. I'll be bruised in the morning.

Once or twice I return the attack, but Itzcuani shrugs off my fists and feet like dead leaves scattered in late autumn.

"Stop," my father commands, his voice cutting through the grunts and slapping of flesh.

I turn and drop to my knees. Hot tears burn at my lowered eyes.

"Your Majesty, I am unworthy."

He clears his throat. "No. Never. Your worth is not the issue, Son. Your values are." He pauses, and draws in a breath. "Because you love order, the composing of songs, the drawing of glyphs, the building of monuments. . . . You hesitate before violence and destruction, as if they were the antithesis of everything that you hold dear. Yet you know this to be a lie. Look at me, Acolmiztli."

I lift my head. His face is full of hard love, and measured compassion.

"Nothing can be created without something being destroyed. Order cannot be achieved until violence quells disorder. Hence our temples to the twin creators, Tezcatlipoca and Quetzalcoatl—brothers and enemies, both. Until you feel the profound truth of this paradox— and feel it in your very soul—you will remain blind to the fact that battle is a dance. To learn its harrowing yet beautiful steps, you must find the chaos at the center of your being, occluded now by your obsession with creative endeavors, and channel it as you one day will the voice of gods. Like leadership, warfare requires you to become a conduit for violence. Your people need you to fight for them, to protect them unstintingly. You feel shame, confusion, perhaps anger at this moment, do you not?"

I cannot deny the dark emotions roiling in my chest, so I just nod.

"Good. Let that rise. Let it become fury, but not wild and undisciplined. The trick is to focus violence through the lens of skill, tempered by wisdom. Let order wield chaos, my child."

The contradiction strikes me as almost disgusting. Impossible, and sacrilegious. But I trust my father more than any man in the world.

"Now stand and face the commander. Hurt him, however you can. We shall not leave this courtyard until you do." He pauses again. "Understand that he will show you no mercy. Your enemies—abroad and in this city—would see you dead. Mercy is a luxury we cannot afford."

Itzcuani resumes his battering. But this time, the pain blends with my shame. With my fear of what my older half-siblings may have planned for me. With my outrage at Chimalpopoca's designs on our homeland.

I don't anger easily. Now, however? I am furious.

And this damn obsidian-eating son of a bitch won't stop punching me.

So I try to stop him. I pretend we're dancing—that he's someone I want to get close to, whose flesh I want to caress.

Before he knows it, I've blocked his latest blow and left him open. The bare skin of his abdomen glistens in the twilight like an invitation.

Funneling all the rage burning along my nerves, I slam my fist into his solar plexus.

The commander staggers, loosing a grunt of pain.

"Well done, Acolmiztli!" the king calls, signaling an end to the match. His sternness has softened. He is my father once more. "Remember what you've learned here. I had hoped to wait to have this conversation, but things are too perilous. I have just received word that the armistice has officially ended. Our blockade continues, but the Tepaneca and Mexica may still break through and attack us here at home."

The idea horrifies me. I am suddenly glad of today's examination.

Itzcuani has recovered and addresses me. "So this lesson may save your life. You receive a passing mark, Your Royal Highness. I recommend you for the calmecac, where your instructors will further hone your abilities." I allow myself a moment of internal joy while remaining outwardly composed.

"However," the king adds ominously, "there is also the matter of my bastard son."

I turn to stare at him. Father has refused over the years to speak of Yancuilli and his attempts at abuse.

"You may believe I have left you alone in that struggle. Yet I swear my eyes were always upon you, ready to intervene should it become necessary. I preferred for you to handle the conflict on your own, as you have. Now, however, you two will be beyond my reach. I do not trust that boy. And neither should you. There are political reasons I cannot eliminate him from our lives, so you sadly must grapple with him alone. Be wary, but be confident. You are better than he, by far."

At these words, I begin to kneel, ready to place my hands on his feet in filial respect. But my father stops me and pulls me into a gruff embrace.

"Come, Crown Prince Acolmiztli. Let us dine."

Bidding farewell to Itzcuani and exchanging pleasantries with me about the weather and an upcoming musical festival, the king walks us to our dining hall, where a feast awaits.

"Sit, my beloved men," Mother says. Her voice echoes slightly in the broad stone chamber. Light slanting in from high windows reveals that most of thirteen guest tables are empty, straw mats rolled up beneath them. "You have exerted yourselves in spirit and flesh. Come rest your sinews, fill your bellies, and let me ease the tension in your hearts."

I don't need any further encouragement. I unroll a mat across the royal table from them and begin to pile my plate high with delicious food from the royal kitchen.

Mother kneads at Father's shoulders. He leans back into her palms, half-closing his eyes. Only in her presence, for a time, can he drop the shield of propriety that as a king he must always hold before him. The fact that I'm sitting here makes no difference.

That's another lesson I've learned from them. Don't be stinting with your affection when it's just family. The kind touch or kiss of your beloved, surrounded by your children, is one of the most beautiful experiences the gods have granted humanity.

"Right there," he murmurs. "That's the spot, dearest one. Feed me, yes?"

She laughs, winking at me.

"How easily your father slips into childhood in my hands. Here, Your Incorrigible Majesty. I've unwrapped a tamalli for you."

She pops a piece into his mouth and he grunts with delight.

"Is that a bruise rising on your cheek, Acolmiztli?" she asks.

I'm in the midst of scooping up shrimp molli with a tortilla, but I stop to rub at my face with the back of my hand.

"I had to get Commander Itzcuani's approval before entering the calmecac. His test was . . . tough, but Father gave me the insight I needed to pass muster."

"Ah. Let me guess. The 'chaos conduit' speech," she quips, leaning forward to peck Father's cheek. "I thought you were going to avoid that one."

The king opens his eyes to give her a playful sideways glare.

"Woman, how dare you mock a tradition of the House of Quinatzin? Every crown prince must receive this wisdom from the man who sits on the throne."

Leaning forward, Mother whispers: "He means that he was a terrible fighter when he was your age, so his father had to consult with multiple priests to develop that little pep talk he just gave you."

"Foolish wench!" Father cries, turning and tickling her mercilessly. "Let's see whether your bladder can withstand my chaos-wielding fingers!"

I just shake my head. "Let's hope no one important walks in right now. You two are like teenagers."

After they've wiped away the tears and gotten their giggling under control, my mother addresses me. "I may jest about the origins of that lesson, but please take it to heart, Son."

I nod. Of course I understand. That's another lesson my wonderful parents have taught me. Humor takes the edge off the harsh truths. It's not a sign of disrespect to poke a little fun.

{7} GOODBYES

A T DAWN THE FOLLOWING DAY, I rise with a mixture of antic-ipation and trepidation. It has been too long since I met with the acolyte. I would like to drink in that beautiful face and voice once more before I move into the calmecac.

Fortunately, the person in question is also my instructor on palace protocol, royal etiquette and rites, all things relating to the elegant performance of my duties—including my ritual transition to boarding school.

I reach the study chamber of the small temple of Xochiteotl right as the first daylight watch begins. Izcalloh is poring over a painted book in which the patterns of princely behavior are prescribed.

They are as stunning as ever, dressed in richly embroidered skirt and blouse, with a sort of flowery triangular yoke draped over wide shoulders, pointing toward that slender waist.

Izcalloh's face, delicately painted with gold dust and rouge, is all planes and squares until they see me and smile. Then, suddenly, dimples soften the hard angles, and butterflies flutter in my gut. Even before becoming my tutor, back when I was a toddler, Izcalloh—four and a half years older—often cared for me, teaching me clever games and spellbinding me with fantastical tales. Is it any wonder I became infatuated?

"Crown Prince Acolmiztzin," they say, standing. "It has been too long, Your Royal Highness."

"Indeed, cherished acolyte and teacher. I was disappointed that you weren't in charge of at least some of my examinations."

They tilt their head and pause, as if considering their words carefully.

"As was I. But the Chief Counselor and your royal father thought it best."

I lift my eyebrows, but say nothing negative. "In any event, I'm here to receive your guidance once more. Tomorrow I must leave the palace for the calmecac of Tetzcoco. Please teach me the proper procedure."

They lower their head briefly, and I am entranced at the winding pattern of the braid piled impossibly high on their head. "As ever, it will be my honor and pleasure. This afternoon, you should begin taking your leave of those closest to you. In short order, you will be living at school, with no chance to visit your royal parents or siblings until the harvest armistice."

I grit my teeth to keep my emotions in check. "The calmecac sits at the northernmost edge of the sacred district, yet it seems I'm being sent to a distant land, cut off from everyone I . . . everyone I cherish."

"The separation is necessary for you to grow into the fullness of your personhood, without relying on loved ones, Your Royal Highness. Believe me, your days and nights will be rather occupied, to the point that you may find yourself unable to dwell on homesickness. Nevertheless, it is your duty to ensure that those you leave behind have a pleasant memory of your parting. Once you have taken your leave, the ritual journey to the calmecac begins. Come, let me show you what is required."

They gesture me over, and I struggle to focus on the diagrams in the codex despite the sweet, flowery scent that floats delicately from their sandy skin.

I nod, however, grasping the essentials of the ritual.

"I suppose my first farewell is to you, Izcallohtzin. The gods reward you richly for the guidance you have given me these last eight years. I hope to see you at the harvesttime dance. Maybe we can whirl through all those wild steps, like we did when we were younger."

A strange shadow clouds their face, features tightening into sadness. "Ah, Your Royal Highness has not heard. Given the unyielding stance of Tenochtitlan's new sovereign, the king has asked my father to serve as ambassador to Chalco. The Chalca have come into greater and greater conflict with the Mexica, and His Majesty believes they may be willing to ally with us. And my father—ah, he has asked me to join Mother and him in this work."

Izcalloh's mother is a Chalca noblewoman from the city of Tlalmanalco, so the appointment makes perfect sense. And Izcalloh is one of the most brilliant minds in Tetzcoco, knowledgeable about the intricate histories of Anahuac's many kingdoms, adept at the diplomatic niceties that can curb violence and change minds.

So why do I feel so disappointed?

Noting my disappointment, the acolyte touches my arm gently. "The post is not eternal, Acolmiztzin. I swear to return by the time you finish your studies, to serve you, as my father has served yours. Our families are bound to each other."

Before I can stop myself, I blurt out my revealing question.

"Has a xochihuah ever served as consort to an Acolhua king? Or concubine?"

I am not expecting Izcalloh to blush, but the rouge on their cheeks glows ruddier as they cast down their eyes.

"Not as a consort, for that goes against the divine mandate of procreation. But as a concubine, yes. Your namesake, former king of Coatlichan, did indeed take a xochihuah as his lover, then elevated them to a position of authority among his concubines. There is a song about them, I believe. 'Petals and Scales.' A ballad."

Of course. I know the piece. The Master of Song performed it, long ago, during a festival in honor of the flowery gods.

Clearing my throat, I reach out a trembling hand and lift Izcalloh's chin. "Just carry out your mission, do you hear me? Then come back, free of heart and mind. Your crown prince commands it."

Izcalloh, overcome at my unexpected display, just nods.

Worried about what other foolishness I might start doing if I linger, I hurry off to take my leave of the others in my life.

I have two sisters, but I only love one—Tozquen, named for our grandmother. Barely ten years old, she's bright and chatty like a parrot.

"Big Brother!" she cries as I enter the garden where she's tending flowers. A big green and yellow huipil almost reaches her knobby ankles.

"Good morning, Little Sib. Come give me a hug."

She wraps her thin arms around my waist, her head pressing against my chest.

"Don't go, Big Brother." Her muffled voice is full of tears.

"I have to, Little Sib. But the time will pass quickly. You'll be watching Tochpilli by yourself now, and he's a handful. I promise I'll bring you something pretty when I visit."

She's sniffling as she pulls away, but her eyes are full of determination.

"I'm your favorite, right? The only princess in Tetzcoco? Even when you're king?"

I can't help but laugh.

"Do you really think that I would ever make *Atototl* a princess?"

Our older half-sister, born to the daughter of a prominent merchant who slept with our father when he was a general, well before he got married. Though she's not royalty, being a royal bastard caught her a reputable husband, Lord Nonohualcatl, from a minor noble family in the Chimalpaneca borough.

Now she's determined to be designated a legitimate child of the king. A princess. But no. Never. She's conniving. Cruel. Ambitious. Crude. Only twenty-two, she acts like some gum-chewing madame running a house of pleasure, greedy for wealth.

"Until I have daughters," I promise Tozquen, tousling her long, black hair, "you will be the only Princess of Tetzcoco."

"I love you, Big Brother," she whispers, hugging me again.

"Me, too, Precious Parrot," I reply, kissing the top of her head.

I have younger brothers, but most of them are toddlers living in the concubine complex to the south of the palace. My mother was the one who insisted my father follow this tradition.

"You'll need more sons," she insisted, "if you are to cement your control of Acolhuacan. Legitimate issue you can marry off to Acolhua princesses so that our royal house is ascendant in every city. Thus have emperors ever held sway in Anahuac."

The memory makes me smile a little. My father is the romantic idealist. My mother, though she adores that side of him, remains as pragmatic as any Mexica noblewoman. She has given the king another royal son, however. Tochpilli, a boy of only three. Today I visit him in the nursery, fixing the string on his wheeled dog toy so he can lead it around, shouting "chichiton, chichiton!"

I watch him play for a while, heart full of chagrin.

"Bye, Little Sib," I say at last, standing to leave.

He doesn't notice.

I hope my older brother doesn't notice me, either.

Yancuilli is nineteen, a student in his final year at the calmecac. He's not illegitimate—not exactly. His mother was a Tepaneca concubine that my grandfather gave my father, to curry favor with the Emperor.

We have never gotten along. When we were younger, visiting the imperial hunting lands with our father, uncles, and cousins, he consistently beat me at every physical competition the older boys designed—races, wrestling, rabbit-snaring. Upon each victory, he would crow about his superiority. I still remember when I was eleven and he fifteen. Pinning me down with his knees, he laughed from above me.

"Not really fit to be a king, are you?"

I tried to wriggle free. "Perhaps, but a king I'll be, whether you like it or not."

"You'll die before Father does. You won't even make it to the age of twenty."

"You'd better pray that's true, bastard, because the first thing I'll do once crowned is order you beheaded," I spat.

"Oh, I pray. Every day. To Tezcatlipoca, Lord of Chaos and Destruction."

Thrusting up with my knees, I managed to make him tilt so far that he had to clutch at the ground to stay atop me.

"Then you're just as stupid as you are illegitimate," I answered. "There's a reason they call him the Enemy of Both Sides. He could turn on you in a second. Only a fool would put his destiny in the hands of a trickster god."

Laughing, Yancuilli punched me one last time before leaping to his feet and acting like he'd done nothing wrong. It was his typical routine.

Luckily, I've been mostly free of him for four years, except when his more recent duties have put him in proximity to me. Two months after he left for school, his mother died. Her manor at the edge of the royal estate stands empty. He has no reason to visit. And father will not grant him official status as a prince. He's merely a lord.

But at the calmecac he has risen to a position of power—one of the Tiyahcahuan, the youth leaders. He's already seen battle, conscripted last year to fight against the Mexica, so now he gets to wield authority over the younger students.

Like me, soon enough.

As much as I look forward to life at the calmecac, I dread the moment when he and I come face to face again. Father's warning yesterday, though welcome, was a bit superfluous. I know I have to be on my guard against him.

Saying goodbye to my parents is hardest of all. Izcalloh's voice echoes in my head as I steel my courage: "Tradition dictates the words and forms, but the timing is the adolescent's choice. He who leaves must speak first."

I wait until after dinner, as we sip chocolate served by royal attendants, leaning back on our feathered mats and sharing the day's events. I stare at them lovingly for a moment. Mother's black hair hangs loose and lovely over her exquisitely embroidered long-sleeve huipil. She seems ageless in her beauty. Father is wearing a simple white teucxicolli, the long tunic reaching his knees. His greying hair is pulled back with a cozoyahualolli—a rosette of white heron feathers worn by most Acolhua kings, heritage of the Chichimeca.

"Tomorrow I turn sixteen. I'll be leaving you, beloved parents," I say without preamble. "I entrust you to the people of Tetzcoco while I'm away. Yet my heart is heavy. My entire life has been lived at your side. More than the tribulations that await me at the calmecac, I fear your absence from my days will hurt the most."

Mother wipes a tear from her cheek. Father clears his throat and speaks to me, using the old words the Tolteca left behind. There is both sadness and pride on his face—open, unhidden.

"Though you came from the loins of your mother, and your father, it is the Duality, the Source, the Sovereign of the Near and the Nigh who winged down your soul from on high. Though your mother nurtured and reared you, though your father trained you and opened your mind to science, our skills and knowledge come from the heavens."

He looks at his queen, nodding, and she takes up the thread, looking at me with a wistful smile full of love and joy and nostalgia.

"When you were born, precious jewel, knowing our debt, we dedicated you to the Feathered Serpent, presenting you as an offering to his sacred school, the calmecac. Now it is time for us to relinquish our hold on you, to turn you over to whom you truly belong: the creative force whose sole property and possession is every human heart."

Father continues as she falls silent. "When you were young, nail of my finger and hair of my head, you were too weak to stand alone. Your mother lifted you in her arms, fed you, clothed you. Yet now you are nearly a man, strong and brave and true. When the sun rises, go without possessions, without another word to us, unshod and fasting, to the House of Tears. In that sacred school, noble boys are cast like copper, drilled like jade beads, carved like copil wood. There you will bud and blossom in time, becoming a flower that the Giver of Life will string into a necklace for divine glory. You will emerge a man, a noble, one ready to rule and to protect our people, to be a looming cypress that gives them shade."

A soft sob escapes my mother's lips as she puts her hands upon mine.

"Acolmiztli, my dearest son, do not look back lovingly at this palace as you go. Forget for a while that we your parents live here, that your prized drums and trumpets and whistles lie awaiting your touch, that the servants and siblings who so love you will spend their days in sorrow at your absence. Tonight, your childhood ends. Harden yourself against the trials that await you. Love is delicate, fragile. Learn to keep it deep in your heart, surrounded by disciplined flesh, sharp mind, resolute and sober defenses. In this life, there is no other way than to fight to protect what matters to you. In the depths of your despair, remember. You must become a shield against the wind for the fluttering flame of devotion."

They embrace me then, and I weep as a child for the last time.

{8} STARTING SCHOOL

THE DAY IS 5 REED. I wake before dawn, and, wearing just a loincloth, leave the palace as everyone sleeps except for guards, who say nothing at my departure.

As I cross the wooden bridge, however, I can make out figures in the dim light—hundreds of Tetzcoca lining the main road. In a human wave, they all bow at my arrival. In unison, they lift their voices.

"O Feathered Serpent, accept our child as your own. Make of him a king."

My people. I am overwhelmed by their love. The need to protect and nurture them. The welcome but daunting weight of that responsibility.

"Thank you, Uncles and Aunts," I respond, voice quavering.

Clenching my fists against tears, I step into the road.

It has been strewn with flowers, a final touch of softness for my royal feet. Head high, I walk toward the pyramid, rounding it to come to the complex of buildings where the priests of our city live and teach. The sky is already blushing with morning as I step under the archway leading onto the campus.

Awaiting me is the high priest, Cocohtli.

"Welcome, Acolmiztli," he says, raising hands dark with soot, "to the calmecac. Here there is no rank, save what one earns. You are a first-year, a postulant, and I mark you as such."

He rubs his palms over my forehead, cheeks, and chin, blackening my face.

"Each morning, after prayer and ritual washing at the river, you will obscure your visage in the central plaza, symbolizing your benighted mind, which we will illuminate."

As if on cue, a dozen boys my age emerge from the woods to the east of the campus, some still dripping wet. I see rivulets of blood running from ears or chest or thighs; part of our predawn ritual is piercing our flesh with thorns, just as the gods once spilled their own blood to set the sun in motion. The boys walk toward the banked and smoking ashes of yesterday's fire in the plaza, and each of them spreads soot over his face.

"Join them," Cocohtli commands, and I hurry to obey.

"Your Grace!" someone whispers hoarsely as I approach, waving me to him. I almost don't recognize the boy at first—so much taller, thinner, and harder has he become in the six months since I last saw him.

"Nalquiz?" I confirm as I approach. We've been friends for years. He's the youngest son of my father's top general, who is off at the moment, restarting the blockade of Coyoacan.

"Yes, and Acaxel," he says, pointing to the shorter smiling youth beside him. My heart surges with joy. It's the youngest son of my uncle Acatlohtli—my father's brother, highest judge in Tetzcoco.

"Cousin!" rasps Acaxel in greeting before leaning in close and winking conspiratorially. "Hope you kissed a girl or two before today, because you won't be seeing any for a long time."

Nalquiz just shakes his head in disbelief. "Do you not know your own cousin? Girls, boys, xochihuahqueh, . . . they all throw themselves at him. Of *course* he's kissed a few, idiot."

I cock my head to one side, ignoring their jabs. "Aren't there groups of young women living and working in the temples, training to be priestesses?"

"Our schedules are set so that we never see them," Nalquiz explains. "And if any boy is caught trying to enter their living space, he is beaten by the priest in front of the other students, and expelled from the calmecac."

Before I can express how ridiculous that punishment seems, the two of them seize each of my arms and pull me to where several dozen brooms lean against the wall.

"Grab one," Nalquiz mutters, "and start sweeping. The plaza has to be spotless before the sun peeks over Mount Tlaloc."

Without complaint, I join my friends and the other boys in the work of cleaning ashes, dirt, and leaves from the flagstones. They've developed a system, each student moving to a different part of the plaza to sweep an area that measures between one square hand and one square arrow. No one speaks. It's amazingly efficient. I find an unclaimed bit of dust and sweep it off into the grass that rings the plaza.

The sun's rays crown Mount Tlaloc as we return our brooms and rush to Sunrise Hall, picking up mats from beside the door as we enter and placing them in a pattern the boys have established over time, facing a slightly raised platform at the front. There is some quiet negotiation as Acaxel convinces the others to let me sit beside him, but within a minute of entering the hall, we are seated on our mats, hands on our thighs, awaiting the priest.

My stomach decides to growl. I feel irritated eyes on me.

"You'll get used to it," my cousin whispers. "We fast from dinner to lunch."

"Indeed," comes a strong if wizened voice. An elderly priest makes his way up one side of the hall, ascending the platform with cautious steps. His robes and tonsured silver hair mark him as a cuacuilli—a revered monk given few duties beyond occasional ceremonial chores and teaching. "We chastise the flesh so that it will obey us always. It is your most versatile tool—now used for building, now for warfare— yet it can turn on your heart with vicious deceit if you have not imposed discipline on your bodies. This truth the gods themselves discovered at the dawn of the fifth sun, our present age. Who can tell me how?"

I tap my mat.

"Yes. The new postulant. Speak."

"When they built the bonfire from which the sun and moon were to be born. Beautiful Tecciztecatl, son of Tlaloc, volunteered to leap into those flames and be transformed. But his divine body betrayed him three times, recoiling from the heat. Ugly Nanahuatzin, son of Quetzalcoatl—having lived his life covered in boils—knew how to endure pain. So he walked into the bonfire and sat amid the coals, word-lessly allowing his flesh to be consumed. Therefore is he the sun."

The old monk lifts his right hand in praise. "A wise answer. Does your cousin beside you know the price of Tecciztecatl's undisciplined flesh?"

Acaxel hesitates for a moment, then responds.

"Ashamed at Nanahuatzin's self-sacrifice, he leaps into the smolder-ing ashes. It takes much longer for him to burn, every second of it agony. Then both are reborn as glowing orbs on the horizon. The gods agree it isn't fair that both should shine with equal glory, so Quetzal-coatl takes a rabbit and hurls it at Tecciztecatl, darkening his face a bit. He becomes the moon, and Nanahuatzin the sun."

Our teacher, whose name I later learn is Iztacmitzin, then begins to build a lesson around the birth of the sun, seemingly pulling the connections out of thin air. Finishing the story of the birth of the heavenly lights, he reminds us that for a time the new sun just wobbled on the horizon, unable to start his course across the sky. The heat became atrocious, drying up the land, burning clouds into smoke. Then did the Lord of the Dawn—the morning star who heralds the morning—begin to shoot arrows at Nanahuatzin out of anger, screaming for him to move before the whole world was aflame. The missiles missed the sun, who instinctively hurled down his own darts, transforming the Lord of the Dawn into the God of Frost.

"Only when the gods allowed Quetzalcoatl to sacrifice them all," Iztacmitzin tells us, "could he use his aspect as Lord of the Wind to channel the divine energy of their blood into a blast that set the sun in motion at last. What rituals derive from these events, do you think?"

Several boys tap their mats. Our teacher looks at one, who responds, "Our daily bloodletting with maguey spines and mesquite thorns. If the gods were willing to spill their ichor to give us light and warmth, how could we not do the same for them?"

The teacher selects Nalquiz next.

"We're about to begin the month of Tepopochtli," he muses, "meant to ease us from the dry to rainy seasons. Unlike the foul Mexica, who claim their tribal god Huitzilopochtli is the sun, we'll revere Nanahuatzin Tonatiuh, who gives us just enough of his blazing heat to grow crops and survive."

The rest of the morning is spent poring over the Book of Days, learning the auspicious dates in the coming month and which ominous times to watch out for. Iztacmitzin also shows us diagrams of the sun's passage across the sky during mid-spring, as well as an almanac for tracking the movements of the Morning Star.

In a moment that leaves me dumbfounded, Iztacmitzin reveals a deep secret: the Morning Star and the Evening Star that appears in its absence *are the same god!* Quetzalcoatl and his double—his animal self, Xolotl, the dog-headed divinity, for whom my Chichimeca ancestor was named.

"One of many dualities that make up the hidden reality of the universe," the old monk concludes. "Which is why all leaders of Tetzcoco—religious, civic, or military—must be trained as priests, my young postulants. You cannot lead in Acolhuacan if you are blind to the innerworkings of the cosmos."

He dismisses us, and my friends lead me to the Mess Hall.

"Time to break our fast," Nalquiz says, his already pale face lighting up with excitement. He shakes his gangly limbs in hilarious anticipation of food.

Acaxel pushes his long bangs from his dark eyes and puts a hand on my arm. "But let me warn you, Acolmiztli—it's not much, and we have to make it ourselves. The good thing is we get to talk as much as we want for the next hour."

I laugh. "That means we just listen to you babble on like a chachalaca, doesn't it? I was almost shocked at your self-control all morning."

"I . . . uh . . . may have an opinion or two, yes," he replies, winking at us.

"You should've seen him during first thirteen days," Nalquiz tells me. "He got into *so much trouble.* How many times did they make you hold your head over a pot of chilis? Five? Eventually there was so much mucus, so many tears—and his throat was so sore—he couldn't speak a word!"

We make our way to a large stone griddle where the other boys are gathered. A fire blazes beneath the stone. Beside it on a table sit a few balls of maize dough. I notice students are patting theirs into tortillas, so I snatch one up and do the same. Acaxel glances around and grabs two, then tosses me another as I drop my tortilla onto the hot stone.

"Some of these fools can't count," he tells me, winking. "For dinner we get to make and eat more food, but lunch is always this light."

Balancing our hot tortillas on our fingertips when they're ready, we find a corner of the mess hall and eat slowly, relishing each bite. My friends catch me up on the gossip, naming most of the other soot-faced postulants to me and reciting their noble lineages. I know most of them, of course. The only total strangers are the two commoner boys whose excellence at their borough's telpochcalli schools earned them a place among us.

"I really enjoyed this morning's studies," I tell them. "I never expected learning in a group could be like that. Even for subjects I already know, the teachers delve deep and reveal all sorts of connections and hidden knowledge. When I'm king, I'm going to lower the age for admittance into the calmecac. I wish I'd spent the last five years here!"

Nalquiz pops his last bit of tortilla into his mouth and sighs. "Do you think you could marry me off to some noble family in Coatlichan or something? I don't want my sons growing up under your tyranny."

Kicking his feet against the packed earth, Acaxel giggles. "He can't stand it here. I'm not sure how he's going to make it all four years, to be honest."

"I'm the crown prince, Nalquiz. I'll take care of you."

"Uh, that doesn't really matter here," Acaxel warns. "You'll see soon enough."

After lunch, we proceed to the larger Sunset Hall on the western side of campus. Our movement from building to building allows the other students to receive instruction as well. There are postulants, beginners like me who start attending on their sixteenth birthday. After a year or so of study, postulants become novices, officially accepted into a priestly order, who can assist with basic religious ceremonies. Next they are promoted to cadets, allowing them to serve as squires to established knights. After proving themselves, cadets become initiates—fledgling priests and warriors. I catch

glimpses of these older boys, but we're not to be distracted. The punishments for tardiness are severe.

Two somewhat younger priests, about my father's age, are in charge
of instruction for the afternoon. Emiltzin and Caltzin are their names.
Almost indistinguishable, as if they were twins. Rumors suggest that
they are lovers. In any case, their dry, dense instruction is less enter-
taining that what we received that morning, but I find it even more
intriguing. They put us through our paces, reviewing some advanced
mathematics that I am lucky to have studied on my own. Most of my
fellow postulants fumble and make fools of themselves, despite several
weeks of study.

"Fine," grunts Emiltzin at last. "Brother Iztacmitzin tells us you were
studying the birth of the sun and moon this morning. As you know,
tradition tells us that the gods gathered in Teotihuacan for this event."

Caltzin opens a painted book, showing a map of Eastern Anahuac.
The glyphs of all major city-states indicate their location.

"That ancient city," he adds, pointing to the very edge of the map,
"lies roughly ten thousand rods to the north-northwest of Tetzcoco.
We will now divide you into three competing subcommittees of a
council. Each group is to present a recommendation to the king and
his prime minister—"

"For the purposes of the calmecac," Emiltzin interjects unnecessarily, "that means us."

"—recommending the route assigned to you. Calculate the speed
with which an army of five thousand warriors and their attendant
auxiliaries could travel the distance, and prove that yours is the best
option."

I tap my mat. "What if it isn't the best option?"

Emiltzin looks at me dispassionately. "Then find a way to make it
the best option."

As if to assess my ability, he assigns the worst mountain route—
not through passes, but over summits—to my friends and me, with a

few other boys who glare at me with naked anger. But I have literally studied military strategy with generals. I know I can find a solution.

I stare at the blank square of amate paper we're gathered around, thinking. Then I look up at them.

"No one expects an army to come over the summit of a mountain. It's counterintuitive and wasteful. And that's why it's the best option."

Nalquiz cocks his head at me. "Explain."

"We drop the auxiliaries. No cooks, tents, squires. Just five thousand elite troops—Shorn Ones and Otontin, mainly, plus the best of the other knightly orders. A forced march. No stopping."

Acaxel nods. "It's uphill for the first three-quarters of the way, but then it's a fast descent toward Teotihuacan."

Taking up a paintbrush, I do the math. "We could have soldiers at their gates in three hours. They'd be watching the plains here and the pass here, but they would be blindsided when our forces emerge here. No time to prepare for a siege. We would overrun them within another half hour. Use their local resources afterward."

The other boys are stunned, then excited. We spend a few more minutes hammering out the details, then offer to present first. The priests are thoroughly impressed, and the groups arguing for the remaining routes do so halfheartedly. Our success earns me some grim looks, but I am not at the calmecac to be these boys' friend.

I am not like them. I have been specially groomed, tutored, and trained—every moment of my life engineered to prepare me for a singular purpose.

I am the crown prince. I will rule Tetzcoco one day.

My duty is to be the best.

The rest of class is equally fascinating. We learn some essential surveying techniques for marshy land. Then we study several species of cane from the lakeshore, processing one of them for its medicinal use. Finally, the priests teach us to recite the history of the fall of Teotihuacan, looking at the images in a painted book to prompt our memory of those conflicts among the giants, who once lived there a thousand years and more ago.

Once dismissed, we march double time to the nearby woods. "To collect firewood," Acaxel explains. "Load your arms up with whatever thicker pine branches you see fallen. We'd rather not make two trips."

A cluster of young priests is waiting for us in the plaza when we return. I discover that they keep a bonfire lit all night, providing torches to the groups who awaken at different dark hours to do penance.

Hunger is gnawing at my belly, but though the sun is about to drop behind the western mountains, it is still not time for dinner. Instead, we rush to a large square of packed dirt just north of the Great Hall. Racks of weapons have been set on the perimeter. A battle-scarred war hero stands at the center. I recognize him at once—Captain Tenich, veteran of many battles with imperial forces.

Behind him are four older students. Initiates, well into their fourth and final year.

The youth leaders of the calmecac, I realize. One of them is Yancuilli. He sneers at me over the captain's shoulder.

"Postulants, a bit of sparring to warm the blood!" Tenich shouts, his eyes twinkling. "Grab your practice swords and square off against your partner."

I hesitate for a moment as my classmates march toward the racks. The captain nods at me in recognition.

"I see there's a new boy in your group," he calls. "Yancuilli, put him through his paces. Let's see what his father and yours have taught him."

"Yes, sir," my half-brother replies, bending to draw a macana from the weapons rack and tossing it to me. I snatch it from the air by its handle as he pulls another and rushes me with no further warning.

Fear and anger explode in my gut. I try to do as my father told me—to channel those dark feelings through the prism of fencing skills the commander of the royal guard has drilled into me since my coronation. I put it all to use: parry and riposte, lunge and attack, feint and remise.

But Yancuilli doesn't respond the way I expect him to. His moves are unpredictable, leaving my guard open again and again. He slaps the flat of his wooden blade against my stomach twice, pops its edge against my arms and legs, and finally slams it into my groin, sending me sprawling in a fetal ball of pain.

"You," I gasp, "don't fight honorably."

My half-brother spits and drops down to whisper in my ear. "And you fight like a child. Hear me, *brother*. You're not getting pampered here. You'll learn to defend yourself well, or you'll piss blood every morning from the beatings you'll get when sparring."

I see Captain Tenich shaking his head as I roll over and pick myself up. "Enough of that. Acolmiztli, it's a shock for everyone, how dirty warfare can be. But remember—the only honor on the battlefield is staying alive long enough to kill or capture as many enemy soldiers as you can. When you're face to face with the Tepaneca, we need you to think ferociously. Now take up your position. Let's walk through your mistakes."

He has memorized my every move. While the youth leaders supervise other sparring bouts, Tenich shows me where my guard was too high, when my body wasn't turned enough, how to shorten the arc of my attacks.

"Postulant," he says, after I've practiced the adjustments, "I've seen you play the drums. Seen you dance at different celebrations. I know you grasp rhythm, deep in your bones."

"Yes, sir. I do."

●◖◯◗●

"Good. Because combat has a beat. It's different every time. Some opponents waltz, while others jig. Watch them closely, Acolmiztli. You have to gauge that rhythm, fast, in order to dance them to defeat. To death. Understood?"

Heeding the captain's words, I glance at the sparring boys with new eyes. Their feet slap against the ground, sending up little puffs of dust. And I can feel them, sudden and clear: competing beats, thrumming through earth and air into my senses.

Gooseflesh rises along my arms and legs. He has helped me find my personal key to combat.

"Understood, sir. Thank you."

With a dubious smile, the captain nods at me. Then he makes the entire group drill together, carrying out a series of synchronized movements with our practice swords he calls a cemolin. With every repetition of this cemolin, I start to feel its essential rhythm.

There are fifty-two cemolintin, I will discover in time. Thirteen of these sequential series of movements are for the obsidian sword, and on this first day of my time at the calmecac, I learn the seventh by heart.

I will be ready for Yancuilli soon. Then we'll see whether I'm just a spoiled brat with mediocre martial arts.

When we slide our practice swords back into the rack, it's time to make dinner. In the mess hall, we work together to boil beans that have been soaking all day, adding chilis and a bit of venison we're given. Acaxel, Nalquiz and I split duties so we can eat faster and more—my job is to pat out and quickly cook the tortillas.

Our stomachs full and our bodies briefly rested, we walk, slowly for once, to the campus temple, which is dedicated to both Quetzalcoatl and his female counterpart, Cihuacoatl. After the older students have entered, we postulants arrange ourselves at the far left, looking up at the statues of our gods, who rise above altars covered in food prepared by the female students we never see. They've both been painted black with liquid rubber, though her face is half red while his bears swirling wind glyphs. Each is ornately dressed in dazzling white with red fringes.

The temple priest uses a jeweled ladle to scoop up burning copal incense from a copper bowl. Waving the smoke to the four directions, he intones a prayer, asking Quetzalcoatl to blow sweet winds down the mountain slopes to ease the heat and prepare the way for the tlaloqueh, who bring the rain late each spring. Next he appeals to Cihuacoatl, who protects her children like all mothers—with fierce abandon—requesting that she hold her shield up just a little longer to keep Tetzcoco safe from our enemies.

Then we students sing the sacred hymns of Teocoatl, naming this divine duality, to the slow and hypnotic beat played by another priest.

I feel someone looking at me. Without moving my head, I lift my gaze and scan the wall behind the images of the gods.

An eye is peering from the edge of the curtain that hangs on our end. Delicate fingers have curled around the fabric, pulling it taut to hide the spy.

A girl. Looking at me. When my eyes meet hers, she doesn't jerk away. She returns my stare with unabashed interest. Then she extends three fingers of her hand and wiggles them.

It takes me a moment to understand.

The number three? Motion? Ah, 3 Movement. A day. Her birthdate.

Her calendrical birthname, which most girls in Tetzcoco use all their lives.

Eyolin. Lovely syllables.

I know her, I think. The eldest daughter of Acacihtli, a minor judge from the Mexihtin borough.

A shiver of guilt makes me avert my eyes toward Cihuacoatl.

Keep these unchaste thoughts away, Divine Mother, I pray.

●❰❰❱●

As if in response, the gong sounds. It's time for bed. We postulants wind our way through the campus to the House of Pine, where each of us grabs a rolled sleeping mat and finds his place on the dirt floor. Nalquiz and Acaxel arrange for me to lie between them.

Sleep comes easy, but it is light and full of dreams in which Eyolin pulls the curtain back and steps toward me, lips parting as if to speak or kiss. Then she transforms, becoming Izcalloh, beckoning me closer. I'm awakened several times by the moans and muffled weeping of boys who have held their emotions in check as long as possible, and who now vent them softly.

Doing my best not to think about my own yearnings, or my parents' faces, I drop into dreamless unconsciousness for a while, until a priest awakens us with insistent calls.

It is midnight. Our turn to sweep the plaza once more. The bonfire burns bright, spreading ash in the light wind. Wordlessly, but with genuine vigor, we use our brooms to fight against the ever-encroaching entropy of the world: Tezcatlipoca's principal tool of chaos.

So much of our lives is spent like this, asserting order against decay.

A tired part of myself wonders why we even bother. But of course, I know the answer. We have no choice. We were born to impose our vision upon the wildness of the world, no matter how futile it seems. Thus did Quetzalcoatl and Cihuacoatl shape us at the beginning of this age, grinding the bones of the failed attempts at humanity that had gone before, bleeding divine ichor into that flour to form humans in their image.

Humans driven to create and to protect their creation.

Our turn done, we return to our mats for another four hours. Then, before dawn, another priest awakens us for the morning ritual.

At the plaza, we light pine torches in the bonfire and head into the woods.

"Two fir branches," Acaxel tells me, yawning, "and two maguey spines. You understand the ritual, yes?"

I nod. Of course I do. My father and tutors prepared me for schooling—taught me my solemn obligation to the gods.

Pulling away from the other boys, I scoop up the branches, snap spines from a battered plant. I walk fifty rods, down to the river and toward the east, and find a boulder behind which to keep myself unseen.

I extinguish my torch in the river and kneel, laying the fir branches like a blanket of green before me. Then, I puncture the skin of first my right and then my left thigh. The pain is bright and sharp, but brief. Soaking the spines with my welling blood, I set them carefully in the form of an X on the fir needles.

"I spill my essence," I whisper to the night that lingers before the coming of the sun, quivering darkness swirling around me, "in pay-ment for my life, to keep the wheels of the cosmos turning, and to show my devotion to the gods who died so all might thrive."

As if in response, the wind blows suddenly stronger, and above Mount Tlaloc the first gleam of morning veins the black sky with violet.

{9} CLASHES

THE CYCLES OF THIRTEEN days pass one after another, our quotidian routine repeated with small variations. One novelty is that after practice, Captain Tenich updates us from time to time on our continuing conflict with the Empire. The news is spellbinding: details about the blockade and siege of Azcapotzalco and Coyoacan, where Emperor Tezozomoc and his son King Maxtla rule. Hundreds of Tepaneca warriors have fallen. The cities suffer from a lack of supplies. The Mexica once again attempt to distract with attacks here in Acolhuacan, but they are harried back home over and over by reserve troops from our southern cities.

The dry season ends once High Priest Cocohtli leads the ceremonies atop Mount Tlaloc to appease its namesake, the God of Rain. Storms begin to roll in from the coast, breaking upon the summits to drench Acolhuacan. We students endeavor to face the regular downpours as we do all obstacles—with grim determination, never ceasing the rites and work we have been assigned, practicing even during the heaviest of showers.

Yet at night, faced with solitude in the darkness inside and the calamitous clash of water sprites in the thunderheads above, we sink into bereavement and fear. At times I swear I can smell my mother's perfume—as if she has ducked her head through the doorway to ensure that I am safely asleep. I thrust my homesickness down deep, but other boys cannot control their emotions. Some cry out for their parents at the worst of the thunderclaps. Others seek solace in each other's arms. I smile at those twisting shadows and look away. My mother's people condemn such intimacy between men, but in Tetzcoco, we judge it less harshly.

"The heart wants what the heart wants," my father often says. "Who are the rest of us to gainsay a person's desires and loves?"

In the end, my own desires get the best of me too.

It's one of the two commoner boys that discovers the absence of guards during the first night watch, when rain is the heaviest. I see him slip out twice before I follow to confirm my suspicions.

Just as I thought, he arcs his way along the perimeter of the campus in the pouring rain, till he comes to the small temple with its attendant dorms.

A girl is waiting for him under the eaves of a storage hut. When I interrupt their kiss, she almost screams. Then her eyes widen in recognition, and she almost screams again.

"Hush. I won't tell anyone about your little tryst. But go inside and awaken Eyolin. I need to speak with her."

My classmate stares at me as we wait. "Forgive me, Your Highness. I didn't mean to—"

I wave his apology away. "Tonight I'm a sinner, just like you. Later we can ask forgiveness of the gods."

"Acolmiztli," a sweet voice croons above the din of the rain. I turn to face Eyolin, who has emerged from the nearest dormitory. Her black hair is loose and damp, as is her cotton shift, which reveals her body in ways that make my heart pound.

I take her hand and pull her into the hut. It is dark, but dry. Though I can barely make out her delicate features and pomegranate lips, Eyolin's warmth and scent fill the closed air of the space, driving all else from my mind.

"I have thought about you every night," I confess, "since your lovely eye fell upon me from behind that curtain."

"And I have dreamed about you, dearest prince, for the past three years. Since your coronation, when you stood tall and handsome before us all."

Her voice is both soft and strong, like a babbling brook that slowly wears down the stones with its current. In that music are harmonics of desire that set the strings of my own flesh to quivering.

We have little time. No further words are needed. My mouth finds hers in the darkness, and we come together with a moaning hunger, ignoring the chaos of lightning and thunder, howling wind, and torrential rain.

In the heat of lovemaking, I almost call her by Izcalloh's name.

But she is Eyolin. Precious in her own way.

We melt together till the fire in our veins cools. Then we lie side by side on the dirt floor, holding hands, until my gut tells me I must leave or be discovered.

"Every night that it rains," I whisper in her ear, before giving her one last kiss and slipping into the slackening drizzle. The storm in the heavens, like the one in my heart, has spent itself for the moment, and the moon winks at me from gaps in the clouds.

My furtive encounters with Eyolin become a regular part of my school life, as dangerous as sparring with my brother. But as my father says, a man need not fear danger. He need only face it with courage and skill. I have begun to acquire both.

During battle practice, I find that my talent lies less with the obsidian sword than with dual macuahuitzoctli—the short wooden swords almost like knives. For warfare, their triangular heads are edged and tipped with obsidian razors, but my sparring pair just have blunt wooden points.

In my hands, they become mallets of percussive pain. I leave many boys bruised as I slide in close, my nimble hands stabbing them over and over with a speed learned from so many years at the drum.

Still, the larger obsidian sword and thrusting spear are the standard-issue weapons for warriors throughout Anahuac, so we get drilled on their use every day. Every fortnight or so, the captain obliges me to cross blades with my bastard half-brother. I use the opportunities to study his fighting carefully. There's a clear rhythm emerging to his style, one he likely doesn't know, given his blind arrogance. And like slapping out counterpoint on a drum alongside another percussionist, I suspect I will one day be able to slip inside the beats of his attacking dance and finally best him.

I bide my time, however, even after learning all thirteen of the cemolintin for the obsidian sword. With every victory against me, Yancuilli grows more arrogant and careless.

"Why are you holding back?" Captain Tenich whispers as he pulls me to my feet after our fourth match, wiping blood from a vicious gash in my forehead that my half-brother has just given me.

"Commander Itzcuani once told me, 'Never let your enemy see your full strength until you know you can defeat him.' The lesson has stayed with me, along with the memory of his punishments."

Tenich chuckles. "Yeah, I went to school with that hard-ass. Good advice. Just make sure your full strength is enough before Yancuilli sends you to the medics."

At last, three months into my schooling, I face off against my rival for what I hope is the last time. Ominous grey clouds hang above us, like a funeral shroud that would bundle us forever. A drop of rain splashes against my face as Yancuilli assumes his stance. I ignore the weather, focusing on his feet and shoulders, which I can now read like the glyphs in a painted book.

"Are you ready for another beating, kitten of the Acolhua?" he sneers.

"Shut up," I snarl without looking at his face, "and fight me, you bastard."

With an enraged grunt, he attacks, a downward stroke that I parry, only to have him spin so that his blade comes around again in an arc. I have to hop backward to avoid being struck, and he immediately lunges for me again. As I parry and dance away, I grasp that he is using a variation on the eleventh cemolin. It's as if a drummer has taken a 4/4 rhythm and stretched it into 7/8, shifting the downbeats, inserting more pauses. My half-brother probably believes that he has made his moves random, unpredictable, but once I feel the cadence, I immediately adapt to it.

At first we move as one, my mirroring of his moves forcing a curse through his clenched teeth. Then I slip in and out of his defenses, tapping him with the flat of my blade, feeling out his defensive strategy. It is weak. The fake haphazardness of his style is all about attacking.

So I count the beats until it's time for one particular move—the centlacolmetztli, or half-moon. As Yancuilli swings his macana in that 180-degree sidecut, I turn my back to him, dropping to my knees so that the wooden blade passes above my head. At the same time, I thrust backward with my own sword, slamming its broader end into his groin.

He falls to his knees, gasping in pain.

Lightning forks across the darkling sky above us.

I spin on one knee and next smash the pommel of my weapon into his throat. He topples backward, wheezing, his eyes shutting against the pain.

The clouds open up then, and curtains of water blur the world. All I can see is Yancuilli, writhing in the mud. I jump onto his chest, pinning his arms. My heart is thundering louder than the storm around us. A need I have never felt rises within me.

To humiliate. To obliterate.

It overwhelms skill, order, ethics. My nerves twitch with unfiltered chaos.

I slam my fist into Yancuilli's face. Once. Twice. But as I pull my arm back for a third blow, Captain Tenich pulls me off, hauling me to my feet and shouting above the pounding of the rain.

"Enough! You've proven your worth and made your point!"

Then his look of anger and worry dissolves. Turning his head so only I can see his smile, the captain leans close and says softly, "Well done, Your Highness. Well done, indeed."

The other youth leaders help my half-brother up. As he stumbles woozily through the rain, the rest of us carry the practice weapons back to the armory. There, Tenich gathers us round to let us know the latest, just in from a messenger.

"Joyful tidings," he says, winking to us in that impish way of his. "Emperor Tezozomoc has waved the white flag. He sues for peace. The long war has ended, boys. Acolhuacan has won!"

Cheers go up all around. I join in, exuberant.

"Our forces have ended the blockade and will be returning soon," the captain continues. "Once they've been feted and have rested, I shall convince some of those heroes to pay you a visit, to tell you of their exploits and tutor you in the fine points of establishing siegeworks."

Though I now feel confident that I could go into battle and survive, I still sigh and slump in relief. A weight has lifted from my shoulders. Fifteen years of war is quite enough. Let us have peace in which to make music, write poetry, plant new gardens, build great monuments and buildings.

I yearn to see Tetzcoco brimming with artists and philosophers, engineers and actors. Too many years have been spent on war; too many men.

To rule over such a paradise is my grandest dream.

Not a full week of thirteen days has passed before the whispers start. At lunch and before prayers, I begin to hear to word *usurper* repeated in hushed tones. It's one thing for malcontents throughout Alcohua-can to grumble about the losses they've incurred due to their Over-lord's war. Patriotism doesn't require blind obedience. Criticism and debate are necessary and useful. But a Tepaneca slur against my father? Repeated in the most elite school in his city?

I decide to ignore it, figuring I may be overreacting to what are probably harmless conversations. But then at practice one day, I hear Yancuilli mutter to one of the other youth leaders, "If I'm at all related to Xolotl, it's through my mother's blood. My father is a usurper."

Now I understand the source of the whispered slurs. Yancuilli—son of a Tepaneca concubine, enraged by his humiliation at my hands and Tezozomoc's defeat—has decided to wage a war of gossip against his own father's legitimacy in a bid to harm me. I'm tempted to con-front him, but instead I wait until dinnertime and interrogate my friends, who are more attuned to gossip than I am.

"It's that old lie," says my cousin Acaxel. "You know, how your father and mine aren't truly descended from the imperial Chichimeca family."

I sigh: "Ah, that foolishness again. Some Tepaneca will believe any damn thing to claim *their Emperor* should be named Chichimeca Chieftain."

"And that's not," Nalquiz observes, "the way Chichimeca titles work!"

"Tezozomoc has never cared about the rules of peerage," I reply. "He's spent fifteen years attempting to sow chaos in Acolhuacan and turn people against my father."

"Let's hope this new peace is lasting," Acaxel muses.

I have my doubts, but before I can express them, Nalquiz interjects.

"Oh! The initiates are finishing the repairs to the Hall of Song this week, friends. The priests are going to host a celebration there on the thirteenth day. Singing and dancing, at long last! Maybe even some rogue will smuggle in a gourd of wine or two," he finishes with a smile.

{10} THE HALL OF SONG

Eyolin's Question

The night before the dedication
we're laying in the dark,
Eyolin's head nestled
in the crook of my arm.

"Do you love me?"
she asks, her voice quavering.
There's another question
hidden in those words:
will you make me your queen?

Thunder claps before
I can answer.
As its echoes dies,
I kiss the crown
of her head.

"You are precious to me,"
I say at last.
The words *love*
and *precious*
are so close
in our native tongue—
tlazohtla
tlazohtli.

But her silence tells me
that she hears the difference
and understands.

Dedication

All the male students gather at last
in the Hall of Song, a smaller replica
of the House of Flowers,
which I know so well.

The Master of Song arrives
and we bow as he makes his way
to the sacred spot
where the drum will soon stand.

"Though fire once gutted
this holy hall, silencing its harmonies,
stilling its rhythms—your hands
have lifted it once more,
in echo of the work of the gods
at the beginning of each new age
when they repaired
the destruction
of the last.

"Today we celebrate its rebirth
and rededicate this building
to Huehuehcoyotl,
that Old Coyote,
Sovereign of Dance and Song."

He gestures to the image
of the prankster deity
on the wall behind him.

"Before them must stand a drum
to please their pointed ears
with beautiful beats. Who better
to set it here than acolytes
of their favorite lovers,
Xochipilli and Xochiquetzal,
god and goddess of every pleasure?"

At this signal, two temple attendants
enter, carrying a drum between them.
Not men or women, but two-spirit folk—
one a xochihuah, the other a patlacheh.
Such dual beings play special roles
in our rich Tetzcoca faith.

I think of Izcalloh, so far away now,
but ever-present in my heart and memory,
brilliant and elegant and spiritual,
partaker of divine mysteries.

The instrument itself appears
scorched by fire and ancient.
Olmaitl mallets hang
by a leather thong.

As they set the drum before
the Master of Song, he speaks again.
"The gods have willed that today
the greatest drummer in Tetzcoco
stand in our midst. I call upon him
to seal this dedication

with a song we all
can dance to."

He looks at me and gestures.
"Crown Prince Acolmiztzin,
come stand at the drum
and make the gods rejoice."

At the Drum

All eyes are on me
as I make my way forward
without hesitation.
Though I couldn't know
I would be called upon,
for music I am ever ready.
It is a pivotal moment,
and I shall do my duty,
certain that my skill
and confidence
will never falter.

I remember my father's words to me
as we ate dinner after our final fast:
"If you hope to one day lead men into battle
they must do more than trust or fear you.
They must admire you, must love you.
You have no choice but to be the best.
Then will they lay their very lives down
at your command. Then will Tetzcoco
bend its knee gladly, knowing a man
like a god lifts himself above them
so they might find protection
and might feel relief
in the ample shade
of his mighty
branches."

It is time for me
to be more than a boy,

more than a man.
I must make them hear
the divine song itself.

My hands settle on the worn wood
and then begin to slap out a rhythm.
It's an old song, from my father's youth.
Everyone knows it. They soon join in.

My First Song

Let us all be friends,
let us steal away a heart.
Only here can we snatch
such love like a bloom.

So stand my friends
and beat your drums!
Come, shake your rattles!
Yes, stamp your feet!
Let's seize those flowers
while there's still time!

Let your passions rise at last,
bundle up your heart with joy.
The blossoms fall into your hands—
frangipanis, gold and sweet,
petals scatter as you dance!

They sing with gorgeous voice,
all those sacred birds in flight—
the cotinga, the ibis, the oriole,
the quetzal, the parrot, the mockingbird!

The ibis calls first,
then all respond—
rattles and drums,
hands and feet!

Now stand my friends
and beat your drums!

Come, shake your rattles
and ring your bells!
Yes, clap your hands
and stamp your feet!

Feel the rhythm
of the song divine—
let's seize those flowers
while there's still time!

The Students

All the boys have been
dancing in a frenzy,
shouting out the chorus,
stamping their feet
and clapping their hands.
Like a puppeteer, I hold
the threads of their souls
in my hands.

I don't want the dance to stop.

So I grab the olmaitl,
wooden mallets with rubber ends,
and I send them spinning
to my own rhythm,
frenzied and complex
like making love
at the heart of a storm.

My Second Song

Fire-red parrot,
you keep flaring up,
the blaze of your crest
has set me aflame
till I groan your name!

Sweet-smelling incense,
dazzling popcorn bloom,
you swear your love is true:
but everything's impermanent,
even me and even you.

We're born to be abandoned,
so I know you will leave at last,
as will I, when heaven calls.
Such is the fate of everyone—
to be shorn of all our flesh.

I see you arrive
among these nobles,
gentle, lovely creature.
You perch, my blue cotinga,
resting on my feathered mat.

I ache as you croon,
my golden oriole,
sweet frangipani bloom—
you swear your love is true,
but I have only borrowed you.

As when cocoa is crushed
and blended with medicine,
or I am offered a tobacco tube—
if my heart takes her in,
she will make my heart drunk.

But battle is waiting,
a man's holy destiny—
what if I return to find
that she's left this earth
forever, my nobles?

When fighting, will I refuse to go
to the Place of the Shorn?
"My heart is now precious,
for I am a poet in love—
and my flower is golden."

Or will I leave her behind,
for my heavenly home,
surrounded by blooms?
Will emeralds and feathers
be my eternal reward?

I surrender to the will of the gods.
Let me live or let me pass away!
Let me be bundled and burned,
poet though I be! But, I beg—
let my heart not be her captive!

{11} BATTLE

AS IF MY SONG were prophecy, tragic news comes a few days later.

My friends and I are eating our meager breakfast when Captain Tenich enters the mess hall and approaches us. There is no trace of his accustomed humor on that face.

"Acaxel, Acolmiztli—you need to come with me, boys."

Bewildered, we follow him. But he doesn't lead us to any of the many halls on campus. Instead, we walk out the north entrance of the calmecac and head for the armory, which doubles as Tetzcoco's military headquarters.

"Are we going to see my father?" Acaxel asks, but the captain just quickens his pace in response.

Inside the fortified building, we are led to the strategy room, where troop movements are being tracked on the large map of Anahuac painted onto the floor, an even larger replica of the one in the palace strategy room.

Standing over it is my father. Flanking him are his commanders, including my cousin Zoacuecuenotl, hollow-eyed and unshaven.

"Elder Brother," Acaxel says. "You've returned from the siege. Thank the gods."

The king glances up at us, his features drawn and grim.

"My dearest son. My beloved nephew. It pains me to pull you from your studies for such ill tidings. Yet thus have the gods ordained."

Acaxel's eyes are going red, glistening with prescient grief. His voice rasps as he speaks.

"Where is my father, Your Majesty? Why is he not by your side, Elder Brother, here where he can defend Tetzcoco and all of Acolhuacan?"

What have you two done with him? My cousin doesn't say those words—would never dare—but we all hear them just the same. Zoacuecuenotl pulls his cape tighter around him, as if to keep the chill of tragedy from sinking into his flesh.

"When Emperor Tezozomoc surrendered," my father begins, "he was at first quiet. After thirteen days, however, he extended an invitation. A feast, to celebrate the new peace between Tepanecapan and Acolhuacan. To be held at the old retreat in the forest of Temamatlac, in the southern reaches of our territory."

I can't keep quiet. "A trick, surely."

"Thus did General Acatlohtzin conclude as well," Zoacuecuenotl says, his jaw clenching as if barely able to contain his emotions. "Though custom makes it impossible to ignore such an invitation, my father refused to let the king attend, offering to go in his stead with the Shorn Ones. It is only due to their fierce hardiness and courage that we know what befell my father there."

Acaxel falls to his knees, eyes wide, tears rolling down his face. But he says nothing, shuddering in silent sorrow as he awaits the rest of the news.

The king grits his teeth and balls his hands into fists. A grunt of rage and bereavement escapes his lips.

Acatlohtli is his most beloved sibling.

Was.

"It appears," he rasps, "that while half our troops were off in Tepanecapan and most of the rest were keeping the Mexica at bay, rebel factions have gradually seized control of four major Acolhua cities: Chimalhuacan, Acolman, Huexotla, . . . and Coatlichan."

More than any other news today, the loss of our biggest, most powerful city is an unfathomable blow. Without Coatlichan, Tetzcoco—and all of Acolhuacan—is in serious jeopardy.

"Acatlohtzin arrived at the retreat only to find gathered there the new leaders of those cities, as well as contingents from the Mexica and the Colhuahqueh. Most distressing was the presence of noblemen from Tetzcoco itself, . . . including the entire leadership of the Chimalpaneca borough."

The king turns his head to spit in rage before continuing, his voice rough with emotion. "My brother delivered my message: The Tepaneca are to no longer cross Moon Lake or otherwise set foot in Acolhuacan. Peace does not mean alliance. Then, that despicable Maxtla, who was overseeing the supposed celebration in his father's name, growled that the Emperor had not summoned General Acatlohtzin, but King Ixtlilxochitzin. 'Yet we are glad to kill you in his stead, for now,' the monster declared. 'Acolhua, show your loyalty.' Upon which our own people fell upon my brother and killed him, along with most of his warriors. Only two escaped to bring me this dire report."

My father slumps, grief overwhelming indignation as his hands and lips quiver.

Acaxel begins weeping in earnest now, punching at the tiled floor and howling. I kneel beside him, attempting to give him comfort. I can't fathom what he is feeling. I don't want to imagine the loss of my father.

Later I learn the details my father has omitted. Maxtla had the Acolhua traitors flay my uncle alive, then drape his skin across a boulder. His elite soldiers received similar treatment.

Commander Zoacuecuenotl steps to his younger brother's side, pulling him to his feet and embracing him gruffly.

"Our revered father accompanies the sun now, Younger Sibling. Weep not for him. The ultimate glory is his. Free of this sorrowful, slippery earth, he has found true joy and honor beyond death."

Father watches, eyes full of compassion, as they console each other. After a moment, Acaxel's sobs subside, and the commander releases him. My father, setting aside his own bereavement, taps at the map before us with the wooden pole. I notice at last the fleet of canoes coming from Tenochtitlan, the stone figures representing battalions arrayed to our south and north.

"They are coming to this city. From three sides. Our troops deployed in Tepanecapan will not arrive in time to protect us, and the new king of Coatlichan has mustered the southern Acolhua batallions in support of the Emperor."

Thinking of Izcalloh, I ask, "What of Chalco? Has Ambassador Cihtzin had any success in rallying the Chalca Confederation to our aid?"

"None of the messengers I sent south have returned with word, Son. And the Republic of Tlaxcallan will only offer asylum, not military support. We could empty the city and retreat east over the mountains into that foreign land, but . . . to what purpose? We are Tetzcoca, heirs of Toltecayotl and Chichimecayotl." His voice begins to rise and harden as he makes his case. "We shall not renounce our Way. We shall stand and defend this city at all costs. Every man old enough and every woman strong enough will fight."

Acaxel, his voice shaking, looks up with burning resolve. "Even postulants?"

The kings nods. "You two will accompany us into battle. Acaxel, you will go with your brother south to meet the traitorous Acolhua. Avenge your father's betrayal. Stop their advance. Acolmiztli, Captain Tenich assures me you have made much progress. Good. We march at dawn, to the lakeshore. We shall push the Mexica into the rotting sediment they so love to dredge up."

Instead of the calmecac, we are escorted to our homes. Acaxel follows his brother to the family manor to console his mother and sisters. Soldiers walk me to the palace, where my mother is waiting with kisses, food, and more distressing news. It has been four months since last we saw each other, but we have little time for pleasantries or catching up. Peril is upon us.

"Rumors are flying," she tells me as she urges me to eat. "Support for the emperor is spreading like wildfire throughout Tetzcoco. Your father has sent soldiers into the boroughs of the Mexihtin, Tepaneca, and Chimalpaneca. It was a necessary move: imposing a curfew and keeping groups from congregating to plot against us. Yet it seems to be worsening rebellious sentiment in the other neighborhoods."

I take a sip of water. "Then we have to win on all three fronts. Mexica on the shore; Acolhua to the south; Tepaneca from the north. If any of those armies reaches the city, Mother—"

She lifts a hand. "I know. Tetzcoco will tear itself apart. The common folk are tired of conflict. They would rather give in to Tezozomoc. And many noble factions see this as their opportunity at last to seize more power."

I think about my bastard brother and the whispers at school. I wonder how much my conniving sister is involved with this rebellion; if she has drawn him into her machinations.

"We should keep a close eye on Yancuilli and Atototl."

She taps her heart. "I already convinced your father to have them watched by his best merchant spies. I trust neither of them myself. But now, off to your room, my son. Your father will be addressing the city before dusk. Clean up and dress well. Let's leave together at the end of this watch."

Once in my room, I dismiss my attendants and run my eyes over my possessions: instruments from all over Anahuac, including multiple drums and conches and flutes; statues of not only gods, but of beautiful women and men and xochihuahqueh from our greatest legends; paintings of landscapes both familiar and strange; clothing for every season, every occasion, every social class. Running my hands over such wonderful objects, I imagine them burning as the city is sacked. A sobering thought. But I am more than these things. I am the Crown Prince of Tetzcoco, son of the Chichimeca Chieftain, Overlord of Acolhuacan.

And tomorrow I march into battle alongside my father.

My gut roils at the thought. The palms of my hands tingle.

Am I ready? To fight? To perhaps lay down my life for Tetzcoco?

An old war song reminds us: "Ignore the braggart and his boasts— no man knows his mettle until a blade is flung his way in battle."

But what I feel isn't fear, I realize. At least not entirely. It's anticipation. I'm about to be measured, weighed, judged by the gods on the burnt and bloodied field.

The calmecac has done all it can to prepare me. I pray that I am truly worthy of my lineage, of my people.

Not much later, we're crossing the wooden bridges and heading toward the sacred square at the foot of the pyramid. It feels strange to wear a cape, vest, and sandals again, after so many months barefoot and with only a loincloth. Already my skin has become used to hardship and exposure. How much more so after a long winter—after another three and a half years at the calmecac?

If I can make it that long, of course. If my city, my people, can withstand the onslaught.

The remaining nobles of Tetzcoco are arranged in front. Mother and I are led by royal guards through the throng of commoners to our designated place. The pyramid looms above us, its double summit scintillating in the golden-pink light of the setting sun.

My father emerges from the interior of the pyramid to stand between the twin temples, as if to symbolize his dilemma: whether lineage—Quetzalcoatl's way—or crisis—overseen by Tezcatlipoca—will decide the future of Tetzcoco's leadership. Resplendent in his royal attire, a blend of Toltec and Chichimeca traditions, the king addresses the gathered crowd.

"Years ago, upon the death of my noble father, this city selected me to succeed him. On the day of my coronation, I humbled myself, admitting my inadequacy, conscious that the Lord of Chaos might seek a replacement for me. Yet I swore to do my utmost to protect you—to rise to the occasion and become a towering cypress that gave Tetzcoco and all of Acolhuacan shade. Graced for a time with the gift of rulership that flows from the source—the Great Duality, Sovereign of the Near and the Nigh—I have sought to honor my fleeting role as your king, to bring glory to this turquoise diadem set upon my head. I have spread my wings and tailfeathers to protect you while using talons and beak to keep the enemy at bay."

There are shouts of encouragement and love, but also hissing and jeers. A part of me wants to take the guards and hunt through the crowd for the dissenters. But Mother is right. Taking action against other Tetzcoca right now will only worsen the situation.

"I know, ye nobles and commoners who have entrusted to me the care of this city, that even now I am being watched from the heavens above, from the Land of the Dead below, and from every nation across the sea-ringed world. The duty to prove my worthiness to rule is my own. The Mexica approach over Moon Lake. Rebel Acolhua march from Temamatlac to our south. And round Lake Xaltocan to our north come rushing the hordes of Tepaneca, eager to expand their empire.

"Harken, my beloved Tetzcoca—I shall never yield!" The shout booms throughout the sacred plaza, amplified by his courage and engineered acoustics till it sets our very bones vibrating. "My family's patron god, whose altar stands at the heart of the palace, is the Feathered Serpent—who values royalty and lineage, traditions passed down generation after generation, knowledge of rulership and deep wisdom inscribed in our hearts. Not meekly shall I abandon the mat of power. Nor shall I easily permit any man other than the Crown Prince—the greatest mind our people have ever known—to succeed me. We are the heirs to Toltecayotl, to Chichimecayotl. And on the morrow, we march to war!"

A roar of approval goes up from the sacred plaza then, and my heart is filled with hope.

A full watch before dawn the next morning, a page helps me into the battle gear my father had artisans make for me. First the padded cotton armor, then over that a feathered tunic and kilt—the iridescent red and green of quetzal plumage. Copper greaves to protect my legs, matching bands for my upper arms and wrists. A sturdy wooden helmet in the shape of a puma's head, covered in yellow parrot plumes.

As the page straps on my sandals, I slide a pair of macuahuitzoctli knives into the belt of my kilt. I'm hefting my obsidian sword and shield, getting a feel for their weight, and trying to ignore the jangling of my nerves when my father enters with a small drum in his hands.

"You look like a true warrior, Son," he says with a wistful smile.

I bow my head and tap my heart with the pommel of my sword.

"You honor me, Father. Is that a signal drum?"

"Indeed," he says, strapping it to my back with a leather harness. The weight is light, natural, as if I'm meant to bear it. "I want you at my side during the battle, communicating my commands with the appropriate rhythms. You know them, I trust?"

"By heart," I assure him.

"Then let us be off, Acolmiztli. The latest report has the fleet of war canoes closing on our marshes. They have come slowly, expecting a naval response, but I want them in the water while we're on land. I must use our smaller numbers as strategically as possible."

The troops have already been arrayed in two columns along the western road. We make our way to the vanguard, and I see that the king has organized a nauhtzontli—four units of four hundred men. A unit of archers; another armed with spears and atlatls; and two units of infantry—a full forty pantin, each of those twenty-man squads comprised of a seasoned veteran leader, younger warriors, and students from the calmecac and various commoner schools.

An impressive job of organization on such short notice. Our military is among the best.

We reach the commanders, bannermen, and god-bearers at the front. Father turns to me and gestures at the army behind us.

"I need a forced march. I want us to cover the distance in half a watch. Can you set an appropriate beat?"

I hand my sword and shield to my page.

"Yes, Your Majesty," I reply, slinging the signal drum in front of me. Then, conjuring up the pace for sixteen hundred souls, I begin to slap out ringing sixteenth notes.

Someone sounds a conch. The army surges into movement like a fire wyrm, tail stretched out for hundreds of rods as it writhes its fast way down the road.

The inky black of the forest gives way to brambles and grass, then the reeds and canes of the marshes. Before long, under the dual light of the setting moon and the smears of dawn in the eastern sky, I can make out the narrow forms of Mexica war canoes. Some have reached the far edge of the marshes and are attempting to navigate the twisting passageway to shore.

Anticipation kneads at my stomach. In moments, my first battle will begin.

"Signal to the centzontli of archers: Take up your positions!"

I pound out the rhythms. In the distance behind me, the order is repeated with flags. Twenty pantin of archers array themselves along the marsh in front of us.

"Nock your arrows!"

My hands slap out the command.

"Take aim!"

A flurry of notes.

"Release!"

At my signal, four hundred bowstrings twang in unison, and arrows hiss over the marshes toward the canoes. I hear distant cries. It looks as if shields have gone up, but the occasional scream suggests that coverage isn't complete.

"Nock!" my father shouts again. "Aim! Release!"

Together, we send volley after volley. The Mexica return fire, a trickier proposition from drifting boats. Still, many of our archers are struck. Some fall forever amid the mud.

Once the commanders determine that the archers have done what they can, and before their arrows are depleted, my father orders the wielders of atlatl and spear to the frontline, to be protected by a centzontli of infantry with larger shields.

There are several tense moments of exposure as we wait for the Mexica to come within forty rods of the shore, the maximum reach of a spear hurled by an atlatl. Enemy arrows thud into shields, the mud, and Tetzcoca bodies. The commanders have the king and me retreat a few rods, just to be certain.

Then come the shouted commands, which I echo in the language of beats:

"Set!"

The warriors place the butt of their spear in the cup at one end of the atlatl.

"Reach!"

Holding a spear balanced in their atlatl, they reach back their arms.

"Hurl!"

Thrusting arms forward in an arc as they grip their atlatl, they send their spears flying through the air at tremendous speeds. I can now make out individual Mexica on the canoes. Many are pierced by the javelins, falling into Moon Lake or dropping dead in their boats.

We cycle through several more iterations of *set, reach, hurl*. With each volley, the Mexica lose dozens, since their shields cannot withstand the speed and force of our spears. But they also come closer.

The commanders' scouts report that several canoes have forced their way through the maze. Mexica warriors are spilling onto the shore.

Father orders the other centzontli of infantry to advance on the invading force.

Now the battle depends on the cohesion of our units, of the ability of these young men to follow their captains' orders, and the years of drilling they've received at their respective schools.

Again I am convinced that we need to start boys' formal education off earlier.

Yet our warriors acquit themselves well, pushing the Mexica back into the reeds and mud, slicing and beating them into a retreat.

Some enemy break through the line, rushing at the command post. That is when the arrows we've held in reserve are loosed by archers watching from either side.

But they can't get everyone. A trio of Mexica Jaguar Knights hurtles toward us. I fling the signal drum onto my back and take sword

and shield from my page. Heart pounding, I hurry to put myself between the attackers and my father.

The commanders and their staff take on two of the elite warriors, whose moves are so fast and accurate they seem a blur.

The third gives a ululating cry as he comes running right at me, sword raised.

Rather than try to block his blow, I step into it, crouching to slam my head into his solar plexus. He stumbles back, and I swing my sword in an arc that should slice through his abdomen. But this is no mere boy. He spins to one side, thrusting his own sword out.

The edge of his weapon meets the flat of mine, which shatters into splinters. He lifts his sword again, and I drop to the ground in a crouch, my back to him. With a horrible boom, his weapon smashes the signal drum. My instrument slows and softens the blow enough that the obsidian blades only nick my skin through the tunic and quilted armor.

My unusual defense confuses him for a few seconds, enough time for me to pull the obsidian daggers from my belt and begin hammering them repeatedly into his feet and legs.

He screams and tries to grapple with me, but the bloody thud of destruction runs along my nerves. Into strong hands that have been trained for more than a decade.

My muscles know exactly what to do.

I stand and beat out a deadly rhythm on his abdomen and chest. Blood is spraying everywhere, reddening the world.

I do not stop until I reach his throat and silence his howling.

{12} SIEGE

THE IMMENSITY OF WHAT I've done doesn't hit me until long after the Mexica have withdrawn from the shore and the main contingent of our forces have marched back to Tetzcoco. In fact, it's not until I'm being bathed by my attendants at the palace that I find myself unable to distract my mind any further.

I have killed a man.

The widening of his eyes as he toppled backward, a bloody mess. The dead thud of his body against the packed earth of the road. The weight of my father's hand on my shoulder as he praised my speed. *Nomiccamaé*, he called me. It's a word we use to refer to the unseen hands of our revered dead that protect us from harm.

Hands of Death.

Grabbing a sponge from the grip of one startled old palace woman, I scrub the blood from those fingers, unnatural in their speed.

I know the Jaguar Knight was honored by his death. I know his soul has winged its way to the House of the Sun—the just reward of all men fallen in battle. I know my own merit has increased by my act of valor. I know I saved the king's life.

But these hands have now destroyed, rather than created. And that destruction weighs upon me like I never expected.

Fate, however, gives me little time to feel depressed.

Both our other armies are herded back to Tetzcoco in bloodied retreat. My cousin's men are harried north by the devastating combi-nation of our Mexica enemies and the Acolhua who are now allied with Tezozomoc. The soldiers under General Xicaltzin are driven south by Maxtla's invading force. Our battalions are hemorrhaging soldiers as men from rebel cities defect to the Emperor's cause.

When they reach our city, my father has me accompany him to debrief those commanders.

Zoacuecuenotl speaks first.

"It brings me great shame to have been routed, Your Majesty, but we have learned much. The legitimate kings of Huexotla, Coatlichan, and Coatepec—still loyal to their Overlord—have fled into the moun-tains with some of their citizens, hoping to make their way to relative safety in the Republic of Tlaxcallan."

General Xicaltzin has a similar tale.

"While most of the smaller villages stand empty now—our people having escaped over the foothills into Tlaxcallan too—the rebel city of Acolman added its thousands of soldiers to Maxtla's forces. We should have been overwhelmed had we remained. Limiting our losses, I thought it best to return and seek the support of other allies."

But there are no allies.

Instead our army, some six thousand men, is all that's left to create a defensive ring around Tetzcoco.

For two non-stop days, they dig trenches and erect earthworks, palisades, and timber fences between the stone towers that dot the perimeter.

Then the enemy arrives, and the siege begins.

For two cycles of thirteen days, a routine develops. The Emperor's forces feint or attack. They are blocked or driven back. Injuries and deaths befall both sides, but we feel the losses more keenly. Earthworks are damaged and must be rebuilt in the dead of night by teams of sturdy women and boys.

I remain with my father: serving as his squire, carrying important messages to his generals, sounding the large municipal signal drum to communicate general commands to all troops, and helping with strategy.

One of the enemy's main objectives is the destruction of farms on the edge of Tetzcoco. Fiery arrows rain down with regularity, setting crops ablaze. Yet no attempt is made to burn down buildings within the city.

"Chimalpopoca wants Tetzcoco intact," my father tells me. "It's the jewel his grandfather has promised him. So they'll attempt to break us in other ways."

As if to prove him right, Maxtla dams the river next, but not before we have filled every available cistern and receptacle with water. Still, gardens within the city begin to wither. Food has been gathered and is rationed by a corps of noblewomen, led by my mother. Yet the siege takes its toll. Hunger spreads. By the twentieth day, the guardians of the queen's larder have begun fending off attacks on the stores. Multiple citizens are jailed, a handful killed on the spot or executed later.

Unrest starts to roil in the city like a disease. Father has established squads of young warriors and students to patrol the streets, especially in the three districts with deepest ties to the Empire. Fortunately, my team is assigned the Chimalpaneca borough, so I can keep an eye on my bastard sister Atototl. Mother's spies have reported strange gatherings in the house of her husband, Nonohualcatl.

Though the siege and my duties occupy most of my time, other matters demand attention. Twice a lady-in-waiting from the household of Judge Acacihtli greets me near the pyramid, bearing messages from her mistress Eyolin. Because of her Mexihtin ethnicity, she is confined to her borough, but she is desperate to see me, her handmaid confides.

I won't lie. I ache to hold the girl in my arms—to fend off the nightmares with her kisses, her scent. But the relationship is a luxury I cannot afford until Tetzcoco is triumphant. I send my affection, and promise to see her once this crisis has ended.

After the second such exchange, Eyolin sends no more messages. I'm both disappointed and relieved.

Today, as is my new custom, I awaken before dawn, put on my gear, pick up my sword, and head for the morning rendezvous point near the temple. Acaxel is waiting in an alcove, partially hidden by a low wall and a cypress tree.

"I keep trying to arrive first, but you always manage to beat me," I laugh.

My cousin gives a yawn that ends with a grin. "You're going to be my king one day. And there's not much else I can compete against you in. Grant me these small victories with grace, Crown Prince Acolmiztzin."

Before I can device a proper retort, something moves in the shadows. A person exits an alley, and, jerking their head around erratically, turns onto the road that leads to the Mexihtin borough.

"Didn't see us. Suspicious," Acaxel mutters.

"Yes. Nervous, maybe? The curfew is still in effect until next watch. No one should be on the streets."

"Should we follow? Wait for the others?"

I hesitate, considering the drawbacks to both options.

More movement. I pull Acaxel down and peer over the low wall. The figure steps away from the building for a moment, into the hazy moonlight. I recognize him at once.

Yancuilli.

"That can't be a good sign," my cousin hisses. "Didn't your father assign him to temple security?"

"Shit," I grunt. "Don't let him out of your sight."

As quietly as we can, we follow Yancuilli, tracking him from a safe distance as he takes several turns and reaches the noble section of the borough. At last he enters the courtyard of a sizeable manor.

Acaxel and I duck into the shadows of a shrine across the street, as people with torches emerge from the house to meet the newcomer. The flickering flame illuminates their visages.

Three Mexihtin officials, one of them Judge Acacihtli—Eyolin's father. Beside these stand Atototl and her husband, Lord Nonohualcatl.

Rebels, I'm certain. In league with the Emperor.

"Welcome, Lord Yancuiltzin," the judge says, gifting the bastard the formality and titles he so craves. "I see you have been followed, just as you promised."

Muttering a curse, I take a step back, right into the steely chest and arms of a warrior who has emerged from the shrine. He locks me in a brutal embrace, pinning my hands to my sides.

I grunt in pain. Acaxel spins to look at me, raising his obsidian sword.

But he is too late, too slow. Out of the pre-dawn dark swing other blades, glittering in the torchlight.

One hacks off my cousin's hand; the other slices across his abdomen. For an eternal second, he stands quivering, his stump spurting, the gash gaping wider and wider like some gruesome, speechless maw. Then he drops to his knees, his intestines spilling all over the cobblestones.

"No!" I scream, filled with horror. I kick and writhe, trying to break free, to no avail.

Blood bubbles from Acaxel's lips. His eyes go glassy and empty.

"His head will serve as proof," the judge calls. "Leave the body on the street. Many more will soon join it."

An uprising, I manage to think, amid my fury and despair.

Then a blade swings again, a mighty arc that rips through my cousin's neck.

His head tumbles to the ground.

My struggling hands find their way at last to my belt. I pull my daggers free and slam them into the thighs of the man who restrains me.

Howling, I whirl about to kill him—to kill them all—but then something hard crunches against the back of my head and the dark swirls thick around me, till I tumble senseless to the ground.

"Wake up, you arrogant piece of shit."

My eyes flutter open as I try to surge to my feet, only to slump back, dizzy at the pain in my skull. Standing over me is Yancuilli, his thin lips twisted into a rictus of sick glee.

"They've asked me to negotiate with you," he says, scoffing. "The city is about to fall, and in the aftermath, various families will be vying for control."

Gasping at the throbbing of my head, I manage to snarl: "Father won't trade away his throne for my freedom, you bastard. Tetzcoco is more important than one life."

"Oh, everyone knows how self-righteous the Usurper is, kitten. They wouldn't dream of such negotiation. But the judge thinks he will have the better claim before Chimalpopoca to be appointed Governor Regent, over other Tetzcoca pretenders. He just wants you to confirm that you've deflowered his daughter."

I manage to sit up. Dawn has lit up the shadows of the room they've dragged me to. It is empty of everything save a few ceramic pots, and the mat I'm on.

"Eyolin? In the midst of your revolution, he wastes time attacking me for sleeping with her?"

"Ah. Thank you." Yancuilli pulls aside the curtain at the doorway. Beyond it stand a guard and a scribe. "You heard the confirmation. Go let the judge know. And don't look at me like that. I'll be fine. He can't even stand."

They give curt bows and rush away.

Yancuilli turns to me again. "I'm truly disappointed. The king calls you the greatest mind in Tetzcoco. Yet you fail to understand why I lured you here. The Mexihtin Tetzcoca feel certain that if they are in possession of the 'legitimate' heir to the throne—born of a Mexihtli noble girl—then your uncles in Tenochtitlan will allow them to serve as regents here."

My mind whirls, this time not from the wound to my head.

Why did I ignore her messages? May the gods curse me for a fool.

"You're saying that Eyolin is *pregnant*?"

Yancuilli rubs his hands together in delight. He crouches down, tilting his head as if to see me better.

"Oh, the look on your face! I have waited long years to see you brought down, Acolmizton." My hands twist into fists at the insulting diminutive of my name. "Look at you! Younger than me. Weaker. Child of that mongrel princess our father *dared* to make queen while he relegated my mother to the margins. Why should you be heir to the throne?"

I spit in his face. "Fucking bastard. Do you think the Mexihtin in this city will give you any power even if I'm dead?"

Yancuilli wipes my saliva from his face and reaches for my throat. "Oh, let me make your despair complete, *Brother*. I promise that no child of yours will ever breathe air outside the womb. I have my own plans for Tetzcoco, you see."

The movement behind him comes so fast, I can hardly credit my eyes. A hallucination, surely, brought on by pain and rage.

But the pot comes slamming down on Yancuilli's head, and my bastard half-brother tumbles, moaning.

Standing over him, dropping pieces of fired clay to the ground beside her, is Eyolin.

"Acolmiztzin, Beloved, hurry!" she whispers hoarsely, voice quavering with worry and shock. "You have to get out of this borough before the fighting begins. My father and his allies have let the Tepaneca into the city. They'll be converging on the sacred center by next watch at the latest!"

She reaches her hand out. I take it, warm and soft, a promise of peace beyond the siege—of a glorious future I refuse to renounce.

"Is it true?" I whisper. "Is my child in your womb?"

Eyolin lowers her eyes. "Yes, my Lord."

She's trembling. My heart is filled with compassion and longing.

"Then come with me, precious flower. Be mine."

A smile spreads across her pretty face as she begins to pull me to my feet.

Then, a silhouette rises behind her.

A hand slips around her shoulder, gripping a shard of ceramic.

In a single movement that lays bare my soul, the point slashes across Eyolin's throat. She collapses, blood bubbling from mouth and neck. Her hand slips from mine.

Yancuilli grunts a bitter laugh, pulling himself to his full height.

"Don't get too attached to anything, kitten. I plan on taking it all away."

My mind is a hive of buzzing noise and blurry abstraction.

All I can see are the bits of broken clay scattered around her dying form. Everything in the universe shrinks to a single desire.

Of its own accord, my hand snatches up a shard as I roll and surge, tottering to my feet, rushing at Yancuilli with the zigzagging determination of a legendary monster.

●◖◗●

Just then, shouts and forms spread around me. The judge and other Mexihtin, bursting into the room.

"He killed her!" screams Yancuilli. "Swore no child of his would live among the Mexihtin!"

I hear swords slice the morning air, like hawks upon an easterly wind.

I cannot die in this place. I need focus. I must fight.

Gritting my teeth, I jab the shard I hold into my thigh. The bright ache relieves my confusion for a moment.

"I spill my essence!" I scream. "In payment for my life! Let me live, and I shall send many souls winging to Your side!"

Heedless of their obsidian blades, I spin into the Mexihtin guards, beating out patterns of punches and stabs, gouging and ducking, biting and butting my head against them till I've made it through the door.

Then, guided by the gods or sheer luck, I make it to the street and begin to run.

{13} ESCAPE

THE MEXIHTIN ARE HARD on my heels. My head wound begins to grind at my thoughts again. My strength is being sapped by blood flowing from the multiple cuts I received during my escape.

I turn a corner. Whether through fate or supplication, the rest of my patrol squad comes rushing in my direction.

"Crown Prince!" someone shouts as I founder from relief and weakness. Their arms seize and lift me just as darkness wraps its tendrils around my mind and drags my mind into the caverns of oblivion.

I spend an eternity there, watching their deaths play out again and again.

Acaxel, on his knees, intestines spilling from the gaping cut.

Eyolin, smiling as her throat is sliced open.

No! I scream and scream, unable to move—unable to keep them from dying.

Unable to die and join them.

When I awaken at last, surgeons are changing poultices on my various wounds. All women—as is our tradition—the surgeons wear long huipils of undyed cotton, but the dark blood of wounded warriors has stained most of them.

"I must warn," I rasp, "the King. Enemy in the city. Traitors aiding them."

One of the surgeons places a gnarled finger on my lips.

"Hush, Crown Prince. All of Tetzcoco knows. The battle is raging in the streets at this very moment." She looks at one of her younger colleagues. "Bring the Queen."

As if she's been pacing outside the chamber, my mother rushes in to take my hand and kiss it, her eyes full of tears.

"Acolmiztli, my dearest son, thank the gods you're awake. They've overrun the city, invaders from without and traitors from within. At any moment, they'll breach the sacred precinct and storm the palace."

Taking a sharp breath, I grip her hand more tightly. "You need to flee. With Tozquen and Tochpilli. Yancuilli—he's determined to be regent, I think. He won't stop until every other pretender to the throne is dead."

Mother nods. "Yes, we have surmised as much. Your father has been hoping you'd regain consciousness soon. He plans to draw the enemy into the foothills, giving the rest of us a chance to escape."

I'm able to sit up now with just a dull throb, making me wince. "Where will you go?"

"It's better you don't know, Acolmiztli. You understand me, yes?"

Of course I understand. What I don't know can't be tortured out of me, should I fall into the hands of the Emperor. My chest aches from a surge of sadness. I want to rebel—to follow my family into whatever exile she has chosen for them.

Yet the weight of the entire city rests on my father and me. If the Tetzcoca are to survive, including this beautiful woman and her precious children—if we are to ever get another chance to reclaim our collective birthright—I have to set aside my emotions. I must become an impassive mountain. Cold granite. Unbreakable.

"Then let us say farewell, Mother. I place you and my younger siblings in my heart of hearts and lift a shield to protect my love, until we meet again, in this life or the Unknowable Realm."

She bites her lip and embraces me tightly, before calling waiting guards to escort me to my father's side.

The troops are arranged in the reverse order of normal battle, with inexperienced infantry keeping the enemy at bay as my father, dressed in full battle regalia with banners flying high, is at the very back, with the godbearers and Zoacuecuenotl.

My page begins to dress me in my armor as the king and my older cousin approach me.

"Blessed be the Duality!" Father exclaims. "I hear that you barely escaped the Mexihtin traitors and the bastard who has spat poison into our mouths."

I lower my head. "Yes, Your Majesty. But it gives me great shame to report that I was unable to protect Acaxel. I pray my cousin's forgiveness."

Zoacuecuenotl's jaw tightens grimly. "The enemy and their turncoat allies are to blame, Acolmiztzin. Many great men fell today in the surprise attack. General Xicaltzin was dragged from his home and hacked to pieces in the streets. Lords Iztactecpoyotzin and Huitzili-huitzin were slain upon their sleeping mats."

The mention of my beloved tutor almost undoes my composure. Instead, I take my helmet from my page and slam it onto my head. The waves of pain erase for a moment the emotional shock.

"We have no more time to lose," the king says. "I need you to take up the signal drum, Crown Prince. Sound the retreat. The bulk of our forces under my command will flee to the hilltop fortress of Cuauhya-cac. As the enemy follows, a thousand soldiers will regroup and lead the civilians to safety over the mountains. A smaller elite guard will spirit your mother and siblings to safety."

My page hands me a new drum, and I begin to tattoo a vigorous, rolling beat.

The line of infantry breaks apart, scattering. The invaders ignore them.

The rest of the army, just eleven thousand strong, surges west-ward as one.

Fifty thousand enemy troops give chase.

Night has already fallen by the time we ascend the slopes and hide ourselves among the quarried stone and deep caves of Cuauhyacac. After resting, I join my father and cousin on a heavily wooded but-tress. We look out at the fires dotting the floodplain, on both sides of the river that flows from farther above us.

"We shall not hold them at bay for long." My father's voice is quiet, but undaunted. "When they overwhelm our defenses, we shall then fall back to Tzinacanoztoc, the hunting retreat where I was born. At that point, we shall require allies, or we shall be destroyed. Let us hope that the spies I dispatched to Chalco will help Ambassador Cihtzin convince the Chalca ruling council to give us aid."

My cousin drops to one knee.

"Your Majesty, what if they are not successful? All reports suggest that our forces in Tepanecapan have been boxed in by the Emperor and are bleeding entire battalions of defectors! We must seek the support of the Otomi people."

I dare to speak. "Will they come? They have never fully bent the knee to Acolhuacan or its Overlord. I understood they've been seeking an alliance with the Emperor."

My father scrapes his fingers along his chin in thought. "We have no choice but to send an envoy to Otompan. And Zoacuecuenotzin, it must be you. That fierce folk will heed no one with less power or fame. Go tell the Otomi rulers of our plight. As my grandfather shielded them from the Emperor a generation ago, so now his son pleads the intervention of their mighty warriors, for whom we have named the most elite class of our own army."

My cousin lowers his eyes. "I am honored by the favor Your Highness shows by appointing me. Willingly I shall go and do all that can be done to win them to our cause. Yet should I fail to return, put the army under the command of Tzontecomatzin and flee with the Crown Prince over the mountains. Our efforts come to naught if you both die in these hills. You are Tetzcoco, sire. As long as one of you lives, the city lives." He pauses then. And finishes: "The Acolhua live."

My father's face twitches with emotion, starlight glittering in the tears he cannot control. There is a moment of silence. From far below, the sound of laughter and music floats upward, and distorted by distance, it turns into something ominous, like the gruesome chuckling of some Underworld giant.

"My beloved nephew, may the Sovereign of the Near and the Nigh watch over and favor you. If you fall in valiant combat, I shall see you triumphant in the House of the Sun."

The men embrace.

"Before you gather a team and leave, Zoacuecuenotzin," I interrupt, "I have something that may help."

I explain the route I devised at school for a party of similar size to follow toward the Valley of Teotihuacan. My cousin places both his hands on my shoulders.

"You are indeed knowledgeable," he says. "I feel confident that with you by his side, my uncle the king will receive the strategic advice that I cannot provide him while away. Yet harken well, Acolmiztzin. If the tide turns against you, I give you but one commission. Run. Run and do not stop until you are safe. Do you hear me? My family is dead. It is possible I now go to die myself. Our deaths must not be in vain."

I embrace him, once. Then he turns and dissolves into the darkness of night.

When the attack begins, it is unceasing. The enemy has the numbers to assault the hill in waves of a third, keeping fresh soldiers rested and in reserve. We managed to hold out for three days, making new arrows and spears from fallen trees in shifts while our archers and lancers rain projectiles on every attempt to ascend the slope. We even manage to dislodge a few boulders and blocks of quarried stone to crush many dozens of men.

But our resistance is doomed to fail. Our numbers are too small. A squad of Mexica wind their way up the craggy northern slope, hiding under overhangs and beside outcrops until they spring on us. The confusion leaves open another hole in our defenses, and the enemy come streaming up. As squads converge to fight them along the crumbling edge of the hill, we leave more openings. Soon the entire summit is swarming with swinging swords, ringing with battle cries.

A thousand men are sleeping in the network of caves. Enemy soldiers burst in and slaughter most before they awaken.

I can scarcely hear their screams. With half my royal guard dead and the other half fighting for their lives, my world has shrunken to the grimacing faces of my opponents, and the frenzied but predictable rhythms of their lunging offense. Neither logic nor fear dictate my response. I am a conduit for instinct or divine hands as I play my sword and daggers in vicious counterpoint.

As they fall, my enemies' features often shift for a second.

Imposed upon their dying faces flicker the visage of first Acaxel, then Eyolin.

And it is here that I learn the unspoken price of death.

The shadows of the dead linger.

Some three thousand new shadows flit upon that hilltop before we retreat with nothing but the weapons in our hands.

The ancient retreat of Tzinacanoztoc is at a higher altitude, its forests full of gnarled pines and drooping firs. There are supplies stored in my father's well-appointed summer mansion, but not nearly enough for eight thousand bloodied men. Squads are sent out to hunt deer and fish. Earthworks are erected at the edge of the summit. The army settles into a similar routine as before.

Near sunset, a lone nobleman, his cape in tatters, approaches sentries on the western slope. It is Itzcuintlahtlactzin, one of the captains who accompanied my cousin to Otompan.

His tale is harrowing, heartbreaking.

"We had crossed the mountains according to the plans of the Crown Prince and were rushing toward Otompan, when we were ambushed by a company of Otomi warriors from the nearby town of Cuauhtlatzinco. They took our weapons and escorted us before the governor of Otompan, the bearded one we call Yacatzoneh.

"Zoacuecuenotzin then made his plea to the governor, explaining Tetzcoco's plight. But a Tepanecatl stepped forward, one Captain Quetzalcuixtli, imperial envoy. 'You have all heard Ixtlilxochitl's request for aid. But under no circumstances should you comply. You

have agreed to place yourselves under the protection of Emperor Tezozomoc: to accept him as your father, your mother, your great cypress
tree and shield.'

"At these words, the governor nodded and laughed. 'Ixtlilxochitl
claims the title of Acolhua Overlord—of Chichimeca Chieftain. If he
is the legitimate heir of Xolotl, scion of that lofty lineage, let him
defend himself alone! Indeed, he clearly does not even need the help
of his nephew, the mighty hero Zoacuecuenotzin! Since he has sent
the captain general on such an ignoble task, let his messenger have a
similar end. Seize him and tear him limb from limb!'

"And so they did, as I watched in horror. Like dogs they fell on
him and rent him apart, shouting 'Long live Emperor Tezozomoc!'
Then the governor ordered that Zoacuecuenotzin's fingernails be
removed from his severed hands. 'String them together like a necklace
of precious stones,' he mocked, 'as they come from such a noble, august
family!'

"The others of our party were killed in the same way. But the
governor left me alive. 'Bear these tidings to the Overlord: You will
surely perish, Usurper and Oppressor, before another month is gone.
You and your arrogant son both. You will find no succor on the sea-
ringed world. Your end is inevitable.' I cry your pardon, Majesty, for
bringing such inauspicious news."

The loss of Zoacuecuenotzin, yet another loved one, weighs heavy
on my soul. Yet there's little time to grapple with my feelings, as word
comes from sentries that the enemy—with leisurely but implacable
pace—is encroaching like a flood that wends its way through the
forest before uprooting the trees.

Late afternoon, just before that massive host arrives, we get
another messenger: Commander Tezcacoacatl, who led the civilian
evacuation once we had drawn the enemy away from Tetzcoco.

"Your loyal people have made it safely over the mountains, sire,"
he tells my father. "The border cities of Tlaxcallan are giving our

citizens asylum, as promised. And the last message I received from the queen's guard confirmed that your wife and children are still out of harm's way."

The king slumps with relief, as if a great weight has been lifted from his shoulders and he can now focus on something new.

Our survival.

He calls together his remaining military leaders and addresses them.

"We have accomplished our main goal. Our fellow Tetzcoca live on, in exile. Emperor Tezozomoc will not risk taking an army over the volcanoes to invade Tlaxcallan. Such a foolhardy stunt would mean suicide for his men, and Tepanecapan does not desire genocide. They want our cities. Our wealth."

Words and gestures of assent. Generals and commanders all appear to agree with Father's risk assessment. He continues, his now soft voice growing hopeful as he speaks.

"For the moment, we have no allies, no strategy that can beat back and defeat the army that even now roils at the base of this hill. I need time—years—to make new alliances and raise a vast army. I shall now have to defeat the Emperor first, I suspect, before retaking my city."

My father pauses, holding each of their gaze in turn.

"For the moment, however, I must survive. And so must the crown prince. Therefore shall I take a small contingent with me and escape to Tlaxcallan. I need you, mighty Acolhua, to hold off the enemy as long as you can. Give me as many days as possible. When you can resist no longer, scatter like seeds on the wind and meet me a year from now in Tepeticpac."

No fanfare. No gathering of the troops to bid us farewell. The enemy cannot suspect we are slipping away. But word spreads fast across the hilltop, and I am met with many salutes and tear-streaked faces as I prepare to leave.

Father selects just two squads—captained by Totocahuan and Cozamatl, both great leaders and soldiers. Along with Tezcacoacatl, who knows the mountain passes well, these forty men accompany us down the western slope into the depths of Chicocuauhyohcan, a forest so ancient and thick it feels untouched by the hands of man. By nightfall, we reach the ravine of Cuetlachac, taking shelter beneath a large fallen tree against the cold mist that descends from Mount Tlaloc. The captains set sentries and schedule scouting both ahead and behind us.

Sitting in the darkness—as we can light no fire for fear of drawing the enemy's attention—my father asks me a strange question.

"Do you remember the tale of when young Ce Acatl—the human incarnation of the Feathered Serpent himself—spent a year with Mixcoatl, the demi-god he believed was his father?"

"Yes, sire," I reply. "Every time he went out to hunt for his father, his uncles attempted to trick and kill him. But he was too clever by far. Once he hid in a rock to avoid their fiery attacks. Another time, when he was in the highest boughs of a tree and they shot arrows at him, he let himself fall and pretended to be dead. After each attempt on his life, Ce Acatl would get up, capture that day's game with reverence, thank the gods for their bounty, and return to cook for his father."

The pressure of my father's hand on my shoulder is almost shocking in the darkness. "Then, when Mixcoatl learns the truth and at last confronts his devious brothers, they fall on him and kill him, burying him without ritual or rite in the sandy soil."

My chest is tight with premonition, but I continue the story.

"Yes. But the gods send animals to show Ce Acatl where his father's body lies. He takes it to the Temple of Mixcoatl to perform the proper ceremony. And when his uncles try to stop him, those same animals help Ce Acatl to slay the fiends. Their sacrifice undoes the blasphemy, and Mixcoatl ascends to his place in the heavens."

Father squeezes my shoulder. "Indeed. Then Ce Acatl goes on to live a pious life, studying and mortifying the flesh, until he is called to be the next king of the Toltec Empire. Only later does he realize his own divinity.

"Let him always be an example to you, my son."

My voice cracks as I say what I can't stop myself from saying, all formality falling away:

"You won't die, Father. I won't let you."

The king laughs softly. "You cannot decide my fate. Only the Sovereign of the Near and the Nigh has such power. All I ask is that, no matter what the days ahead hold in store for us, you keep yourself safe and prepare yourself for your own fate, Acolmiztli. Tetzcoco needs you to be ready when the time comes for you to lead."

"Yes, sire."

Soldiers urge us to sleep, but my dreams are filled with towering dunes that I dig at with blistered hands, trying to find the body of my father before his soul slips into Mictlan.

No divine animals come to my aid. Just a howling wind that buries me beneath the sand as well.

The strained shouts of Tezcacoacatl awaken me just before dawn.

"Your Majesty! Your Royal Highness! The enemy are upon us!"

In an instant, Father and I are on our feet, obsidian swords in hand. Sleeping soldiers rouse themselves all around us. Tezcacoacatl scrabbles down into the ravine.

"Four hundred Tepaneca and Otomi!" he gasps as he rushes to us. "Just minutes away. I don't know how they found us so quickly—"

My father scans the ravine. "We shall retreat to the narrowest point, upstream. Forty men can hold off four hundred for a time. Acolmiztli, do you see that towering cypress? Climb as high as you can and be still amid the densest of its foliage. Do not descend until the enemy is gone, understand me?"

The tree is ancient, its trunk the thickness of several men, roots snaking through the rocky soil into the river that flows through the gorge. It rises some thirteen rods above the ravine, gnarled and impassive like a giant trapped in amber, or a wizened nature sprite.

"You need me by your side, Father," I protest. "We can defeat them if—"

His raised hand silences me. His features are hard and stony, like a dam that holds back roiling waters of anguish.

"I need you to obey me. There is no time. My beloved son, I can go no farther with you, can shelter you no longer. My misfortune ends today. I am forced to abandon this life. Yet I beg of you—never abandon your city, your subjects. Never forget that you are the heir to both the Chichimeca and Tolteca Way. Spend the rest of your youth wisely. Train. Learn. Endure. Abide. And when the moment presents itself, take back what we have lost."

Tears pour from his eyes now. My knees grow weak. My heart is breaking.

"Avenge the father they take from you today. Hide in that tree now, not as a coward, but as the last hope of the Acolhua people. Watch if you must. Remember my love and my sacrifice, Crown Prince Acolmiztzin . . . my precious jewel."

Unable to keep from sobbing, I throw my arms around my father and king, feeling the steel of his muscles go slack as he returns my embrace.

Then he gives me a single kiss on my forehead, the first since I turned ten.

The last he'll ever give anyone.

"Go, boy. Today fate crowns you king."

My mind reeling, my chest aching, my eyes streaming tears, I scrabble up the sheer wall of the ravine, clinging to root and rock.

Then higher and higher I climb, the cypress like the World Tree itself, the tail of the leviathan Cipactli that was planted into the center of the earth by Quetzalcoatl and Tezcatlipoca at the beginning of time, roots cradling the Underworld, branches holding up the heavens.

I climb till I might as well be sitting among the stars, looking down at the flood of Tepaneca and Otomi warriors along both banks of the narrow and shallow Cuetlachac River.

The clash is mighty. Only twenty men can stand shoulder to shoulder at the narrow point of the defile, and our two squads take turns beating back wave after wave of enemy combatants. But the strategy doesn't work for long. Soon warriors loop around behind our forces, attacking from the other end of the ravine so that both squads have to defend my father, fighting back to back.

Perhaps understanding the futility of these tactics against so many soldiers, the king at last leads a charge up the ravine. A dozen Otomi lancers surround him and begin to slam their spears into his body.

I almost cry out—almost slip from my perch in shocked dismay. Instead, I clamp one hand against my mouth while continuing to cling to the sturdy bough. Father was right. I must live, though it pains me. Though the memories of these deaths may haunt me forever. Though loss bends my head and blackens my soul.

I must endure. I must abide.

Our remaining soldiers keep pushing forward and then suddenly veer up the more gradual slopes downriver. The bulk of the enemy hurries after. Eager to join the pursuit, the Otomi lancers wrench their spears free, and my father's body collapses, lifeless, into the river.

●◖◯◗●

{14} ALONE

Bundle Him

I slip slow from the tree
like a stone hurled
from the fifth heaven
to burn up in the air
or smash to bits
against the earth.

Between combustion
and shattering,
I find myself beside
the river, reaching
into the cold current
to pull my father free.

A rustling behind me
and I whirl about,
sword in hand.
Captain Totocahuan
has returned, bloodied
and battered but whole.

"Acolmiztzin!" he cries.
"You're here, alive!
Come, let us run
while there is still time!"

I raise my hands
to keep him away.
"No closer, Captain.
Where you are, stay."

"But your father desired
that I stay by your side!"
he insists, desperation
bright in his eyes.

"Do not follow me.
I know not where I go
nor who will give me aid.
If my enemies follow,
can you stop them
from killing me?

"They felled my father,
a more powerful man
than you or I.
Only on my own,
as an orphan bereft
of city and sire,
shall I perhaps
survive.

"So take his body,
perform the rites,
let his spirit
wing its way
to paradise.

"You bow to me.
Good. Understand
your duty.
Do it well.

"I am your king.
Bundle him, I command.
Bundle and burn him.
Keep his ashes safe
Until I return."

Road of the Rabbit, Path of the Deer

The range rises before me—
massive, indifferent, cold.
Like harbingers of doom,
peaks neither threaten
nor scold. They simply are,
and in being, they make me
small. Empty. Nothing.

Yet my sorrow looms larger,
consumes every step,
with every waking moment,
subsumes me in despair.

Sovereign of the Near and the Nigh,
as you did for Ce Acatl Topiltzin,
send me a sign, a guide—
help me abide the coming times.

For now, afflicted and alone,
I shall go into the mountains,
the wild places of the world,
following the road of the rabbit,
the path of the deer.

Mother once whispered
a dark tale in the night,
to keep me from wandering.
The Ohuihcan Chanehqueh,
mischievous nature sprites,
dwell in dangerous places

awaiting foolish souls
who dare trespass
in their demesne.

They lead men astray
till they are so lost
they starve or just
slip over the edge
of the world.

To fool my enemies,
to put Emperor
and uncles
off my trail,
I must disappear
into their realm.

O Sovereign
of the Near
and Nigh,
dual source of all,
who reigns on high—
if it be your will,
there I shall die.

But if you let me live
I swear an oath
of utter truth—
this world will ring
forever
with the praises
I shall sing to you.

{II}

EXILE

{15} INTO THE MOUNTAINS

RAIN BEGINS TO FALL as I wend my way through the tall pines of Mount Tlaloc. Though my padded armor grows water-logged and heavy, I am grateful for the intervention of the heavens. Again and again I hear in the distance the signal cries of Tepaneca and Mexica squads, searching for me. Fortunately, the mountainside is too broad for my pursuers to fully scour, and a tor-rential downpour scrubs my tracks from the slippery earth as if I had never traversed this forest.

As if I had never existed.

About halfway up the slope, I find a shallow cave and take refuge. I need to sleep, to recover my focus and energy. But hunger gnaws at my belly, and grief at my mind. When I at last manage to slip from conscious-ness, my dreams are full of ominous sights and sounds that fade from memory when I awaken before dawn, leaving just a vague sense of unease.

The sun never rises. At least, not visibly. Instead, the world goes white all around me, a dense mist that shrouds the pines and occludes the summit. After drinking deeply from rainwater cached in nearby rocks, I continue my ascent, blind to anything beyond the trees a rod or so in front of me.

I imagine the entire sea-ringed world must have looked this way once, before the Feathered Serpent lifted the heavens from the earth with the World Tree.

It's as if I'm walking through the very being of Tlaloc himself, whose name means "lies upon the earth," just as this mist of his does, densely and completely.

As hunger reasserts itself, an insistent ache in my gut, I manage to catch a handful of grasshoppers. Unwilling to risk starting a fire to roast them, I pop them into my mouth and swallow as fast as I can. They provide little in terms of sustenance, but they take the edge off and give me a bit of energy.

Even if I had a slingshot or bow, instead of just this damned obsidian sword, hunting would be a difficult proposition. I can scarcely see the ground in front of me, much less prey at several rods' distance. And I must keep moving. I haven't heard sounds of pursuit since nightfall, but I'm certain the Emperor's men are combing these woods in search of me still.

The calmecac has prepared me for hardship. But not starvation. I try not to think about where my next meal will come from if the divine attendants have abandoned the mountaintop. Fighting my way ever upward against sucking mud and slippery rocks, I focus entirely on the ascent as the slope grows steeper.

The gods will provide. Or they won't. My fate is in their hands.

I will live or die at their whim.

The mountain is still shrouded in low-lying clouds when I reach the summit mid-afternoon. There is smoke curling from the sanctuary that dominates the flat, barren expanse. The main building is a long rectangle that opens at one end onto the open-air temple of Tlaloc.

I approach with caution, sword in hand. It may be that my enemies have arrived before me and are lying in wait within the sanctuary. Fortunately, my uniform is the same as any young noble knight. Nothing marks me as a member of the House of Quinatzin.

"Greetings!" I call. "I'm a weary refugee from Tetzcoco. Perhaps you can spare me some food?"

An older man appears at the entrance. His greying hair lies long and unkempt over his shoulders and back. He is wearing two sky-blue capes, tied at each shoulder in the overlapping style that keeps the cold from the skin of one's torso.

A teopixqui. Holy attendant of the gods of rain.

"You are welcome to share the meager atolli I was about to eat, young warrior. From your uniform and dialect, I can tell you are a noble scion of Tetzcoco. I imagine you have gone through much in these last few days. Word of the city's fall has reached me even here at the edge of heaven. Indeed, refugees from your community passed this way a couple of weeks ago."

"Thank you, Venerable Godkeeper," I say with a bow, letting my sword hang free from the strap around my wrist. "I am indeed from that jewel of Acolhuacan. It has been nearly two days since last I ate, so I accept your atolli with much gratitude."

He gestures for me to follow him inside. Beyond the vestibule, where statues of the four Tlaloqueh crouch upon stones carved to resemble clouds, two holding up jars of rainwater, two cracking whips of lightning—we enter the living area of the godkeepers: a communal cooking space and four shadowy sleeping alcoves.

"Have a seat," the monk says, reaching for another bowl and ladling corn gruel from a pot sitting on the hearth.

I set my sword and helmet aside as I sit cross-legged before the low table where his atolli awaits, still steaming. Placing mine before me, he takes up a spot on the other side. Piled on a rough board in the center of the table are chia and squash seeds. I sprinkle some over my gruel.

"I thank you, Venerable Godkeeper, and heaven itself for the gift of this meal," I intone, waiting for him to eat a spoonful. Forms trump hunger, no matter how frantic the growling of my stomach has become. With a wink, he brings the spoon to his lips, and I begin to dig in, relishing the warmth and simple flavors.

"You were indeed hungry, I see," the monk remarks as I run my fingers along the inside of my bowl, getting every last morsel. "I am reminded of my early days here at the edge of heaven. Or my youth, in the calmecac of Coatlichan."

I look up at the mention of that city, once ruled by my namesake and ancestor.

The godkeeper notices the glimmer in my eyes and smiles.

"You are the crown prince, are you not?"

Something about his tone makes me bristle. He's mocking me.

"Not any longer, no. My father was killed."

He does not seem surprised. Indeed, his grin broadens into a sneer.

"His death does not make you cease to exist 'any longer,' Your Royal Highness."

Befuddled and irritated by his bizarre behavior, I snap at the godkeeper.

"It's not a matter of *existence*, but *succession*. My father has died. I am now king. Overlord of your country. And this temple."

"Ah," he drawls. "Chichimeca Chieftain Acolmiztzin."

I lean toward him. "Yes. Whether you like it or not."

"You misunderstand me, Your Grace. I simply wanted confirmation. We have been expecting you."

Like striking snakes, four Acolhua warriors leap from the sleeping alcoves, swinging their swords. I manage to roll out of their way, grabbing my own blade and my helmet as I scrabble to my feet and rush out into the mist. It has thickened again, forcing its way into my lungs as I sprint toward the edge of the summit, taking gasping breaths.

Ululating cries and a blast from a conch trumpet rally a half dozen other soldiers from their hiding places among boulders and yellowing grass. Rather than try to reach the path that winds down the southern slope, I spin away, jumping over a jutting bit of granite onto a steep incline of loose scree and stunted pine. I try to keep my footing, but I fall backward and begin to slide. Sharp stones slip under my armor, slicing and digging into my skin.

Jumping off a cliff. Not the smartest strategy.

At last the incline levels out a bit, and I regain my feet. I glance up toward the summit and see three soldiers scrabbling down after me, partly shrouded by mist. The rest are probably circling around on the pilgrim path, hoping to cut me off below.

I run as I have never run before, kicking off my sandals to better maintain my balance as I hurtle among sparse trees and wisps of white, the downward slope giving me dangerous momentum.

Yet I am mere seconds ahead of my pursuers. Any misstep or stumble, and they'll be upon me.

The certainty of death helps me ignore the stitch in my side, the burning of my lungs, and the aching of my legs. By luck or fate, however, I am descending along a mostly smooth cleft in the mountain's side, free of trees and boulders.

Soupy and cold, the air around me is growing denser. I can feel it coalescing, as if a water sprite were about to step from the fog and seize me.

Instead, it begins to rain as I keep up the pace. Drizzle at first, condensing from the mist, but then a steady shower that dissolves the white haze and reveals black thunderheads. After a few more minutes, lightning whips through the darkening sky, followed by the crack of great celestial vessels shattering.

A storm. Curtains of rain, blinding me. Yet I cannot halt my progress. I keep caroming downward, one hand outstretched so I don't slam into anything.

Moments later, I learn why this rift is so clear of obstacles.

From behind me comes a rushing roar. Something is heading toward me, the sound of its approach growing louder than the pounding of the rain.

The cold bite of water, rising above my ankles, signals the flood just in time.

Flinging myself toward the gnarled pines to my left, I manage to leap away from the river of muddy water that slices down the channel. The level steadily rises as I wend my careful way through the woods at the edge of the flood. I dart my gaze warily behind me.

The rain slackens for just a moment, long enough to reveal my enemy. Two warriors, shields and swords lifting at the sight of their target.

There's no other choice. I flip my own maccuahuitl into my hand and charge.

The storm redoubles its fierceness. I can scarcely see my opponents as we clash, but flashes of lightning illuminate their movements in choppy rhythms that defy my instincts. Every blow I attempt is blocked, and I fail to parry or dance away fast enough.

Their blades slash at me. My chest is well enough protected, and my copper greaves deflect the obsidian razors twice. But as they harry me backward toward the roiling course of floodwater, the two men nick and slice the skin of my arms, legs, and face, till I'm streaming blood from a dozen minor wounds.

Some sting. Some ache. All of them open up a chasm of despair within me. I have never been hurt this badly in my entire life. The hardships I believed I had endured are nothing compared to the looming specter of almost certain death.

One of these seasoned warriors discards his shield and comes at me harder, screaming above the tumult around us. While blocking the most aggressive of his attacks, I turn my sword at too much of an angle and it bursts into splinters beneath his blow.

Just then, his companion swings his blade against my head.

My helmet shatters as I tumble back into the rushing flood. I feel the swirling black of unconsciousness pull at my mind the way the current does my body, which itself is swept down the mountainside at vertiginous speeds.

I can see nothing, and the rest of my senses are fading.

But then nausea grips my gut as I go over some sort of cliff.

I'm suspended in the air for a miraculous moment, as if Quetzalcoatl has given me wings. Like he did to the survivors of the Third Age, when the world was destroyed by the fire of Tlaloc's raging grief.

Then I drop like a stone along the waterfall.

I black out before my body hits.

{16} THE DEATH OF ACOLMIZTLI

FOR A TIME, THERE IS NOTHING. No sound. No light. No existence.

Then, voices, debating my destiny. One of them thrums and howls like a hurricane wind, stripping away protest like leaves from brittle trees or unrooted soil from the land.

"He is mine. Let him suffer ere he rise."

Then, nothing once more.

Time passes. Maybe hours. Maybe centuries.

I slowly emerge from that black void. I hear birds trilling nearby. The soft lap of water against stone. Ripples upon my body. Rocks beneath my back. A dull, persistent ache in my head.

I try opening my eyes. The world is bright and blurry, but I manage to make out a small lagoon, fed by a slackening cascade of floodwater that falls some ten rods from the cliffs above. From the waist down, I'm lying in the glittering pool. The angle of the sun suggests that I have spent more than half a day unconscious here.

Attempting to sit up, I discover I am too weak, too fatigued. Over the course of a watch, I pull myself in fits and starts from the water, into the shade of an overhang of earth and rock through which the roots of an oak have snaked. Yearning for the water that lies so tantalizingly close.

I take stock of my wounds. Most are shallow and have begun to scab over. But a deeper gash on my left bicep is still seeping blood. Wincing with the pain, I scoop up mud and pack it thick against the cut. One by one, I test my limbs. No bones are broken, though bruises have begun to mottle my skin like cuitlacochin fungus on maize.

My head is the biggest problem, I realize. My helmet kept me from dying, but there is a massive lump, painful to the touch, just behind my left temple. Blood oozes from a cut directly above it. Gently as possible, I apply a mud compress, but the pain is bright and overwhelming.

I close my eyes, my breathing labored, and slip back into sleep.

The following morning, hunger compels me to stand at last. I strip off my still damp and bloodstained cotton armor. The air is brisk on my bare and battered chest, but I feel more comfortable.

It occurs to me that I need to be dead. In the minds of my enemies, at least. So I pull off my bronze greaves and vambraces, my battle kilt as well, and toss them with my armor into the lagoon.

Nothing now marks me as a noble knight. Looking down at my simple loincloth, I nod.

Acolmiztli is dead. Let us see who I become.

The woods are littered with debris from the storm. About a watch or so into my renewed descent, as I stop to forage for pine nuts and mushrooms, I find a ground squirrel, dead for perhaps a day. Part of me is repulsed by the idea, but with a sharp piece of flint I've brought with me from the shore of the lagoon, I skin the little animal and eat as much of it as I can, along with the edible plants I've found.

Though nausea threatens to make me gag a few times, I know I *must* eat. I cast my eyes up and southward, toward the snow-capped ridges of the next dormant volcano, Iztaccihuatl. Like Mount Tlaloc, it is protected by one of the Tepicmeh, the mountain gods. Climbing into those heights will require all my strength and energy. I can't afford to reject any food I find.

"Thank you, Tlaloc, for your hospitality, for the food you've provided," I whisper in prayer, swallowing my nausea. "And Iztaccihuatl, Beloved White Lady, open smooth paths for me as I ascend your slopes. Keep me safe. Keep me fed. When I return to power, my people will visit these slopes every year to give offerings and hold rites in your honor."

By late afternoon I reach the pass between the southern foothills of Mount Tlaloc and the northern slopes of Iztaccihuatl, one of the two major trade routes between Tlaxcallan to the east and Chalco to the west. Perhaps because of the storm, or imperial expansion, there are no merchants tramping along the muddy road. In the distance to my left I see smoke curling from a small village. It's almost unbearable, the temptation to head that way—to be among people again, and to eat a warm meal.

But I cannot expose myself. Cannot be recognized. I must let my enemies relax as they grow convinced I am dead. For the present, this chain of volcanoes must be my home. I have no choice but to learn to survive in their crags.

I am Tetzcoco's only hope. To protect my people—half in exile, half conquered—and to ensure our city shines once more as the jewel of Acolhuacan, I must abandon myself to the wild.

My muscles are groaning and my head is a throbbing mess, so I find a copse of cedars standing like sentinels atop a low rise. I lay within the shadows of their vigil and drop into oblivion.

In my dreams, I lie dismembered. Each of my limbs is a piece of Acolhuacan—disjointed, bloody, rotting.

The hurricane voice twists around me, dark humor undergirding its stark words.

Hate me for breaking you, boy. I thrive on hate. Yet understand this vital truth—nothing new can be shaped without shattering the old. I am your enemy, yes. The enemy of every weak part of every man alive. And I am the only ally who wants to see you triumph, strong and brilliant, your valiant deeds and conquests echoing down the years. Even when you think yourself alone, I am there. I am the Night. I am the Wind.

I awaken at dawn, hardly able to move. My flesh has become one vast ache. But I pull myself to my feet, using a fallen branch as a sort of staff, and begin to ascend once more.

As a child I was mystified by Toltec legends, cultural heritage of the Acolhua people. In the most famous, the king of Tollan offers the hand of his daughter, princess Iztaccihuatl, to brave Captain Popoca . . . but only if he is able to lead an army to victory against a distant enemy. Another captain covets the princess for himself and devises a stratagem: he returns to Tollan early with a contin-gent of warriors loyal to him, announcing that Popoca has died on the battlefield. Iztaccihuatl believes the lie. Brokenhearted, bereft, she kills herself just moments before Captain Popoca returns, unscathed.

To find his promised bride now dead.

To take her in his arms and climb as I climb.

To howl at the heavens, demanding they revive her.

I would beg for the same. To see my father and lover and child returned to me.

Ah, but Tezcatlipoca mocked Popoca as he mocks us all. He instead turned the princess into these snowcapped heights, in profile, like a woman draped in a funeral shroud.

I climb her tresses, garlanded green as if by the loving hand of Mother Earth, bereft at the loss of a beautiful daughter. At the base of her head the forest gives way to grasslands, waving gently on the slopes, the wind ruffling her hair.

A flicker of fire to the south. The other volcano, where Tezacatlipoca has commanded her beloved to stand watch, his roiling heart bursting at times in billowing smoke and red-hot lava. Popocatepetl we call him now, a mountain god whose grief Tezcatlipoca prolongs forever.

A pang of guilt makes me stumble and fall to my knees. For I did nothing. I just ran. Left her body bleeding out upon the floor and saved myself. Will Eyolin forever lie there in my mind, hands clutching her belly as if to protect our unborn child? Or will the Lord of Chaos excise her from my thoughts, a weakness I cannot afford, a stumbling block on the road to my destiny?

I hear a soft snarling. The tearing of flesh. The smell of fresh blood.

At the treeline to my right sprawls the carcass of a deer. Something has taken a massive bite from its throat.

And gnawing at its belly is a coyote, the most striking animal I have ever seen. Golden eyes full of wily wisdom. Reddish-brown coat going nearly black at muzzle, paws and tail.

Around her neck, a thick white ruffle, like a fasting collar affixed by the gods.

With slow, careful steps, muttering soft syllables in low tones to keep her calm, I approach the fresh kill.

"I don't mean to steal or scare you away. I just hope you'll share, Aunt Coyote. I'm as hungry as you. Maybe more."

Keeping her pine-nut eyes on me as I kneel at the deer's throat, the coyote keeps eating, emitting only a low whine. A sound of welcome, if I remember my lessons right.

With my sharp bit of flint, I shred some flesh away, plopping it into my mouth.

I cannot explain how delicious the warm, red meat tastes; how it eases into my stomach like the richest of feasts.

But there is little time to savor this sustenance.

A snarl comes from behind me. I spin on my heels to see a puma crouching, furious. By her side are two lean cubs, maybe five months old, echoing their mother's fury.

The coyote and I are eating her kill.

She lunges forward, and I scramble back using palms and feet.

Then the coyote leaps between us, growling. The puma draws up short, mystified.

A short bark, then my defender, ears back, turns to look at me. She gives a hushed but insistent whoof.

I return her stare and then look at the deer. Without understanding how, I grasp her command. Quickly, ignoring the protest of muscles and bones, I seize the carcass by its legs and fling it over my shoulders.

Then I start running through the tall grass.

I'm a dozen rods away when I turn to see the puma and coyote, still facing off.

"Come on!" I shout, like a man who has lost his mind. "She'll kill you if you stay!"

In mere moments, the coyote is on my heels.

She overtakes me, heading up toward the snowline, twisting her narrow head to check that I'm following.

And suddenly I remember the words of my father after my consecration as the crown prince. We were standing atop the Pyramid of Duality, before the shrine of Tezcatlipoca. There the statue of the Lord of Chaos is flanked by a feathered coyote, gilded bright, teeth bared.

"The god is a trickster, true, ready to upend the world and watch it burn as he laughs. We cannot hope to understand the workings of the divine mind. What he destroys, we must accept as the necessary cost of creation. Yet when the time is right, the old words affirm, he comes to us in the guise of a coyote, leading us from the smoldering ruins of the past, to the better future he has prepared for us.

"Rue not the night, my son. Without the darkness, the dawn could never come."

{17} THE COYOTE WAY

WE ARE NEARLY at the snowline when the coyote barks
again. I stop, turning to find that the puma and her cubs
have given up their pursuit. I drop the deer to the frost-
dusted ground, and, with my ally at my side, begin to eat.

Once we've sated our hunger, she watches me skin the animal—
the chunk of flint no longer awkward in my hands, but steady and
sharp. While she rests, I scrape the inside clean as my father once
taught me, rub it down with snow, and then drape the skin over my
shoulders like a cape, to keep the worst of the cold away.

I have no easy way to transport the rest of the meat, and if I remain
here, the puma may track me down and pounce while I'm asleep.

"It's better we just leave the carcass behind," I say aloud, glancing at the coyote. "Thank you for your protection and for sharing
your food."

The words bring a lump to my throat. Kindness from an animal, when most humans in the region would kill me to be in the good graces of a tyrant. Something in my chest loosens, and I begin to weep openly.

"Did you choose to be alone?" I ask the coyote between sobs. "No time for mating. No pups to care for. Content to wander your territory with no companions. Or . . . did you lose your family, like me? They're all gone. Everyone. My city. My people. Cousins, dead. My lover, dead. Our unborn child. My father . . ."

My voice cracks and I bend over, wracked by overwhelming grief.

Minutes pass. When I look up at last, she is sitting on her haunches, watching me. I gather myself at last.

"Accident, god-sent, or divine double, I am grateful to you, Aunt Coyote. I'll remember you always. Your golden eyes. Coat the color of raw, primal earth. That nezahualli of white fur around your throat."

Perhaps tiring of my yapping, she turns and begins to slink away. I watch her, whispering a prayer of thanks to the heavens.

Then she stops, glances back at me, and gives a shake of her tail.

My chest fills with joy and relief. I hurry to follow.

By dusk, the coyote has drawn me to a ledge under which she curls up to sleep. The breast of Iztaccihuatl looms above us, the snow silvered by the rising moon. I lie down a rod or so from my companion, gazing up at the emerging stars.

Darkness deepens all around, silent and still. It has texture, weight, density—I'm suspended in night like a corpse bobbing in briny water.

A cold wind spins its way through the thick black, swirling around me before rippling down the tall grass, then sweeping along distant treetops.

Lifting into the heavens.

Above the horizon, the Milky Way has risen. The dark seam at its heart is the Black Road, traversed by gods and souls who move between the Heavens and the Underworld.

I remember when wailing arose from the concubines' palace many years ago. My mother explained to me that Lady Xiloxochitl had mis-carried in the third month of her pregnancy. The other women were crying out to the Sovereign of the Near and the Nigh, so they might guide the baby's soul to Chichihuahcuauhtli—the divine orchard that stands in the Realm of Duality—to be nourished at the Nursing Tree until given a second chance at being born.

I imagine the ghostly form of my own child—dead before drawing a single breath—fluttering wispy along the Black Road, all the way to the highest heaven to be sweetly embraced and consoled.

As silent sobs wrack my body once more, the wind blows toward the pearly edges of that divine highway and then coils back,

returning to this frigid ridge at the edge of the world, this uninhabited boundary not just between Acolhuacan and Tlaxcallan—not just between Anahuac and the Eastern Highlands—but between heaven and earth.

And I know myself watched. Sense myself enfolded in the chaotic smoke of Tezcatlipoca's obsidian mirror. Feel myself tumbling in the destructive whirl of his might.

The promise of dawn holds no comfort. I have been abandoned by all but the cruelest of the gods, and his eerie presence thrums around me with inscrutable schemes. I cannot fight despair any longer. Cannot wield my father's wisdom, or my studies, or my people's faith to halt the bleak and bereaved battering in my breast.

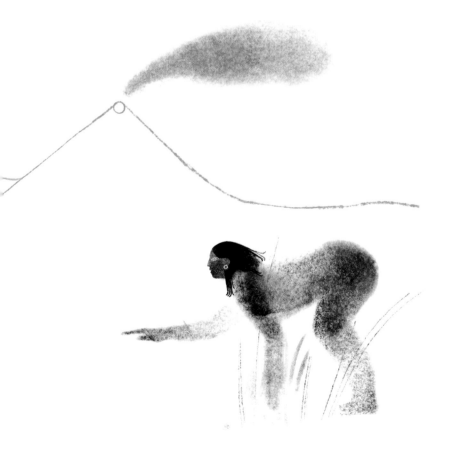

The wind pulls at the unraveling threads of my identity. I feel it suck away the last traces of my name, erode the Tetzcoca dialect from my tongue, lay bare the inconsistent bedrock of my heritage till I no longer know who I am.

A million obscure arrows, spears, swords, and daggers aim themselves at me, threatening to sunder what remains of my soul.

The menace is too great to withstand.

I scream against the violence unleashed upon my being.

Beside me, the coyote starts to howl in poignant harmony with my grief.

I beat my fist against my heart and curse the Enemy of Both Sides, the Mocker of Men.

Tezcatlipoca.

"Bastard! I know what you want! You let them ravage my city and kill my kin. You hope to turn my vengeance into a tool of destruction! To make me pull down the empire, leaving smoking ruins! Then what, you twisted slave master? Will you discard me? Are my dreams just bait to lead me along, till I wreak havoc for you?"

Waves of dark come crashing and crashing, dragging me like floodwaters over the cliffs of sanity.

"Why wait? Annihilate me now!" I wail, surging to my feet and thrusting a fist at the sky. "Or shall I do it myself?"

I bring the flint to my throat, hand trembling. A rivulet of blood blossoms where the tip meets my flesh.

But then I see. Like a caul stripped from a newborn's eyes. An aching revelation.

The wind spins through the eternal night, yes. Destroying everything in its path.

Yet—I look at the stars it leaves in its wake. Those delicate flames, suspended in the void. Flickering. Tenuous.

But tenacious. Unyielding. Refusing to wink out forever.

I fall to my knees, understanding more deeply than I ever have.

●◖◗●

I can almost taste that holiday amaranth dough, shaped into peaks, baked and consumed in honor of the Tepicmeh, our holy mountains down whose forested skirts precious rivers flow.

Pressing my forehead against the ground, and digging my hands into the stony soil, I rasp to Tezcatlipoca, in whose grasp I have always lain.

"You made them divine. Iztaccihuatl and Popocatl. Volcanic gods. Forever ruling these slopes. Side by side eternally. Worshipped by every surrounding nation. You gave them more than they asked of you. It wasn't cruelty, Lord Tezcatlipoca. It was respect."

Then I use the piece of flint, not to slit my throat, but to slice into my thigh. Blood wells, black beneath the moonlight.

"I spill my essence," I whisper to the quivering darkness swirling around me, "in payment for my life, to keep the wheels of the cosmos turning, and to show my devotion to the Lord of Chaos who shatters the rotten and tottering, so his children are forced to rebuild."

Whining softly, the coyote crawls to me on her belly and licks the blood away.

During long weeks, I become her acolyte, learning to track like a coyote, to weather storms and mudslides and smoldering forest fires under her watchful and often reproving eye. Then the dry season comes, cold beneath clear skies that sap warmth from rock and soil. Food becomes even more scarce, but my companion knows how to survive. Under her silent tutelage, I begin to grasp the Coyote Way.

Our staple is the zacatochin, the diminutive volcano rabbit that fits in the palm of my hand. They live in burrows amid clumps of grass near the snowline. The coyote scents them out, begins digging in a frenzy, and shoves her short snout into the widening hole. I seek other entrances, snatching little furry bodies that scramble to escape along their accustomed runways.

She eats hers whole—in a single bite, fur and all. Though it is awkward work, I skin them first and pop them into my mouth. Over time I learn to relish the hot copper of their blood, the crunch of their light bones.

Yet a diet of zacatochin is not enough for either of us. From time to time we come across a deer, and we perfect a strategy for bringing them down. At times I have to chase the animal toward some sort of obstacle—boulder or copse or cliff—tiring it out and cutting off most avenues of escape. Other times it has already been weakened by the cold, left behind by the small herds in which deer tend to congregate during winter, seeking warmth and protection.

The coyote then begins to snap at its legs, hobbling it so that she can more easily lunge upward at the deer's throat. She bounds back and forth, avoiding the antlers if we've targeted an older buck. I watch this dance closely, feeling the rhythm of every encounter, gripping my sturdy spear of pine sharpened to a deadly point by my flint.

Once the deer is bleeding and unable to bolt away, I join the ballet, circling around till I have a clear shot at the animal's left flank. Then I rush in, slamming the spear home at an angle so it goes behind the ribcage and pierces lungs and heart.

It's a technique I perfect after botching the first attempt, when I try hitting the deer's side straight-on and end up snapping my spear on its ribs. The coyote has to finish it off that day, whining at me in irritation. I learn. The next kill is clean.

Winter deepens. I soon have leggings and boots of deer hide, as well as a sort of vest beneath my cape. My hair grows long and unruly. My human stink appears to fade or change, as evidenced by the ease with which I move among the sluggish animals on the slopes of Iztaccihuatl.

When separated from my companion for any length of time, I mark my path the way coyotes do, pissing on boulders and trees, scrabbling at the earth with my hands.

She knows my scent. Always finds me, though my own senses cannot lead me to her.

My human thoughts fade or change as well, rising mostly in dreams. I hunt when the coyote hunts, rest when she rests, give myself completely over to her rhythms.

In the bitter cold of night, under the moon's watchful vigil, we cradle each other's forms, shared heat and comfort surmounting all divisions of man and beast, tame and wild. We are two bundles of warm blood staving off icy death.

The peace I find at her side is indescribable, formless. Heaven-sent.

I know it will not last, but I revel in it while I can.

After several weeks, dark clouds pile up in the north, the direction that the priests say leads to the Land of the Dead. Out of that dismal realm of shades blows a bitterly cold wind so that even the sturdy pines grow brittle with ice.

We should descend from the mountain before the blizzard strikes, but it moves too quickly, and the coyote is off alone somewhere. Before I can find shelter in the dimmed daylight, snow is spinning thick and blindingly white around me. Soon I am struggling through drifts up to my knees, the soft cold becoming frigid needles that plunge into my bones.

A yipping sound. She comes bounding out of the blurry swirl to nip my hand. I follow. In one of the biggest banks of snow gapes a hole. She dives in, and continues burrowing. Then she reappears, looking at me expectantly.

Bury myself in the snow? It's madness.

But I trust her. More than I trust myself.

The space she's cleared is small, just room enough for the two of us. It is cold at first, but the wind isn't cutting against my skin, so that much is a relief. The coyote curls up beside me. Her fur is much thicker now—I suspect she could survive many hours of exposure to this winter storm.

Snow piles up in front of the entrance to this burrow, and soon we're sealed inside in utter darkness, black as the obsidian face of the God of Frost. Amid this absence of light, I cannot help but think of his origin and role. How he was once Lord of Dawn until—angry at the unmoving form of the new sun, Nanahuatzin— he fired arrows at the horizon, hoping to strike that fiery sphere. But the trembling solar deity reacted instinctually, protecting him- self with deadly rays, one of which pierced the forehead of the Lord of Dawn, blackening and hardening his face forever, and curving it into a deadly blade.

The warmth of dawn seeped away from his divine flesh, leaving only cold bones. Setting aside his bow and arrow, the god took up the Broom of Death. Now he sweeps fading life from the world, his icy touch laying bare rock and soil.

"His passing through our land is grim and fearful," my father once told me, as we looked out upon withered fields one especially harsh winter, "but it ensures that spring will draw bright and verdant crops from the earth."

Unending cycles of time. The paradox of death and life.

And I realize another paradox. Our lair has grown warm. The snow melts and refreezes around us, forming thin walls of ice.

The heat of our bodies is trapped inside by several feet of snow, insulating us against the brutal cold. For the first time in months, my hopes for my city awaken. Engineering applications flit through my mind, as well as philosophical implications.

At the heart of destruction, one can find shelter.

In the impenetrable darkness, one can be a light.

Amid the swirling arms of the hurricane, there is stillness.

●❮○❯●

I must remain at the center of the storm. But when I emerge, he will have cleared a path for me. My enemies will be weakened. I shall burst triumphant from the snow and greet the sun-bangled world with a battle cry.

Months pass. Warm air begins to ruffle the pale grass. Streams trickle from the summit as snow melts. I strip off my boots and leggings, relishing the brush of wind and soil and greening plants.

The coyote and I spend time running each evening, exultant. Game becomes plentiful, and we glut ourselves, yipping at the arrival of spring.

Though the music of nature echoes around me, my response brims in my soul with no outlet, until I find a hollow stump and stretch deerskin across it. My new drum booms through the glades and forest as I pound out my joy at all the rebirth.

Words come unbidden, poetry slipping through my lips like a prayer.

> In the House of Holy Writ
> our god composes songs,
> experimenting with sound,
> playful whistles and beats.
> He scatters down flowers
> and delights us with tunes.
>
> His sparkling songs jingle
> as if ankle bells approach.
> Our flower rattles echo
> that rhythm in response.
> He scatters down flowers
> and delights us with tunes.

The sweet chachalaca croons,
its call a mirror of these blooms,
unfolding its raucous sqawk
upon the rippling water.

A bevy of beautiful swans
trumpet in solemn answer
to the scarlet bird of heaven
whose song is enduring truth.

Many green days go by in such primitive musical bliss. Aunt Coyote often joins me with her plaintive cry. We are two singers at the edge of the world, clear voices rising unfiltered through the sky, into the Realm of Duality.

Then one afternoon comes an echo of her voice: distant howling, riding some southerly wind in our direction. In an instant she's on her feet whining. With a single glance at me, she begins running. I follow.

We don't pause to hunt. She is bent on descending toward the pass between Iztaccihuatl and Popocatepetl, so much so that as dusk becomes night, we navigate scree and forests beneath the stars. I have learned to trust her instincts, so my feet echo the placement of her paws in the trickiest of places.

The coyote is still moving forward when dawn breaks. I pull some jerked venison from the leather pouch I made during the winter. I give her a strip and she gulps it down. We stop briefly at a stream to drink bracing water, but then she surges forward again.

The howl comes again, closer. We reach the pass. Standing across from us, on one of the foothills of Popocatepetl, is a male coyote, brawny and brown.

Painful understanding makes me gasp.

"No. You can't leave me, too," I insist, voice raspy from lack of use and sorrow and what might be the onset of grippe.

My companion nuzzles me softly. I bury my hand in the white ruffle around her neck, crouching beside her, leaning my forehead against her snout.

Loss I have learned to forget comes bubbling up inside my heart.

"Very well. I . . . I understand. Go be with your mate. Bear another litter of beautiful pups. But hear me true, dear friend: I will miss you all the days of my life."

She licks the tears from my face, golden eyes full of slanting sunlight. Then she pulls away from my touch, bounding across the stony soil toward her mate as she makes sounds of greeting.

I stand and watch her approach him. Their eyes meet. They make soft noises of recognition. Then, in unison, their inscrutable faces swivel toward me.

"Take care of her and the pups," I call to him, my voice cracking with emotion, "or I'll hunt you down like a fucking deer."

The male draws his ears back, but his mate nudges him softly. Without another sound, they turn and head up the slopes, growing smaller and smaller as I stare, heartbroken.

Then my eyes turn toward the east. Toward Tlaxcallan.

"People," I whisper hoarsely to the wind. "I think I'm ready for them now."

But first, of course, I have to make myself appear more human. I find a pool of water in the foothills of Popocatepetl, fed by a stream of snowmelt. I plunge naked into the icy water, which takes my breath away for a moment. Then I set to scrubbing my body and loincloth with the coarse sand beneath my feet.

Emerging clean and shivering, I realize just how powerful the stench from my fur capes has become. So I avoid them altogether and lie down upon some warm rocks in the sunlight to dry. The early spring air is still crisp, so it takes a while for my trembling to stop.

Toward evening I calm my hunger with venison jerky and pine nuts. But the food fails to give me energy. I feel drained. My head begins to ache. I stumble to a copse of mesquite and lay back on dead seed pods that crunch like the abandoned shells of strange insects.

As the moon peeks over Citlaltepetl—the tallest volcano in this land, a mountain that touches the stars themselves—I find myself dropping into a stupor that leads to turbulent yet formless dreams, tempests of emotions and inscrutable patterns whirling in the recesses of my mind.

Sunlight slanting into my eyes awakens me in the morning. Violent spasms shake my body. I am covered in cold sweat.

A fever. Dangerously high. I know the peril I am in, but there is little I can do save find help. Head pounding, eyes watering, I stumble into the pass and head east.

Every step jars the marrow of my bones. The spring sun is not enough to warm me. I shiver again and again, cursing myself for abandoning my furs, however rank they might have smelled. The shadows of the two volcanoes are still cold, and as the day wears on, I feel liquid pooling in my lungs, swelling behind my eyes, throbbing against my temples.

From time to time I hear her howling. Has her mate abandoned her? Does she know I am ill, guided by some canine instinct I lack?

I catch glimpses of her fur in the dusk. Her golden eyes seem to flash with the failing sun. Rather than waiting to piss every few hours like a man, I stop at each large boulder and tree, leaving my scent for her to follow.

Another ability absent in me. Must see tracks to follow.

Eyes too watery now. Getting darker. Darker. Darker.

Stars wheel overhead. Cannot stop. Smoke in the distance.

Then she leaps from the slope. Lands before me.

No. Too big. The size of a man, crouched on hindquarters.

Fur falls away. White fasting ruffle floats off in the chaotic wind like dandelion seeds.

Golden plumes sprout from the creature's hide.

It is not her. It's Coyotlinahual. Feathered Coyote. Tezcatlipoca's avatar, nahual, companion.

Patron of featherworkers. Forger of the mask that Emperor Ce Acatl used to hide his aging face from his subjects, when he realized his destiny was death after all.

And that holy beast opens its snout and speaks:

Well done, Nameless Prince. You have braved solitude and want, have learned the Coyote Way. Now you return to your own kind. We have more lessons for you, more ways for you to contemplate. You must master the sustaining of life, and the bringing of death.

The smoke is closer now. Can you see it drifting over the face of the moon?

A few steps more, boy. Then you can rest.

{18} THE FARM

I THINK HE'S PRETENDING to be asleep, Mom. Hey, kid—I saw your eyelids flutter just now. Can't fool me."

I ease my eyes open. The world is a little blurry, except for the round face looming above me. Big eyes, a delicate nose, a small mouth twisted in wry humor. The smallest dot of a mole high on the left cheek. I would guess this owl face belongs to a boy of about ten years, were it not for the raspy, feminine voice that keeps rattling away with breathless rhythm.

"See, kid? Not so sick anymore, are you? Not after all the fancy herbal remedies my mother forced down your feverish throat. That kind of medical attention doesn't come for free, you know. Time to get your scrawny self up and start paying your debt. This is a farm. Lots of work needs doing."

"Sekalli!" an older woman scolds, pushing the girl from my field of vision. "The Divine Mother bids us care for every ailing soul that crosses our path in life. We do not demand payment, my daughter."

I try to sit up, pushing my elbows against the mat on which I'm lying.

"I cry your pardon," I whisper, my throat burning with the effort. "I did not intend to impose."

Sekalli harumphs and turns her head. I see that her glossy black hair is pulled back in a single braid. The hairstyle and their accents confirm that I've made it to Tlaxcallan. Near Cholollan, I imagine, given the geography of their republic. It's the closest city to Popocatepetl.

The mother crouches beside me, a cup of water in her hands. "Drink, dear boy, and think nothing of it. That which the gods demand is never an imposition. I am Makwiltoch. This rude and perhaps unmarriageable girl you see pouting before you is my eldest daughter, Sekalli."

I down the water in almost a single gulp.

"My thanks to the Lady my Aunt," I say.

Sekalli stifles a laugh.

"Oh, sure, now he's going to pretend he's a noble. . . . Who are you, the Lost Prince of Tollan?" She nudges me with her bare toes. They are long and delicate. I realize that by instinct I've used the respectful forms I've always employed with commoner women in Tetzcoco. "Just call her 'Auntie' like a normal person, kid."

I am trained to control my anger and to maintain at all times a façade of dignity when dealing with my lessers. But this peasant girl rubs against my nerves with every word and gesture. She speaks coarsely, spitting abrupt rather than reverential verbs, using the blunt pronouns *yehhua* and *yeh* to address me rather than the respectful *yehhuatzin*, or even the neutral *yehhuatl*.

"Why do you insist on lowering your speech with me?" I demand, stern, though still neutral. "We do not know each other, Maiden."

The girl waves her hand dismissively. "You'll survive. And I'm pretty sure we're not on the same level. What year were you born?"

With Madam Makwiltoch's help, I stand, my legs a bit wobbly.

"In 1 Rabbit. On the day 1 Deer."

"A-ha! See? I was born in 13 House, a year before you. So I'm your elder cousin, kid. I'll talk to you any way I want."

I find it hard to believe the scarecrow of a girl before me is seventeen years old. Her threadbare white blouse and skirt hang loose on her small form, like a child dressed up in her mother's clothes.

"Enough, Sekalli. Call your brother and sister in. It's nearly dusk. Your father will be expecting us to have supper together."

Without waiting to be asked, I roll up the mat and place it along one wall, then move the table to the center of the room, close to the hearth. A pot of stew is bubbling there upon a brasier held up by a stone statue of the God of Fire. The typical communal living space of the working class: kitchen, dining, and work room all in one. The western side is dominated by a loom. Two curtains on the eastern wall cover the entrances to sleeping quarters beyond.

From outside come shouts: "Are you stupid? The sun's about to set! There are cihuateteoh in the air, just looking for spoiled urchins like you to steal away."

Sekalli herds in two younger children, both squealing with fear of the legendary revenants who accompany the setting sun after having died during childbirth.

The children rush to their mother's side, glancing at me with suspicion.

"Set out six bowls," Makwiltoch says, pushing them away as she cooks tortillas on a griddle. "Our guest must be very hungry."

As her siblings hurry to obey their mother, Sekalli grabs a ladle and stirs the stew, making quite a show of not looking my way. But she cannot control her urge to keep speaking.

"These brats have no manners, so I'll introduce them. She's Yema-saton. Ten years old." The quieter sister is nearly as tall as Sekalli, and stouter. "And the boy here is Omaka."

"I'm seven," he announces, growing bolder as he sets two bowls on the table. "Are you a warrior? Have you killed anybody?"

His voice is so much like Tochpilli's that I almost crumple, overcome by the sudden memory of my little brother. I've tried to put the fate of my remaining family out of my mind, but now my heart aches with longing.

"I don't think we should—" I begin with a wheezing voice, and then a hand sweeps aside the curtain of the main entrance and Sekalli's father lunges in. He is tall and svelte, with muscular shoulders, contrasting with his shorter, stouter wife. Sun-weathered skin. Craggy features. Kind eyes.

"I see our unexpected guest has arisen at last!" he says, thumping his chest in greeting.

I give a curt bow, fist on my heart. "I am grateful for your hospitality, Uncle."

"Bah," he grunts, coming up to me and putting a hand on my shoulder. "We're people, after all. How could we lay claim to humanity if we didn't help one another? Sit, sit. Let's eat together and share our stories, yes? That's what the gods intended when they gave us mouths."

A smile plays itself, unbidden, across my face. I can see where Sekalli gets her chattiness.

Once the stew has been ladled into our bowls and the tortillas are stacked in the middle of the table, I wait for the farmer to take his first bite, then reach for a tortilla and use it to scoop up the thick stew. It's standard fare—squash, tomatoes, chilis, and beans—but after months of eating like a coyote, I find myself relishing the complex flavors as if the imperial kitchens had prepared the meal.

"Yes, eat up! It does me good to see you enjoy my wife's cooking. It's what convinced me to marry her, you know. She does things with spices that no woman in all of Tlaxcallan can dream of."

"Shush, husband. Your penchant for exaggeration will make him uncomfortable."

He just smiles more broadly.

"I'm sure the others have introduced themselves to you. I am Polok. My clan has dedicated itself to tilling the soil for hundreds of years, here on this fertile plain near the border with Tepeyacac. Our fields are vast, and our neighbors few, so any visitor is cherished."

I lower my tortilla. "I am glad to have stumbled upon your generous family in my illness. Please forgive any misdeeds arising from my fevered state."

"Not at all," Polok says, serving water from a gourd and passing me a wooden cup. "What's your name, lad?"

I take a drink from my cup to give myself a moment. I abandoned Acolmiztli when I set out into the mountains and found myself living the Coyote Way. That princely identity must stay dead for the time being.

I picture my canine companion, her ruffle of white shimmering in the moonlight.

"Nezahualcoyotl," I say, finally.

"Neza what?" Sekalli scoffs, nearly spitting out her mouthful of stew. "No wonder you're gobbling up all our food. Fasting coyote indeed."

Polok gives her a light smack on the head. "Enough, daughter. Nezahualcoyotl, I hear Acolhuacan in your voice. A refugee from the civil war? Partisan of the dead overlord, perhaps?"

I nod, having long ago decided on my new backstory. "My father was a minor judge in Coatlichan. Our family fled once the Mexica and Tepaneca allied with rebels in our city. But my parents and siblings were killed, along with others escaping Emperor Tezozomoc's greed. I wandered for months in the mountains, trying to avoid capture or death. Illness drove me down from their peaks. I walked all day and all night, feverish, till I collapsed at your farm, Uncle."

Sekalli shakes her head and sighs: "So he's sticking to his fanciful story of nobility."

Polok is sizing me up. He taps his index finger on pursed lips, paus‑ing before launching into his offer.

"There are many refugees from your nation throughout Tlaxcallan. You may know some—might even find gainful employ in the new boroughs that have sprung up. But why not stay here? I can offer you room and board, and rewarding work. You may think it beneath you, but hundreds of mouths depend on this family's labor. It will be rich experience, Nezahualcoyotzin."

"Father!" Sekalli whines. "Why are you using honorifics with this kid? Why invite him to stay? Our food stores are growing smaller by the day!"

"Quiet, brat. Ah, . . . ever since your mother gave birth to you on an inauspicious day, you have been a thorn in my side! I am only get‑ting older. I could use another pair of hands in the field while your brother is still too young."

I think on the words of the Feathered Coyote.

You must master the sustaining of life, and the bringing of death.

"What sort of work would you have me do, Uncle?"

"At first, you would be my zacamoh. We rotate our fields, letting some lie fallow each year. It is now time to break up the untended soil and get it ready for planting. You would begin with that task."

Sekalli's big, pretty eyes open even wider as I nod in answer.

"Very well. I shall remain and toil at your side, Uncle."

After Makwiltoch shares a charming bedtime story about a boy and his pet ahuizotl—the magical water dog with a fifth hand at the end of its tail—the children and their parents retire to their respective chambers. I unroll my mat near the hearth and drop into blissful, easy sleep. At some point in the night, I feel eyes upon me, but I ignore them and snuggle deeper into quiet, simple dreams. Let anyone who likes come stare at me throughout the night. I have been scoured free of fear and shame.

Before sunrise the next morning, Polok rouses me. We break our fast with cold tortillas and walk into his fields under dawning skies. Everywhere yellowed corn stalks droop, trellised with brittle vines. Then, at the heart of the patchwork farm, we come to a broad rectangle of empty soil, dotted with wild grasses and cacti.

"Here," the farmer says, handing me a long, pointed piece of oak that reminds me of the makeshift spear I wielded alongside the coyote. I know the name: huitzoctli, planting stick, its ends hardened by fire. "The first task is to break open the hardened earth and remove the weeds. Jab the huitzoctli into the ground thus," he says, showing me, "and then twist as you pull it up. See the result? The soil is loosened so that turning the soil later will be easier."

I jab at the ground, trying to imitate his technique. He corrects me a couple of times, but I am heir to the throne of Tetzcoco. There is no skill I cannot master. Soon my twisting withdrawal of the planting stick leaves loose mounds of soil just like his.

"You have a natural affinity with Mother Earth, Nezahualcoyotzin," he says. "I'm fortunate your hands will prepare my field. I shall leave you to the work, then. I must inspect the existing crops. Life is returning to them quickly after the long winter, and unexpected fruits may already be emerging."

After a watch has passed, my hands are sore and blistering. The repetitive motion, like plunging a spear into the bellies of enemy after enemy, has left my shoulder numb.

Polok returns, his wicker basket brimming with yellow squash and small tomatoes. "I realized I didn't mark out quadrants for you, but I see that you have developed a system yourself. Good. Attainable goals. Never try to travel from one end of field to the other when turning the soil. Always divide it up into manageable squares."

I nod and return to the work. After another half watch, I'm surprised to see Sekalli nearing me as I look up from the ground. She is holding out a stoppered gourd.

"Water," she explains. "The sun is getting high. You must be thirsty."

I take the vessel, and my fingers brush against hers. I feel a thrill along all my nerves. Her big eyes are frank and unwavering as she looks at me. They glitter in the late-morning brightness.

Turning aside, I take a deep draught of the cool water, and let it dribble over my chest. Sekalli sighs. I glance back to see that she is still staring at me, almost avidly.

Annoyed, I thrust the gourd back into her hands. "Here. Quit gawking at me. You're like some overzealous little boy, watching a military parade."

"Boy?" she demands, huffing in feigned offense. "Me?"

I gesture at her. "Yes. With your round face and scrawny body. Chop that hair off and slap a loincloth on you. I doubt anyone would guess you're a woman."

Her features scrunch up. For a second, I regret the insults—the lowering of my speech. It seems certain she's about to burst into tears. But I misjudge Sekalli, to say the least.

"Fair enough, you pretty bastard. We could probably swap clothes right now and folks would think you make a much better girl than me. Those feminine lips of yours: perfect little bow on top, pouty thickness on the bottom. Shapely ears and nose. Honeyed eyes. And your hair is shamefully long. Damn, I bet my father could marry you off in a heartbeat if we dressed you up in my ceremonial skirt and blouse! Sure you're not a xochihuah, Neza?"

She spits at my feet and storms away, leaving me unsure whether to laugh or snap the planting stick across my knee in anger. Clearly, the girl is a more formidable foe than most men I've encountered. I'll need a better strategy to fend her off.

A little after midday, Yemasaton brings me a bowl of cold corn gruel and a half-dozen tortillas. For a moment, her features blurred by sunlight, I mistake her for my beloved sister Tozquen. My breath catches in my throat. Living with a family is dangerous when you're trying to forget your own.

"And Sekalli?" I ask, breaking the awkward pause.

"Shucking corn. Her main job. I get to nixtamalize it. Mother grinds it on the metate."

I crouch, looking at the tortillas and reflecting for a moment on the hours of work that go into producing them. While Yemasaton waits, engrossed with some glossy beetle, I eat the meal, and I relish and appreciate each bite, then drink water from a gourd strapped over the girl's shoulder.

Not much later, Polok joins me. Together, we finish breaking up the soil in one quadrant of the field. He talks the entire time, sharing the male genealogy of his family going back five generations, recounting lessons about planting he learned from his father and grandfather, sharing special prayers to the dual Gods of Corn and Abundance.

I say little beyond occasional phrases of agreement, mined from my own lessons about agriculture and the visits I made with my father to the fields surrounding Tetzcoco. Polok is impressed with the snatches of knowledge I share.

"It is good that the scion of a noble family understands the value of this labor," he observes. "Your father must have impressed such respect upon you at an early age."

Lowering my head as I swallow my grief, I search for a worthy reply.

"He was a man who loved all the people of our city, noble and commoner alike. How could I not emulate him, Uncle? For the next four years, he will look down on me from above, part of the morning retinue of the sun. I shall not make him avert his eyes in shame."

●◖◗●

Silence reigns for a time thereafter, until the sun is low in the west.

"Come, Revered Nephew," Polok says at last. "Let us comfort our souls and flesh with food and family and welcome rest."

At dinner, Sekalli is more reserved. She serves me my food with her eyes down, and is quick to pass me a tortilla or water just as I reach for it. I wonder during the meal and the quiet conversation that follows—weather, gossip, political speculation, the like—whether my working with her father has earned her respect. Perhaps, having spent her snide insults on me this morning, she has abandoned that tactic. Having fended off the advances of many girls during the last few years, I can sense that she is attracted to me. Maybe she will attempt some new strategy to seduce me.

Ah, . . . but I am as wrong as could be.

After her siblings have washed the dishes outside and her father has smoked a tube of tobacco, while sipping on maguey wine, the family retires to their rooms. Sekalli, pausing to bank the fire of hearth, clears her throat pointedly.

I look up from unrolling my mat.

"You slink when you walk, princess," she mutters with a tone of exaggerated seduction. "Your hips sway back and forth. Very cute. Let me know when you want to try on one of my skirts. That round butt of yours will fill it out nicely."

I suddenly remember my uncles, laughing at my ambling steps, naming me Yohyontzin. I bristle. "You unsufferable, shapeless tomboy! You've been saving up your venom all afternoon, haven't you?"

She purses her lips at me. "I hear the noble teens of Acolhuacan have a thing for commoner boys. We can play pretend, you know. I'll be a boy if that's what excites you, Neza."

I surge toward her, lifting my hand, but then she giggles suddenly and pushes past the curtain into the room she shares with her siblings.

I swear to the gods, if she refuses to relent in her twisted teasing, I'll leave this farm and head toward Cholollan. Brazen wench. How dare she talk to me in such a way?

The most annoying thing is that her round face fills my dreams that night, pretty and glowing like the moon itself.

{19} DARLING BOY

I T TAKES ALL WEEK to loosen the soil and remove the weeds. Then we do the same for a second fallow field. For the third week, we switch to using a coahuacatl—a sort of hoe with a curved stone tip—to turn the earth, readying it for planting. It is arduous work, but the days pass with startling speed, and there is always a delicious meal and comforting talk at the end of each.

Sekalli never fails to fling a barb at me when the right moment presents itself, but no longer in front of her family. She chatters away like her father and refuses to address me with neutral or formal speech, but her cruelty softens slightly and she misses no opportunity to take care of my immediate needs.

As for me, I look forward to the end of each day, not just for the chance to rest and laugh, or for the occasional game of patolli or chilling folktale. More and more I find myself admiring the glinting fire of

Sekalli's eyes, the raspy melody of her voice. I know she comes to stand over me in the middle of the night. I'm tempted to reach up and pull her down onto the mat with me. But the memory of Eyolin's curves beneath my hands keeps me from acting on simple urges.

Still, Sekalli is insistent in subtle ways that belie her station and lack of schooling. After the first week, she emerges from the sleeping chamber with a stack of folded fabric right before I lay down to sleep.

"Here, Neza," she says simply, dropping the bundle into my hands. "I wove you some more breechclouts. And a tilma, to keep the worst of the sun off your back. Must be hard for a spoiled noble brat to work the fields."

I ignore the last statement. It's purely reflex, I'm certain.

She has spent hours weaving these for me. I can't help but feel moved.

Lowering my head, I address her with respect. "I thank you, dear Elder Cousin. I shall use this gift well in the service of your family."

She bites her lip with open need. "You'd better, kid."

Polok's milpas, like those of nearly every community in these high-lands, are anchored by maize. The corn stalks have to sprout first. Once they're a bone-length in height, beans are planted so their vines can use the maize as a trellis. A week later, different varieties of squash are added. Then each quadrant receives seeds from a couple of other crops: tomatoes, avocados, chilis, sweet potato, melon.

Grown together, these crops are hardier—more resistant to insects and blight. Strength in diversity, one of Tetzcoco's greatest civic principles, reflected in the real world. One day I'll return to manage my people's lands, a cultivator of human beings.

Halfway through spring, the time for planting comes. Polok gath-ers his entire family and gives each a huictli. Makwiltoch brings a drum out from their sleeping quarters, an ancient wooden instrument whose sound I simply have to hear.

The woman sees the eagerness in my eyes.

"Do you know how to play, Nezahualcoyotzin?" she asks, extend-ing the drum toward me.

"Yes, Auntie. Only tell me the pattern, and I shall beat it true."

Sekalli gives a sigh of relief. "We may actually get the gods' atten-tion this year. Mother has no rhythm to speak of."

Laughing and chatting about previous years' ceremonies, the family follows Polok into the milpa, to the edge of the first field of rich, turned earth.

Yemasaton hands her mother the wicker basket containing the maize seeds. Polok pricks his finger with a maguey spine, letting a drop of blood drip onto the soil.

"Cinteotl! Xilonen!" he begins, invoking the gods of the milpa, a duality whom the ancient prayers name Seven Serpent. "Smile upon this family today as we conjure a healthy, bountiful harvest from this sacred soil, the very flesh of Our Mother the Earth!"

His wife has explained the ritual rhythm, so now I begin to beat it out slow and sure on the old wooden drum. It resonates rich and clear under a morning sky already piling up with clouds. Polok and Makwiltoch exchange a surprise look, nodding appreciatively at my skill.

And then, so unexpectedly that I almost falter, a voice rings out in song beside me. Beautiful. Haunting. Heavenly.

Sekalli. Her eyes are closed as she croons to the fields, our tools, and the seeds.

> O priestly planting sticks
> imbued with holy force—
> the green time is almost here,
> the thunderheads at last appear:
> it's time to do your work!

Our mother's basket swings heavy
with Seven Serpent's sacred gifts,
the seeds she's cherished through the cold.
Come harvest time, she'll carry home
the precious children of this field.

You fields that lie rich and black
like a smoke-dark mirror
in which the future's scried—
receive these seeds, hold them close,
feed their roots, help them grow.

As her last phrases die upon the humid breeze, my hands grow still upon the drum. But that rhythm keeps thrumming in my heart as I take up my huitzoctli and begin jabbing holes alongside Polok and his younger children. Makwiltoch and her eldest follow us with the basket, dropping seeds into each hole. My eyes are drawn to Sekalli's fingers: long and thin, nimble and sure.

It strikes me then that all her movements are graceful, economical. I have mocked her slight form, but there is much skill in her wiry arms.

My mind is filled of a sudden with foolish images: Sekalli dressed richly in sumptuous clothes of bright colors, as befits a concubine of the Chichimeca Chieftain. Hair coiffed in an elaborate fashion, lips gleaming red, her eyes made even more lovely by shadowy makeup.

"What are you staring at?" she mutters, nudging me along. "Poke holes in the damn dirt, Neza."

Habit makes me snap back: "I was just pitying you. Does your family never eat meat? You should gain weight before the wind blows your skin and bones away like a kite."

As if summoned by my barbs, the white tail of a deer flashes among the dried corn stalks of a neighboring field. Months with the coyote have honed my reflexes. Without a word, I heft my planting stick and start to rush toward my prey.

"Father, coyote boy is running off!" I hear behind me. "You worked his spoiled majesty too hard, I guess!"

Stalks whip at me as I pursue the doe. She has caught my human scent and is bounding free of the milpa. I leap into the air, arm cocking back and releasing my makeshift spear.

It rips into her side, piercing lung and heart.

Without any further pain, she drops dead upon the second fallow field, bleeding out on the freshly turned soil.

I bend to touch her still flank.

"We are grateful, Mixcoatl, God of the Hunt," I whisper. "We give thanks, Lord and Lady of Sustenance. We honor you, Aunt Deer, for giving your life so we might live."

As I stand, I find the family surrounding me.

"An auspicious feat if ever I saw one," Polok mutters, placing a hand on my shoulder. "I assume you know how to dress a kill, Nezahualcoyotzin. We shall finish the planting while you take care of her."

I give a curt bow. "Of course, Uncle. And tonight, we shall dine on venison stew."

His smile is broad and proud in turn. "Indeed we shall, Revered Nephew. Indeed we shall."

The meal is hearty and delicious. Sekalli serves herself three times, staring at me pointedly as she devours the blend of meat, tomatoes, and squash.

Is this what you want? Her eyes seem to ask. *I'll be whatever you want, Neza.*

Of course, aloud she continues to rib me, joking about how I run like a coyote with burrs in its tail and other superficial insults. Her mother scolds her. Sekalli ignores the reprimands, continuing to pick at my faults.

It's just her way. And it no longer bothers me. I hear what she's truly saying.

Makwiltoch tells the story of how the fearsome Itzpapalotl disguised herself as a deer and tricked two Tolteca hunters into killing her, so that, burned and bundled as a goddess, she could lead their people across the Chichimeca wastelands toward Anahuac to found Tollan. Then it is time to sleep.

The light of a full moon filters through the cracks in walls and roof. Sleep eludes me as I think about the many deer the coyote and I brought down together. The sense memory of her fur against my fingers makes my heart ache for a moment.

Then, the air begins to echo with howling.

I rise as quiet as I can be from my mat and slip out into the night. It's her, I think. That particular timbre and pitch—the rough rumble as her cry decays.

Where are you? I want to shout. Instead, I try to track the direction of the sound. But as soon as I think I've pinpointed her position, the howls start again elsewhere.

Standing at the edge of the farm, I reach my arms up, pleading.

"Don't do this to me!" I call. "Isn't my suffering enough? Why must you strike at my heart every time it begins to heal? Why must you strip each happiness from me?"

Tears stream from my eyes. My shoulders tremble with sobs I can barely contain.

Then, I feel an embrace enfold me, thin arms reaching from behind to pull me close.

Sekalli's body, warm and small, redolent of grass and mountain flowers.

"Shhh," she whispers against my shoulders, her sweet breath soft in my hair. "It's okay. I'm here, darling boy. I'm here."

My heart unmoored from the world, adrift in this impossible moment, I turn to look upon her face, silvered by the moon until her ethereal beauty is almost unbearable.

The wheels of the cosmos turn like tumblers.

Our fate clicks into place.

I kiss her.

{20} THE WAY OF ORDER

Midnight Walks

When her siblings are fast asleep
and her father's gentle snores
filter through the house,
Sekalli emerges, a cute smile
curling along her mischievous lips.

For an hour—maybe two—
we amble through the milpa,
hand in hand, watched by the stars
as we joke and giggle
hug and snuggle.

It's hardly becoming a prince,
I know. But I remember my father,
holding my mother close,
nuzzling his lips against her neck,
whispering so only she could hear.

I've said it before:
I know what love is.
And it's blossoming in my heart
just as sure as the milpa
burgeons with the rain.

Stay and Create

Sekalli pulls away from my kiss
one cloudy, balmy night.

"I feel the conflict in you.
The loss of your family,
the honor of your nation,
your need for revenge.

"And it may be unfair
but I'm asking you not to go
in search of what to destroy.
Stay and create. Here by my side.

"That's the Way of Order, Neza.
At the beginning of time,
the Feathered Serpent himself
was the first to shape chaos.

"Didn't he take the body of Cipactli,
broken by his brother Tezcatlipoca,
and forge the earth from her flesh?
Prop up the heavens with her tail?

"Didn't he teach the first humans
the double calendar and seasons,
so they would know when to plant
and which prayers to offer up?

"And every time this world was burned,
flooded, scoured by fierce winds—

didn't he patiently pick up the pieces
and rebuild it all again? Oh, darling boy.

"How can it be you don't understand?
He made us for a simple purpose.
To fall in love and forge a duality,
husband and wife, starting a family.

"Building a home, bearing strong children,
laughing together, lights in the darkness.
Ephemeral joys, indelibly human.
Loam between toes, a loom in one's hands.

"Life is too short to waste on destruction.
Once you avenge yourself, what will be left?
I'll give you my body, my heart, and my soul,
all that you need to build a new life.

"Let's compose songs together, boy.
Lullabies for our babies, hymns for the gods,
an epic of love that none can forget,
the tale of a noble who chose to farm
and erected a palace of maize
for his owl-eyed queen."

Tempted

If what I build on earth
will crumble into dust,
why should I strive
to remake Tetzcoco?

The building of things
itself brings me joy.
Could this quiet farm
contain my creativity?

Could I close my ears
to the coyote's call?

Could her melodies
drown it out?

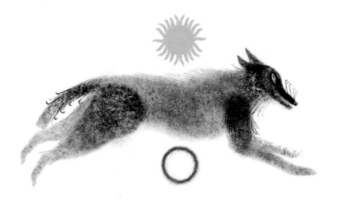

{21} CHOLOLLAN

O UR MIDNIGHT WALKS continue over the next month. From time to time a shower catches us unawares, and we have to duck into the corncrib to stay dry.

The conversations we have are vital—sometimes profound, sometimes silly, always drawing our hearts closer together. I tell as much of the truth about my past as I can, lying mainly by omission. Sekalli lets me avoid certain subjects, big eyes glinting with compassionate comprehension.

Yet talk is preamble, if I'm honest. We crave physical contact. Our embraces grow tighter. Our kisses deeper. At last we find ourselves gasping in the stormy dark, grinding against each other with a need so piercing it makes us cry out.

But I go no further. The rickety wooden structure and pouring rain bring indelible memories. Sweet pleasure in the dim, yes. But also horror. The sight of Eyolin's streaming blood. The thought of our child, snuffed out in the muffled silence of the womb.

Every time I pull away, Sekalli sighs. To my muttered excuses, she gives the same answer, one that fills me with worry and hope:

"It's okay, darling boy. We have a lifetime."

The milpa drinks in rain, drawing sustenance from the long-rested soil. It burgeons almost magically, free of insects and fungus, healthier than we could have hoped.

"Neza's rhythms," Sekalli insists.

"His careful preparation of the soil," her father counters. "And his uncanny intuition about the right blend of crops for each angle of sunlight."

"Our work together as a family," her mother concludes before I can humbly reject their praise. "Each contributing what they can. All success emerges from communal effort. Never forget that truth, my dears."

Harvest for the two new fields is just thirteen days away when Polok announces he will be traveling to his relative's farms to enlist additional pairs of hands for what promises to be an abundant yield.

"Omaka will accompany me," Polok adds. "Time to involve him more in the management of the land. Also, his aunts and uncles have not seen him in more than a year, so they will be delighted."

Though at first the absence of Sekalli's father seems to promise an easier time with our trysts, Makwiltoch is waiting for us that first night, sitting on my sleeping mat when we return at the darkest watch.

"I thought as much," she says without preamble. "Your father snores, but not quite loudly enough for me not to hear these furtive comings and goings."

At a loss, I drop to my knees. "I cry your pardon, Auntie. Our time together has been chaste."

She waves this affirmation away. "I trust my daughter to do with her body what she sees fit. Yet, if you feel affection for her, I encourage you to share it openly, Nezahualcoyotl. My husband and I admire and care for you, young master. We would be honored if you and our daughter decided to form a family together."

I cannot tell this dear woman the truth: that any family I form will be in danger should my identity be revealed. That Tepaneca or Mexica troops could descend on this farm like locusts and obliterate every life and dream. That I have sworn oaths to both my revered dead and the gods themselves to wreak vengeance on the empire and reshape Tetzcoco into an earthly paradise.

That the exiled and conquered people of my city are depending on me to return, triumphant.

I think I love Sekalli. No. I'm sure I do.

But I don't know how those feelings fit into my plans.

As is typical, however, Sekalli speaks first.

"Mother, thank you for being understanding. Can we keep this from Father until after the harvest? Let Neza and me come to an agreement first. We are only just getting to know each other, and we haven't really spoken about the future. Soon, I swear. Just give us a little more time."

Makwiltoch stands and places her hands on both our shoulders.

"Yes. Of course. I too was once a young girl in love. I know there's no commanding the heart, no changing the course of that raging flood. Let yourselves spin in its eddies for the moment. But once this harvest is sold in the marketplace, be ready to tell your father." Here she looks pointedly at me. "Or to say goodbye."

She walks toward her sleeping chambers, then pauses at the curtain, turning to regard us once more.

"Tomorrow I shall go to Cholollan with your sister. We need new threads to weave a set of summer clothes, as you've wasted them all on the young master. Stay behind to cook for him as he tends to the fields. Perhaps you can have that conversation you both have been avoiding."

The woman is wiser than I had imagined. I am up at dawn—walking the fields, pulling weeds, pruning vines that are bending cornstalks, checking for bugs and plague. Mid-morning, Sekalli brings me water. She slowly wipes away the drops that dribble down my chin and onto my chest. She gives me a kiss and a smile.

"Lunch next watch. I'll come get you. You can rest and eat inside the house."

The meal is simple but savory. Sekalli uses more spices than her mother, and my tongue tingles, delighted, at the piquant pleasure of the chilpoctli she has added to the venison.

It's these simple domestic rhythms that make me waver—that cause me to lose sight of my long-term goals. I imagine a life like this, the two of us, tending to our respective tasks and then coming together in relieved, blissful joy.

I spend the afternoon weeding other fields where later-season corn will be growing soon. We will harvest them at the height of summer. I find myself evaluating which squares of earth need to be allowed to go fallow next.

There's a smile on my face then, that falters suddenly at the sight of an eagle, dropping through the air to snatch a mouse up in its talons.

The avatar of the God of War. Patron deity of the Mexica.

I try to shake the ominous feeling all throughout the afternoon and dinner, but it's not until Sekalli ducks into her parents' room and returns with a stoppered clay jar that these dark premonitions fade.

"Maguey wine," she says. "Ever had any?"

"No. My people are quite strict about forbidding strong drink to noble teens."

She laughs lightly. "Well, let me teach you."

Setting out two copper cups—the costliest objects in the house—she pours us both a drink. "Think of this liquor as a sacrament. When Feathered Serpent buried the remains of his beloved Mayahuel, after her grandmother and the rest of the ferocious tzitzimimeh had torn her to pieces, she became the maguey plant, sprouting from the ground."

"To provide us with those useful fibers and thorns, as well as her *unfermented* sap to refresh our palates," I insist, having already heard this argument from other boys at the calmecac longing for alcohol. "It's her *children*, those Five Hundred Drunken Rabbits, who taught men how to make themselves stupid with maguey wine."

Sekalli shrugs. "Perhaps. But right now, I want you to get a little stupid with me, darling boy. Loosen up. Set aside your troubles and truly *be with me* here and now, free for a moment from all you've lost. Please?"

The promise of oblivion is a temptation I find hard to resist. I reach for the cup.

"Sips? Or all at once?"

"Like this," she says, lifting the drink to her lips and knocking it back in a single gulp. "Ah. Sweet as your nimble tongue, Neza. Try it."

I follow her example. The liquid burns my throat, but it's a pleasant sizzle, like the heat of chilis in her cooking. And the aftertaste is indeed sweet, like honey.

As rain begins to patter against the roof, she pours another round. Then another. Soon we are making foolish jests about her family members, as well as different social and ethnic groups, imitating their quirks. For some reason, I begin to show off the different accents I have mastered, switching between dialects of Nahuatl and even sliding into other languages as I mimic the gestures of Otomi, Popoloca, and Chontal folks.

"Oh, Divine Mother!" she wheezes between guffaws at one point. "Do the Chalca prince again. You sound *just like* one of those arrogant bastards."

Everything makes us laugh. We find ourselves on our backs on my mat, rolling and giggling. Then we're clinging to each other, mouths locked, hands fumbling at our clothes.

Her thin body is more beautiful than I had imagined, fitting against mine with such perfect precision that it seems the gods themselves designed her to be my mate. Even after we have spent our passion with cries that nearly drown out the thunderstorm raging around us, her arms and legs cleave to me, encircling my body as if they have at last found their rightful place.

There's no stopping the words that well up from within me, rushing past my lips.

"I love you, Sekalli."

Her lips close around my earlobe for a second as a shudder passes through her lanky, lovely frame. Then she whispers, voice raspy with emotion:

"Me too, darling boy. Always and forever."

The next day, Makwiltoch and Yemasaton return with spools of thread. Her eyes keep a close watch on her daughter and me. I catch her nodding, as if she intuits the change that has occurred. When she serves me dinner, I give thanks, calling her "Mother" instead of "Auntie," my voice cracking and quavering.

Eyes going red with nascent tears, she touches my hand.

"You are quite welcome, my son."

The following afternoon, Polok and Omaka arrive with four other men—cousins and nephews who will help with the harvest. We lead them on a tour of the fields, followed by a hearty dinner and much family gossip.

Now that five people share the communal living space at night— one of whom has decided he needs to sleep right beside the entrance— Sekalli and I must make do with fleeting moments of touch, furtive kisses amid the milpas, and longing glances. Strangely, the forced separation makes me want her even more, and my dreams are full of her big eyes and slender limbs.

Work keeps us all busy during the day, thankfully. There are implements to repair and sharpen. The corncrib has to be cleaned and swept. New baskets must be woven and old carrying frames restored to transport excess harvest to market.

When the day comes, Polok offers grateful prayers, and Sekalli and I perform a hymn of thanksgiving. Then the entire family plunges into the fields, each person focusing on a particular plant, and we begin reaping this season's bounty.

The work takes us a few days. But at last the corncrib is fairly bulging with food, and other baskets and sacks have been lashed to the carrying frames, ready for the half-day walk to Cholollan.

"You'll be coming with us, of course," Polok tells me after dinner as we watch Omaka and his second cousin—a man of about twenty years—play coyocpatolli. The game consists of two players tossing small stones into a hole in the packed dirt floor.

"Yes, Uncle," I say with a bow of my head, suppressing the urge to call him *Father.* "Whatever you need. I am glad to help and learn."

That night, I emerge from a strange dream full of feathers and talons to see Sekalli kneeling beside me. She places a finger on my lips and points to the house entrance. Its accustomed accidental guardian has rolled to one side, opening a path for us. As stealthily as possible, we make our way outside, where a bright gibbous moon hangs high, lighting our way as we enter one of the older fields. Brittle brown stalks crackle as we pass.

"Not the quietest of places to meet," I mutter, and she hushes me.

"Just wait. You'll understand in a moment."

The old maize gives way and we're standing at the edge of a cleared space. A mat has been unrolled at its center.

"I couldn't stand a single second longer without you," she says, drawing me down with her, eyes luminous with moonlight and desire.

"Come, darling boy. I want to remember the feel of your body while you're away."

Either we are fortunate enough to sneak back in before the rest awaken, or some of the adults simply feign ignorance of our tryst. Whatever the case, the household rises with the sun and breaks its fast. Then Polok and I—along with his kinsmen—shoulder our carrying frames and begin the trek to the market.

I turn several times to find Sekalli's eyes lingering on me. I make farewell gestures, smiling, but a part of me has been conditioned by the past to feel dread at such partings.

Of course I'm coming back, I tell myself. Tezcatlipoca has given me no sign that it is time for the next step. I can still enjoy this warmth for a while longer.

The road to Cholollan is a gradual rise, just enough to make our journey tiring but not arduous. After half a day's brisk walk, the city sprawls before us, white buildings spreading like concentric ripples from three main centers—the sacred plaza, the great market, and the ancient pyramid known as Tlachihualtepetl, the Manmade Mountain.

I think back on the lessons of Izcalloh concerning this city, though something twists inside me at the image of their face. Conquered by an offshoot of Tolteca and Chichimeca society two hundred years ago, they moved the temple of Quetzalcoatl from the ancient pyramid to the new sacred plaza. Then, as Tepanecapan rose in power, Cholollan allowed Tlaxcallan to annex it, becoming part of the republic that refused to bend a knee to the Emperor in the east. Unfortunately, it has also refused to outright *oppose* Tepanecapan, which is why Tlaxcallan never allied with us during the war.

Guards wave us along at the entrance to the city once Polok explains our destination. Soon, we come to the edge of the market, a vast and buzzing riot of colors and smells dominated by the Potters' Guild, whose earthenware bowls can be found on the table of kings.

Polok pays the fee for an unoccupied stall near the featherworkers' quarter, and we begin to unpack. Looming over the spot like a harbinger of my future is a statue of Coyotlinahual, the feathers of the divine avatar painted gold and glistening in the midday sun. I try to ignore it, as I help the others lay out our harvest on mats and tables, but I keep imagining a low thrumming emerging from its stone throat: the hushed growling of the Lord of Chaos, readying himself to upend my life once more.

We do a steady trade for half a watch—bartering for eggs, kitchen implements, spools of thread, and other valuable items—before my fate walks up to me at last and spins me round.

It is my uncle Coyohuah, husband of my father's sister Chochxochitl. He is wearing a colorful cape and loincloth, earplugs, and sandals, all of which mark him as a noble.

"Nephew?" he cries, touching my face and upper arms. "You're alive!"

Polok looks up from the lizard jerky he has just acquired.

"Is this a kinsman of yours?" he asks me.

Not wanting my identity revealed in this way, at this moment, I scramble for a plan.

"Yes, sir. My father's brother-in-law. May I go and speak with him? I promise to be return soon."

Polok stands, regarding my uncle's attire and ducking his head in respect. "Of course you may, Young Master. I would be thankful should you choose to inform me of any developments. My home will ever be yours, but family is family, well I know it."

I reach across the table to grip his arm, suddenly moved to reveal the truth to him.

"I pray your family can be mine, Father. When I return, I shall be on my knees."

His eyes widen at the phrase. Swallowing heavily, he rasps, "We have much to discuss, then, my son."

"Coyohuahtzin," I say to my waiting uncle, who is also surprised at my words, "can we talk somewhere quieter?"

"Yes. Follow me."

Coyohuah leads me out of the market square. A block away, the sound of commerce is muffled enough to permit normal conversation.

"Where have you been?" he demands. "We've been told you were killed by the Emperor's men. I even saw your shattered helmet and bloody cape!"

"I faked my death to put them off my trail," I explain, "then spent the winter on the slopes of Iztaccihuatl. Since spring, I've been living on a farm southwest of Cholollan, under the name Nezahualcoyotl."

"Pretending to be a commoner?"

"No. I told them I am the scion of a minor noble family from Coatli-chan. Enough of the truth to keep me safe."

"But you've been working as a farmhand. And from the sound of it, getting involved with the farmer's daughter?"

I say nothing. It is none of his concern, but I am in no position to assert my authority over him. His eyebrows beetle in frustration.

"Would you like to see your people? Before you go back to the farm? About a thousand refugees ended up here in Cholollan."

I remember the commoners lining the streets as I walked to the calmecac. The honor they have always shown me. If I have hidden myself for all this time, it's so I can take back Acolhuacan more easily, and they can return to their homes. So I can grow into a towering cypress that keeps them all in its shade. These refugees left their homes so as not to bend the knee to Emperor Tezozomoc. I will be safe among them.

"Please," I tell my uncle.

The new calpolli sits on the northwestern side of the city, beside the road to Huexotzinco. Canopies and tents flutter in the late spring breeze. Construction is in full swing, with dozens of new houses being erected among less permanent shacks as we approach.

"For the first month, they were reluctant to build," Coyohuah explains. "They would be going back soon, they argued. Then word reached us that your father had been slain, and you appeared to die as well. Now most have resigned themselves to a new life here. Ah, but look, Acolmiztzin. See how the idle stare at you. How they can hardly credit their eyes. A ghost walks among them, a tenuous symbol of hope."

"The crown prince!" someone cries, and a murmur begins fluttering through the calpolli. Sounds of sawing and hammering cease. Men descend from ladders to get a better glimpse. Coyohuah grabs my reluctant wrist and pulls me through the evolving camp. Hands reach out to touch me. Old women weep for joy. Courage flashes in the eyes of young men.

Nausea rises inside me.

I've made a mistake. I shouldn't be here. It isn't time.

Coyohuah takes my elbow and propels me forward. "Our villa is just ahead. Do not waver. Whatever you feel, they need to see you strong."

Word is spreading like wildfire. The Acolhua refugees line the limestone street now. One man, face scarred from battle, falls to his knees.

"Your Majesty!" he shouts with a Tetzcoca accent, and in a wave my people drop to the ground, lowering their heads into the dust, calling out like lost children to their parents.

"Your Majesty! Chichimeca Chieftain! Acolhua Overlord!"

The weight of their expectations settles onto my shoulders. Though by all rights I should stumble before them, I lift my head higher. To them, I'm not the crafty coyote that bides his time despite the hunger. I am their fierce puma, claws at the ready.

Even if only for a moment, I try to make them believe I will rend our enemies to shreds.

{22} NO CHOICE

I NSIDE MY UNCLE'S VILLA, servants fret over me, wiping the dust and sweat from my body. They help me change into a new breech-clout and cape, commoner-white but fringed with blue patterning. I keep them from cutting my hair, having them braid it instead in the Otomi fashion.

Then they lead me into my aunt's day room, where she waits upon cushions, dressed regally. My uncle has also just entered, and we sit before her.

"Chochxochitzin, it is good to see you," I say in greeting.

Her somber eyes are red with emotion, reaching out to take my hands in hers.

"My blessed nephew, the news of your survival comes just in time to rescue our hearts from despair. As the Tetzcoca see me as their regent-in-exile, I was hard-pressed to ease their bereavement, but your unexpected appearance is a balm to us all."

My uncle clears his throat. "I'm not certain how much he knows, beloved." The two of them share a look, then he continues: "Nephew, the Emperor gave many Acolhua cities to the Mexica: Teopancalco, Atenchicalcan, Tecpan. And, of course, Tetzcoco. King Chimalpopoca then installed your half-brother Yancuilli as ruler of our city in his stead, though the Emperor has taken the titles of Chichimeca Chieftain and Acolhua Overlord."

I wince at the mention of that bastard's name. Eyolin's slit throat flashes across my mind for the briefest of moments. Squeezing my aunt's hands lightly, I try to smile.

"I suspected as much. He was deeply involved in spreading the lies and rumors that turned part of the city against my father. And I'm sure his betrayal and the exile in which we now find ourselves have been difficult for everyone. Yet, beloved aunt and uncle . . . the moment has not come for us to rise back up. It is better you continue to guide them; to settle in and wait here in the Republic of Tlaxcallan."

Chochxochitl closes her eyes for a moment. A single tear rolls down her cheek.

"That much I understand, Your Royal Highness. Apologies. But we have not shared the worst of the news." Her eyes open again, full of sadness and compassion. "When your mother and siblings fled to Tenochtitlan, her brother the king betrayed her, handing the three of them over to the Emperor. Thus did he convince Tezozomoc to deepen the ties between the Tepaneca and the Mexica—elevating the Kingdom of Mexico to a partnership with the Empire. But the Emperor . . ."

Her voice cracks. Her grip grows tight and trembling. Her lips move soundlessly.

My uncle says the words for her:

"Reports claim that Tezozomoc has executed the queen and your young siblings."

The news is a blow to my heart. I pull my hands from my aunt as if from a scorching flame. I'm having trouble breathing. My beautiful, brilliant mother. My adorable, loving sister. My playful, silly brother. Gone forever?

"Acolmiztzin?" my aunt whispers. "Are you . . . going to be okay?"

I shake my head. "No. That damned tyrant has made me an orphan. And he has poisoned the plan I have been crafting. I had hoped that my mother and my aunt Azcatzin would be able to sway enough of the nobility of Tenochtitlan to our cause, despite Chimalpopoca's unpatriotic loyalty to his grandfather. There's no way Itzcoatl or Tlacaellel actually wants this alliance."

My uncle gives a dismissive wave of his hand. "We don't need the House of Acamapichtli or any other Mexica to help. We just need them to stay out of the fight. Then you can lead us Acolhua exiles against the empire!"

I slap my palm against the floor. "We have *no allies*. If we couldn't protect our homeland, we *certainly* won't be able to invade Tepanecapan."

My uncle raises a hand to stop me. "That's where you may be wrong, Your Highness. Yes, the Republic of Tlaxcallan refused to ally with Acolhuacan . . . but over the past year, public sentiment has shifted in our favor. I have developed ties with the kings of several nearby cities who wish to aid us."

It is good news. It lightens my heart a bit. But it's not nearly enough.

"The Mexica will *not* stay out of the fight. Not with control of Tetzcoco in the balance."

"Not willingly," Coyohua agrees. "But at the moment they have a bigger problem. Chalco. Their confederation has watched the rise of the Mexica with hatred for generations. During the conquest of Acolhuacan, the Chalca decided to build a wall across the narrow pass between Colhuacan and Chalco. That strip of land is an important trade route for the Mexica, and now they are enraged. The Emperor has severed ties with the Chalca Confederation and given Chimalpopoca permission to conquer them by force."

I grasp what he is getting at immediately. With its former ally and current partner at war with each other, Tepanecapan is vulnerable.

"Are you certain the Tlaxcaltecah will support us?" I ask, returning to his earlier words.

"Their republic has allowed Acolhua leaders in exile to become members of its ruling council. Our numbers are strong in every allied city-state in the area, especially Huexotzinco, where King Motoliniatzin of Coatlichan governs the refugees. Tomorrow I head to Tepeticpac for a week-long series of meetings. We Acolhua councilmen plan to solidify support for an assault against Azcapotzalco. I feel confident we can get a resolution passed to call up an army, especially now that you are here in Cholollan."

I am suddenly overwhelmed by all the information; the possibilities; and the waves of sadness and hope that beat against my heart by turns.

Standing, I give a curt bow to my uncle and aunt. "On its face, this plan seems feasible. Yet I need some time to consider all that you have shared with me, to grieve for my mother and siblings, and to consult with the gods."

"Of course!" my aunt says. "Shall I have someone take you to private chambers?"

"No. I need to get out of this calpolli altogether." I glance at my uncle. "Can you lend me some guards? There's a place I want to visit."

Climbing to the summit of Tlachihualtepetl, I am overwhelmed at the scope of human ingenuity. There are fools who mutter that only giants could have built this massive pyramid—and, partly overgrown by Mother Earth's green leaves and roots, it does indeed seem formed by greater forces. But they say the same of the mighty structures of Teotihuacan and Tollan. And I am certain the minds and muscle of people like us built them all. We suffice, I believe. The gods made us stewards of the sea-ringed world precisely because such skills are within our grasp.

This broad, artificial plateau was once erected in honor of Quetzalcoatl, but a new shrine to the Tlaxcalteca rain goddess Chiconquiyahuitl has been built here, now that the Feathered Serpent is worshipped in the sacred precinct. His old, crumbling temple stands a few rods away, hung with vines, filled with shadows.

Beyond, at the eastern foot of the pyramid, a graveyard sprawls— full of bundled bones and ashes, sepulchers of nobles beside unmarked plots. Taken by itself, the site strikes me as a testament to the power of decay, destruction, death. As if Tezcatlipoca were winking at the world. *Even your worship of order and creation is doomed to crumble,* he seems to whisper.

In the end, entropy wins.

But, after all has decayed, new shoots emerge from the soil.

Dusk is settling over Cholollan, the shadows of the volcanoes reaching for the distant sea. My uncle's men light torches as I stand contemplating my choices. One walks over to illuminate my path, but the flickering flames bring little comfort. We have always built upon the ruins of the kingdoms that fell before us. Surely, the gods will smile upon my new vision for Tetzcoco as the glittering and glorious cultural heart of Anahuac. But intuition or the whispering of Duality tells me that now is not the moment; that rushing toward Tezozomoc too early will be our undoing.

My thoughts are shattered suddenly by shouts and the crash of swords against shields.

A few rods away, a group of men is clashing with my uncle's guards. They wear bloodred tilmas and breechclouts. Their heads are shaven, their bodies painted completely black.

"The Deadly Hand!" the guard beside me grunts, pushing me behind him. "A guild of assassins. Controlled by nobles who want Cholollan to ally with Tepanecapan. Hurry, Your Majesty. If they catch you, it will be—"

A spear rips through his throat. He drops in a heap before me, and the Deadly Hand charges.

I wrench the spear free from his neck and send it hurtling through the darkling air. It slams into the chest of the foremost assassin. Not waiting to see him fall, I pick up the torch and sword of my fallen guard and begin to run toward the only structure near enough to provide cover—the ruined temple of Quetzalcoatl.

Arrows and spears slap against the stone and earth around me as I zigzag my haphazard way along the pyramid. A flake of obsidian slices my left bicep, right as I plunge into the vine-festooned interior of the shrine.

I have mere moments before they converge on me.

Ancient kings were crowned in this place, after spending four days in its holy heart.

There has to be a stairwell. I swing the torch back and forth, my years of study and geometry training kicking in, my brain reconstructing the temple's architecture based on these blasted remnants.

Behind the base where his statue once stood. That black maw in the darkness.

Trusting my instincts, I rush around the cracked basalt pilar and step into the void.

There are stairs, fearfully steep, slimy beneath my sandals. The torch reveals them in guttering flashes as I hurry down into the bowels of the pyramid, every step threatening to send me tumbling to my death.

As I reach the bottom, I hear cursing above and then feet on the steps.

I am in a large chamber, walls covered with frescoes that moisture and time have destroyed. Three tunnels lead away. I poke my torch into each.

The walls of one depict, in a mosaic of brilliant colors, the never-ending coils of the Feathered Serpent.

The walls of the second, eternal swirls of black obsidian, the smoke curling from the Smoking Mirror himself.

And in the third, the two patterns twining about each other, a braid of bright and dark.

A sign from Duality.

Taking a deep breath, I plunge my torch into a pool of water that has accumulated over the centuries. Then, in total darkness, I rush down the third tunnel, right hand outstretched, left lightly touching the mosaic.

For what seems a quarter watch, all I can hear is the hushed crunch of my shod feet against the sandy floor. Then a panting seems to come from everywhere, echoing eerily in the confines of the stone passageway.

Before me, golden eyes flash in the gloom. I pull to a halt, doubling over to catch my breath. Without warning, something massive takes a step toward me, the rock thrumming all around at its movement.

Then a breeze caresses my face. The night wind, blowing at me sideways. I feel along the wall and find an opening that leads me, after a few twists and turns, into the graveyard east of the pyramid. There is no one near. I am safe, for the moment.

The moon has risen, casting silver light upon the tombs.

My mother's people believe that their patron god—Huitzilopochtli, Lord of War and the Sun—waged war against his elder sister Coyolxauhqui and their four hundred brothers.

He slew every one of his siblings, hurling their bodies into the sky to become the southern stars. But, with his sister, he went one step further.

He dismembered her, kicking her limbs down the slopes of Coate-pec, mountain home of demigods.

But before he could send her head sailing after, he heard his mother weeping in grief.

"I shall never look upon the face of my beloved daughter again," she wailed.

And so, in a moment of uncharacteristic compassion, Huitzilo-pochtli hurled his sister's head into the heavens, where it became the moon. Every night, the Mexica say, mother and daughter stare at each other, content for even that distant, fleeting connection.

But I . . .

I . . .

I will never look upon my mother's face again. Never get to watch my sister and brother grow into great leaders.

Who else will die as the tyrant hunts me down?

I'm not just Tezcatlipoca's instrument of destruction. I also leave a wake of death behind me wherever I go.

I cannot return to the farm. Those good people do not deserve to have their lives ruined because of my bleak destiny. Sekalli . . . the thought of her dying twists like a knife in my gut.

Once more, I have no choice, though it breaks my heart.

I love her. Like no one else I've ever known.

But I must flee. For her sake.

{23} FLIGHT

Orphan

In vain was I born.
In vain my spirit left
the Realm of Duality
to emerge on this earth
and live a wretched life.

I should never have emerged.
Better I had never been born.
So I say. Yet what shall I do?
Like the nobles who remain,
must I live in the public eye?
Be prudent and wise, they advise.

Will I arise at last upon this earth
to claim my throne, my birthright?
Now I feel nothing but suffering.
My heart aches, howling friend,
for it is hard to walk
this slippery earth alone.

Yet how to exist together?
We're thoughtless and cruel,
every man for himself.
If I would live in joyful peace
among people once again,
I must bow my head
in meek obedience.

So I just weep and grieve,
orphaned amidst the human throng.
How can your heart choose
such a fate for me, cruel god
by whose whim we all live?
If only your anger would wane,
but misery flowers in your presence,
Tezcatlipoca—you want me dead.

Are we truly happy,
those who live on earth?
If so, then just with friends
is there joy on this plane.
Thus it is for all who suffer,
for all who are lonely
at the heart of a crowd.

Do not despair, my heart.
Stop your fruitless pondering.
There is little compassion
to be had in this world.
Even when I feel you near,
O god by whose whim we all live,
pain flowers in your presence.

I can only search for, remember
the loved ones I have lost.
Will they return?
Will they live again?
No, a single time do we perish,
just once here on this earth.

I hope their hearts
feel no more pain now—
in his presence, right beside
the god by whose whim we all live.

●◖○◗●

Where?

I wish I could return to her,
to that peaceful farm
in the shadow of a volcano.
But I swore an oath to my father
to take back what we have lost
and to avenge his brutal death.
And to honor my siblings and
my mother,
their lives snatched by the
Emperor's claws—
joy and love will have to wait.

My hand alone will not suffice
to bring that ancient monster down.
I need to raise a mighty army.
But what warriors would follow me?

Yes, I must flee. Must prepare.
Find more allies. But where?
Deeper into Tlaxcallan?
No. My uncle has much to do
and I should leave him to it.
Let him believe me dead again—
he will work that much harder.

Not farther south. Not the coast.
My homeland is a viper's pit,
and Mexico is perilous, too.

●◖◗●

Where? Where can I go?
Where do I have friends?

A remembered scent
floods my senses.
Izcalloh. Their father.
Their mother's connections.
The conflict with Mexico.
Chalco, then. That's where.

I know how to kill. But there,
perhaps, I will learn to lead.

Leaving Like a Coyote

Avoiding farms and waystations,
I run through forests
toward volcano shadow,
toward that high pass again,
to cross into Chalco
and embrace my fate.

As I scramble along the edges
of that well-traveled path,
I swear I catch glimpses
of my former companion,
slinking through the hills,
white ruffle flashing.

At times it seems golden plumes
glint amidst the trees,
and once I imagine a jaguar
the size of a grizzly bear,
its every step a drumbeat—
Tezcatlipoca's avatars.

They urge me onward.
I cannot stop to rest.

Like a coyote who leaves
mate and pups behind
for a season of solitude,
knowing he will return
unless this slippery earth
robs him of his life—

So do I abandon the girl
and the Way of Order,
praying beyond hope
to make my way back
when the Mocker of Men
decides my work is done.

{24} SOLDIER OF CHALCO

GETTING INTO THE ARMY of Chalco is easier than I imagined. I spend weeks lurking around the margins of Tlalmanalco, helping small farms with their harvests and catching every bit of gossip possible. Then, a month after abandoning Tlaxcallan, I finally encounter a traveling merchant who tells me what I need to know in the archaic dialect of the southlands.

"Hast thou heard? Our brave and beloved Prince Quetzalmazatl— may he vanquish every enemy—is leading a fresh army against those whoreson Mexica that keep encroaching on the confederation!"

"Whereabouts, wouldst thou say?" I ask, drawing up a mental map of southern Anahuac.

"Northwest of here, on the plains between Tlalmanalco and Chalco City. Why? Hungry for battle, art thou?"

"Mayhaps," I say, as I bid him goodbye, heading back into the nearby pine forest. There I retrieve the sword and noble tilma I've hidden.

Then I make my way to the battlefront, guided by sun, and the sound of clashing swords and screams.

The Mexica are being led by my uncle Moteuczoma. He is pushing the Chalca back south, toward Tlalmanalco, leaving wounded and dead in his wake. As night falls and both sides prepare for a tempo-rary halt in the fighting, I slip among the fallen soldiers and retrieve a breastplate, shield, and kilt.

Snarling comes from nearby. A wolf and a coyote are facing off over a corpse.

The dead man's helmet catches my eye. Shooing the predator and scavenger off with swings of my sword, I pull it off his head, wincing at the sounds of squelching wounds.

It's sturdy, painted blue with a fringe of feathers at the back.

From two conical projections, like coyote ears, dangle red tassels.

A perfect fit.

I head toward the Chalca encampment, giving my uncle's troops a wide berth. I almost get caught by a Mexica sentry, but I drop into the tall grass just in time and crawl past him before resuming my running crouch.

When I stumble into a Chalca perimeter guard, I slip into the accent of a noble from Amaquehmecan, one of the cities in the federation.

"Gods! Plead your pardon. I got quite a knock on the head perhaps a watch ago. Woke up to find myself surrounded by poor dead sods. Nearly ran into the damned Mexica getting back."

"Name?" the guard says.

"Nezahualcoyotl, son of Nezahualpilli."

I imagine Sekalli smiling at my clipped consonants and breathy vowels, and the outlandish name I have chosen for my father—typical of Amaquehmecan. The echo of her remembered laughter resounds achingly in my heart.

The guard, however, doesn't even bat an eye at my lies.

"Go visit the medical tent before reporting to your squad. Doctor's got her hands full with real wounded, but the last thing we need is for you to collapse again on the battlefield with a concussion. One of her aides can check your skull for dents."

"Yes, sir," I say, ambling off.

And like that, I become a Chalca soldier.

From the doctor's aides, I learn that entire support squads from my purported city of origin were wiped out in the battle, so I claim to be the only survivor of a group led by one Captain Amimitzin, who has just died during surgery.

I weep over his mangled body. It isn't hard to summon the tears.

Along with two other orphaned soldiers, I'm assigned the following day to a squad from Acxotlan, one of the three districts of Tlalmon-alco. The captain—a veteran in his thirties named Oton—gives us a gruff and abrupt welcome.

"I need you to stay alive long enough to kill at least one of those bastards. Do that for your country, and then you can go riding across the sky with the sun with the other fallen, if that's what you want. Personally, I prefer a long life to celestial flight. So, if you're like me, then after you fulfill your patriot duty, just keep killing every gods-damned Mexica warrior that crosses your path."

Sage advice. And once the sun has cleared the summit of Iztacci-huatl to the east of us, the two armies march toward each other. When only about forty rods separate us, everyone begins to hurl projectiles—some arrows, others stones from slings, still others spears from atlatl. I quickly run out of things to throw and lift my shield above my head. Two arrows thud into it as I crouch.

Somewhere a conch announces the next wave of attacks—the elite warriors of Chalco and Mexico slamming together in a vicious melee. Then, one after another, successive surges of increasingly less talented, less experienced, and less equipped soldiers join the fray, till the battlefield is a writhing mass of chaos.

As my squad, one of the last, moves into the center of that maelstrom, my eyes and heart scan the movement, seeking out patterns. There's a rhythm to the ebb and flow of battle, and I smile once I feel it. I have come a long way from the pampered prince who almost didn't pass his martial arts examination. Now the complex beat fills every niche of my being, body, and soul, and I slip into the unconscious choreography, whirling amid the swinging blades, slaying each man unfortunate enough to become my partner in this deadly dance upon the bloody battlefield.

The fourth Mexica I face has a pair of macuahuitzoctli knives tucked into a sash at his waist. As I step into his attempted blow, I pull the obsidian daggers free and thrust them into both sides of his neck.

Then, wielding my weapon of choice, I truly become an avatar of destruction.

After two watches of violence, someone pulls at my arm, and I swing around, burying a knife in the shield of my captain.

"Didn't you hear the retreat being sounded?" Oton shouts, slapping me. "Get your ass moving, boy!"

We fall back to camp, receiving orders to pack up and head slightly east. The other members of my squad bombard me with questions, somewhat in awe of what they've seen me accomplish on the battlefield.

"I don't know if you'd be any good in a flower war," one of them grunts. "But in a life-or-death battle, you're pretty formidable."

"At the calmecac, they called me Hands of Death," I half lie, repressing a shudder at the memory of my father's pride and the band of assassins—the Deadly Hand—that have driven me from my beloved's side.

They chuckle, amused, but soon they're all using "Tomiccama" instead of Nezahualcoyotl to refer to me.

Our Hands of Death. Lovely.

No sooner have we settled in against an outcropping than our captain rounds us up.

"The prince has gotten mortality reports, and our kill rate was the highest today, men—better even than the elite squads. So he wants to review you crazy punks in person. Come on."

He leads us up a hill where we find Prince Quetzalmazatl looking out at the enemy army, which has withdrawn to allow us to drag the dead from the battlefield before vultures, wolves, and coyotes begin to pick at their corpses. I size him up. Our commander is dressed regally, a cape of scarlet ibis feathers over a full-body uniform of black and green. His helmet bears thirteen-point buck horns.

But my eye is drawn to my uncle Moteuczoma's troops, which are drilling for the next battle in the distance ahead.

"Utterly predictable," I mutter.

Captain Oton catches my words and looks askance at me as we come to a halt, some rods away from the prince and his retinue.

"What do you mean?"

"General Moteuczoma. He is merely twenty-one. His strategies are taken right from the manuals of Tenochtitlan's calmecac, drilled into him as a student there. No variation permitted, no adaptation. If our commander decided to flout those norms, he'd catch the fool flatfooted."

One of my fellow squad members clears his throat. "I know he's out of line, Captain, but you saw him fight. He sees stuff we can't. Moves different. The enemy don't know what to do."

As the prince makes some final consultation with his generals, Oton leans closer.

"And what would you change, were you in command?"

"I would send commoners against the Mexica elite in the first wave, but armed with lances so they have greater reach than the obsidian swords and fists of the enemy. Meanwhile, I'd split our best warriors into two groups. Send one through the hills to attack the Mexica elite from the east, while the other half, having left before dawn toward the west, circles around from behind. Box those top fighters in. Decimate them, and Moteuczoma will retreat all the way back to Tenochtitlan."

The captain considers my words with a blank expression, glancing at the distant troop movements of the Mexica before turning to regard our commander.

The prince is making his way toward us now. We salute, hands on chests, heads lowered for the space of four heartbeats. He has seen maybe four more summers than my Mexica uncle, but he is still relatively young to be leading such a large force against such a formidable enemy.

"So these are your boys, Oton," the prince says. His voice is deep, but kind, and his eyes fill with care and admiration as he looks us over.

"Yes, Your Highness. Chalco's best fighters outside the military orders."

As he walks along our line, Quetzalmazatl examines each soldier's weapons and uniform. He stops in front of me.

"The one with the obsidian daggers. I hear you were particularly deadly today."

"It was my honor, Your Highness, to transform many Mexica dogs into butterflies on their way to the House of the Sun. I doubt any were worthy enough to become hummingbirds, much less eagles."

He chuckles at my deprecation. "Your name, soldier?"

"Nezahualcoyotl, Your Highness. From Amaquehmecan."

"Yes, I hear it in your accent. Well done, Nezahualcoyotzin. Continue the heroics on the morrow."

I bow low in response.

The prince has his people give us extra rations—actual meat, and six tortillas each—before dismissing us. Our captain lingers to consult with him in private.

The following day, I learn why.

Our squad is given thrusting spears, as are all the commoner foot soldiers, whom we are instructed to lead against the Mexica elite the moment the barrage of arrows and stones ceases. As we crouch beneath our shields, I give a knowing look to the captain, who gestures me to silence. He wants all the credit, I suppose.

When the final volley is in the air, I make a further whispered suggestion.

"Let's rush them now. They'll be even more shocked."

He stands and gives the command without hesitation. In moments, we have closed the gap between our two armies, just as the top enemy fighters—Shorn Ones, Otontin, Eagle Knights, Jaguar Warriors—step forward to engage.

None expect our halberds to come thrusting at their bellies. Most receive only minor wounds, but some of us manage to disembowel our opponent. At the very least, we fight them from a distance that renders their sword moves, blows, and kicks ineffectual. Our inexperienced infantry is on a level playing field with their best.

Still, they are masterful fighters, and they find ways to slip under, around, and over our spears. I drop mine and begin to defend my squad with an obsidian dagger in each fist.

I find myself squaring off against an Eagle Knight who parries my every blow with his own knives. The violence of his defense soon has me taking steps backward, and I feel panic rising as he switches to offensive tactics I can barely counter.

Just then, our elite fighters converge from east and west. Trapped between our spears and their swords, the Mexica vanguard begins to fall like a doe and its fawns, surrounded by hunters.

The frantic pounding of drums commands the survivors to retreat. Flags from Moteuczoma's generals request a halt to the fighting.

By the end of the day, his army marches back toward Tenochtitlan indeed.

That evening, the prince invites us to dine beside the command tent. He plies us with maguey wine and venison, praising our captain's strategy and our valor.

"Tomorrow, when we return to Tlalmanalco, double wages will await you boys!" He lifts a cup to salute us. "Enjoy yourselves while the enemy licks their wounds."

We thank him, downing another cup and gorging ourselves. I try not to think of Sekalli's cooking—of sneaking sips of her father's wine with her, and the feel of her slender body against mine. I wish the Mexica would return now. Keeping myself alive leaves no time for regrets. The moments of introspection between battles are what is hard.

"Nezahualcoyotzin," the captain whispers sharply, and I glance up, suddenly aware that I have not been paying attention. "Prince Quetzalmazatl is addressing you."

"Pardon, Your Highness. I was reliving the heat of battle in my mind."

He smiles. "Not to worry. I merely asked whether you will be returning to Amaquehmecan."

"Ah." I nod, having prepared myself for this eventuality. "I should rather not go home just yet. My father is a minor priest, and what he lacks in influence on the city, he makes up for by being outrageously strict with his children and wife. I have never experienced such freedom my entire life. I am loathe to end it."

"I should recommend your staying at the calmecac," the prince responds, "but I suspect your desire for greater freedom would be hampered by such an environment."

The captain scoffs gently. "I happen to know of a widow—the wife of a crooked judge who passed away, leaving her nothing but debts. Now she rents out rooms in their manor and sells maguey wine to survive. I'll introduce you to her."

So that is how I come to live with Cillamiyauh. Though age would stoop her shoulders and back, she holds her head high while she goes about her business, scowling at the world with haughtiness as if the grey streaks in her hair were pure silver.

"If you drink, be quiet about it," she instructs as I pay her a month's rent in advance. "No noise after nightfall. No girls in my house."

"Of course, Cillamiyauhtzin. I should never dream of such a thing, Revered Aunt."

"And don't lie to me, young sir. I despise liars and tricksters most of all. My late husband deceived me for more than a decade. I'll not be made a fool again; not by any man."

For the better part of a month, just shy of twenty days, I live the life of a young, feted warrior. My many kills permit me to wear finer clothing, to get my hair cut shoulder-length, to sit in a better section of the audience when watching ballgames or concerts or plays when we return to the city. And I do all of it, filling my days with frivolity, food, and drink, letting veterans who admire my courage spend hours sharing their own tales of valor, accepting the invitation of every noble who learns of my reputation and wishes to meet me.

The city of Tlalmanalco is divided into three wards, each with its own minor king. Together, these men rule the city as a triumvirate. Cillamiyauh's manor is in Acxotlan, where the king is Toteocih—older brother of Prince Quetzalmazatl.

Word spreads through the ward about my squad's crucial role in routing the Mexica army. People treat me with deference I haven't enjoyed since before the siege of Tetzcoco. As the prince esteems us, so must the king, rumor suggests.

How do I know these murmurings? Cillamiyauh makes certain to tell me, squinting disapprovingly at my features as if she might uncover some secret buried beneath the mask of my kindness.

"Oh, you've become quite the little mystery, lad. Noble mothers throughout the ward wonder about your age and background, imagining their daughters betrothed to you one day. Little boys fashion fasting collars for themselves before playing at soldiers, each giving himself your unusual name. You are a cipher they fill with their secret longings. You mean nothing on your own . . . you're just juxtaposed with those fantasies. Ah, but I have my suspicions, yes I do. You've insinuated yourself entirely too quickly into the noble circles of this ward. I have a friend who works at the king's palace. I'll ask him to warn His Majesty. He should be wary of his younger brother's acquaintances."

She doesn't seem a real threat to me, so I ignore her ramblings. But I do become overwhelmed by strangers wanting to curry favor with the royal family. Sometimes I ignore people on the street who attempt to get my attention. But, one day, I feel someone staring at me with such intensity that I cannot help but look up.

It's Izcalloh. I haven't seen them for a year and a half. They are dressed beautifully in the flower-embroidered skirt and long blouse worn by clerics of Xochiteotl, the Flowery Duality.

I should have been more careful. Their mother is from this city, this ward. I had hoped to wait longer before contacting them, but the gods have other plans.

They stare at me, in shock. Then joy begins to dawn upon their face, their eyes filling with happy tears. That is until I raise my hand in discrete warning and shake my head, once. A nascent smile fades from their lips.

I continue walking, drawing near them on the broad street. Their perfume fills my mind with memories, my heart with longing for a simpler time, when they taught me the intricacies of court intrigue and giggled at my foolish imitations of Acolhua nobles.

"Tell your parents," I mutter, passing alongside them, "that I am Nezahualcoyotl of Amaquehmecan, should they ever encounter me. Bide your time, dear Izcalloh. The moment has not yet come."

Then, without turning back, I leave my tutor and friend behind.

On the eighteenth day since the Mexica retreat, our squad is called up for duty once more. A new battle has broken out near the narrow pass between Iztapayocan Hill and Lake Chalco. The Mexica are trying to tear down the wall, and Prince Quetzalmazatl has been asked to lead an army to support the confederation's besieged forces there.

After a day's march, we arrive to find the soldiers of Iztapayo-can and Chalco City spread thin, trying to protect hill, wall, and lake from invasion—as well as the broader pass through Colhuacan on the north side of the hill, which Moteuczoma's army used to reach us.

The prince has Captain Oton accompany him on a tour of the four fronts, presumably expecting some off his strategic genius—ideas he steals from me and passes off as his—to provide solutions to the multi-pronged attack. While they're away, I do some digging on my own, getting a feel for what has happened during the last three days of fighting.

What's clear is that Moteuczoma is *not* leading these Mexica. These tactics have sprung from a mind much more capable and flexi-ble than his. Stolid, stubborn, and mean, my Uncle Moteuczoma pre-fers to face everything head-on, with unnuanced force. When rain fell on his thirteenth birthday—ruining the feast planned in his honor—he sought to slay the tlaloqueh themselves with his bow, loosing arrow after arrow into the clouds.

That earned him the nickname Ilhuicamina—*he shoots at heaven.*

Not the sharpest blade in Tenochtitlan's intellectual arsenal.

I have my suspicions about the identity of the new Mexica commander, and they are confirmed when Oton returns, breathless, and pulls me behind a moss-crusted boulder to confer in private.

"Nezahualcoyotzin, I need your unparalleled eye for tactics. The mad Mexica have put a fire priest in charge of this army, one Prince Tlacaellel. No one is quite sure to make of his tactics."

I scoff, remembering my uncle's twisted, devious pranks. He never got caught. Everyone believed him too pious, too noble. Afterward, he would just smile at his victim. Wink at them.

Infuriating.

"Tlacaellel is a dangerous, dastardly man. Can you see what he has done? He's forced Chalco to remain in a defensive posture on four different fronts. He will not permit us to attack. Once he has worn us down enough with his feinting, he will pour his forces past our weakened defenses."

A voice interrupts from behind us. "And what shall we do to stop him, Nezahualcoyotl? It *is* you I should ask, isn't it?"

Prince Quetzalmazatl has rounded the boulder. My captain drops to his knees and beats his forehead against the sandy soil.

"I plead your pardon, Your Highness. My error is great and deserves great punishment. I put my life in the hands of my prince. Do with me as you will."

The prince waves this apology away with a smirk.

"I am annoyed, but I choose to believe that you have conveyed this young man's ideas to me as your own, because you knew how difficult it would be to accept military advice from one so inexperienced. Nezahualcoyotzin, how old are you?"

"Seventeen, Your Highness," I reply, not daring to lie. My birthday has come and gone, uncelebrated. I do my best not to reflect on where I was just one year ago. My heart might break forever.

"Amazing. I suppose your father's discipline and guidance has tapped into some innate talent of yours. Yet let us reserve that conversation for another time. At this moment, I need your guid-ance, no matter how young or strange you may be. Speak freely, soldier."

I take a deep breath. So much depends on these words I'm about to speak. The outcome of the battle. My position within the army. My relationship with this prince. Our possible future alliance. If I am wrong, my people are damned.

"Pull everyone back," I say in a rush, giving myself no more time for self-doubt. "Especially the canoes. Tlacaellel will assume we have bottled ourselves up in the pass out of exhaustion, and he will trigger an attack. But it will be an ambush. Archers and spearcasters will await his boats, supported by pikemen who can use their thrusting spears to keep any surviving Mexica at bay. The other half of our forces will hide on the east side of Iztapayocan Hill, so that when the Mexica come over it and round its northern edge, we shall meet them with brutal surprise."

Quetzalmazatl scratches his chin. "These seem more barbarous Chichimeca tactics than honorable Tolteca warfare."

I lower my eyes, hoping this man will indulge my breach of decorum.

"Like the Acolhua people, we Chalca are heirs to both traditions, though through the more elegant Nonohualca. Do you know the Mexica Way, Your Highness? What matters most is survival, *then* vic-tory. Honor is superfluous. That is what Tlacaellel believes. We must embrace the same attitude or suffer defeat at his hands."

After a moment of consideration, when I suspect I may be exe-cuted, the prince sighs.

"Having trusted your unaccountable wisdom before, I should be foolish not to do so again. Captain Oton, I require you and your squad to support my own royal guard. This risky stratagem cannot result in the deaths of our commanders. Or princes."

Two watches later, hunkered down among boulders at the base of Iztapayocan Hill, we hear the ostensibly quiet movement of the Mexica army as they attempt to slip behind the enemy they believe trapped between hill and lake. Instead, they find themselves face-to-face with five thousand Chalca soldiers.

The fray is intense, spattering blood tinted purple by the encroaching twilight. The fighting is in such close quarters that soon all distinctions between squads are gone. As another Mexica drops dead beneath my obsidian daggers, I pause to look for the prince, who should be inside the protective circle we have formed.

But that defense has crumpled on one side, and an Eagle Knight leaps through the gap, swinging his sword at Quetzalmazatl's head. I fling one of my knives at him. It thuds into the flat of his weapon, twisting it in his grip so that his blow only grazes the prince's breastplate. Pushing my way past dueling warriors, I scoop up a broken halberd and leap at the knight, thrusting the point at his throat. He parries with his shield, knocking the spear from my right hand and opening himself up just enough for me to land close and slit his throat with the dagger in my left.

"Are you unharmed?" I ask the prince, scanning the area around him. Another Chalca warrior has stepped into the gap in his defense, keeping the enemy at bay.

"Yes. Thank you. Stay here with me, Nezahualcoyotzin. Rest a moment."

We watch as the Mexica falter finally and then begin to retreat—not called by drums, but by the dawning realization that they have been bested. Runners come from the lakeshore to inform us that the enemy canoes have been destroyed and most of those combatants slain.

As Tlacaellel pulls his forces back into Colhuacan, heading toward the causeway that leads to Tenochtitlan, I can imagine him wondering, perplexed, just what freak twist of fate has placed a military genius in the midst of Chalco. One day, I hope to tell him the truth to his face.

When we return to Tlalmanalco, the prince bids me accompany him to his villa: a brightly frescoed manor beside one of the nine streams of this city, on an estate thick with pines.

The prince's personal attendant is waiting as we enter.

"Welcome home, Your Highness."

"It is good to be back, Micnomah. Would you please fetch the cedar chest from my dressing room?"

"At once."

As he leaves, the prince turns to me. "You intrigue me, Nezahualcoyotzin. Indeed, your fighting prowess is matched only by your sharp intellect. I need a person like you at my side, protecting me while engaging me in challenging conversation. So, I have already informed Captain Oton of a promotion and transfer. You will now be a member of my royal guard, assigned specifically to accompany me during military and state matters."

I bow my head, trying not to consider the complications of such a post.

"Your Highness honors me."

Micnomah returns at that moment, carrying a wooden box. Quetzalmazatl removes the lid and pulls out an ornate netted cape, covered with small white shells. He motions me over with a tilt of his head.

"You must look the part."

I take the cape, and he pulls out a new kilt and vest: the same green as his own uniform, with a black design along the edges, and a repeating pattern of deer horns and quetzal feathers.

"You are now one of my people. Do you understand the import?"

Indeed. I grew up surrounded by tecpantlacah, courtiers sworn to my father. Nobles without titles whose lives revolved around the palace. Wholly dependent on the royal figure to whom they held a duty of homage. Susceptible to his every daily whim.

"I do. My life is yours, my liege."

Of course, my pledge is a lie. Though the deception pains me a bit, my only fealty is to the Acolhua people and the gods we worship. Yet I admire this prince; his open heart and mind.

In different times, we would be friends.

{25} THE WAY OF CHAOS

Friendship

"Friends are like flowers,"
a singer chants to pounding drums.
"Blooming briefly, they brighten
our lives as we pluck them
and braid them into our hair.
Then those sweet-smelling petals
wither and fade, forever gone."

Beside the prince, I sing along, hands
tapping on the pommel of my sword.
He arches an eyebrow in surprise.
"You know this piece? It's Acolhua."

A week after our big battle,
we are standing in his city's
House of Song, among a throng
of elite warriors, celebrating victory
against the Mexica. I nod and smile.

"Music is what makes me good
in battle. All the lessons I learn
for one can be applied to the other."

The notion is novel to him,
but intriguing, and we talk later,
sipping maguey wine at his villa
as the stars wheel across the sky
and night deepens into silence.

We discover we love the same poets,
have studied the same philosophers,
prefer the varied voice of the mockingbird
to the bright feathers of the quetzal,
believe in the essential beauty of humans
despite the ugliness often on display.
It's the first of many long nights
spent chatting by his side
sometimes wandering the woods
that surround his manor, teeming
with deer and birds that remind me
of my time on the volcano that now
looms above us, cold and dormant.

And I see the worthy core of his character
at meetings with the ruling council,
especially soothing the roiling heart
of his brother, the king, whose haughty
spite often threatens to cause a rift.

Everywhere we go, it's clear his people
adore him, see him as their true leader,
one not concerned with renown or applause,
but working behind the scenes, alongside
brilliant nobles and commoners alike,
for the good of the ward, the city,
the Chalca Confederation as a whole.

It's impossible not to admire the man.
Bit by bit I come to care for him
as if he were friend or kin,

the older brother I always dreamed of,
rather than the monstruous bastard
who actually plagued my childhood.

One night we get thoroughly drunk,
and I actually call him *notiyachcauhtzin*,
beloved older brother, a phrase that
has never passed my lips before.

Throwing one arm around my shoulders,
he lifts his cup with the other and shouts,
"To friendship! To brotherhood!"

And for the first time since Acaxel's death,
I feel myself bound by fraternal love
to the heart of another like myself.

The Revelation

Almost two months to the day
after we repulsed Tlacaellel's troops,
Prince Quetzalmazatl arrives at the house
of Lady Cillamiyauh, face cold and hard
as he pushes aside the curtain to my room.

"Your Highness!" I say, rising to bow.
"What an unexpected surprise.
Should I get changed? Do you need me
to accompany you somewhere?"

I reach for my uniform, draped on a peg,
but his hand, firm on my forearm, stops me.
His jaw is tight. Something is terribly wrong.

"Nezahualcoyotl," he says simply,
lowering his speech as if to underscore
the difference in our social rank.
"Perhaps you do not know,
though such unawareness
is itself a clue, but I am betrothed
to the lovely Princess Maquiztli,
daughter of my namesake,
Quetzalmazatzin the Great
King of the Itztlacozauhcan Ward
of Amaquemehcan.
Chichimeca Chieftain,
we Chalca name him,
in defiance of Tepaneca
and Acolhua both."

Without taking his eyes off me,
he pulls a dagger from his belt,
begins to slowly twirl it
in his long fingers.

My heart is fluttering
like a maddened
hummingbird
trapped in a cage,
sensing its doom.

"Imagine my surprise
when, after sending a messenger
to the woman I love
asking her to reward your father,
I discovered that there is no man
named Nezahualpilli in her city,
much less a minor priest."

As he says the last word,
the prince quickly steps close
and places his blade against
my throat, eyes widening,
breath coming in angry gasps.

I could free myself, kill him.
But I do not wish to do so.
He is my friend. And possibly
my ally. If he lets me explain.

"Your Highness," I plead,
"it was never my intention

to spread these lies so far.
I simply sought to survive.
I am planning no evil
against you or your people."

His blade presses harder
against my skin, drawing blood.

"Then tell me who you are."

"I am Nezahualcoyotl," I begin,
"but I was born Acolmiztli,
son of King Ixtlilxochitl of Tetzcoco,
Overlord of Acolhua,
Chichimeca Chieftain."

Then I relate my story,
beginning to end—
the happenings,
not the visions,
not my dreams.

As I speak, Quetzalmazatl
pulls his knife from my throat,
paces slowly before me,
eyes growing distant with thought.

When I have finished,
there is a moment of silence
before he poses a crucial question.

"Are you my friend, Acolhua?"

●◖○◗●

"Yes, Quetzalmazatzin."

It is the first time I have used
his name. Even the honorific
cannot lessen the danger
of addressing him thus.

"Am I truly an older brother to you?"

"Yes, Quetzalmazatzin."

He stares into my eyes for the space
of several seconds, gauging my honesty.
Then he slides his blade back into his belt.

"Before your father was killed," he says,
"he sent an ambassador, hoping for an alliance.
The council decided the risk was too great,
but circumstances have changed, my friend.
Is this still your wish? That Chalco
and Acolhuacan stand together against
Tepanecapan and Mexico?"

"Though I do not know when
the right moment will present itself,
yes, that is still my wish, made stronger
by the admiration you inspire in me."
Despite the tension,
taut like a drumhead,
the prince begins to laugh,
waggling his finger at me.

"If there's one thing
you've taught me,
Little Sibling,
it's that there is
no right moment.
Just the right strategy."

Then, unexpectedly,
he pulls me into a hug.

"There's a reason you're here.
There's a reason we're friends.
Let's unleash chaos on the bastards."

Thunder in Your Heart
(Prince Quetzalmazatl Speaks)

Nezahualcoyotzin, you cannot hide
in the dim light of lies any longer.
I can see it in your whirling attacks
on the blacked, bloody battlefield.
I can hear it in your hoarse voice
as you speak of siege and slaughter.

There is thunder in your heart,
waiting to burst your foes asunder.
Should you fail to release it soon,
it will crack your soul in twain.

No need to say the words.
I know you yearn for beauty,
for creation and order,
for love unfettered by hate.
Yet you have been forsaken
by everything but destruction.

You may be a singer, a drummer,
an architect, an anointed leader,
but you must now compose a dirge,
must intone a ululating battle cry!

Enough wavering. Embrace the dark.
Be a conduit for chaos and war.
Obliterate your enemies so completely
that no one will dare lift a weapon

against your kingdom again.
Fast no more. Glut on their blood.

I know you. Before I knew your identity,
I knew you. You are so like me, Brother.
Built to love, to aid, to lead a city
into peaceful, enduring prosperity.

Yet the gods have placed people
beneath the shadow of our wings
and tail feathers, divine charges
whom we must protect with talons
and beak and fierce speed, dropping
like predators from above to slay.

So turn from the Feathered Serpent.
Show Tezcatlipoca that you can retake
by force and wiles what he allowed
the Emperor to wrest from your kin.

You are Acolhua, yes, but also Mexica.
Heed the call of the violent patron god
of your mother's people, Huitzilopochtli,
born on a shield with a sword in his hand.
We Chalca shall shrug off the hated yoke,
rise to smash our oppressors beside you.

Let your fasting end. Feast on their fear.
Hold back no more. Let that flood
of fiery wrath pour forth from within
till it effaces traitors and usurpers alike.

Betrayal

Almost two whole watches
we sit and make plans
in my rented room,
never imagining
that Cillamiyauh,
my nosy landlady,
has overheard
everything.

She, too, plots chaos.
Seeking to curry favor,
she scurries to the palace
where her younger sister
serves as lady-in-waiting
to a minor princess.
The message is urgent.
It spreads like wildfire
through the network.
King Toteocih
fairly fumes
in fury.

The prince has just left,
ordering me to rest,
promising we shall
meet on the morrow
and begin to reveal
my true identity
to key nobles.

Then the king's men
burst into my room
and arrest me.

{ III }

RETURN

{26} PRISONER

I AM DRAGGED THROUGH the streets of Acxotlan to the royal
palace. The guards refuse to answer my questions, so I have to
wait until they deposit me on the polished wooden floor of the
audience chamber. Keeping my head low, I glance up at Toteocih,
seated on his jade throne at the center of a raised dais. A jade diadem
perches awkwardly on his mohawk. Emerald plugs in his earlobes and
bottom lip sparkle ostentatiously. Despite his finery, his wide face is
purple with rage and his hands are clenched into trembling fists.

"Acolmiztli," he spits. "Son of Ixtlilxochitl. Crown prince of
Tetzcoco. How dare you live in my city under a false identity, fighting in my army, joining my younger brother's personal guard? What
sort of Acolhua madness or adolescent arrogance compels you to
mock Chalco in this way? Do you have a death wish? Suicide by
execution?"

"I cry your pardon, sire!" I press my head against the cedar planks. "If I fought for Chalco, it is because I believe in the cause and despise the Mexica."

"Why not announce yourself to the government, then? Liars have much to hide. Their work as spies, for instance."

I clasp my hands together in supplication. I have never begged for anything in my life—but I know the expected gestures.

"If Your Majesty would but summon your brother," I begin. "Much could be explained."

"Ah, so Quetzalmazatzin has concealed your identity from me all these months?"

"No, sire. Not at all. He only just discovered who I am."

The king scoffs, leaning back with a gesture of incredulity.

"Yet you still live? Clear evidence of collusion. Lady Cillamiyauh reports that the two of you had begun plotting an alliance between Acolhuacan and Chalco. How many troops had you agreed to commit to my deposal? Once my brother was installed as king, what were your next steps meant to be?"

I realize the peril to which I have exposed Quetzalmazatl. His elder brother will now perceive his every word as a slight—will suspect treachery in his every act.

"Your Majesty, never have I sought your removal, nor has the prince. Indeed, we had hoped to come before you soon with the truth, and with a proposal for ridding both our nations of the threat posed by Tepanecapan and Mexico."

A mocking laugh escapes the king's twisting lips.

"Goodness, *thank you*, Your Royal Highness, for deigning to share your superior plots and schemes with me. It is truly an honor to have a great Acolhua intellect among our less refined southern thinkers. However, I have quite a different plan in mind." Toteocih stands and descends with slow steps from his dais, approaching me. "Rather than

continue to fight with the Mexica, at great cost to our federation's coffers, I shall offer you to Emperor Tezozomoc in exchange for a return
to normality. Chalco as his favorite vassal; Mexico as the minor hive
of mercenaries and mutts. Full access to imperial trade routes from sea
to shining sea. Rumors have been pouring out of Tlaxcallan for
months about you, and the old tyrant has been desperate to track you
down. He will be quite relieved . . . quite ecstatic that I am holding
you for him."

The maw of fate opens before me, ready to devour all my hopes.

The king grips me by my hair and hauls me painfully to my feet.

"Nezahualcoyotl, eh? Let us see what a week of fasting does to your
arrogance. You will beg me to hand you over to the Emperor soon
enough."

The cuauhcalco is nearby, in the judicial complex. The guards thrust
me inside one of its sturdiest cells, with thick oak bars and an ingenious locking mechanism of crossbars that can't be reached from inside.

The king keeps his promise to make me starve. The first two days,
guards bring me nothing but water once a day, a small bowl that I
ration into several tantalizing sips.

None of the nearby cells are occupied, so I am left alone in the
gloom with my thoughts and growing hunger. It has been nearly a
year since I felt such brutal solitude. The mountain, the farm, and the
army—Aunt Coyote, Sekalli, and Quetzalmazatl, to be precise—have
kept me sane, kept my spirits high, kept my hopes alive.

This silent darkness allows no comfort. My failings are laid bare. I
am forced to face my recklessness and the pain it causes others. Has
Quetzalmazatl's brother punished him as well, I wonder?

At the height of my self-hatred, in the depths of my second night
in prison, I wonder if it might not be for the best that I am given to
the Emperor, executed publicly by his tremulous old hand. To warn

others against dreaming too big; against pitting their pitiful small selves against the churning wheels of the world.

Then, the following morning, a miracle brings wonder and light back into my life.

I hear movement somewhere, steps and clattering, swinging inner doors that separate sections of the cuauhcalco and keep prisoners from escaping. Yesterday, similar sounds announced my bowl of water, but there is something enticingly familiar about the footsteps that now approach: a gentle slip and slide, instead of the clomping of brute soldiers.

The perfume reaches me first, and I can't stop the tears that rise to my eyes.

Oh, by the Thirteen Heavens, it's Izcalloh. Somehow, they've come.

"Your Majesty?" they whisper, probing the darkness with tentative music, making my kingship a fact with a few melodic syllables. "Are you here, Acolmiztzin?"

Light flickers as they lift a small torch, like dawn on the very first morning of the world when the sun sat hovering on the horizon. Izcalloh is wearing their clerical uniform, the same long embroidered skirt and billowing blouse I saw on the street some months ago.

"Yes, Noble Izcalloh, Precious Flower, dearest friend and mentor. I'm here, in the darkness again."

They rush to my cell, sliding the torch into a sconce on the nearby wall before thrusting their hands between the bars and grabbing my own.

"My Lord, forgive me! I have taken entirely too long to come to your side. I am undeserving of your mercy, but I swear I have endeavored daily to enter this prison. Only this morning, however, was I able to win the support of enough members of the priestly and judicial guilds. The influence of Prince Quetzalmazatl was key. Many in this ward respect him, despite his brother's accusations of treason."

Relieved to hear my Chalca friend unscathed, I squeeze Izcalloh's strong but soft hands. "So you've met with him? I mentioned you several times, as we discussed plans for an alliance. He laughed and nodded, but would not explain what he found so amusing."

"My mother is his second cousin," Izcalloh says. "Thanks to that royal connection, my father and I have been relatively safe since the fall of Tetzcoco. Though the prince and I are not close, we have been at several events together since I arrived. The moment he learned of your arrest, before being summoned himself, he came to visit me at the temple of the Flowery Duality. Since then, I have been petitioning to meet with you as a cleric—to help you offer up your confession to the Eater of Sin before you are executed by Emperor Tezozomoc."

The starkness of those words makes me tremble and almost fall to my knees, but Izcalloh holds me up, their hands sliding up my arms to grip me more tightly.

"Peace, Acolmiztzin. I shall see myself flayed alive as a sacrifice to Xipe Totec before I permit Chalco to turn you over."

I have not seen this fierceness on their features since I was a little boy, surprised at the scolding they gave me one day for mocking some important noble.

"I am moved by your loyalty."

They pull their hands back slowly, and I'm forced to lean against the bars to support my shaky legs. Izcalloh kneels before me, pressing their pretty forehead to the flagstones.

"Forgive my boldness, but I am not driven by simple loyalty, Your Majesty. My homage, my fate, my heart await your command." Their voices cracks slightly, quavering with emotion. "I exist for you alone. I have since we were children. I shall put my body and soul between you and danger, sire. You are my king, my overlord, my chieftain. I dedicate my existence now to returning you to your proper role as the mighty cypress, whose broad branches provide comfort and shade to the Acolhua people. All that must be done, I shall do. Without remorse. Without regret." They lift their tear-streaked face to look me in the eyes. "Hear me, sire. I am yours."

I swallow heavily. Izcalloh themself taught me long ago how to respond to such a declaration.

"Stand, loyal subject. Your king receives your homage with a glad heart. Our love for you knows no limits. Come into the crook of our arm. Lie beneath the shade of our wing. As you swear to defend us with your life, so we declare you our person, untouchable by all on pain of death."

Izcalloh stands, takes my hands, and kisses them.

"No harm will come to you," they say less formally. "The prince and I have the beginnings of a plan. Before this cycle of thirteen days has ended, you will be free."

They reach into the wide sleeves of their blouse and pull out a tamalli, still wrapped in its corn husk.

"I must be careful about how much food I attempt to smuggle in," they explain, "as the guards are quite thorough in their search. But I will get you some sustenance every day."

I devour the tamalli immediately, savoring the cornmeal and the spicy bean filling. The guards have also given Izcalloh my bowl of water, which they pass to me. I sip carefully, a small amount.

"Prince Quetzalmazatzin related an abbreviated version of your story, but I was hoping, if you are not too tired, that you could expand on what has befallen you this past year?"

I catch a hint of nervous worry, as if Izcalloh is reluctant but resigned.

They need to know. Everything. I am tired of my secrets, and Izcalloh is the one person in the universe in whom I can completely confide. So I begin to speak. The story takes the better part of the watch, and afterward we sit in silence.

Something twitches in Izcalloh's face, a hint of sadness or disappointment.

"What," they mutter breathily, after the space of several awkward moments, "does Your Majesty plan to do about the Chololteca farm girl? Do . . . do you still love her, sire?"

Shit. I had not considered this reaction a possibility. There are ways I could avoid the conversation altogether . . . but I need Izcalloh. I care for them deeply, in complex ways that are different from what I feel for Sekalli. So, I decide to be as straightforward as possible, without insulting them.

"Does my love for her change anything for you?"

Izcalloh shakes their head immediately. "No. Never. I am simply . . . confused. Before I left Tetzcoco, you intimated that I . . ."

Ah. Now I understand. Perhaps Izcalloh had imagined a period of exclusivity as they guided me toward the right marriage alliance. They never expected to share my affections so early on.

"That you would become my concubine. Yes. I still want you at my side, Izcalloh. As my closest advisor. And more. Release those fears; you have my heart. But don't ask me to forget about Sekalli too. I can't turn my back on that love. She changed me in profound ways, Izcalloh. Made me understand things about myself that were hidden. I'll be a better ruler because of her family and her."

Izcalloh's larynx bobs as they swallow and nod. "And I cannot bear you children. It is an understandable impulse, sire. Your Majesty is the king of Tetzcoco, Chichimeca Chieftain, Acolhua Overlord. I dare not gainsay your right to love whomever you please—however many people your heart is capable of loving. I have always known that you will gather multiple concubines and wives to your side. Thus have kings always lived and ruled. Yet . . . to keep a commoner as your consort?" They pause and look me in the eye. "It is highly unusual."

This moment is critical. I must act with wisdom, balancing my emotions and needs with those of the people I care about. My father serves as my best model. I think of what he might say in my position.

"Come closer," I say, gesturing Izcalloh to my cell.

●◖◉◗●

Almost shyly, they approach. I reach between the bars, put my hands on their cheeks. My index fingers lightly touch the corners of their eyes, where the folds of their eyelids overlap and turn up slightly, as if eternally smiling. At my touch, Izcalloh's lips spread in a shy smile as well, and the feel of dimples forming beneath my palms thrills me in ways I can't explain.

"I abandoned Sekalli. She may never want to see me again. But even if she consents to be with me, Noble Izcalloh, I make a solemn oath. I shall make no decision before you meet her and can fully advise me. I hope to balance my love and my responsibilities with your help."

Izcalloh nods, laying their hands atop mine.

Then, fulfilling a desire I've felt since my tenth summer, I pull their face closer and kiss them through the bars.

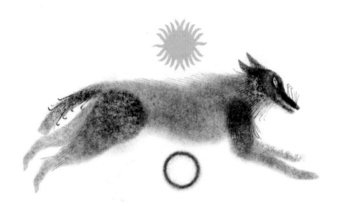

{27} THE WAY OF DUALITY

●◖◗●

Blossoming Sun

Once again, I am a child,
wincing at the pitch black
in which forms roil and squirm
like bleak, unspeakable wyrms.

Intimations of higher reality
or projections of my hunger
and thirst and solitude,
they remind me of monsters.

The nexquimilli, that bundle
of human ash, rolling and groaning,
leaving dark billows in its wake.

The centlapachton, crooked goblin
whose small size belies its wickedness,
creeping about, dragging its hair.

The tzontecomatl, severed head
that follows children, bouncing
and rattling, teeth snapping.

Just as you would hear me scream
and rush into my chambers
to hold me tight and shush away
every babbling fear, lighting candles
to dispel the imagined bugbears—

So now you glide into this prison,
torch held high like some divinity,

like the sun, blossoming as it emerges
from the gloomy Land of the Dead
to pour its life-giving rays upon us.

Today, overcome with the overlap
of past and present, fear and relief,
I cry out to you in inchoate despair.

"Elder sibling! Dearest friend!
Am I a being of shadows or light?
Shall I create or destroy?"

Your smile dispels the dark
that still lingers in my heart.
"Neither," you whisper. "Both."

Sovereign of the Near and Nigh
(Cleric Izcalloh Speaks)

Who says you have to make a choice?
Who says those paths are different?
Remember the way of your father the king,
the Source that he worshipped, Duality.

Everywhere we look, a continuum
between two polar opposites,
each of which contains the other.

I stand before you, thought a boy
at birth by parents and priests,
but carrying the flower in my heart
that pulls me toward the feminine
so I exist in the middle, a xochihuah.

And the divinity I serve, Xochiteotl,
comprises male and female,
Xochipilli and Xochiquetzal,
one yet two at once,
loved wholly and separately
by Huehuehcoyotl,
themself of fluid gender,
ever-shifting orientation,
encompassing both
wisdom and foolishness,
old age and youth,
good and evil.

Creation? Destruction?
They are mere creases
in the robe of the Sovereign
of the Near and the Nigh,
mere unfoldings of the All.

Order cannot even exist
without chaos to organize.
Chaos whirls to naught
without order to destroy.

You must embrace rot and growth,
exist in the tension between extremes.
You must stand on both sides.

I love and serve you, but understand—
you are not what matters most.
Tetzcoco is.

You exist to preserve it,
to protect its people,
to help us prosper
and understand
and bloom.

The city—water, land, folk—
it is the jewel that the gods
entrusted unto your hands.

You must do everything
in your power, destructive
or creative, to preserve
the lives and livelihoods
of the greatest number
of souls who entwine
to make Tetzcoco great.

That is your Way, sire.
I shall help you walk it.

Remembering My Father's Words

It is a lesson
I've learned
again and
again.

I must channel
the destruction
at the center
of my being,
letting it whirl
within the strictures
of discipline,
aiming it sure
at my enemy.

Warfare means
I become a conduit,
focusing violence
through the lens of skill—
order wielding chaos.

My father was right.
Izcalloh speaks truth.
And after two years,
I finally feel
it is time.

{28} RESCUE

O N THE SEVENTH DAY of my captivity, Izcalloh comes accompanied by the prince.

"Quetzalmazatzin!" I exclaim. "How did you manage this
feat? Izcalloh told me the council had forbidden you to visit me while
your claims were being investigated."

He waves away my questions. "We don't have long, Nezahualcoyotzin. A new guard has been assigned last minute to this watch, as
the soldier posted has fallen suddenly ill."

Izcalloh winks at me. Clearly, the illness is not from natural causes.

"A supervisor will no doubt arrive shortly to ensure he adheres to
the restrictions on your visitation rights. We must act quickly."

The prince moves the two crossbars, unlocking the door to my
cell. As he pulls it open, he gestures at me with his chin.

"Take off those clothes. We need to swap outfits."

"Pardon me?"

Izcalloh interrupts. "Prince Quetzalmazatzin will remain here in your place while I escort you out. The guards won't notice what's happened for at least a half watch. Or, if the gods look upon us with favor, perhaps not until nightfall. By that time, we shall be past the border of Chalco, in the high pass between the volcanoes."

I untie my cape, but then hesitate.

"Why?" I ask. "Why do this for me?"

"It is the honorable thing," Quetzalmazatl replies. "And you have earned my respect and affection. Besides—songs will be sung about this day, my friend. We are about to transform Anahuac forever, you and I."

"What about the consequences? Freeing me is treason. Your brother will not hold back because of family ties or your military victories."

The prince has begun to strip off his more elegant cape and tunic.

"At first I shall claim you feigned illness, only to overpower me when I entered your cell to check on you. Those who have seen you in action will credit the story. Afterwards, I am confident that my allies throughout the confederation can sway political sentiment in my favor."

Izcalloh, who has turned their back to give us some privacy, scolds me lightly. "I have told Your Majesty daily that a plan was being formulated. Please trust that we have considered all options and lighted upon the course of action that is safest for all involved."

Sighing, I start to untie my breechclout. "Far be it from me to gainsay Your Highness. Should you require me to punch you in the face to make your story more credible, I shall muster up the nerve."

Quetzalmazatl can't help but laugh. "Perfect. Stay feisty, Little Sib. And when you're free, please move quickly to organize an official state visit from the Acolhua government-in-exile. My allies' support depends on the fulfillment of our agreements."

Awkward though it may feel, I start to don his sweeter-smelling and more luxurious garments. "As soon as I return to Cholollan, I'll meet with my uncle and begin preparations."

Once we have completely swapped clothing, Izcalloh locks the prince inside my cell.

"You look enough like me to fool the guard, who won't dare to raise his eyes to your face. I've dismissed my retinue for the day, so just follow Izcalloh's lead and get out of Tlalmanalco as quickly as you can."

We grip each other's forearms through the bars.

"Be well, Elder Brother," I say. "We shall meet again soon."

Leaving the cuauhcalco is easy if nerve-wracking. Izcalloh picks up the pace some twenty yards away, and soon we find ourselves beside one of the streams that flow through the city, heading eastward toward the fields surrounding Tlalmanalco.

"Wait," I call to them, a sudden thought crossing my mind. "You can't come with me. Your parents will be in danger."

"Do not command me to stay, sire," they plead. "Now that Your Majesty's identity has been revealed, you will be in need of political protection from those opposed to the Emperor. And you have promised Quetzalmazatzin that you will send a team of diplomats to negotiate a treaty. You are a brilliant young man, but you lack the statesmanship required for such negotiations. I shall be your advisor—your voice when needed. I swear upon my destiny to protect yours."

"Still. The moment Chalco discovers you've helped me escape . . . your parents will be seized and imprisoned."

Izcalloh gestures ahead. "I've thought of that outcome. And not wanting to inform my parents until you were securely free and at my side, I arranged for their majordomo to meet us nearby."

A thin man in his fifties is waiting beside a shrine where the stream bends slightly north. He bows as we approach. I remember him from visits to Izcalloh's home as a child. Tetzcoca, from the Colhuahqueh borough. His name escapes me.

"Cleric. Majesty. We are well met. I take it I am meant to convey a message to the Lord and Lady?"

"Yes," Izcalloh says. "They need to leave Chalco as soon as possible. Within the next day, I would say. As you can see, I am helping our king escape to Tlaxcallan. Once my complicity is discovered, my parents will be in danger. Lead them, faithful Tocual. Get them to safety."

My father would want me to do everything possible to protect his oldest, dearest friend. I immediately interrupt.

"To be precise, take them along the southern route to the border of Tepeyacac and Tlaxcallan. Between there and Cholollan is a family farm, belonging to Polok the Chololteca. Ask the commoners in the area. They will gladly point the way. We'll await you there and then escort you to the Acolhua borough of Cholollan."

"As you command, Your Majesty," Tocual responds. "If the gods will it, we shall see you in a few days' time."

The sun has begun to set when I judge we are far enough from Tlalmanalco to rest. We are deep in the foothills of Iztaccihuatl. The stream we have followed drops in a short cascade ahead of us, forming a shallow pool before continuing west toward the city.

"I desperately need to bathe," I say, untying the prince's cape from my shoulders. "The stench of a week in that prison still clings to me."

Izcalloh grins. "You are indeed unpleasant to walk behind, sire. Undress and enter the water. I believe I saw a copalxocotl tree a few rods back. I shall collect some of its fruit so you can scrub yourself clean."

As they leave, I strip off the rest of my borrowed clothes and plunge into the water, keeping head and body submerged to soften the shock of the cold. Then I find a perfect nook to lean in, stretching my legs out and leaning my head back against a perpendicular stone.

"Here," says Izcalloh, handing me two halves of the soapy, fibrous fruit. While I lather up and scrub away, I hear them building a small fire close by. I'm relieved, because emerging from this water as night falls will be unpleasant without a source of heat.

"When I was a boy," I say, after I feel sufficiently clean, "you would wash my hair. Could you do that for me again?"

"Of course, sire."

Izcalloh kneels on the bank, behind the stone where I'm resting. Soon I feel their supple fingers, massaging the suds from another fruit into my tangles, kneading warmly at my scalp, and running gently down my neck, along my ears.

To surrender myself like this to someone I trust completely—it's intoxicating. Arousing. There's an unexpected intimacy to Izcalloh's fingers in my hair. And when their wrists brush against my face, I can smell the sweet, flowery scent that has long haunted my dreams. Every fiber of my being comes alive, tingling, yearning. Finally, I can bear the tension no more. I reach up and put my wet hands on Izcalloh's neck, pulling them toward me into a long, warm kiss.

How many nights have I imagined these lips, that tongue?

Izcalloh's hand slips from my hair onto my chest, gliding downward with nervous fluttering twitches along my belly.

There's no stopping now, for either of us.

"Come here," I rasp against their cheek.

"Yes, Beloved."

Nothing more, just the rustling of their clothes falling to the earth.

Then Izcalloh is in the water with me, their limbs tangling with mine, our lips sliding across each other's bodies until we surge together, my eager arms encircling their chest as the stars wink in bright delight at our lovemaking.

{29} BACK ON THE FARM

The Ashes

I awaken, head cradled
in the crook of Izcalloh's arm.
Beside us, the fire has died
leaving hot ash.

I pull aside the blanket,
staring for a moment
at our lovely naked forms
before rising to quench
the lingering heat
with piss.

"Majesty!" Izcalloh objects,
awakening with a start
as steam puffs
from the banked fire.
"Some decorum, please.
I know I taught you better."

Laughing, I find the bundle
of my clothes and begin
to get dressed.
"If I can't let my guard down
with you, dear friend,
then with whom?"

Izcalloh sighs,
gathers the blanket
about them,
and goes off

into the bushes
to discreetly take care
of their needs
and dress where
none can see.

Into Tlaxcallan

Once more through the pass,
eyes roving the rocks
hoping for a glimpse
of that white ruffle.

Izcalloh's pack is full
of delicious provisions.
Perhaps my lack of hunger
keeps the coyote away.

As we cross into Tlaxcallan
my gaze drifts to Huexotzinco,
a blur in the distance,
and I think I see her running.

"What is it, Your Majesty?"
I sigh and put my hand
on Izcalloh's shoulder.
"Nothing. A mere mirage."

We turn south into the shadow
of fuming Popocatepetl.
When I glance back
the silhouette is gone.

With Child

It is nearly evening of the second day when
we reach the farm, the sprawl of buildings—
house, barn, corncrib—with milpas fanning
copper-brown like the tailfeathers of a turkey.

Omaka is playing with a rubber ball beside
the worn dirt road. He looks up to see me
and shouts with excitement, dashing inside.
The family pours out as we approach.

The kids are taller, smiles stretching taut.
The eyes of Makwiltoch are full of relief.
But Polok's jaw is hard, his gaze blazing,
and Sekalli steps out from among them.

As lovely as ever, haughty disdain
sketched across those lips and owl eyes,
small and wiry thin, except—
her belly bulges big beneath her skirt.

Pushing past the others, she steps close,
hands balled into fists that smack
against the rich fabric covering my chest
until, tiring, I gently seize her wrists.

"Are you with child? Is it mine?" I ask.

"Whose else would it be, bastard?
Who else have I loved? Who else
seduced me with his sweetness?"

●◖○◗●

Izcalloh, perhaps unwisely, interrupts.
"Speak not thus to His Majesty, girl.
He has returned, after all, even with
the weight of a nation on his shoulders."

Sekalli looks them up and down, seething.
"Who in nine hells are you, cleric,
to silence my disappointment in the father
of my unborn child? Stay out of this."

I gesture at Izcalloh. They step back, bowing.
"Sekalli, forgive me. My mother and siblings were slain,
assassins sought to kill me. I had to run, love.
For your protection. And your family's, too."

"Wait, 'love'? Will you continue that lie?
I doubt you were honest with me at all.
We were just a convenient refuge for
'Your Majesty.' And I was an easy wench."

Her mother gasps and pulls her back.
"Sekalli, stop. You go too far, child."
The woman I love begins to weep,
clutching at her belly and shaking.

"Crown Prince? Exiled Tetzcoca King?
How could you hide such things from me?
Why did I have to find out from strangers
after you abandoned me without a word?"

"I couldn't let anyone know I was alive,"
I try to explain. "For the sake of my people.

I hated lying to you about my identity.
But everything else was the truth."

"Let's say I believe you. You loved me.
Put your child in me. So? You've returned
with this noble xochihuah, whose eyes
drip honey when they look at you.

"Will you make them your royal consort?
Will you marry some princess to seal
an alliance that will help you retake
the kingdom your father lost?

"Where in your life is there room for me,
a farmer's daughter? What future awaits
your child by a mere commoner?
You have blithely destroyed my life!

My soul swells with all the words
I long to say. But I swore an oath.
I turn pleading eyes to Izcalloh.
Sighing, they give a single nod.

And I drop to my knees.

My Consort

Marry a princess? Never.
Not while you draw breath.
I will bring down the empire,
reclaim my city and my throne,
bring the Acolhua together again,
my birthright as Chichimeca Chieftain.
And you will be at my side. Forever.
No one will ever take your place.

Hear me well, beloved Sekalli—
I want you as my royal consort,
the one who bears my children.
Your daughters will be ladies,
your sons Acolhua princes,
rulers of mighty cities,
councilors and generals,
clerics and judges.

I will carve a paradise
into the rocky hills for you,
divert rivers to water gardens
where your love for nature
can flourish like the flowers
I shall gather from all corners
of the sea-ringed world.

If you accept this place
in my heart, at my side,
if you accept my love,

your parents and siblings
will never want for anything.

Polok, my new father,
I will make a cuauhpilli,
honorary knight, elevating
Omaka and Yemasaton
to nobility as well,
granting them lands and titles.

I owe you all so much,
I love each of you dearly.
I will pay whatever price
for my lies, if only you will
deign to forgive me.

You are the family I choose.
I long to make you part
of the family I've inherited.

●◖○◗●

Bound to Him

They are all visibly moved, even Polok,
whose jaw slackens while his eyes go red.
Sekalli for once is speechless.
Her mother pulls her aside and whispers
in furious insistence as her father
kneads her tense shoulders,
kisses the top of her head.

"Even this farm can be perilous,"
Polok mutters to me as they confer.
"Raids, invasions, drought—
I'm willing to consider
another option."

Then he leads his family indoors,
leaving Sekalli alone with Izcalloh and me.
With a rueful smile she reaches down
and pulls me to my feet. "Kiss me, darling boy."
Our lips meet for a long, yearning moment.
Then Sekalli turns to address Izcalloh.

"I can't agree to anything until I understand.
Who are you? What is your role here?"

"Our fathers were childhood friends.
I have been Acolmiztzin's tutor and guide
since he was a child, devoted to him
completely at the king's command.
Yet I shan't pretend that's all there is.
I love His Majesty, though for reasons

that perhaps you would fail to grasp,
not mere attraction or obsession."

"And does he love you? I really don't want
to share his love. That royal tradition
has always seemed odd to me."

"Love me or not, the king must have others,
Maiden Sekalli. As much as we may want him
for ourselves, he is more important than that.
He belongs to his people, of course, but also
he must open his palace to many women
for political reasons I shall gladly teach you."

Sekalli looks at us both, weighing these words.
"I can accept that. But, darling boy, I can feel
your affection for them. It's nearly palpable,
like the sun on my skin or wind in my hair.
Do you deny it, Neza? That you love them?"

The urge to lie is strong, to spin out a web
of fanciful distractions that obscure truth.
But this moment requires honesty.

"Of course I love Izcalloh. I have for years.
Yet there is nothing in that love to fear.
It doesn't change what I feel for you,
It poses no danger or rivalry at all."

Sekalli sniffles. "But you still plan,
do you not, to take them

as your concubine?
Don't lie to me."

It is hard for her, I know.
Commoners have one spouse,
though death or divorce
may lead them to another
and many take lovers as well.
But the polygamy of kings
is alien to them.

Izcalloh makes a daring move,
reaching out to touch Sekalli's arm.

"I am bound to him by duty,
heritage, and deep respect.
He needs me by his side.
That is where I belong."

"You don't need to be a concubine
to be by his side, cleric. Unless
you want to share his bed as well."

"Maiden Sekalli, in this slippery world
upon which we live, there is no other way
for me to be with him at all times.
Perhaps together we can build a new one
in which that is no longer true."

Before Sekalli can retort,
a caravan comes hurrying
in a cloud of dust.

How Many Will Die for Me?

Izcalloh recognizes the group at once.
"Father! Mother!" they cry in relief
as a palanquin is lowered to the ground.
The majordomo, Tocual, accompanies
his master and mistress, Izcalloh's parents.

As Lady Azcalxoch embraces her child,
Lord Cihtli addresses me, glancing
briefly at barefoot Sekalli.

"Acolmiztzin, my liege, we have come
as you commanded, abandoning all.
Know, however, that Chalco follows.
We were making preparations
when the news reached us—
Prince Quetzalmazatzin was beheaded
for treason by his brother the king."

The words are blows to my heart.
I take a stumbling step forward.
"No trial? Did the council approve?
And what do you mean by saying
that Chalco follows? Pursuit?"

"Many of those conspiring with our
Izcalloh, and the prince, turned on you,
and the king deemed action a priority.
After the execution, he sent soldiers
to our home. We scarcely escaped.

They have been on our trail since,
perhaps three watches behind us."

Horrified, I look at Sekalli, Izcalloh,
the unfortified farm glowing red
in the dying light of sunset, as if
already bloodied by the conflict.

We have till dawn, at the most.
How many more will die for me?

{30} UNEXPECTED VISITORS

SCAPE IS OUT of the question. The closest city is Cholollan, and there the Deadly Hand await my return. Instead, I dispatch Tocual and two of Lord Cihtli's guards to Cholollan to inform my uncle and request immediate aid. It is difficult for anyone to sleep that night, and not just because of the looming threat of a company of Chalca warriors descending on the farm. Even subtracting the three messengers I've sent, there are still eighteen of us to bed down.

Lady Azcalxoch has her household staff sleep out of doors, where the remaining three guards will rotate a vigil. Polok and Makwiltoch cede their sleeping chambers to Izcalloh's parents, taking their mats into the children's room.

That leaves Sekalli, Izcalloh, and me in the communal space on the west side of the hearth, awkwardly trying to arrange our mats without further damaging our uncertain relationships.

"Damn it," Sekalli says at last. "Just put your mat between us, Neza. I'll sleep closer to the coal. The cleric can hug the wall if they get lonely."

"If she were to slip up and address Your Majesty thus in front of others," Izcalloh mutters, "it could trigger a political crisis. Or at least a scandal that would not soon fade."

"I'm a commoner, not an idiot," Sekalli hisses. "I am perfectly capable of using reverential speech when necessary. But I'll be damned if I do it just to satisfy your worshipful urges. Ply him with pretty words all you want, Izcalloh. If I own his heart, then when we're alone, we'll speak as equals. Clear enough for you? Or should I rephrase it using honorifics?"

"Sekalli, peace." I unroll my mat between them. "Of course I want you to speak to me informally when we're alone. Izcalloh, please stop being so combative."

For a moment, the prospect of spending the next few decades refereeing their conflicts makes me shudder. Then I think of how my mother eventually found a way to treat Father's concubines like younger sisters, and I take comfort in the old adage that custom makes every strange taste palatable.

The looks of irritation they give me, followed by the quickest little smile they exchange, suggest that maybe Sekalli and Izcalloh will find common ground in time.

We lie there in silence for what seems ages. My mind keeps going back to Quetzalmazatl, his courage in taking my place, and the vicious cruelty of his execution. I have so many souls to grieve . . . so many deaths to avenge.

But first I must survive. This night, and all the others between now and the day I re-enter Tetzcoco, triumphant.

I'm startled to feel Sekalli's hand reach for mine. Our fingers interlock in the dim light of the hearth, and I turn on my side to look at her.

"Keep my family safe," she whispers. "I'm going to trust you, believe what you've said is true. But don't let the Chalca harm my parents or my siblings, darling boy. I won't forgive you if they do."

I bring her hand to my lips and kiss those slender fingers.

"I swear it."

After two watches of troubled sleep, most of us are awake, long before dawn. Despite Makwiltoch's objections, Lady Azcalxoch has her staff prepare breakfast, though the compromise is that the farmer's wife gets to prepare the tortillas, her culinary pride.

After I inform Lord Cihtli that Polok is now a Tetzcoca cuauh-pilli, the noble raises his speech and treats my father-in-law with the respect he would afford any peer. The tensions of the previous evening and night fade as dawn emerges from its home below the horizon, painting the sky with a riot of bright color.

We've not quite finished our meal when a guard bursts into the house.

"The Chalca are here, sweeping through the milpas!"

I snatch up Quetzalmazatl's sword and rush outside, followed by the guard and Lord Cihtli. Rounding the house, I see movement in three different fields.

"Three squads. Sixty men."

"Terrible odds for the five of us," Lord Cihtli drawls.

"Six," says a voice behind us. Polok has emerged, carrying a huge club with obsidian razors imbedded in its bulbous head. "I studied at a telpochcalli in Cholollan as a teen. Fought against the Tepaneca as a young man. I'll not let these bastards touch my wife or children."

Cihtli accepts a sword from one of the guards. We spread out to provide the broadest protection possible.

"We just have to hold out till my uncle brings reinforcements," I remind them, mentally recalculating the time to and from Cholollan. "Which, gods willing, should be any minute."

Then the Chalca erupt from among the cornstalks, and the fight begins. Lord Cihtli's guards are courageous, but rusty. Their attackers push them back, and within seconds all three are bleeding from multiple wounds.

Though Lord Cihtli is in his early sixties, he was once a general of Tetzcoco, veteran of multiple wars. Military instincts kick in, and he mounts a berserker attack against the Chalca, advancing *into* the squad before him, slashing and hacking in a fighting style that lacks elegance but burgeons with deadly violence.

Polok simply stands his ground and smashes his heavy weapon into any Chalca soldier foolish enough to come close. Forty years as boy and man working the soil have given my father-in-law the sinews of a jaguar, and his blows are devastating.

All this I see from the edges of my perception. My heart swells with the words my mother spoke on the last night of my childhood:

"Love is delicate, fragile. Learn to keep it deep in your heart, surrounded by disciplined flesh, sharp mind, resolute and sober defenses. In this life, there is no other way than to fight to protect what matters to you. In the depths of your despair, remember. You must become a shield against the wind for the fluttering flame of devotion."

I watch the enemy for a moment. Then I have it: the rhythm of these brutal whoreson invaders, these beasts who would take the last bit of joy from me, who would snuff out the divine light in my people's eyes.

Howling my love to the heavens, I become a whirlwind of destruction.

The pull of gravity loosens. I leap and spin, the edge of my blade slitting throats, opening the veins of arms, ripping through cartilage and bone.

Five men fall before me. Ten.

An eleventh, rage and horror on his face, comes at me with a halberd, determined to keep me at bay, seeking to skewer me like a rat.

But I rush him and flip myself over the stabbing spear, swinging my sword with every ounce of strength as I drop through the air, every bit of grief and ire.

●◖◉◗●

The sword passes right through his neck, sending his head tumbling into the very earth I worked alongside my beloved's family. Blood erupts from the man's empty shoulders, spraying that rich soil, which drinks up his life as if desperate to slake some infernal thirst.

A scream behind me.

The guards have fallen. A dozen Chalca surround Polok, who is spinning about, blinded by a cut in his forehead that dribbles blood into his eyes.

I rush to his aid, leaping into the circle and fighting back-to-back with him, shouting instructions.

"There's one coming at you south-southwest! Another directly in front! Swing now!"

The situation is getting dire. The remaining twenty-some-odd soldiers break from Lord Cihtli—who has fallen, gripping his leg—and join the attack against us. Polok drops to his knees. I stand over him, spinning my sword to deflect the attacks.

But I'm getting tired.

There are too many of them.

I feel a blade bite into my side. Blood spills from the stinging cut.

Another on my right leg. Then my left.

No. Not here. Not like this. If my death is all you wanted, why delay so long?

I have done as you wanted. I have become an agent of your will.

Are you not listening? Damn you, Tezcatlipoca. I knew you would forsake me.

And, as if in answer, a familiar snarl breaks through the din of the melee.

My coyote.

My heart swells with love and relief at the sight of her white collar, flashing as she leaps.

She flings herself onto the unbelieving soldiers, snapping her mighty teeth, ripping at arms and legs, howling like a monster emerged from Mictlan itself.

Startled, screaming in pain, the soldiers retreat for a moment.

Auntie Coyote, whimpering to see me hurt, nuzzles close and licks my wounds.

"Are you okay, girl?" I ask, looking her over. "That was madness. Why would you risk yourself so? These are not deer, Auntie."

She presses her nose against mine, those intelligent eyes of gold looking deep into my soul. Then she yips as if to say, "Fool. You are my friend. Of course I should come to your aid."

Lord Cihtli limps over. His wound is thankfully only superficial.

"Remarkable beast, Your Majesty. Yet the respite she has earned us will be brief. Look. The Chalca return."

Staring at the encroaching enemy, he reaches down to pull me to my feet. Polok, wiping blood from his forehead, struggles to stand beside us.

With knowing nods to one another, we form a triangle, shoulder to shoulder, facing out.

Auntie Coyote growls, crouching at my feet.

The soldiers surround us, begin to tighten their circle, approaching with sword and spears outstretched.

"Let's kill as many of these fuckers as we can," Lord Cihtli spits, shockingly crude. "So that songs will be sung about what we do here today."

We raise our weapons.

And the air is suddenly filled by a whistling hiss.

Thud. Thud. Thud.

Arrow after arrow rip into our attackers' chests, arms, and legs. Shrieking or dead, they drop to the ground one by one.

I look back, toward the road.

I am wholly unprepared for the sight that awaits me.

Twenty Mexica archers are notching their bows for another volley. Behind them stands my uncle Zacatl, fist in the air.

"Again!" he cries.

The twanging of bowstrings. The thwack of obsidian points against armor and skin.

In seconds, all the remaining Chalca lie dead or writhing.

"Never in a thousand years could I have predicted this," I mutter, kneeling to touch the blood-soaked earth. "Is this your doing, Mother? Are you advocating for me even there, in the Underworld, pleading with the gods?"

Polok doesn't wait for an explanation. He dashes into the house, calling the names of his wife and children. Lord Cihtli drops the point of his sword against the ground, leaning hard on the pommel as one would a walking staff.

The coyote nuzzles me with a soft whine. I pat the ground and stand.

"Zacatzin?" I call, still stupefied. "What? How?"

The Mexica lower their bows, letting their commander through. He crosses the rods between us with a smile.

"Acolmiztzin, my dearest nephew. It's so good to see you alive."

We embrace for a moment. I tremble with emotion, but quickly get myself under control as we pull apart to stare at each other in wonder.

"You go first," I say simply. "Just tell me everything."

Zacatl cocks his head and takes a deep breath. "Yes, that's sensible. About . . . half a year ago? Yes, ten solar months back. A message from Cholollan reached your aunt Azcatzin in Tenochtitlan. It was your father's sister, explaining that you were indeed alive and had been living on a farm here at the edge of Tlaxcallan. She explained that the Deadly Hand was after you, and she pled for help keeping you safe. You know Azcatzin. She immediately went round to the houses of all her sisters and half-sisters, all her sisters-in-law and cousins. Her words and reputation had a powerful impact—all those Tenochca women, most of them related to the Emperor, stood in solidarity with her as she petitioned Tezozomoc."

"You mean . . . directly? In Azcapotzalco? What did they ask him for?"

"To forgive you. To spare your life. To allow you conditional freedom. That old bastard took his time thinking about it. Probably had his shitty son whispering all sorts of hate in his ear. But then he received a message from King Toteocih in Chalco, apparently saying you were a prisoner there. A foolish move on Toteocih's part, trying to use you to blackmail the Emperor. He hates the Chalca much more than he hates you. It's one of the reasons he asked us to wage war on them. To spite the confederation, he declared that you were no longer a wanted man, granting you freedom as long as you move to Tenochtitlan and remain there."

For a moment I just stand there, mouth slack. The very man I am determined to kill, the person responsible for the slaughter of my family, the fall of my city, the exile of my people . . . that vicious tyrant is withdrawing the threat of death, in exchange for *what?* My lifelong confinement to the Isle of Mexico? Does the Emperor really believe that I will consent to be one of his pets? Bastard. His arrogance and cruelty are without bounds.

At the same time, Tezozomoc has just done me an incredible favor.

A sly smile twists at my lips. I no longer have to run, and neither do those I love. And not only that, the doddering fool is putting me right where I've always planned to go.

I am almost overwhelmed again by a sense of divine destiny—as if the Sovereign of the Near and Nigh has turned the cosmic wheels one more click toward some unseen future.

Zacatl is narrowing his eyes at the strange play of emotions on my face. Before he starts questioning me, I need to understand fully what has happened.

"How did you manage to find me *here?*"

"Though King Chimalpopoca wasn't particularly pleased with the imperial command, he knew he had to comply. So he ordered me, his least favorite sibling, to go fetch you from Tlalmanalco. Of course, when we arrived, we learned that you had escaped with the help of some prince. I hear he was beheaded."

The reminder of Quetzalmazatl's death staggers me again. I rub at my eyes, cursing under my breath. "I shouldn't have let him free me. He'd still be alive."

Zacatl leans in close, concern tightening his features.

"Ah, Acolmiztzin, but you likely would have been beheaded instead. He was your friend, this Chalcan prince?"

I simply nod.

"Well, he gave his life for you. Now he wings his way through the heavens alongside the sun. Be of good cheer. Not all men can choose such a noble end."

For a moment I hear Quetzalmazatl's voice, deeper than mine, signing along with that sad chorus: "Friends are like flowers—blooming briefly, then forever gone."

"Why the farm?" I ask, once I've gained my composure.

"Oh, I know how you think, my dearest nephew. The farm is the closest, most logical choice. So we rushed through the pass and to Tlaxcallan's border with Tepeyacac. Other folks pointed us here, and then we arrived to find you getting your ass kicked."

I laugh, despite myself, drawn into our accustomed banter.

"Uncle, that's hardly fair. I personally killed fifteen men in less than a quarter watch."

He shrugs and gestures at his men. "You would have been dead in less than *that* time if we hadn't killed the rest. You can be a mighty warrior and still get trounced, Crown Prince."

"He is no crown prince," Izcalloh calls, emerging from the house with the others in tow. "He is the King of Tetzcoco, Acolhua Overlord, Chichimeca Chieftain."

Zacatl slaps his hands together in response. "Nice titles. Unfortunately, other men now claim them, so he's got a way to go before I call him *sire*. Right now, his most important moniker is Nephew of the Tenochca King. We'll work on the rest later."

Sekalli and Izcalloh fret over my wounds for the better part of a watch, washing and bandaging the cuts. Sekalli curses at me for daring to get hurt. Izcalloh lets me know their displeasure in less direct, more courtly ways. But I feel their love, warm and reassuring. And they work together, in tandem, united in their desire to heal and chastise me.

Watching them from a distance, tail bouncing from time to time against the cornstalks, sits the coyote, as if waiting to confirm that I am fine.

When I stand and wave at her, she yips brightly, ducks her head one last time, then dashes off toward the volcano. I have to fight back tears. Sekalli and Izcalloh, understanding instinctively, each hold one of my hands as I watch her go.

We humans who remain begin dragging the Chalca bodies to a bonfire in the midst of a fallow field. Then another group of soldiers comes rushing onto the farm, demanding to see me.

Wiping soot from my face, I round the barn to meet them.

Acolhua warriors from Chololan, led by my uncle Coyohuah, accompanied by Tocual and the two guards I sent with him. At last.

"Majesty!" my uncle cries, hurrying to my side. "Have we come too late? I see bandaged wounds. Were you badly hurt, sire?"

"No, Coyohuahtzin. Reinforcements arrived." I gesture at the Mexica carrying dead Chalca. "My mother's younger brother, Zacatzin."

I explain the situation as the other men gather—Lord Cihtli, Polok, Zacatl. I glance around for Izcalloh, gesture them over.

"I am glad you are here, Coyohuahtzin. You will remember Cihtzin, my father's closest friend. I entrust him and his wife to your care.

Take them to our calpolli in Cholollan. See to it they have a worthy manor. I shall send valuable goods as recompense for your investment, soon." I turn to Izcalloh's father. "I must ask you to perform two important services, Lord. First, continue as my ambassador in your new home. We have much to coordinate and arrange."

"Of course, Your Majesty. As I served your father, so shall I serve you. What is the second service you would have me perform?"

I take a deep breath. "Grant me your child, Izcalloh, as my principal concubine. I need them, and I shall treat them with the utmost love and respect. I know they have never left your side. I know that Lady Azcaxoch will miss them dearly. But you will see them often, as they will be my spokesperson with the Acolhua refugees. Izcalloh will travel to Tlaxcallan twice a year, to help you prepare for whatever day the gods ordain for our glorious return to the homeland."

Lord Cihtli turns to Izcalloh, his normally stolid expression softening with affection. "Is this destiny the one you desire, my precious jewel?"

"Yes, Father. I love him and wish to serve him always."

The veteran general then drops to his knees.

"It being their will and yours, sire, I am honored to place my only child in your hands. Keep them well, as their mother and I have done."

By evening, they have all left for Cholollan. Zacatzin and his men set up a camp outside. A teary Izcalloh retires to Polok and Makwiltoch's sleeping chambers to nurse their grief at the parting, and Sekalli and I sit together, watching the dying flames of the hearth.

"You kept your promise," she says at last, taking my hand in hers.

"Lord Polok *was* lightly wounded," I say, smiling as she giggles at the title, "but I did indeed protect him with my life. And I kept the Chalca from entering this house. Which is why I hope you can believe my next promise—Beloved, I will keep you safe, as long as I live. You. Our children. Your parents. Your siblings."

Sekalli squeezes my hands. "You certainly know how to give speeches, Neza."

"All you have to do—" I continue.

"And here comes the catch," she quips, though I can see she is just being playful, whistling in the unknowable dark of our future.

"All you have to do," I repeat, raising an eyebrow in feigned frustration, "is say yes. That you'll be my royal consort, at my side, loving me for as long as we can love. Then tomorrow we'll head to our new home, at the heart of Moon Lake."

Those round owl eyes glitter with joyful tears, and the reflection of dancing sparks.

"Okay," she breathes into the cool night air. "Let's do it, darling boy."

{31} VISION

Arriving in Tenochtitlan

After a prayer of thanksgiving at dawn,
we leave the multiple milpas behind
to travel through the pass and into
Mexica-controlled Colhuacan.

The next morning, we take canoes
from the city of Iztapalapan
across southern Moon Lake
to the Isle of Mexico, all green
gardens and white stucco,
highlights of frescoes and willows.

The newcomers are awed
as we ply the broad canals
of Tenochtitlan, expanding
a bit more each day as silt
is dredged and deposited
on its stretching edges.

For me, the arrival is fraught.
Good memories and bad,
layered in a palimpsest:
family and enemies,
childhood and present.

At last, we reach Zacatl's villa
to be greeted by my aunts
and all the other noblewomen
who have struggled to win
freedom for me and mine.

Once we have settled in,
a welcoming feast begins—
my aunt Azcatl gives a speech,
tipping out wine to the gods
in worshipful appreciation
of a reunited family.

For now, at least,
we are all of us,
while clearly
not Mexica,
Tenochca.

War Averted

The following day, it is time
to present myself, my consort,
and my concubine to the king.

Chimalpopoca's haughty sneer eases
into a condescending smile
as the three of us kneel.

"It breaks our heart, Nephew,
that your father elected this fate
for himself and for you.

"Yet now we spread our wing
to gather your little family close
and protect you, talon and beak.

"We have even controlled the crisis
you precipitated in Chalco. Tlacaellel,
our brother, fire priest of Mexico—

"He has agreed to wed Maquiztli,
once betrothed to the very prince
who lost his life aiding your escape.

"Her father, king of Amaquehmecan,
will be bound to us by this marriage,
will end the conflict, usher in peace.

"Believe it or not, that is our royal will:
peace, under the wise and watchful eye
of our grandfather, the Emperor.

"There is room for you in our world,
but soon you must reverse the statement
you made on the day of our coronation."

Chimalpopoca leans forward on this throne.
"You must declare yourself Mexica, boy.
Only then shall we be sure of your allegiance."

I swallow hard, my stomach churning.
"Before Your Majesty and Huitzilopochtli,
Supreme God, Lord of Sun and War—"

I pause, placing fist over heart.
"I affirm to all that I am a proud Mexica,
scion of the House of Acamapichtli."

My uncle grins, satisfied at last
now that my humiliation is complete.
"Welcome to the Empire, Nephew."

The Golden Eagle

That night, after tossing and turning
beside Sekalli in our ample quarters,
I have a dream. Perhaps a vision.

A voice from a hurricane thrums:
"Awaken to your nahualli forms,
Chichimeca Chieftain, and strike!"

The morning star rises above
that swirling dark storm,
blinking magic at me.

My body begins to tremble,
and suddenly glittering feathers
sprout from my shivering skin,
like the plumes of Coyotlinahual,
and I am transformed into
a massive golden eagle.

I lift into the skies, catch the wind,
which flings me, soaring high
toward Azcapotzalco.

The imperial palace spreads below,
and I drop like a catapulted stone
bursting into the throne room.
Old Tezozomoc screams
as I leap upon him,
beak tearing.

While he watches, dying,
I devour his heart.

Then again I shake and transform,
fur bursting, claws and maw emerging
as I become a jaguar that gnaws
at his feet and legs
while ants scurry.

The emperor dead,
I tear down his palace,
then bound into the mountains,
burrowing deep with
thundering growls
to become their
hot, beating
heart.

{32} THE FUTURE BLOOMING

O NLY ONE MAN I know can interpret this dream. But approaching him could be dangerous. His motives have always been inscrutable, even when he was a teenager. Revealing my dream to him now could have catastrophic consequences, if I am misjudging his character. But I need powerful allies if I am going to right the wrongs done to me and mine. People who can shape the political realities of Tenochtitlan in my favor.

So as soon as I can, I visit my uncle Tlacaellel in his manor, where courtiers and household staff make preparations to receive his new bride.

"Acolmiztzin," he begins, as we sit in his meditation chamber, "or rather, Nezahual-coyotzin. A name I much prefer. I am glad of your visit, Nephew. Since learning that you were the one whose strategy gave the Chalca army the upper hand against Moteuczoma and me, I have felt both relief and great pride. It comes as no surprise to me that you have blossomed into such an effective military leader. My respects."

I suspect he is being sincere. The military philosophy both our peoples inherited from the Toltecs emphasizes respect for honorable opponents. Neither Tlacaellel or I have behaved ourselves like Tezozomoc and his ilk upon the battlefield. We have no reason to feel anger toward each other.

"Thank you, Tlacaelleltzin. I also admire your keen intellect and insight. Therefore would I like your opinion on a dream I recently had."

I recount the details, which have been burned into my mind as if they actually happened to me. He taps a brush absentmindedly against the writing table beside him. After several moments of silent contemplation, he pulls a folded book from a reed chest beside him, consulting various glyphs as he moves his lips mutely.

Then he sets the codex aside and speaks at last.

"A vision. A message from three gods. You are indeed blessed." There is the slightest hint of envy or irritation in his voice. "The morning star is Quetzalcoatl, patron god of your father's people, whose creative energy triggers such transformations. The golden harpy eagle is the nahualli of Huitzilopochtli, patron god of the Mexica, your mother's people. The message is clear—Tezozomoc will die if you embrace that part of your identity."

He adjusts his lanky form upon his mat, drawing the fingers of his right hand through the long hair that hangs over his priestly robes and into his lap. After sizing me up carefully, as he untangles a strand, Tlacaellel continues with his interpretation.

"Finally, the jaguar is one of Tezcatlipoca's many animal forms. The nahualli's name is key. Tepeyollotl. Mountainheart. In that form you destroy the Emperor's legs and palace, and thus you are destined to bring down the Tepaneca Empire after his death, avenging your family, eliminating his possible heirs." The hatred in his eyes startles me, but it suggests that I've made the right choice. My uncle has no love for Tezozomoc, I can see. "Only after that happens will Tezcatli-poca be content that you are the rightful ruler of Acolhuacan, and he will plunge his rage at humanity into the mountains for a time, giving you surcease."

His interpretation leaves me stunned. Yet, I can hardly begin to ponder my next steps now, for fear that he will reveal this destiny to his brother the king.

Tlacaellel narrows his eyes at me, his thin lips curving into a mys-terious grin.

"You are afraid, as indeed you should be. You have no way of knowing what I might do with this information." Then he reaches out his hand and lays it on mine, a most uncharacteristic gesture of affec-tion. "Fortunately for you . . . I also desire the destruction of that old bastard and his decrepit empire."

I can't hide my shock at this news.

"You . . . what?"

"Mexico is destined for more than vassalage to the Tepaneca, Nezahualcoyotzin. I have scried heaven's will again and again, in the entrails of birds, in mirrors of obsidian and water. Every divination reveals the same truth: Huitzilopochtli intends for us to dominate the sea-ringed world, from shore to shore, north to the Land of the Dead, south to Tlaloc's water paradise. All of it."

My mind boggles. I never imagined that he had such aspirations.

"You say Huitzilopochtli wants Mexico to rise up against Tepanecapan?"

Tlacaellel runs his fingers over a painted book on the writing table. The glyphs on the first fold tell me it is a history of the Mexica.

"My late sister no doubt shared our people's story with you, Nephew. A great chieftain, Mexihtli, led our tribe out of Chichimeca lands centuries ago. We spent generations wandering through Cuextecapan, adopting some of their gods, learning their language. Mexihtli left this earthly plane and was revered as a god. Our ancestors carried his bundled remains as they made their way into Anahuac, this region of lakes. We angered the local Nahuas with our brutal ways, but they hired us as mercenaries, until at last we ended up in captivity in Colhuacan, blending with that people, forgetting our original tongue. Then we escaped, made our exodus to this isle, named it Mexico—Place of Mexihtli. But by then, of course, we had begun to call him Huitzilopochtli, as he had drawn us south to this new homeland."

I nod in answer. It is hardly an auspicious history, though certainly a testament to the hardiness of the Mexica.

"I shall rewrite that tale," Tlacaellel announces, a startling declaration. "Huitzilopochtli has given me a vision as well. We Mexica, like all the Nahua nations and the Tolteca before us, emerged from the nine caves of Chicomoztoc a thousand years ago. We were simply the last to leave that sacred place. And before our time in Chicomoztoc, we all of us lived in Aztlan, under the brutal regime of the Azteca, whose tyranny we fled for this promised land. We are a *single people*, Nezahualcoyotzin. And I intend to unify all Nahuas under a single government, guided by the Mexica. Or rather, by this family. The House of Acamapichtli, to which you belong."

It is a bold, brazen, impossible idea. Yet, the cold smoldering of my uncle's eyes suggests that it may come to pass, just as he says.

"Rewriting history, though," I muse. "Will people accept such a thing?"

Tlacaellel taps his chest. "Your father was devoted to the Sovereign of the Near and the Nigh, was he not? Why do we call that divine source *Self-Making* and not *Self-Made*?"

Though he stares at me expectantly, I have no easy answer.

"Because," he answers with a satisfied smirk, "creation of identity is *ongoing*, Nephew. *Who we were* is destroyed as time passes, replaced by *who we are*. My brother the king needs you to be Mexica, for example. Can you be?"

Given his brutal honesty, I can only speak the truth. "At this point, I am willing to be anything to regain my throne. And as you say, Uncle, I am a descendant of Acamapichtli. A member of this family that you would elevate above all others."

Tlacaellel's face lights up with genuine joy. "Ah, that is good, very good. You see . . . King Chimalpopoca is blind to the divine fate I've described. He is wholly a creature of his grandfather, dedicated to the crumbling House of Tezozomoc. Still, I am working on my other brothers. It will take patience and time to win them to our cause. But your presence in Tenochtitlan is a gift from the gods. I require your assistance to fortify Mexico. To prepare it for its glorious future."

My hands are shaking with a mix of anxiety and excitement. I want to trust my uncle. I want to believe that everything I have endured has brought me *here*, at *this moment*.

I decide to have faith. To trust his vision and my own.

"Yes. I shall join hands with you, Tlacaelleltzin. While we work in secret, I shall also ready my people in exile. When the moment comes, Acolhuacan will stand with Mexico."

"Excellent. Though I shan't lie to you, Nezahualcoyotzin. I intend for our alliance to be lopsided. Tenochtitlan will be first among equals, so to speak. But you will have Tetzcoco and Acolhuacan—that I swear on my life, Your Majesty."

His words bring tears to my eyes and warmth to my heart. My dream has never been to make Tetzcoco the most powerful city in Anahuac. Just the most beautiful: a sanctuary for artists, musicians, and philosophers. If Tenochtitlan wants the political glory, they can have it.

Tlacaellel stands, pulling me to my feet, and for the first time in our entire lives . . . the two of us embrace.

Two months later, I am pacing outside of the birthing chamber while Sekalli groans, choking back the vulgarities she has sworn to curb in the presence of nobility. The midwife has given her both cihuapahtli and a drink infused with ground opossum tail, but her hips are narrow, so still she suffers.

One last grunting scream, and I hear our baby cry.

The midwife shouts and whoops like a warrior. Then the curtains part. Izcalloh, who has been assisting the midwife, waves me in.

"Sekalli has fought a good battle, sire. She has captured a son for you."

Inside, my beloved is smiling, hair pasted by sweat to her forehead. We watch as the midwife lifts our son from the mat and recites the old words to him:

"You have arrived on earth, youngest one, beloved boy. May the Sovereign of the Near and the Nigh keep you whole and hale, so that you may meet your family and learn your lineage. Welcome, precious prince, to this slippery world, full of hardship and sorrow, but also love and light."

My heart filling with pride and affection, I wonder for a moment whether the soul of the unborn child I lost in Tetzcoco might have been winged down by the Sovereign of the Near and Nigh, to quicken the flesh of our son.

Impossible to know. But I like to think the Source adds balance to the sadness of the world this way.

Lowering the newborn to the mat again, the midwife cuts the umbilical cord with a deft motion and wraps him in swaddling clothes, putting him in Sekalli's arms.

She then deposits the placenta in clay jar, which Izcalloh takes from her.

"Lord Nezahualcoytzin," says the old woman, standing. "Have you chosen a name for this your firstborn son?"

The date is 1 Cipactli, the sign that honors the primordial leviathan upon whose back the earth was formed by Quetzalcoatl and Tezcatlipoca. I think of the new Tetzcoco I plan to mold alongside this boy.

"I shall call him Cipactli," I answer.

She puts his umbilical cord in my hands.

"Noble Izcalloh will bury Lady Sekalli's afterbirth in a corner of your family's home. Your Highness must keep this cord safe, until the gods lead you to the battlefield once more. There, amid the fire and flood of war, you must let it drop. Only then will Cipactli's future as a brave and virtuous man be assured."

I look at the twisted, bloody umbilicus for a long time, imagining it lying in the shattered ruins of Azcapotzalco.

Then I kneel at Sekalli's side and kiss my son upon his pointed little head.

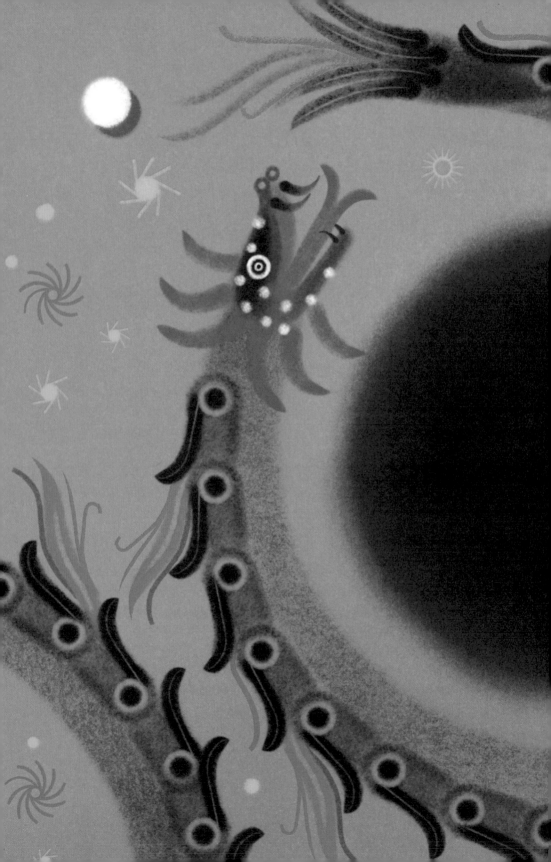

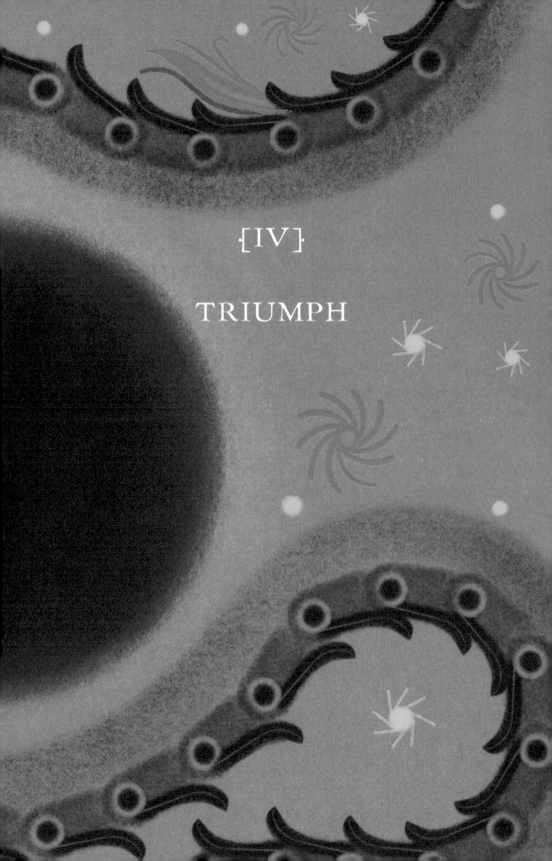

{IV}

TRIUMPH

{33} THE LONG WAIT

Never Forgive, Never Forget

Time passes
as it always does,
cycles spinning eternal,
our two calendars like wheels
with interlocking cogs
that align every fifty-two years.

As they turn,
they pull me ever forward,
further from the outrages
of the past.

Wounds scab over,
love and work and
the dance of days
healing hurt while
leaving sacred scars.

But I never forgive,
never forget—
the fire of my vengeance
never dies, stoked to blazing
by every bit of news
about the cruel rule
of my bastard brother,
Yancuilli.

It becomes a litany—
The capture of my city.
The exile of my people.

The loss of my country.
The death of my father.
The death of my mother.
The death of my brother.
The death of my sister.
The death of my lover.
The death of my son.
I repeat these offenses
over and over again
while my plans, laid in secret,
gestate slow and strong,
fed by my people's need,
the self-satisfied glee
of my enemies,
until my schemes
are solid and tightly wound,
like the spiraling coils
of a baby snake
curled within its egg
waiting to burst forth
and strike.

The Things I Do to Keep Myself Busy

6 Flint is the year I turn eighteen.
Having scoured the royal library
to absorb all the knowledge I can,
I enter Tenochtitlan's calmecac
and present myself before the priests.
I pass their tests with perfect scores,
confirming my worth to the city's nobility.

7 House is the fourth year
since my father's assassination.
I move my family to an estate
on the crest of Chapoltec Hill
where I have built a sprawling manor
for consort, concubine, child, in-laws.
There we perform the last memorial,
greet Father's soul one final time
before it moves on, forever,
to the Unknowable Realm.

8 Rabbit is when Chimalpopoca,
having witnessed my great skills
in the building of my own manor
and two others for his siblings,
appoints me Royal Architect.
My first task is to construct
a new causeway between our city
and Tlacopan, Tepaneca stronghold.
The work consumes my time,
but Izcalloh oversees the slow simmer
of our plots while also caring for Sekalli,

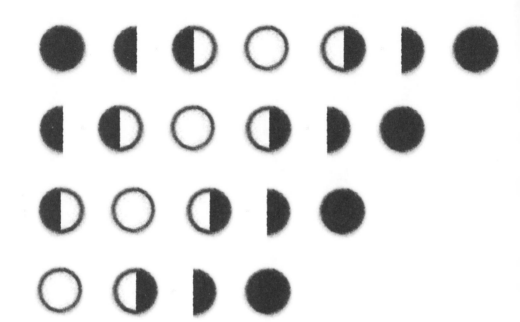

who becomes pregnant once more,
and Tlacaellel swears that any fears
the Emperor had about me dissolve
at the sight of his new direct route
into Tenochtitlan being fashioned
by my own hands and mind.
Bastard can't imagine what
the bridge is really for.

9 Reed is the year my second son
comes into the world, screaming
and red-faced as if a god of flame.
Tlecoyotl, I name him—fire coyote.
And just as he begins to toddle,
the causeway is completed.
Tezozomoc pays our city a visit,
commending me with shaky voice
as I kneel before his aging bulk,
wishing I could yank a sword
from a guard's hands and
slit his throat. But, I wait.
I'm getting good
at waiting.

10 Flint presents a dilemma.
An uprising in Chimalhuacan,
Acolhua city on the shore
of Moon Lake—the Emperor
orders Moteuczoma to intervene
with me as second-in-command
and my young uncle Temictli
as my eager squire. It's a test,

but Izcalloh's network of spies
gets word to the rebels in time,
who scatter to the wind or hide
so I just wind up aiding my uncle
in tracking down the rebel leaders.
When I'm forced to execute them,
I tell myself it's necessary—
their impatience has endangered
my plans and my people.
But now some conquered Acolhua
lose their faith in me,
and the Emperor is delighted
that his new Mexica pawn
moves as he wills.

11 House affords me the chance
to begin building an aqueduct
from the springs near our manor
to Tenochtitlan to the northeast.
A massive project punctuated
by the finalization of many parts
of our massive, ambitious plan
and a happy new marriage between
my youngest uncle Temictli,
his time at calmecac done,
and Sekalli's sister Yemasaton.

In what both seems an eternity
and a blink of an eye,
I go from exiled youth
to man of twenty-three.

But deep in my heart
I'm still just sixteen,
up in that tree,
watching
Father
fall.

{34} CELEBRATIONS

SIX YEARS TO THE DAY after my first son is born, I'm awakened by Sekalli's fluttering kisses.

"I know you worked until late," she whispers in my ear. "But the sun is almost up. The manor will soon be bustling with people and preparations. The briefest of moments, just you and me. Before the controlled chaos of celebrations."

With a sleepy grin, I reach for her. Motherhood and the passing of years have smoothed and rounded her angles, softened her in all the right places. Yet we still fit together as though fated by the gods. Quick but satisfying intimacy—one of the strange paradoxes of domestic life.

"Mmm," Sekalli says after we've lain in each other's arms a while. "That was nice. But I've got to get moving. Your boys will sleep through the morning watches if I don't rouse them."

I kiss the top of her head. "As lazy as their maternal uncle."

"Ha! There are a bunch of loafers in the House of Acamapichtli, too, I'll have you know. My brother-in-law, for example."

I have to laugh. When Temictli was my squire, I literally had to drag him from our tent each dawn for battle campaigns. The Night Axe, everyone called him—annoyingly active well past midnight, and then not a peep in the morning.

"Okay, my sweet. I'm going to get cleaned up and dressed. I'll see you downstairs for breakfast."

After taking my time to wash, I enter my room—a separate space I keep for my books and instruments, tools and writing table—to find Izcalloh setting out a set of clothes that manage to be elegant without seeming overly formal.

"Let me dress you, Majesty," they say, so I stand obediently and let them. I know that, given the months we have to spend apart while they're coordinating with our people in Tlaxcallan, these small tasks bring them comfort and joy, drawing us close for a few moments each day Izcalloh spends at home.

"I saw a courier come up the hill yesterday evening. What's the latest from your father?" I ask. "Has Huexotzinco agreed to add some of their troops to our army when the moment comes?"

Adjusting my loincloth, they nod. "Tentatively, yes. Depending on the timetable. Do we know anything more about the Emperor's health?"

I lift my left foot so Izcalloh can slip on a sandal. "Just the same rumors. The Tepaneca are doing their damnedest to keep his illness under wraps. But it's a safe bet it is indeed serious."

They slip a soft blue vest over my head and extended arms, smoothing it in a sensual way that makes me laugh.

"What, sire?"

"Don't start something we have no time for, Beloved. Neither of us wants to face Lady Sekalli's wrath if we're not down for breakfast soon."

Izcalloh feigns a pout, before slinging my cape over my shoulders.

"Lady Sekalli, Lady Sekalli," they mutter, grumpy. "I suppose I should consult the schedule she has prepared for us. Perhaps I shall actually get to spend a night with you at some point this year."

"Come," I urge with a laugh, taking their hand. "Let's hurry down. It's a day to celebrate, not moan and groan. In any sense of the words."

Sekalli is herding the boys to the low table when we enter the dining room. Tlecoyotl is only three and a half, but he's nearly as tall as his brother. Sekalli insists he takes after her father, and Lord Polok is certainly taller than most men in my family.

"Father!" Cipactli shouts. "Come sit beside me. It's my birthday and Mother says you're to abide by my wishes."

"Izcallohtzin!" Tlecoyotl burbles, pulling free of Sekalli to be swept up in my concubine's arms. Just like I did as a little boy, he adores the noble's storytelling.

Makwiltoch comes out of the kitchen, followed by two of the staff, all laden with steaming bowls of atolli. "Come, my grandsons. Enough pestering your parents. You'll need lots of energy for all the day's festivities, so eat up."

I let Cipactli pull me to a spot at the table. As we sit, he gestures with an imperious hand. "This is all we're eating for breakfast?"

I tousle his hair. "Trust me, there will be plenty of food later today, little sea monster. Better not to get too full so you can enjoy all the treats."

Not long after breakfast, the guests start to arrive, each announced by our majordomo.

"Lady Azcatzin!"

I rush to greet my aunt, who singlehandedly pulled me and my family out of our dangerous exile, giving us a chance at a new life—and possibly a new empire.

Her ladies-in-waiting carry many gifts for my oldest son. Izcalloh guides them to the table in the courtyard set aside as a place for presents.

"Dear Aunt," I say, dropping to one knee in recognition of her status and age. "You have tired yourself in arriving. I welcome you to our humble abode."

She lifts me with a gentle hand. "Revered Nephew, it is good to see you. I pray the Sovereign of the Near and the Nigh has bestowed a measure of health upon you and your household."

"Indeed, we have been granted the grace of Duality. Sons, come and offer your greetings."

My boys hurry over and bow deeply. Cipactli speaks the words Izcalloh has drilled into him. "Honored Personage, we your pages greet you. You have come a great distance, and we humbly thank you. We hope the heavens have caused you to rise this day feeling somewhat well. Please enter and take your rest."

It is a ritual repeated for many of the older members of the House of Acamapichtli. But when Uncle Zacatl arrives with his wife Nazohuatl, I dispense with formalities and hug them both tightly.

"I hear you have picked up a few new instruments imported from abroad," Zacatl mutters with a wink as we pull apart. "I trust you and I will get a chance to liven up the festivities later?"

I give an enthusiastic nod. "Yes. I've already tasked some of my staff with setting them up at the far end of the courtyard. Looking forward to celebrating both the birthday of my son *and* the completion of the aqueduct with you!"

Zacatl's children are a little older than my sons, but the group of kids greets each other excitedly, dashing outside to play far away from the prying eyes of adults. Laughing at the sight, Sekalli and Nazohuatl lean their heads together, chatting up a storm until the majordomo announces loudly:

"Lady Yemasaton!"

Sekalli's sister is now a beautiful young woman of seventeen years. Her handmaiden helps her through the entrance, fretting over her like a worried mother.

"I have great news," she calls to us all, our eyes drawn. "The midwife confirmed it just this morning. I am with child!"

Sekalli leaps to hug her, teary-eyed but joyful. The other women—guests and family—encircle them, touching her belly and offering blessings.

"Congratulations," I call out over everyone. "Where is the future father? Don't tell me he hasn't gotten out of bed yet."

Yemasaton ignores the loving jab. "He'll be coming a little later, with Tlacaellel and Moteuczoma too. He rushed to the palace to give them the good news, and then a messenger brought word to me that he was helping the general and prime minister with something important."

The news is intriguing. A bit worrisome, if I'm honest. I'm on the council now and used to being involved with weighty matters; it feels wrong to be excluded, even on my son's birthday.

As staff begin to decorate the courtyard, I try to ignore the gnawing feeling of wrongness at the back of my mind. I busy myself with stringing up the clay pot full of fruits and sweets the children will attempt to shatter later on—after the banquet, before the music and dancing.

I've just finished when Lord Polok shows up, brushing plaster dust off his cotton jerkin. He gives me a wink and a smile before we clasp forearms in greeting.

"Well, Father?" I ask, expectantly.

"It's ready whenever you want to show them, Nezahualcoyotzin."

Clearing my throat, I call out to my guests, gathering them round. The older members of Mother's family regard me either coolly, or with an expression of bemusement, as if I'm an oddity they've come to tolerate or begrudgingly respect. But the eyes of those closest to me shine with real love and admiration. They're the ones who ultimately matter most.

"As you know, today marks the completion not only of the sixth year of my firstborn's life, but also of the aqueduct that will forever provide our beloved Tenochtitlan with fresh water from this very hill. Follow me so you can see our glorious feat of engineering."

Like a master painter eager to unveil his latest work, I guide several dozen Mexica nobles to the springs near my manor, which now feed into the most ingenious mechanism I have ever built: the very idea that occurred to me on a boat during the last trip I ever made with my mother and father, rowing from this rocky isle to the swampy shores of our homeland. That it is now a reality—that I have actually constructed something that will help the Mexica for generations, despite all the tragedy of the intervening years—is almost too hard to believe.

Made of pine and other hardwoods, the aqueduct runs from the crest of Chapoltepec Hill along a narrow support of dredged-up silt and stone to the little islet of Mazatzintamalco. There it turns at a ninety-degree angle and continues eastward, along the broad causeway I have built between Tenochtitlan and the Tepaneca city of Tlacopan.

An army of soldiers could march four abreast down that bridge.

Its size is deliberate, of course. Tlacaellel and I have been laying the groundwork for the war to come. If Chimalpopoca suspects anything, he doesn't let on.

Moteuczoma has joined the cabal. So has their uncle, scarred and aging Itzcoatl. We are tantalizingly close to turning the tables on Tepanecapan forever.

I wish my uncles were already here to behold this achievement. Once water is flowing through these pipes, we'll fill cisterns throughout Tenochtitlan and Tlatelolco. The final piece will be in place. We Mexica will be able to withstand a siege for at least a hundred days.

●◖◗●

"The last section was just installed," Lord Polok tells everyone as they *ooh* and *aah* over the size and extent of the aqueduct. He has served as overseer in all the various infrastructure projects I have completed during the last half decade. His knowledge and skill have turned out to encompass much more than just soil and irrigation. "We are ready to release."

"Then give the word, Lord Polok. Let's show our guests what this contraption can do!"

He ambles off to order the sluice gates opened.

"I'm sure you've all had to drink some murky, slightly briny water over the years," I tell my gathered friends and relatives. "The gods willing, those days are over."

As if on cue, water comes rushing down the aqueduct, heading toward my adoptive city.

A general cheer goes up all around as people squint against the sun, trying to watch the water's progress. "An auspicious sign!" I declare. "I assume the rest of today's festivities will be equally exciting and successful. Let us return and celebrate young Prince Cipactli!"

Amid their cheers, I lead the group looping back around to our manor. But before we reach the courtyard, my uncle and former squire Temictli comes rushing alone up the winding path that leads to the summit. I'm about to ask where Tlacaellel and the others are, when a weird, strangled urgency in his features causes the entire group to stop and fall silent.

"What, Temic?" I ask. "You look like you're going to burst with some monumental news. Spit it out, already, before you frighten these good people."

It takes him a head-shaking moment to catch his breath after the long climb, but then he waves his hand toward the north. Toward Azcapotzalco.

"Tezozomoc," he gasps, "is dead."

My guests draw sharp breaths, or mutter their shock and disbelief.

For that bastard not to die beneath my blade . . . feels unacceptable. Yet Tlacaellel and I have discussed this possibility. The Emperor turned ninety-two this year. He had gone mostly deaf and blind—had to be carried from place to place by attendants, wrapped in swaddling clothes like an infant to stave off the cold that he swore he could feel in his very bones.

But Tezozomoc has sons. Dozens of them. Most just as vile as their father. And just as guilty of crimes against my people.

Vengeance is still possible.

"Are you certain?" I demand.

Temictli nods. "He's dead. And his son Quetzalayatzin has been crowned Emperor."

Not Maxtla. Interesting. Important, too. Either he'll be easier to defeat, or his selection will trigger a schism in Tepanecapan. Both options work for me.

"Let's get you inside, Temic." I force a smile. "You deserve a drink for running all that way with this news."

But my young uncle takes a step toward me. His breathing is slowing, and there's something ecstatic still looming in his eyes.

"There's more," Temictli continues. "It's the reason they sent me now. Quetzalayatzin entered his father's palace—its inner chambers—and that's where he found her."

Icy knives of premonition carve their way up my spine.

"Who? Who, damn you?!"

Temictli places a trembling hand on my shoulder. "My sister. Your mother. Matlalcihuatl, Your Majesty. She isn't dead. She's been a slave to the Emperor all these years."

It takes all of them to hold me down.

{35} A NEW TYRANT RISES

FIVE DAYS LATER, Izcalloh and I enter the audience chamber of the king. The throne is empty, but the governing council is present: high priests, borough leaders, chief justices, and of course, General Moteuczoma, General Itzcoatl, and Prime Minister Tlacaellel.

Each council member brings his retinue of courtiers and aides to meetings. Whenever possible, I bring Izcalloh, whose advice has not once failed me.

About half the council is part of our Mexico Ascendant cabal. The rest are Chimalpopoca's men, unwavering in loyalty to king and emperor.

"Where is the king?" I demand as we take up our place on the east side of the chamber. "Has the imperial envoy returned with my mother?"

Though I was adamant about going in person to escort my mother home, King Chimalpopoca forbade me, assuring me that the new Emperor would be sending her back under military escort to ensure her safety.

I nearly disobeyed him, but the cabal members convinced me otherwise, to not upend all our carefully laid plans by enraging the king now.

Seeing me, Tlacaellel bursts into movement like a fluttering crow, all black robes and long hair. His long legs carry him quickly across the space that divides east and west councilors—military from civic. There is uncharacteristic sorrow and compassion in his eyes as he takes my hands in his.

The pressure of his fingers on mine let me know this is partly a ruse. I listen closely for the message he will hide in his words.

"Revered Nephew, grim tidings have just arrived. Maxtla has seized power in Azcapotzalco, removing his younger brother from the imperial throne and installing his son Tecollotzin as king of Coyoacan."

A civil war. Our chance, at last. I should be elated—but still all I can think of is my mother, languishing forgotten for a decade . . . until the sweet little faces of Tozquen and Tochpilli rise unbidden to my memory.

"And your sister, Prime Minister? The Queen of Tetzcoco? What of her? What of her children?" My voice trails off in a sob. I feel Izcalloh place the palm of their hand on my back, trying to comfort me.

"We do not know, Royal Architect. The king sent word for us to assemble before disappearing. I assume he will explain—"

Voices come from behind the screen that obscures the king's private entrance at the back of the chamber. As we all turn, Chimalpopoca steps onto the dais with two other men, one dressed in the Emperor's garb, the other a little person, bearing his scepter and a bundle of writing materials.

A confused babble rises from the gathered council. I rub my eyes and tilt my head at the newcomers, trying to understand just what is going on.

"Indeed, I shall explain the situation, Prime Minister Tlacaellel." Chimalpopoca looks at us smugly as he speaks, appearing content to have surprised us, grinning at his own cleverness. "Council members, for those of you who have never met him, I present Quetzalayatzin, son of Tezozomoctzin and rightful heir to the imperial throne."

Quetzalayatl indicates his companion. "This is Tetontli, my scribe and aide."

"We are providing the Emperor asylum while we help devise a plan to remove or kill Maxtla, so that my grandfather's chosen successor rules the empire."

Ignoring Izcalloh's cautionary hand on my arm, I step forward to address them both.

"Your Imperial Majesty, I was given assurances that my mother would be returned to Tenochtitlan. Did your men escort her from the palace before this rebellion occurred?"

"I am afraid not, Royal Architect Nezahualcoyotzin." There is disdain and disinterest in his eyes, as if the life of my mother were an uncalled-for distraction at the moment. "She was, uh, being fed and cared for when the usurper took control. If we are to free her, I shall need your help retaking my throne."

Seething, I repress the desire to spit in his face.

His scribe pulls at his cape. Quetzalalyatl leans down to let the man whisper in his ear.

"Ah! Yes. As added incentive for your aid: my men discovered that not only has your mother been in the slave's quarters of the temple—but so have your two younger siblings."

I stumble back a step. Izcalloh is quick to catch me and lead me back to my position.

Through the confused haze that clouds my eyes, I see Tlacaellel cock his head before turning to respond for me.

"You can rest assured that this council will do all it can to stop Maxtla."

They begin to discuss options. Multiple ideas are suggested, most unfeasible without a massive invasion of Tepanecapan, which neither the king nor the deposed emperor are in favor of. I try to focus, but I keep imagining Tozquen and Tochpilli, laboring for six long years under the cruel hand of a tyrant, with never a word from the older brother who blithely started a family and built monuments for the city that betrayed them.

How they must hate me. How broken they must be.

Izcalloh leans close, muttering to me. "You could not have known."

"Does it matter?" I rasp. "My inaction has kept them enslaved. That's all the three of them will know."

Chimalpopoca gestures at us. "Have you two come up with a possibility?" he calls.

Izcalloh is fast on their feet. "I was suggesting a deadly trap. Something the Royal Architect might be able to build."

For a moment these words strike me as foolish, but the wheels of my mind turn till the gears click into place. A brash idea takes shape. It may ultimately be unfeasible, but it is worth the attempt.

At the very least, I suspect it will excite the king enough to put an end to this meeting and allow the cabal to set our plans in motion. Only overthrowing the empire completely will free my enslaved family.

"Your Imperial Majesty, did Maxtla offer you land in exchange for your loss of title?"

"Yes. Control of a vast estate between Azcapotzalco and Tlacopan. A small portion of the taxes from a few nearby villages. Insulting, really."

"Why not build an estate there and then invite him to its inauguration?"

Tetontli again whispers into Quetzalayatl's ear.

"It will be just as impossible to get an assassin close enough there as in his own palace," he answers. "The imperial guard is legendary."

"Ah," I retort, "but I don't mean to send an assassin. I mean to bring the palace down around his ears. I can design a building for you that will collapse with the removal of a single weight-bearing beam. The false emperor enters with his retinue, you excuse yourself for a moment, then with a yank of a rope, you bring the stone roof down upon their heads."

Both Quetzalayatl and Chimalpopoca sit up straighter.

"How long?" the king asks.

"A week to craft the plans. Then I can send my best construction crew and have the building ready in roughly a hundred days."

"What does Your Imperial Majesty think?" Chimapopoca asks.

Quetzalayatl reflects for a moment, taking his scribe's counsel. Then he lifts his scepter.

"We approve."

A week later, the plans are done. When I deliver them to the king, however, he looks distressed.

"That bastard is planning something," Chimalpopoca mutters, pulling at his hair. "Maxtla, I mean. I just received an invitation to the dedication of a refurbished palace near the sacred precinct of Azcapotzalco. Though intended for Maxtla's concubines, he is making quite a show of giving it to Quetzalayatzin, whom he promises will be named steward of the city while Maxtla focuses on the empire at large."

My gut roils with premonition. Maxtla knows. And if he knows, he knows who proposed the idea. He hated me before. Now he will want me dead. My family could be in danger.

I think of all the people present at the meeting.

"The scribe. He must have revealed our plan to Maxtla. It's a trap, Your Majesty."

Chimalpopoca slams his hand against the wall. "Yes. A bloody trap for the Emperor and for me. I sent a messenger to His Imperial Majesty, warning him. Another to Maxtla, begging his pardon that I cannot attend due to an important religious ceremony."

"It will be impossible for Quetzalayatzin not to present himself. Maxtla will call it treason and have him executed anyway. A no-win situation, sire."

Chimalpopoca groans in desperate rage.

I could almost feel sorry for him, were it not for the mental image of my mother, Tozquen, and Tochpilli, in dirty rags and darkness.

A few days later, news of Quetzalayatl's death spreads throughout Tepanecapan and Mexico. A week of mourning is ordered by the new tyrant.

None of us is foolish enough to attend the cremation and funeral rites of Quetzalayatl, off in Azcapotzalco. Yet by staying in Tenochtitlan, we play right into Maxtla's devious hands.

Another imperial decree comes. King Chimalpopoca of Tenochtitlan and his uncle King Tlacateotl of Tlatelolco are to personally offer sacrifices at the temple of Huitzilopochtli to ensure the ascension of Quetzalayatl's soul to the House of the Sun—as he did not fall in battle, and might otherwise be consigned to four years in Mictlan.

With the decree comes a set of clothing for Chimalpopoca. Undyed cotton tilma and breechclout, beneath the dignity of a king.

"Wear this commoner white as a humble mourner," the imperial messenger repeats. "Rid yourself of false vanity and pride when you stand before your god."

I meet with Tlacaellel, appalled by this course of events.

"You realize Maxtla plans to kill him, don't you?"

Tlacaellel gives a grim laugh. "This destiny he has sought for himself, Nephew. Even now, he attempts to rationalize Maxtla's actions, wondering how he might bend the knee and retain some dignity. He is no sovereign. He has no courage to be at the pinnacle. He would rather be a lapdog—a hairless itzcuintli stroked by its master."

I wave these words away. "That's not what I mean, Uncle. Chimalpopoca *handed my mother and siblings over to the Emperor*! Thank heaven they are alive, but they've lived as slaves for six years. By rights, Chimalpopoca should die at *my* hands."

Tlacaellel sighs, bringing his palms together and touching his lips in thought.

"I understand your frustration. First Tezozomoc, now Chimalpopoca. But the gods have their own ways of meting out justice. When they decide you are the tool for the task, they will put your enemy in front of you." He puts both his bony hands on my shoulder and looks down into my eyes. "As things stand, if we try to eliminate or warn the king, the work of six years may come to naught. Maxtla might win."

There is no denying the truth of his words, as hard as they are to hear.

Something else is bothering me, though.

"Maxtla *must* know that I drew up plans for a death trap, intending to kill him. Why was I not invited to this farcical sacrifice?"

"To begin with," Tlacaellel explains, letting me go as he turns to look out the window at the Great Pyramid, "he doesn't want to include you with two kings. No legitimacy to your claim of succession. You are the Royal Architect of the Mexica, not the King of Tetzcoco. And he's not ready to make you a martyr just yet, I imagine. You've seen the way jaguars play with their prey, yes? Maxtla is just such a predator."

I groan. "He wants me nervous about my family, both here in Tenochtitlan and there in Azcapotzalco. Hamstrung by worry, I will be less likely to attack him. More likely to make mistakes. And when I least expect it, when I'm at my most befuddled . . ."

"Maxtla will strike," Tlacaellel finishes, turning back to face me. "But you're already prepared, aren't you?"

I nod. "That I am. But I could do with some good news, Uncle."

"Well, I've got some. I've received a message from our man in Tlacopan."

Tlacopan is the closest Tepaneca city to Tenochtitlan, just to our west, on the shore of Moon Lake. We have spent years cultivating relationships with its merchants and nobles. Many of them are ready to support us against their nation's imperial regime. Our primary con-tact is General Totoquihuaztli, who has promised us all ten thousand of his troops. All we need is the king, who is unfortunately one of Tezozomoc's sons.

"How have they reacted to recent events?" I ask Tlacaellel.

"This despotic behavior by Maxtla has turned his elder brother King Tzacualcatl against him, making him more amenable to the pro-Mexica sentiment in Tlacopan. We shall have an openly supportive ally soon, instead of just a band of Tepaneca rebels."

I mutter thanks to the heavens. The three prongs of our strategy are nearly ready.

On the next auspicious day, the kings of the twin cities of Mexico, dressed in their white mourning clothes, ascend the steps of the Great Pyramid in Tenochtitlan's sacred precinct with an Otomi warrior cap-tured in a recent skirmish. His honorable death, as a sacrificial victim, will serve as a proxy to replace Quetzalayatl's ignoble end.

Just as the kings place the man's heart in the jaguar basin, troops barge into the plaza through the western gate.

Tepaneca soldiers. Sent by the Emperor, right up the causeway I built to Tlacopan.

Neither Moteuczoma nor Itzcoatl call for Mexica warriors to engage them. Chimalpopoca glares at them, rage in his eyes at their betrayal.

The imperial force deploys itself around the base of the pyramid. They carry with them a wooden cage. The commander of the forces, General Huecanmecatl, ascends the steps partway and makes an announcement to everyone in the square.

"By order of Emperor Maxtlatzin, Kings Chimalpopoca and Tlaca-teotl are to surrender themselves immediately into my custody, for crimes of conspiracy and treason against the empire. Other conspira-tors will be dealt with at his imperial leisure and should prepare their souls for the full weight of his wrath."

Tlacaellel was right. And the bastard even announces his inten-tions to me!

"Nobles not involved in the attempted assassination should pre-pare a demonstration of their loyalty. Now descend, sovereigns of Mexico. We must escort you to Azcapotzalco to give an accounting to the Emperor and receive his justice."

While the city watches in horror, Tepaneca soldiers herd the two kings at spearpoint into the cage, where they are forced to sit with their bowed heads between their knees.

The imperial troops march away. Silence hangs like a shroud over the sacred precinct, until somewhere, a woman begins to wail with inconsolable grief.

While Chimalpopoca's trumped-up trial is conducted in Tepanecapan, the council debates his successor. His supporters suggest installing his ten-year-old son Xihuitl Temoc, with Itzcoatl as regent, but the rest of us push back against the idea. The boy is too sickly and too firmly in the grasp of his Tepaneca relatives. Eventually, we reach an agree-ment: Itzcoatl will be the next ruler of Tenochtitlan.

Those of us in the cabal meet multiple times, concluding again and again that the king will be executed. Avoiding Chimalpopoca's men, who are distraught and keep sending pleading missives to Maxtla, we ensure that Tlacateotl's successor in our sister city still believes in the cause. Regent Cuauhtlahtoa assures us that he does, and that his troops are ready to move out at a moment's notice.

"The canoes?" I ask Tlacaellel.

"Sitting in a warehouse in Tlalmanalco, ready to be picked up."

"As you might imagine," I tell him, "I'm anxious, and want to get started *now*, but Izcalloh cautions me to wait for the right moment."

Tlacaellel nods. "Their counsel is right, as ever. Setting things in motion too early could draw Maxtla's suspicions. Let him imagine us, cowering here in fear, totally at his mercy. He will be less prepared. Your mother, sister, and brother live in that palace. A false step from you, and he could easily have them killed."

His reminder sobers me. I am desperate to set my family free, to retake my throne, but not desperate enough to risk their lives unnecessarily.

I'll wait for the right moment. And it comes soon enough.

Within five days, Chimalpopoca is executed.

Rumors claim that Tlacateotl managed to escape, but was riddled with arrows on a canoe not far from shore by the Tepaneca who pursued him.

Itzcoatl immediately convenes the governing council.

The Master of the Marketplace is the first to get to his feet, wringing his hands with glum grief and defeat, speaking for Chimalpopoca's men.

"You lords all heard the message delivered in the sacred precinct. We have to demonstrate our loyalty to the Tepaneca throne. There is no choice but submit utterly to Emperor Maxtlatzin. To avoid annihilation, we must arrange an envoy of nobles to Azcapotzalco. The godbearers will carry Huitzilopochtli to His Imperial Majesty, and we shall throw ourselves on his mercy. Perhaps he will spare some of the Mexica aristocracy, even if only to serve as courtesans or slaves in his palace."

Objectively, I understand this cowardly reasoning. Maxtla has two hundred thousand warriors under his command. Should they converge on this city, our twenty-five thousand Mexica troops would be obliterated.

But Tlacaellel leaps up, livid. "Have you lost your minds? What cowardice has been snarling in the hearts of the Mexica for you to utter such irrational nonsense? Instead of offering ourselves up the humiliating fashion you describe, let us be steadfast—fighting to the last to defend our kingdom and our honor!"

He glances up at Itzcoatl through wild strands of hair that cover his face.

The high priest interrupts, a sly smile on his face. "Itzcoatzin, if you refuse to agree to send an envoy to the Emperor, we shan't approve your coronation as king. Long have you and your brothers worked in secret against Chimalpopoca. Did you think none of us noticed? You are delighted the king is dead. But hear me well: you shall not rule legitimately unless you petition the Emperor for his forgiveness and guidance, just as he commanded in the message read aloud at Chimalpopoca's apprehension. Do not attempt to wrest power from the people with half the council objecting. You would tear this kingdom apart."

Tlacaellel tilts his head back and laughs.

"Oh, perfect. The fools think they have bounced the ball off their hips and through the hoop. Itzcoatzin, revered uncle and regent, let us concede the issue. We should indeed know the will of Maxtlaton." He uses the diminutive, making the pro-Tepaneca councilors squirm. "Send me as your ambassador with a witness from that spineless faction."

"Such bravura," the high priest mutters. "You will be dead the moment you step foot in the imperial palace."

●◖◑◗●

"Then so be it!" exclaims Tlacaellel. "I am not afraid of death. We all must die. What do I care whether I meet my destiny today or tomorrow? For what occasion should I keep myself alive? When and where could my life be put to better use than here and now? I choose to die honorably in defense of this kingdom. Send me, Itzcoatzin. I wish to go."

Itzcoatl stands and embraces him. "You make me proud, Tlacael- leltzin. Should you die on this mission, I swear that your wife and children will never want for anything, so that they forever remember this moment, when my valiant nephew elected to lay down his life for the honor of Mexico."

Then, pointing to the high priest, Itzcoatl commands: "You shall accompany him. At once. Take a squad of royal guards. And suffi- cient chalk and feathers."

Chalk and feathers. Applied to the faces of warriors who face cer- tain death.

As the high priest blanches and stutters, Tlacaellel turns to me and mouths one word.

Tomorrow.

{36} TO HUEXOTZINCO

SEKALLI IS AS STUBBORN as ever when I give the word that evening.

"Why, Neza?" she asks in the privacy of our chambers. "I don't *want* to drag everyone to Mixcoac. It's just a fishing village, but it's damn close to Coyoacan. And what about our staff? Even if no Tepaneca see us before we load ourselves into the canoes, we'll be very cramped in Zacatl's villa. Can't we just stay here? Can't you just, I don't know, post a guard or something?"

I take her face in my hands and kiss her gently. "Precisely why we're doing this under cover of darkness. What's more, Izcalloh and I will accompany you to the docks at Mixcoac. And Zacatl has added another wing to his villa, so you'll have plenty of room. Trust me, this hill is a strategic target. It will be one of the first things Maxtla attacks if he decides to take Tenochtitlan by force. Ask Izcalloh if you doubt me."

With a sigh, she lets her shoulders droop. "Fine. I won't gainsay the tactical knowledge of the tremendous Tetzcoca Twins. I surrender. Let me pack some essentials. Can you check on them? I'll have the majordomo gather their clothes and games."

I find my sons in the central garden of the retreat, trying to catch frogs in a pond while their teenage uncle Omaka looks on, laughing at their antics.

"Ah!" I cry. "My fire coyote and my sea monster, frog-hunting together! Why didn't you invite your father, boys?"

"Daddy!" they both shout, rushing over to hug my legs and excitedly explaining about the two different kinds of amphibians that live in our pond.

"Brilliant," I say, kissing the tops of their heads. "Just brilliant. And you know where there are even *more* species of frogs—and even squirmy pink axolotls? At Uncle Zacatzin's home, in Tenochtitlan!"

The boys' faces light up with excitement.

"I want to go there, Father," Cipactli says diplomatically.

"Now!" adds his little brother, in tones that echo his mother's endearing willfulness.

"Okay, then let us go! Omaka, we're going to hop into canoes and cross the lake, so toss some clothes into a satchel and meet us at the main entrance."

The teen arches a suspicious eyebrow, but nods his agreement.

As I take the boys to wash their hands, sounds of distant thudding, smashing, and screaming drift into the palatial retreat.

"What is that, Father?" Cipactli asks.

"I'm not sure, but let's hurry. Come, boys."

We rush toward the entrance. My mother-in-law is already there with the cooking staff. Sekalli comes running as well.

"Did you hear—" she begins, but Lord Polok comes bursting through the entrance, panting, an axe in his hand.

"Nezahualcoyotzin! Several hundred Tepaneca have converged on the hill! They just closed the sluice gates and smashed several rods of the aqueduct to bits. A half dozen workers just fell beneath their swords."

"Did they follow you?" I demand.

"Yes! They are mere moments behind me!"

I gesture at everyone. "Quickly, to my study. Hurry!"

Lifting my sons into my arms, I lead the way. Kicking aside my writing table, I crouch, setting Cipactli down, and yanking up on the copper ring set into one of the wooden planks. It lifts on hinges, revealing a staircase leading downward.

"Into the tunnels! They'll be upon us at any instant!"

Whimpering, crying, or cursing, my family makes its way down into the escape route I dug into this hill before the construction of the manor was complete. There was no way I'd have had my family living in what is essentially Tepanecapan without some sort of secret exit.

Lowering the boys into their grandfather's arms, I pull the trap-door shut above me and secure it with a series of bolts and bars. Sekalli has already lit torches and is leading the way through the twists and turns.

No one speaks as we approach the hidden doorway at the far end of the maze. I make my way to the front of our party and open the gate, disguised with clumps of earth and grass.

"Okay, the way is clear," I whisper. "Down the path as fast as possible. Once we reach the shoreline . . ."

Izcalloh puts her hand on my arm. "No, Beloved. That path leaves us completely exposed. We cannot run scores of rods in the open like that. And the Tepaneca may be waiting at the boats, anyway."

Sekalli turns to her father. "Aren't there two walkways of wooden planks running along the aqueduct, all the way to Mazatzintamalco?"

Lord Polok nods excitedly. "Yes, and we built in many gaps along the way, just like with the causeway. We can dump those wooden bridges into the water once we pass . . ."

". . . and any pursuers will either be stopped, or so stupid they'll attempt to travel along the wooden pipes, which will break under their weight," Sekalli concludes, scratching her temple for effect. "If I remember the boring science of it all correctly."

I glance lovingly at the people gathered around me. "The gods truly favor me. What better family could a king in exile ever hope for? Let's do it."

We run uphill, through the forested slope, and soon reach the shattered remnants of the aqueduct's last stretch to the springs. There are no Tepaneca in sight, so we make our way to the beginning of the support structure and start stepping with great care onto the walkway.

I'm helping Cipactli clamber on with his grandfather's help when a sharp cry comes from behind me. A Tepaneca soldier has sprung from some hiding place, and is trying to wrench Tecoyotl from Sekalli's arms. Before I can move to help, my youngest bites the enemy's arm, and his mother hefts a chunk of rock from the soil, bringing it smashing against the soldier's temple.

He drops like a dead man. He probably is.

"Keep your gods-damned hands," Sekalli spits, "off my children!"

We make our way along down the gentle slope, leaning against the aqueduct for balance, tossing the three bridges we cross into the water below, just in case.

But the gods smile on us. No further enemy follow. At Mazatzinta-malco, we startle a guard by leaping down onto the causeway to Tlacopan, but he recognizes me at once.

"Can you escort us to the villa of Prince Zacatzin?" I ask. "I think the city is about to fall under siege."

In the morning, after just a few hours' sleep in my uncle's home in Tenochtitlan—abuzz half the night because of our sudden and riotous arrival—I receive word that Tlacaellel has returned to the city, requesting that all the bridges on the causeways be lifted to prevent invasion of the island. The Tepaneca troops that attacked our home at Chapoltepec have been sighted, camped right outside Mixcoac. There comes a general summons from Itzcoatl, requesting that all Tenochca who are able come together in the sacred precinct.

"Sekalli," I whisper, shaking my consort lightly. Her eyes flutter open. "It's time. I must leave with Izcalloh before the city is surrounded."

She nods sleepily and touches my cheek. "Be safe, darling boy. I love you more than life itself."

"As I love you, Little Owl." Our kiss is sweet if short. I pray the gods will not make it be our last.

Izcalloh in tow, I head for the eastern docks, stopping at the sacred precinct to see what Tlacaellel will say to his city.

Our regent and his brother stand atop the Great Pyramid. The precise acoustics engineered over the decades allows them to address the crowd clearly, as the sun clears the mountains to the east.

"I have returned from my audience with Emperor Maxtla," Tlacaellel announces. "When I demanded of him what he planned to do with the Mexica, thus did he reply: 'Though I rule Tepanecapan, my dear nephew, it is the will of my people that I wage war against your nation. If I refuse them, I put my family at risk. Your treason has angered my sons and councilors. They would see the Mexica obliterated from the sea-ringed world.'"

Tlacaellel lifts a handful of feathers in a hand dusted white with chalk.

"To that message, I simply replied: 'Then we Mexica have no choice but to defy you, tyrant, declaring you our mortal enemy. Either we shall fall on the battlefield and be enslaved, or you the Tepaneca will. Our god tells me you have started a war you cannot win. I have brought the chalk and feathers, the shield and arrows. Permit me to prepare you for certain death."

I choke back a laugh. It is quite unlikely that Tlacaellel actually appeared before Maxtla, much less so that the Emperor permitted him to perform that particular ritual. But it is good theater. The Mexica roar with excitement, imagining the humiliation of the ruler they despise.

Yet amid the cheers come cries of sorrow and fear. Itzcoatl addresses them.

"Fear not, children. We shall earn your freedom without harm befalling a single non-combatant."

"What if you fail?" someone shouts.

Tlacaellel grins in his manic way. "If we fail, we noblemen of the city shall place ourselves in your hands, to do with as you wish. Devour us upon broken, dirty plates, if that seems a fitting punish- ment. But if we succeed, then understand: *your lives are ours.* You must swear to serve and render tribute to us, laboring as we see fit, swearing homage forever to us, your lords. If you agree, let me hear your voices as one, repeating the battle cry of our ancestors: MEXIHCO TIHUEHCAHUAH! MEXICO ENDURES!"

As the unison shouts reverberate through Tenochtitlan, Izcalloh and I slip toward the docks. A canoe is waiting for us, stocked with provisions. We paddle away, pointing the stern toward the southeast- ern shore.

Though we've planned for this moment for six years, working out every detail with Tlacaellel and the others, I can scarcely believe that it's finally happening. I am going to bring down the Tepaneca Empire. I am going to retake my city. My entire country.

I have my back to Tenochtitlan, so I don't see what makes Izcal- loh's eyes widen and lips tremble.

"Majesty—it's begun," they say, pointing behind me.

I turn to behold a fleet of Tepaneca canoes fanning out to the north and south of the island, many dozens curving farther to completely encircle the Kingdom of Mexico.

The siege is underway. The countdown starts now. Speed is of the essence.

It takes us almost two days to reach Huexotzinco, first crossing into Chalco to avoid Acolhua patrols now loyal to the Emperor, then making our way back through the pass between the volcanoes.

Izcalloh is a frequent visitor of the city, so the guards greet them with a salute.

"But who is this fellow with you, Noble Izcalloh?" one asks. "He has the look of a Mexica noble."

My concubine and advisor cannot resist a small laugh. "This young man is none other than Acolmiztzin Nezahualcoyotzin, Tetzcoca King, Acolhua Overlord, Chichimeca Chieftain."

The men stiffen, bow, and step aside.

"You really like saying all that, don't you?" I mutter after we pass the gate.

"Oh, yes," they reply with a coquettish wink. "I almost shudder with pleasure."

"Ha!" I cry, elbowing them gently. "The minute Sekalli's not around, you suddenly want to flirt. She scares you, doesn't she? Even after all these years."

"A little," Izcalloh admits. "But I admire her now. And she treats me like a dear friend or sibling. That helps."

The Acolhua calpolli is on the northwestern edge of Huexotzinco. We try to be inconspicuous as we wind along its streets, heading for the manor of Motoliniatzin, former king of Coatlichan. Yet our identities are quickly discovered, and word spreads. My people emerge from their homes, standing silent and expectant as I pass.

Finally, one dares to call out.

"Is it time, Your Majesty? Is it finally time?"

I stop and look around at the hundreds of faces waiting to hear my voice, waiting to receive the long-awaited news.

"Yes, my beloved Acolhua. It is time. I am here to lead our troops to victory. We topple the Tepaneca, then we retake our homeland."

The cry that goes up puts the shouting of the Mexica to shame.

So much they have endured. To see their suffering perhaps coming to an end overwhelms even me. My eyes fill with tears, and Izcalloh whisks me quickly toward a manor on the nearby hill.

King Motoliniatzin, normally staid and serious, is breathless with excitement when he greets us. "We heard that the old tyrant was dead, but your ambassador and spokesperson has been clear over the years. His death was only one of the conditions to trigger our invasion of Tepanecapan—have the rest been met?"

"Yes," I tell him. "Tenochtitlan has food and water enough to resist a siege. And a Tepaneca city has allied with us in secret. Tlacopan. As soon as we can summon the other four xiquipiltin here, we shall march forth at once."

I still can hardly believe the incredible work Izcalloh and their father have done these six years, in coordination with the kings-in-exile. Five xiquipiltin. Forty thousand soldiers, nobles and commoners alike, amassed far from the prying eyes of Tepanecapan and fully armed and armored, ready and raring to fight.

Together with the Mexica and other allies, we comprise a military host that cannot lose. I almost feel sorry for the Tepaneca.

Almost.

It takes three days for the other legions to march to Huexotzinco from other cities in the Republic of Tlaxcallan. Izcalloh and I spend much of the wait meeting with key leaders in the calpolli, making plans for the restoration of rightful governments in Acolhua cities, removing rebel puppet kings so that the original rulers, long exiled, can sit again on those thrones.

In our free time, however, we explore some of the beautiful springs and lakes in the eastern shadow of Iztaccihuatl, attend a large-scale dance depicting the creation of the earth, and enjoy the cuisine of Huexotzinco. Delicacies like grilled cactus paddles and wild turkey in cacao sauce delight our palates and make us eager for more pleasures.

The nights we spend together in our ample chambers in the king's manor are magical and sweet, as if the rest of the world has faded for a time, leaving only the two of us.

On that last morning, in the darkness of near-dawn, ritual incense seeps in under the door—the sort clerics offer to the gods mid-watch six times a day throughout Anahuac. A sweet-smelling religious tradition.

Perhaps roused by a scent they know so well, Izcalloh nuzzles me, making small contented noises like an ocelot or puppy. Half-asleep, I kiss their forehead.

"What is it, precious flower?"

"So happy right now," they murmur, lowering their speech in a way that seldom happens. "Wish it could last longer. But everything is about to change. Your exile is ending. Alliances. Daughters of princes and kings. Alliances."

"Shhh," I say, pulling them to me and patting their soft back. "You and I will never change. I will always need you. As my advisor. As my lover."

Though their voice is muffled against my chest, I can make out their whispered words.

"I choose to believe you."

Forty thousand men move much more slowly than two or ten or a hundred.

Even with each exiled king leading a xiquipilli in the orderly fashion and direction we have planned, getting through the pass takes two days.

On the morning of the second, I hear a familiar howling. Peeling off from King Motoliniatzin's legion, I hurry into the foothills, Izcalloh beside me.

I am right. It is her.

Old now, her muzzle as white as the ruff around her neck. But the coyote knows me at once; she limps over to lick my face as I kneel to greet her.

"Auntie Coyote," I mutter, unable to stop the tears or the sobs that wrack my chest. "You've come to see me off to war, haven't you? Dearest friend, thank you. For this goodbye and for everything else."

Nuzzling me, she yips softly—almost inaudibly—jerking her head up.

On an outcropping not far away stand two other females.

Her daughters.

We all regard each other for a moment, then I take her narrow face in my hands.

"I have children now, too. So I make a vow, Auntie. As you have protected me, thus will my family protect yours. I'll be overlord of the humans in these lands soon enough. You will be my glyph: my standard. And my royal command will keep these slopes free for your descendants, as long as my lineage holds sway."

I stand and bow to her then. She twitches her tail and ducks her head. Then, with a low whine, she turns to make her laborious way up toward her kin.

Izcalloh stares at me, dumbfounded.

"She . . . it seemed she understood you, sire."

I take their hand and kiss it, overwhelmed by an epiphany.

"Of course she did. She's no ordinary coyote, Beloved. She's my guide, my double, my animal soul. My nahualli."

Another sob shudders through my body.

"She goes to die, she wanted me to know. To return to where she belongs. To the depths of my soul: from where the gods plucked her in my darkest hour."

Our army is about to swing south toward Tlalmanalco when a group of Tepaneca rangers, guarding the border between occupied Acolhua-can and Chalco, catches sight of us.

"Shit!" I exclaim, signaling to a group of elite Otontin traveling alongside me. "We have to stop them!"

They have a considerable lead on us, but we are more desperate. If they get word to one of the cities, it could ruin the crucial element of surprise.

I run like I never have in my life, flying across the rocky soil. My soldiers press forward, keeping up with my speed, flowing as it does from some new fount inside me, the golden coyote at the center of my being.

The Tepaneca tire, stumble. We keep coming, in silent agreement that we shall rest when these bastards are dead, and not a moment before.

After nearly two watches of pursuit, we are upon them, screaming like zohuaehecah, the wailing ghosts of wronged women that are said to haunt the foothills to our east.

Swords whirling, we slice and hack our enemies to oblivion.

Then we collapse in the blood-stained dirt, wheezing and dizzy.

The trip back is slow, almost agonizing. By the time we rejoin the host, Izcalloh has already procured the canoes, which are carried now in the air above our soldier's heads.

Ten thousand boats, each seating four men. Six years for Chalco to build them under the auspices of King Quetzalmazatzin of Amaqueh-mecan, whose son-in-law Tlacaellel paid the federation handsomely for its cooperation and silence.

And by dusk the next day, we stand at the southeastern shore of Moon Lake, ready to launch ourselves within those canoes against the greatest empire since the Toltecs.

The Tepaneca surrounded the island the day Izcalloh and I left.

The Kingdom of Mexico has endured this siege for thirteen days. We are about to end it.

{37} TOPPLING THE TEPANECA

Down the Causeway

We wait until Tepaneca forces
withdraw for the night
to rest and replenish arrows.
Then, splitting into two fleets
of twenty thousand fighters,
we head north and south,
hugging the shores
as our oars ply the water.

Except for Izcalloh and me.
Leaving the kings in charge,
we head straight for Tenochtitlan
swimming silently through mists
that lift in curtains from the lake.

Izcalloh returns to the villa
to let our family know we're well,
and I hurry to the royal palace
where the council is gathered
reviewing the day's damage.

"Nezahualcoyotzin!" the king cries.
"Tell us that your army has arrived."
I confirm. "Landing within the watch,
half north of Azcapotzalco
and half near Chapoltepec,
ready to converge at near-dawn."

Though the city's forces have fought
at the fringes all day, pushing back

attempts at invasion, we rouse them,
array them in the sacred precinct,
and lead them marching
down the causeway
toward Tlacopan.

Rebel Tepaneca sentries keep watch
on the other side, not to stop
but to urge us forward,
sending word ahead to their king
that the ruse he has sustained
can come to an end.

General Totoquihuaztli meets us
just outside Tlacopan, saluting.
"Your warriors can rest here
while we muster our own.
Is the plan still to strike during
the third night watch?"

I return his salute.
"Yes, Revered General.
But first, may I borrow
an officer's uniform?
And an elite squad
disguised as infantry?
I must sneak behind
enemy lines."

Behind the Lines

With my squad of Tlacopaneca,
I travel brazenly through the night
northwestward, to Azcapotzalco.
We take our time, deliberately.
Two thousand rods. Half a watch.

Tlacopaneca King Tzacualcatl
has informed the Mexica
that my mother and siblings
are kept in the courtesan wing
of the imperial palace.

My plan is audacious, mad.
We head for the palace entrance,
present ourselves to the guards.
I do my best Tepaneca accent,
add that supercilious swagger.

"I am Commander Ce Mazatl
of Tlacopan, with urgent intel
for His Imperial Majesty, which
we tortured out of a Mexica spy
caught infiltrating our city."

Escorted to the audience chamber,
we wait under armed guard,
our weapons confiscated,
for someone with authority
to arrive and debrief us.

In my heart I mutter prayers
promising incense and praise
and sacrifice if only once more
the Lord of Chaos will deign
to stand on my side.

Lo and behold!
Maxtla comes striding in,
a sneer on his face.

Caught

"That is no Tepaneca commander,"
he spits at his men. "Are you fools?
Why would you let Acolmiztli
just walk into my home?"

Most of the soldiers bow or kneel,
barking their apologies, pleading
pardon from their emperor.
I follow suit. Part of the plan.

"Maxtlatzin, Emperor of the World,
well do I deserve your spite and wrath.
Yet I am a desperate man whose family
rests in your hands. Forgive my madness."

"What is your purpose here, traitor?
I cannot imagine you have come to beg."

"Oh, but I have! For the lives of my mother,
my sister and brother. To make an exchange."

His interest is piqued. As two guards
raise blades to my throat, he approaches.

"What would you exchange for them?
I warn you—they are dearer than gems."

"The Mexica and Chalca have allied.
They plan an invasion. I know when.

Have my family brought here, please.
If they are whole, I will tell all."

He cocks his head and smiles, bemused.
"If you are lying to me, little kitten,
I will kill you four without remorse
and put an end to Ixtlilxochitl's lineage."

The Sack Begins

Maxtla sends two guards
to the courtesan wing,
orders a battalion arrayed
around the palace.

"Your reputation has grown,"
he explains with a snarl.
"But you will not leave here
unless I permit it, kitten."

Soon, his men drag three
new people into the room.
Mother has aged two decades
in just six years, it seems.

I barely recognize Tozquen,
tall and beautiful, woman grown.
Beside her stands a sleepy boy
of eleven summers: Tochpilli.

"Acolmiztli!" Mother cries,
rushing to kneel before me
and cover my face with kisses.
Tozquen's eyes go wide.

"Here they are," Maxtla says,
grabbing my siblings' shoulders,
holding them back. "Now speak,
or watch them all die."

If I have timed this right,
there are just minutes left.
A few more lies, and then
chaos will unleash itself.

"It began with Tlacaellel.
After the wedding. He dreams
of a Mexica Empire, of rebelling
and rewriting history.

"His father-in-law agreed,
convinced the federation
to ally in secret, hoarding
weapons, building canoes."

Just enough of the truth
to make the lie feel real,
to jibe with information
he may already possess.

"The obstacle was the king,
but Tlacaellel tricked you
into eliminating him. Siege?
To let you believe you've won."

Through the open door I see
a cleric pass, censer swinging,
the ritual incense offered nightly
at the midpoint of near-dawn.

It's time. I glance at my squad.
Each blinks his readiness.

"When will they strike, whoreson?"
growls Maxtla, gone apoplectic.

I stand, stopping Mother with one hand.
"Right about now, you fucking bastard."

The gods love dramatic coincidence.
Just then, conch trumpets sound
and signal drums boom—*alarum!*
Shouts and screams from all around.

The elite Tepaneca rebels leap into action,
using fists and feet to smash the guards.
I pivot and punch the one to my right,
wrenching a stone dagger from his belt.

Then spinning, I slice through the throat
of the fool to my left, grabbing Mother
by the arm and dashing toward Maxtla.
She hugs the kids as I seize the emperor.

"Let's go," I grunt, blade to his neck.
"Tell all we meet to stand down.
I'm taking my family back, you scum,
and you're my imperial passport."

Azcapotzalco in Ruins

When we at last back our way out
into what should be faint dawn,
Azcapotzalco is burning brightly.

The guards that have been creeping
in our wake, held at bay by this blade
and their master's commands, balk.

Some of them run. To fight or flee.
The streets are glutted with warriors:
Acolhua, Mexica, Tlacopaneca.

In the plaza before the palace stand our generals,
with ten fierce squads providing protection.
Mother sees Uncle Coyohuah, hurries to his side.

"Surprise," I mutter in Maxtla's ear. "Surrender.
Or don't, if you prefer. Either way, it's over."
I raise my voice. "Let us tear it all down!

"Let the women and children flee, and
take what prisoners lay down their arms,
but the city of Azcapotzalco dies today!"

"Raze all buildings to the ground!
Not one stone left upon the other!
May nothing but ants ever live here!"

Kicking the back of his legs,
I force Maxtla to kneel
before his enemies.

"What say you, friends? Family?
Allies? What is your verdict?
What sentence must he receive?"

The sneer of arrogance is gone
from Maxtla's traitorous lips.
They now quiver with bleak certainty.

Tlacaellel crosses the space between us,
handing me his double-handed sword.
"Guilty, Nezahualcoyotzin. Death."

Raising the sword, I feel Tezcatlipoca
flowing into my sinews: roiling smoke,
chaotic force, destructive might.

"This is for my father, you piece of shit!"
I shout, swinging at his trembling neck,
severing his head with one blow.

But for the sounds of distant fighting,
there is a moment of silence as we watch
his body tumble slowly to one side.

Then I open a pouch at my waist,
take out my sons' umbilical cords,
drop them onto the bloody earth.

"We are almost done," I whisper
to the Night and the Wind, both fading
with the sun and the morning heat.

"One last task for you, and I turn away
from all the death and devastation
that you so relish, Enemy of Both Sides."

No answer. No matter.
I run, eyes full of tears,
to embrace the ones I love.

{38} THE TRIPLE ALLIANCE

MAXTLA'S SONS AND COUSINS and uncles are less easily dispatched. The war wages for months, our army moving from town to town, mopping up the ever-shrinking Tepaneca forces. Upon learning of the death of Maxtla and the destruction of Azcapotzalco, many commoner soldiers lay down their weapons or defect to our side. In this way, our allied forces swell from an equal two hundred thousand to nearly two hundred and fifty, while those still loyal to the imperial cause number less than forty.

I do my part, but first I take my mother and siblings to Tenochtitlan.

"I thought I should never taste freedom again," the queen tells me as we glide across the lake in our canoe. "Yet I endured, trusting in the Sovereign of the Near and the Nigh, believing that you would find a way, my dear Acolmiztli."

Tozquen takes my hand. "I can scarcely credit my eyes, Older Brother. How I've longed to see your face; to feel your warm embrace.

I have done all I can to help Tochpilli remember, but the Emperor and his sons plied him every day with stories and treats and promises."

Tochpilli frowns, his hands tightening into fists. "You don't know a thing. Neither of you! By letting them wheedle and tempt me, I kept them *away from you both!*"

I see the horror in his eyes and understand that he, more than anyone, needs my love. I grab his shoulders and pull him nearer to me.

"I'm proud of you, Prince Tochpiltzin. You fought with your mind and heart. That warfare is the hardest to learn, yet as boy you have mastered strategy that generals would envy."

The tenseness in his body slackens, and he leans into me, relieved. Then the tears start to flow, and his arms go around my chest, squeezing tight.

It will take so much love to heal him. Fortunately, the rest of my family is waiting, hearts open, brimming with affection.

At Zacatl's villa, we all gather. Mother embraces the sisters and brothers with whom she has finally been reunited, and then I begin introductions for the rest.

"Dowager Queen Matlalcihuatzin, meet Lady Sekaltzin. She is my Royal Consort, mother of my two sons—Cipactli and Tlecoyotl. Boys, this is your grandmother."

Mother kneels, weeping, to hug the little ones to her breast. Wiping her eyes, she stands to greet Sekalli.

"Thank you, Lady Sekaltzin, for being a helpmeet for my husband, and for bearing his beautiful heirs. I look forward to a time of peace, when we can spend time together and become friends."

Sekalli curtsies as if born to nobility. "As do I, Your Majesty."

"And you will remember Izcalloh, child of Lord Cihtzin, once my nanny and tutor. They are my Chief Concubine—"

"—only concubine," mutters Sekalli softly, eliciting chuckles—

"—and my principal adviser."

Izcalloh bows deeply. "I am honored to be part of His Majesty's family. Please look to me whenever you need anything at all, Dowager Queen."

"Ah, sweet Izcallohtzin! What a pleasure to see such a lovely, refined person again. I might have expected His Majesty to seduce you. He was always rather obsessed with your charms, was he not?"

Sekalli looks askance at me, but refrains from further sarcasm. I breathe a sigh of relief.

And so the introductions continue. Before long Omaka has taken Tochpilli on a tour of the neighborhood; Tozquen has been "adopted" by Sekalli's sister Yemasaton, who drags her off to meet other young Mexica wives; and Aunt Azcatzin sweeps mother into the kitchen to oversee the midday meal and share a decade's worth of gossip.

"My heart is so full," I tell Sekalli and Izcalloh, "that I think I might burst."

They each take one of my hands. We stand watching the others for a long time.

Tepanecapan is at last brought to heel, but not without tragedies. King Tzacualcatl falls beneath the blade of one of his nephews. Itzcoatl and I agree that Totoquihuaztli should take his place as king of Tlacopan.

With relative order restored, we finally hold a small constitutional convention. We have torn down one government. Now it is time to forge a new one.

Mexico is represented, of course, by Itzcoatl—now officially king—and his nephews Tlacaellel and Moteuczoma. Cuauhtlahtoa of Tlatelolco and his prime minister join them. Representing Tlacopan is King Totoquihuaztli and his prime minister. I, of course, represent Acolhuacan. Izcalloh accompanies me, as do several Acolhua kings-in-exile.

Scribes from each of the three nations are present to paint images and inscribe glyphs that represent the structures accorded today.

Tlacaellel leads the discussion, being the primary architect of the proposal.

"We have all discussed these terms separately and together in various clandestine settings, yet I am glad to see us gathered officially at last, having achieved several of our multiple objectives. I shall summarize what we have all tentatively agreed to, then we can begin to negotiate some of the details."

I lean toward Izcalloh and whisper, "I'll leave this to you. Listen close and help me get a good deal, without ruining our reconquest of Acolhuacan. I need the Mexica. Let them have what they want."

"Two separate structures must exist," Tlacaellel continues. "First is the political one. The core of our cabal has been the leadership of a trio of cities: Tenochtitlan, Tetzcoco, and Tlacopan. Political power will rest in each of them. Three places of power. A triple alliance."

With a gesture, he has a scribe unfold a map of Anahuac before us. The borders of our existing nations—Mexico, Acolhuacan, Tepanecapan— have been extended out to the edges.

"Each king will control the city states within his region of control, with the caveat that the Mexica sovereign is first among his peers. A king of kings, if you will. Judicial power will flow from Tenochtitlan, with courts in Tlacopan and Tetzcoco being regional divisions of the principal Mexica one. As the territory of this Triple Alliance happens to expand, western and northwestern conquests will fall under the administration of Tlacopan, eastern and southeastern under Tetzcoco, and northern and northeastern under Tenochtitlan."

Tlacaellel pauses. There are no objections so far.

"As to those possible conquests, they will principally be driven by the vision of the Tenochca king—with the counsel of his two peers. Once a conflict is agreed upon, Tlacopan and Tetzcoco must contribute troops and materiel.

"Now for the second system. Tribute. You'll note the red lines, dividing Anahuac into seven tax districts. Tenochtitlan will be in charge of appointing tax collectors and of setting rates, taking into account the needs and preferences of the other two places of power. Then we shall distribute the collected tribute in a proportional way. Mexico will receive the greatest share, followed by Tetzcoco, and finally Tlacopan. I have suggested 50-30-20, but we shall negotiate that in a while."

Though I am fine with Mexico leading and receiving the most tribute, there is one condition I want to impose:

"During a previous conversation, you mentioned that there would be three collection centers where tribute would be brought together for distribution. I shall be frank: I should rather *not* have the 'places of power' also serve as collection centers. Let other kings grapple with the logistical nightmare of storing and guarding tribute."

Totoquihuaztli taps his table. "Yes, agreed."

Tlacaellel grins. "Acceptable. Now, if we all agree on these broad strokes, let us now dive into the details."

Stifling a sigh, I glance at Izcalloh. The expression of excitement on their face almost makes me laugh.

I'd rather be anywhere, frankly. Preferably the House of Song in Tetzcoco, but a construction site would work nicely too. Nine hells, even the battlefield is better than the mind-numbing minutiae of socioeconomic planning. Apparently, I've discovered the limits of my intellectual pursuits. Let others grapple with bureaucracy!

Not long after the agreement is sealed, Itzcoatl announces I am to be crowned king of Tetzcoco in Tenochtitlan's sacred precinct.

"I think we can dispense with the ritual of fasting and meta-phorical descent," he jokes, as we dine together at his palace that evening. "From the stories you tell, you have experienced more than your share of preparatory hardships."

I give an exaggerated sigh. "Ah, I thank you, Great Uncle. I was already beginning to dread the coronation ceremony."

Itzcoatl gives me a sidways glance. "It goes without saying, I hope, that we are supporting you not just because of the love we feel for you. It is in the best interests of the Mexica people. You are as much one of us as you are Acolhua, and though we allow Tlacopan to play its minimal part, you and I both know the truth of things. This is not an equally divided Triple Alliance."

"Of course, Itzcoatzin." I try not to sound exasperated at this same conversation again. "I know this is a Mexica empire, and I am an integral part of the vision you and Tlacaelleltzin seek to spread throughout the sea-ringed world. Nahuas united, under Mexica leadership."

The new king—new *emperor*—pats my hand. "Correction: under *this family's leadership*. Ours alone. Forever. The House of Acamapichtli will continue to grow. New princes and princesses will arise, needing manors and lands, serfs to care for them, tribute to build their wealth."

I keep my thoughts to myself as to what an extravagant waste of effort empire strikes me, because I see the logic too in ensuring our family's ascendancy. Rather than putting them into words, I let the Tenochca king infer my feelings for himself.

"Yes, sire. And you will have my full support as your kinsman and fellow Mexica, always. In exchange, I hope Your Majesty will allow me to focus on the Acolhua people. The city of Tetzcoco. My own vision for a cultural renaissance in the towns under my leadership, that will, of course, redound to the benefit of Tenochtitlan as well."

A smile splits his scarred and aging visage. "I hear you well, Royal Architect Acolmiztzin Nezahualcoyotzin. Once you wear the Acolhua crown, we your allies and brethren shall ride with you into your father's native lands, reverting to your hands the cities we once conquered for Tezozomoc and Chimalpopoca. After installing you in Tetzoco, the Mexica will not interfere with your work, as long as I rule."

"Thank you, sire."

Itzcoatl leans forward, almost conspiratorially now.

"There remains the matter of the future queen of Tetzcoco, however. Tlacaellel tells me you have rejected his suggestions of suitable Mexica princesses. You sent back the concubines proffered by the king of Tlacopan. Should we be concerned? Your choice of concubine suggests certain proclivities."

The damn Mexica and their prejudices.

I remember Itzcoatl's parentage. His mother, like Sekalli, was a commoner. He might understand my wanting to give her sons a chance to shine before forcing them to compete with fully noble half-brothers.

Still, I doubt that he or any of my uncles could understand my deeper reason.

I've found the woman I love. I've promised not to marry as long as she lives.

And I'm willing, like my father, to fight the world to keep that promise.

"When I am secure in my palace," I answer instead, "I shall gladly accept your choice of concubines and his. As for a queen, however— I shall wait until I find the perfect woman at the perfect moment. I trust you will respect that decision."

Itzcoatl's eyes narrow for a moment. Then he gives a gentle laugh that almost starts as a scoff.

"You are an odd one, Yohyontzin," he remarks, pointedly using the old nickname I haven't heard since childhood. "But of course. Live your life as you please. It has worked for you so far."

{39} RETAKING TETZCOCO

A FTER THE GRANDEUR of the coronation—looking down at that teeming multitude from atop the Great Pyramid being the most overwhelming moment for me—and the days of celebratory feasts, the ten thousand canoes full of soldiers seems a familiar, quotidian sight.

An interesting situation awaits me. Most Acolhua cities are in the grips of an ironic uprising. Through clever spies, Itzcoatl has sent word to Mexica warriors occupying them. The king of Tlacopan has also dis-patched orders to Tepaneca troops in the other cities of my homeland. Now those soldiers, installed by Emperor Tezozomoc years ago to pro-tect his puppet kings, have turned against the usurpers, taking over the occupied cities and preparing the way for my army.

Our army, I suppose. Moteuczoma leads a legion of Mexica. A few companies of Tepaneca accompany us as well.

But we are mostly Acolhua, forced out of our homes after seeing our families slaughtered, exiled for a decade. Our partners and children wait with bated breath, desperate to walk those familiar streets—to return to lives their ancestors have lived for generations.

Morning slants across the mountains, striking the surface of Moon Lake, which glitters gold and green as if sparked by flint points flung from the sun itself. The wind picks up out of the east, pushing gently against us like a lover who feigns disinterest before yielding to passion.

The rhythm of oars in the water is sluggish and sleepy. It will not do.

Izcalloh holds my signal drum in their lap. I take it from them with a winking smile. Standing in the prow, I begin to beat out a tempo, loud and clear, infectious. I imagine the sound waves curling through the air in every direction, sinking into water and land, rising into the heavens, until every wheel in the cosmos spins to my beat.

"Come, brothers!" I shout. "Row with your souls! Ma Acolhuacan tihuiyan! Ma Tetzcoco tihuiyan! To Acolhuacan! To Tetzcoco!"

Other signal drums throughout the fleet begin to pound out the same rhythm. Oars sink deeper, move faster.

Like a fire wyrm from the time of demigods, we surge as one across the ripples.

Homeward.

Nearly one hundred thousand troops of the Triple Alliance hit the fourteen major cities of Acolhuacan at once, converging with the forces already attempting to wrest control of each from the imperial usurpers. I, needless to say, have chosen Tetzcoco.

Mansions and temples still rise above the verdant tops of pines, but they are no longer white like the snow capping the nearby mountains. Yancuilli has had them painted red, green, and blue after the Mexica fashion.

Izcalloh and I approach the eastern gate. It is partly crumbling and shattered, but the giant stone warriors still stand proud and tall on either side.

"This is the compromise I spoke of," Izcalloh tells me as we stride into the city, soldiers having cleared the path. "Doing what must be done."

Fires are being put out here and there. The thatched roofs of shrines and working-class houses, smoldering and charred. There is a strange silence. Dogs slink away, tails between their legs.

Warehouse doors stand open, gutted and looted.

But the mansions? Their stone walls still stand, imposing and impassive, even as my soldiers drag usurpers from inside.

"Look what has happened to my city, Izcalloh," I gasp.

"To rid a home of pestilence, one must burn all the mats," they remind me. "Your Majesty became Mexica. You facilitated their ascendancy. Without you, they could never have achieved dominance. Now here we stand at the heart of our city, my beloved king. Behold the Temple of Duality before you. Testament to the faith you showed the Sovereign of the Near and the Nigh."

I look up at the summit. Predictably, Yancuilli has shuttered the shrine of Quetzalcoatl and annointed the temple of Tezcatlipoca with untold buckets of human blood.

The Lord of Chaos is not quite sated, Brother. Let's give him dessert, shall we?

I take Izcalloh's hand. "Thank you, Beloved. For being by my side, guiding me forward, believing in me always. But we are not quite done. There is one last matter I must address."

I tilt my head back and shout at the top of my lungs.

"Yancuilli! Come forth, you miserable bastard, and face me!"

As the echo of my voice fades, a soldier rushes to my side.

"Majesty, he has taken refuge inside the pyramid, descending the winding stair that leads from the temple of Tezcatlipoca to the inner chambers."

"A coward to the end. Have every man with his hands free bring firewood and pine resin to the temple. Dump it down the stairwell. Then light the shrine on fire."

The man's eyes widen.

"Sire, that will surely—"

"Destroy the temple, yes. Perhaps the pyramid itself. I shall build another. Grander. Towering to the very heavens. But right now . . . *burn that building to the ground and flush Yancuilli out!* Am I clear?"

No hesitation. He hastens to obey. Hundreds of men come running up the steps on all four sides, arms laden.

They turn the temple into kindling.

And at a gesture from me, they set it alight.

Smoke billows from both shrines. They creak and moan and finally collapse, hurling angry sparks at the bright blue afternoon sky. Like stars that fail to break the bonds of earth and hover for a sick moment of glory, before falling to the ground.

The stone and concrete Pyramid of Duality was built over a previous platform of timber and mud. The interior is so blazing hot, my men have to descend from the steps or risk serious burns to the soles of their feet.

I stand, staring at the door in the base of the pyramid, the one priests use to slip out unseen during certain rituals.

It opens at last. Black soot and smoke burst forth, and in their midst, a man.

Yancuilli.

"Do not let him escape!" I shout. "But herd him toward me."

Yancuilli takes several gasping breaths and raises his eyes. Hatred roils in them.

"Hello, bastard." I raise my hand in mocking welcome. "I'm back."

"Come to have me executed, then?" he scoffs.

"No. Not at all. I've come to kill you myself. A duel."

Yancuilli gestures at himself. His royal garments are blackened and burnt.

"I have no weapons, Little Sib."

Glancing around at the soldiers lining the city plaza where we stand, I gesture at the former puppet sovereign of Tetzcoco.

"Someone give him a pair of daggers."

Unclasping my cape, I hand it to Izcalloh along with my halberd.

"Be careful, sire," they caution me.

"A coyote always is."

Pulling my obsidian daggers from my belt, I run toward Yancuilli, who has just scooped up a pair thrown his way.

I leap into the air, bringing my blades down as I fall toward him.

With a single arm he blocks me, slashing across my abdomen. My padded armor keeps the point of his knife from touching my skin.

Then comes an exchange of jabs and slashes, a furious flurry of obsidian razors slipping dangerously close to the skin. He has not grown rusty during the past eight years on the throne. He has practiced, gotten better.

Ah, but so have I.

I study his shuffling steps, his lunges and spins.

His stretched-out meter is as clear to me as the first day I deciphered it.

So I begin to dance, weaving in and out of his downbeats.

Slash. I open a vein on his right arm.

Knick. Blood dribbles from a cut on his neck.

Jab. I wound his left thigh, making him limp.

Flick. Rip. Slice. Stab.

Stepping back, he glares at me, with glassy, empty eyes.

Then he begins to run.

"Stop him!" I shout. "Do not let him leave the plaza!"

But that is not his plan. Too late, I see him swerve toward Izcalloh.

His hands snatch at their ornate clerical headdress, yanking back on the long, winding hair. Izcalloh drops my cape and halberd as Yancuilli drags them away from me, toward the main road, holding the obsidian dagger so tightly against their neck that it punctures their sandy skin, raising bubbles of blood.

Eyolin's face flashes over their features, a horrific portent.

"No," I gasp.

"Stay back, you son of a bitch, or I'll slit your xochihuah's lovely throat."

My heart thuds with erratic terror. Izcalloh's hands twitch as if they might attempt to struggle. I shake my head.

"No. Be still. Just let him drag you, Izcalloh. Don't struggle."

Yancuilli smiles. "Yes, very wise. Now drop your daggers and give the word. Tell them to let me leave. I'll release this pretty cleric of yours outside the city. Promise."

He snickers, sounding just like the broken bully that tortured me as a child.

Then the haze of fear that clouds my sight clears, and I see.

The coyote, harrying the deer.

Waiting for me.

Okay.

Deep breath.

I drop my blades, take a few steps toward him.

"Stop, Acolmiztli. Don't follow me. Just give the word."

"No one approach," I call, my voice clear and strong, the coyote swelling in my heart, pushing out all human frailties and concerns, leaving just the prey before me. "Let him go."

Another step. Another.

Yancuilli keeps dragging them back, laughing. "They'll be dead before you reach me. Just stop. There's nothing you can do unless you're willing to sacrifice one you love. Ah, but you've done that before, haven't you? Couldn't stop me then. Can't stop me now."

I should feel rage, but my eyes are glinting gold. I smell his blood, hear the frightened beat of his heart.

My toes bump against it.

My lips curl back, black gums and canines.

"Don't move, Izcalloh!" I howl. "Don't you dare move!"

Scooping up the spear at my feet, I hurl it with all the might in my hybrid flesh.

The air sings with the speed of its passing.

And it slams into Yancuilli's right eye, destroying his brain, the point ripping through the back of his skull. His limbs fall slack, their sinews loosened forever.

The blade slips from Izcalloh's neck as the man who once stole my father's throne drops dead to the ground.

"That's for Eyolin," I whisper to his departing soul. "And our child."

I run to my precious flower then, taking their face in my hands.

"Are you okay?" we both ask at once.

The coyote is still strong in me. I laugh at the urge I feel to lick their wound.

Instead, I kiss them before the gods and all my men.

It's done. We're done. Let me go, now.

As if in answer to my prayer, the Temple of Duality collapses on itself.

{40} KING

Six months later, Tetzcoco is teeming
with construction crews drawn
from all over Anahuac.

But this morning, I am not in the city.
Instead, I walk with Sekalli up the slopes
of Tetzcohtzinco, a rocky hill nearby.

"It's a beautiful view," she says at the summit,
turning to smile at me, owl eyes bright,
"but why have you brought me here, darling?"

"To share what I see, what I shall build, Beloved."
My arm sweeps toward the forest rising above,
toward the distant peak of Mount Tlaloc.

"I shall bring you a river, Lady Sekaltin, carve
a new course for it through rock and soil,
spill into pools I shall hew into this very hill.

"I shall shape its slopes into steps for your feet,
hang flowering vines on every naked boulder,
fill the streams and ponds with fish and lilies.

"A paradise for my consort, owner of my heart,
a refuge for you from the cares of the world.
And there, where the woods begin, a home.

"But unlike anything you have ever beheld.
Round like the temple of Ehecatl, no angles,
all soft and smooth like your flawless skin.

●◖◯◗●

"At its heart, our bedchamber, warm and dark,
away from the politics, away from the children,
away from my concubines and all of the gossip.

"For a while in that space we can imagine the farm,
those midnight walks, those drunken encounters.
We can live in the moment, just you and I."

Sekalli wipes tears from her cheek, laughing.
"I can see it, darling boy. But I also understand
that such a wondrous work won't be just for me.

"You belong to the people, and they will flock
to look on his His Majesty's latest feat.
Long after I'm forgotten, they will come."

My Sekalli is wise, but now I pull her close
to kiss shut her wisdom as birds softly trill
and, muffled by distance, a coyote howls.

"Yes, they will come and marvel, amazed,
wondering who the special woman was
who owned the heart of such a king."

We descend hand in hand to a waiting litter
and then, trailing guards and attendants,
we reenter our city, rising in splendor—

like the jeweled heart of Quetzalcoatl,
which soared from the ashes of immolation
to set itself like a smoking star in the sky.

●❮◯❯●

At my family's ancestral residence,
I kiss Sekalli. "Go inside, Beloved.
I must linger for a while longer."

Not far away, a sprawling palatial complex
is taking shape—Hueyitecpan, my sons call it.
The Big Castle, to contrast with Father's Cillan.

Beyond its lavish residence for king and consort,
the spacious wing for concubines, two courts,
audience chambers and guest houses, gardens—

In the sacred precinct, a new pyramid
rises level by level from the holy ground.
Its dual shrines will rival Tenochtitlan's.

At its heart, I have buried the bundled ashes
of my father, guarded for almost a decade.
by the faithful Totocahuan, now a general.

Out of deference for my Mexica kin,
it will house the idols of rainy Tlaloc
and Huitzilopochtli, war and sun.

Four spaces matter most to me. A small temple
to the Sovereign of the Near and the Nigh,
dual source of all that exists, unfolding forever.

The Ministry of Science and Music, wherein
Tetzcoco's cultural flourishing will take shape,
our knowledge and art recorded for all time.

The College of Philosophers, where the wisest folk
of Anahuac will gather to probe the great mysteries
that haunt the minds of thinkers everywhere.

And my Mansion of Song, brimming with drums
and flutes and trumpets, instruments imported
from every corner of the sea-ringed world.

I smile, though tears prick at my eyes.
I cannot wait to hear the music
that my people will entone.

For I love the song of the mockingbird,
bird of four hundred voices;

I love the howl of the coyote,
echoing upon snow-capped peaks;

I love the color of jade
and the drowsy perfume of flowers;

but more than all these lovely things
I love my fellow human beings.

—*IN TLAMILIZTLI*—

—THE END—

AUTHOR'S NOTE

In 2001, I was thirty-one years old and had just begun studying
Nahuatl, an Indigenous language from Mexico spoken at the time of
the Spanish invasion by the people we commonly call Aztecs and in
the present day by 1.5 million ethnic Nahuas. The language had been
used briefly in my native borderlands, towns established on both
banks of the Río Grande in the mid 1700s by Mestizo families from
Saltillo . . . and Tlaxcaltecah Nahuas from the neighboring community of San Esteban de Nueva Tlaxcala.

While my fascination arose from an exploration of Nahua strands
in my Mexican American community, I had already begun trying to
read colonial-era Nahuatl texts, which led me deeper into an exploration of Mesoamerica before Europeans arrived. In the midst of this
exploration of mine, the Mexican government revamped its currency,
changing "nuevo pesos" to just "pesos" and tweaking the colors and
design. It was then that I paid attention for the first time to the

100-peso bill. On the front was the image of an Indigenous king—Nezahualcoyotl, about whom I knew very little. To his left was an intriguing glyph: a ruler on a throne with a coyote's head floating above him, its neck surrounded by a strange collar. And to his right, in print so small I needed a magnifying glass to read it, was a poem.

When I read those lines, tears came to my eyes. They were the words of a person who understood the value of other human beings, who loved them above all the beauty and riches of the world. Who *was this man?* Why had I, in all my years of schooling in deep South Texas, never learned about him?

I started digging. The more I researched, the more amazed I became. Nezahualcoyotl appeared by all accounts to have been one of the most brilliant Indigenous minds in the history of the Americas. An engineer, architect, statesman, soldier, general, musician . . . and *poet.* One of the few Native poets from before European contact whose work has survived into the present.

And his most amazing accomplishments happened when he was *young.* Many during his teenage years, when he had conceived a plan to overthrow the dictatorship that had murdered his father and create a new Triple Alliance of Anahuac: the Aztec Empire. And as part of this powerful new Mesoamerican nation, Nezahualcoyotl had turned his native city-state of Tetzcoco into a multiethnic center of art, literature, and music. A veritable Camelot of the Americas.

But my amazement came with frustration. How had this figure been erased from my community's knowledge? While revered in Mexico, he is barely mentioned in the US, even among Chicanos. Certainly very few popular books about him have been written.

I spent twenty years learning everything I could about a figure that represented, to my mind, the very best of Nahua—Aztec—culture.

Then I began writing this book you hold in your hands, taking the stories about his life that survived the Conquest and weaving them together with fictional but period-accurate additions to flesh out his world. I think you'll find Acolmiztli Nezahualcoyotl as compelling a person as I have. His actions and words—some of which are actually woven into this story—may even bring a tear to your eyes, too.

You'll certainly never forget about him.

—David Bowles
April 27, 2023

ACKNOWLEDGMENTS

This book, perhaps more so than others I've worked on, exists because of the support and research of many other people. First and foremost I need to thank Amanda Mijangos, whose stunning artwork breathes vibrant authenticity into *The Prince & the Coyote*. It is an honor to work with you on a second book, amiga!

My depiction of Nezahualcoyotl's journey and culture was enriched by the research of fantastic anthropologists, historians, archeologists, and Nahuatl experts, more people than I could possibly list. But I will single out as particularly influential Jongsoo Lee, David Carrasco, Camilla Townsend, Alfredo Federico López Austin, Caroline Dodds Pennock, Miguel León-Portilla, Matthew Restall, Eloise Quiñones Keber, Ross Hassig, Susan Schroeder, and Michael E. Smith, some of whom were even kind enough to answer questions I had along the way.

Finally, a writer is nothing without a team that stands alongside them. For me, that means my wife, Angélica; my children—Loba,

Charlene, Angelo; my children-in-law, Jesse and Rachel; my agents, Taylor Martindale Kean and Stefanie Von Borstel; and the editor and co-editor of this book, Nick Thomas and Irene Vázquez, along with the rest of the amazing folks at Levine Querido.

Tlazohcamati, ammochintin! Thanks to you all!

●◖◗●

GUIDE TO UNFAMILIAR CONCEPTS

Prologue

Tetzcoco—Now known as Texcoco, the city was founded on a hill that the Chichimeca—a group of conquerors from the northwest who invaded the area—called "Tetzcotl." The meaning of that word has been lost, though it was apparently the name of a flower that grew in the area.

Feathered Serpent—"Quetzalcoatl" literally indicates a snake covered with the plumage of a quetzal bird. It's the name of the God of Creation and Order, brother of Tezcatlipoca, God of Destruction and Chaos.

Duality—Rather than binaries, Nahuas believed in the simultaneous co-existence of two sides . . . and a sliding scale between them. So, for example, male and female were both one, separate, and mixed together to various degrees in the universe.

Harbinger of death—Owls were seen as agents of Mictlanteuctli, Lord of the Underworld and God of Death.

Obsidian sword—The maccuauhuitl (baton-in-the-hand) was between the size and shape of a cricket bat and an oar. It had obsidian razors glued into a groove all around its flat blade.

Chapter 1

Calmecac—Literally "string of houses," this was a school for aristocratic youths, attached to the main temples of a city.

Tepaneca—"People of the Place of the Rock," a group who arose from the blending of nomadic Chichimeca with Toltecs, a civilization whose empire fell around 1200 CE. They lived on the eastern side of Anahuac, and claimed to have first arisen in Tepan (Place of the Rock). Their capital was Azcapotzalco.

Acolhua—"The Strong-Shouldered Ones," a group of Toltec-Chichimeca Nahuas living on the western side of Anahuac. Their capital was Tetzcoco.

Mexica—"People of Mexico," a Nahuatl-speaking group formerly known as the Mexihtin, who entered Anahuac after the fall of the Toltec Empire and the rise of the Acolhua and Tepaneca. They were captives of the Colhuahqueh for years before making an exodus toward the Isle of Mexico.

Moon Lake—Later known as Lake Texcoco, this body of water was called "Metztli iapan" [literally "Moon its-lake"] by the Nahuas.

Chapter 2

Gods of wind and rain sweep away—The God of Wind (Ehecatl) and the minor gods of rain (Tlaloqueh) were thought to clear the way for the changing of seasons.

Huitzilopochtli: born a man, made divine—The Mexica believed that Huitzilopochtli had originally been the mortal leader of the Mexihtin, the man who led them out of Aztlan.

Our Lord the Sun—The sun itself was known as Tonatiuh ("He Goes Giving Warmth") and had originally been called Nanahuatzin, the son of Quetzalcoatl.

Descend in order to rise—The sun was believed to make its way into the Underworld to be stoked for its return the following dawn. And Quetzalcoatl descended into the Underworld at least twice, in order to emerge with vital tools.

Causeways—The Isle of Mexico was connected to the mainland by wide bridges of compacted silt and stone, with gaps across which wooden planks were laid.

Chinampas and the Xochimilca—The first floating gardens were created in Xochimilco, a city that produced most of the region's flowers.

Goodman—To give some of the flavor of different dialects of Nahuatl, I'm using different dialects of English, some archaic or rural.

Sacred precinct—At the heart of each Nahua city was a ceremonial plaza with various temples and the calmecac.

Toltec—A Nahua civilization that collapsed a couple of hundred years before Nezahualcoyotl was born.

Each night of the month—Months in the Nahua calendar had twenty days.

Chapter 3
Coatepec, birthplace of Huitzilopochtli—The Mexica believed that mountain Coatepec, to the northwest of Anahuac, was where their patron god had been born to the goddess Coatlicue.

Smoking Mirror—Literal translation of "Tezcatlipoca," God of Destruction and Chaos.

Jaguar Knights—"Ocelomeh," an elite military order.

Chapter 4

Tetzcoca—Because of the multi-ethnic nature of Tetzcoco, it was important for the city's kings to promote a sort of collective identity for all citizens of the kingdom.

Anahuac—"Beside the Waters," the name for the massive lake-filled valley where the action of this book takes place. Now known as the Valley of Mexico, it is mostly filled with Mexico City.

Toltec Way—A translation of "Toltecayotl," the traditions of the Toltec people.

Acolhua Overlord—"Ahcolhuah Teuctli." The title of the king who leads the alliance of Acolhua kingdoms. He is considered first among peers.

Chapter 5

The celestial chorus—"In yectli cuicatl." Nahua poets claimed that they could hear a divine song being sung by birds who were the souls of fallen warriors.

Unknowable Realm—After death, Nahuas believed they would spend four years in one of several possible spiritual realms before passing beyond into a place or state that they could not imagine.

Chapter 6

Sovereign of the Near and Nigh—"Tloqueh Nahuaqueh," a title for the Duality—the divine source of everything—which exists in the highest tier of heaven, Omeyocan (Place of Duality).

Chapter 7

Xochihuah—A queer gender in Nahua culture that doesn't quite align to modern perceptions. Assigned male at birth, but either transfeminine or non-binary . . . often also bisexual or gay.

Flowery gods—The male-female duality of Xochiteotl, which unfolds into Xochiquetzal and Xochipilli.

Little sib—"Niuc." The term for young sibling is ungendered in Nahuatl. One cannot say "little sister" or "little brother."

Tozquen, named for our grandmother—Their paternal grandmother was Princess Tozquentli of Coatlichan.

Gum-chewing—Among Nahuas, chewing gum in public was seen as unseemly and unrefined.

Wheeled dog toy—Though Nahuas never used vehicles with wheels, they created many toys that used them.

Chichiton—Nahuatl for doggy or puppy.

The old words—"Huehuetlahtolli," ritual speeches reserved for important occasions.

Chapter 8
The day is 5 Reed—Nahua dates consisted of a number between 1 and 13 plus one of twenty day signs.

Uncles and Aunts—These are titles a noble boy would use with commoners as a form of respectful address.

High priest—Each calmecac was run by priests.

Xochihuahqueh—The plural of xochichuah.

Fifth Age—Known as "Nahui Olin" (4 Movement), this is our present epoch. The sun was destroyed at the end of the last, hence this ritual.

Month of Tepopochtli—This is one of eighteen 20-day months (metztli, also meaning "moon") that make up the solar calendar, followed by five to six "swelling days" (nemontemi) meant to round out the 365 to 366 days in a year.

Chachalaca—This is a species of bird that chatters a lot.

Pot of chilis—Having one's face held over such a pot was a common punishment for children.

Teotihuacan—A massive city located to the northeast of modern Mexico City. It was old even in Nezahualcoyotl's time.

Cemolin—The word means "single set of movements." The plural is "cemolintin."

Teocoatl—The unified duality of Quetzalcoatl and Cihuacoatl.

Chapter 9

Cycles of thirteen days—"Cencalli," more commonly known by the Spanish name "trecena." There were twenty, making up the sacred calendar of 260 days, which aligns with the solar calendar once every 52 years.

Glyphs in a painted book—Nahua books used a combination of illustrations and glyphs that represented actual words or sounds. They did not have an alphabet or syllabary.

Chapter 10

Tlazohtla versus tlazohtli—In Nahuatl, this exchange goes . . . "Tinechtlazohtla?" "Tinotlazohtli." He echoes her word with one that sounds similar, but disappointing.

House of Song and House of Flowers—Music played a very important ritual role in students' and warriors' lives.

Patlacheh—A queer gender in Nahua culture. Assigned female at birth, but either transmasculine or non-binary . . . often also bisexual or lesbian.

The ample shade—Nahua leaders were often compared to large cypress trees in Nahuatl metaphors.

"My First Song"—Adapts parts of song LII from the codex *Songs of Mexico*. It was common among Nahua poets to use flowers as metaphor for fleeting friendship.

"My Second Song"—Adapts parts of song VI from the codex *Ballads of the Lords of New Spain*. The codex claims it was composed by Tlaltecatl, a poet friend of Acolmiztli's paternal grandfather Telchotlala.

Chapter 11
Colhuahqueh—An ethnicity squeezed between Chalco and Mexico, who had held the Mexica in captivity for several generations before they won their freedom and settled on the Isle of Mexico.

Toltecayotl—"The Toltec Way," which entailed a dedication to elegant culture, complex architecture, fine artistry, sophisticated music.

Chichimecayotl—"The Chichimeca Way," which entailed fierce aggression on the battlefield combined with a strict military code of honor.

Nauhtzontli, centzontli—The root -tzontli literally means "hair." It's used to count multiples of four hundred.

Pantin—Singular "pantli" (literally "banner"). Twenty-man squads.

Chapter 12
Nomiccama—Literally "my" (no-) "beloved dead one's" (micca) "hands" (ma)

Chapter 13
Surgeons—Among the Nahua, it was common for doctors to be women.

The House of the Sun—"Tonatiuh ichan," the spiritual realm where the souls of fallen warriors go, to accompany the sun each morning in the form of birds and butterflies as it rises to its zenith.

Accept him as your father, your mother, your shield—These are more metaphors for a great ruler.

Ce Acatl, the human incarnation of the Feathered Serpent—Many Nahuas believed that Quetzalcoatl had been incarnated as a Toltec king, also known as Topiltzin (Our Beloved Noble).

The World Tree—The massive ceiba, created from the severed tail of Cipactli—the primordial leviathan—which holds up the thirteen layers of heaven.

Chapter 14

Bundle and burn him—The traditional practice for nobles upon their death was to be wrapped tight and cremated; the ashes would then be stored in a special bag.

The road of the rabbit, the path of the deer—Nahua metaphors for a dangerous and irresponsible life outside the confines of tradition and civilization.

Ohuihcan Chanehqueh—Literally "homeowners of dangerous places." To this day, these trickster spirits of the wild are known as "chaneques" in Mexican Spanish.

Chapter 15

Teopixqui—literally "god-keeper"

Tlaloqueh—the sons of Tlaloc, who control rain and storms.

Atolli—A hot dish of boiled cornmeal, known in Mexican Spanish as atole.

Survivors of the Third Age—The third iteration of the earth was destroyed by Tlaloc in a rain of fire after his wife was abducted by Tezcatlipoca. Not wanting all life extinguished, Quetzalcoatl saved a group of people by giving them wings so they could fly above the burning land.

●◖○◗●

Chapter 16

Cuitlacochin fungus—This delicacy, still eaten throughout Mexico, is known as Huitlacoche in Mexican Spanish.

Tepicmeh—The Nahuas revered the greatest of the surrounding mountains as the homes or incarnations of certain gods, and they would make amaranth cookies in the shape of peaks to honor them.

Iztaccihuatl and Popocatepetl—"White Woman" and "Smoking Mountain," respectively, these volcanoes are thought to be what remains of two star-crossed lovers.

Chapter 17

The Black Road—In Mesoamerica, the apparent dark rift in the Milky Way was a path into the spiritual realm.

The Nursing Tree—Chichihuahcuauhtli, a tree in the highest level of heaven where the souls of children are nursed and cared for until they can be reborn.

The smoke of Tezcatlipoca's obsidian mirror—The God of Chaos had a mirror that floated behind his head or was attached to his left leg. Smoke curled from it, hence his name. He could use it to see anything in the cosmos.

The Enemy of Both Sides, the Mocker of Men—Epithets or titles given to Tezcatlipoca because he is the trickster God of Chaos, who both lifts up and tears all people down according to whims they cannot comprehend.

North—Called Mictlampa, "toward the Land of the Dead."

God of Frost—Called Itztlacoliuhqui, "curved obsidian blade," as if his cold touch were as deadly sharp.

"*In the House of Holy Writ*"—A translation and adaptation of song XXXII of *Ballads of the Lords of New Spain*. Attributed to Nezahualcoyotl in that codex.

Citlaltepetl—"Star Mountain," today also known as Orizaba.

Coyotlinahual—"A Coyote is His Double." Tezcatlipoca—differently from other gods who had only one animal form—could assume multiple guises, including this feathered coyote.

Chapter 18
Sekalli—Her name means "1 House," the date of her birth. Most commoners used only their birthdate as their name.

Makwiltoch—"5 Rabbit."

13 House versus 1 Rabbit—The number at the beginning of year names would reset after number thirteen, going back to one.

Cihuateteoh—These were the spirits of women who died in childbirth. Considered warriors, they would accompany the sun as it set each day. Close to dusk, they often attempted to steal children, longing for the maternal role they never got to play.

Yemasaton—"3 Deer," with a diminutive suffix (-ton) to show endearment.

Omaka—"2 Reed."

Polok—This name isn't a birthdate. We can assume that the farmer earned a personalized name because of some deed in battle when he was younger. "Polok" is related to the verb for "conquer."

Ahuizotl—A legendary aquatic creature that had a fourth hand at the end of its tail.

Nixtamalize—To boil maize with lime, increasing its nutritional value.

For the next four years—Warriors upon death would spend four years in the House of the Sun.

Tube of tobacco—Cigars were invented in Mesoamerica.

Chapter 19
Patolli—A board game somewhat like checkers or Go.

Tilma—A cotton cape.

Cinteotl—"Corn God."

Xilonen—God of green ears of corn.

"O priestly planting sticks"—This song is adapted from a ritual reported in *Treatise on the Heathen Superstitions* by Hernando Ruiz De Alarcón.

Itzpapalotl—"Obsidian Butterfly," patron goddess of the Toltec people.

Chapter 20
Cipactli—After this transformation, the great primordial Leviathan became "Tlalteuctli" or "Sovereign of the Earth," one of the most important goddesses.

Double calendar—the solar and sacred systems of keeping time, whose cycles line up every fifty-two years. Quetzalcoatl taught it to the first woman and man, Oxomoco and Cipactonal.

Chapter 21
Chilpoctli—Known in modern times as "chipotle," smoked jalapeño peppers.

Mayahuel—The sacred story tells that Quetzalcoatl fell in love with this granddaughter of Tzitzimitl, a fierce goddess of destruction. When she followed the couple to Earth, he transformed his beloved and himself into trees. But the fierce goddess wasn't fooled and tore Mayahuel to pieces. Quetzalcoatl then planted the pieces of his beloved, and they became agave plants.

Four Hundred Drunken Rabbits—"Centzontotochtin," minor gods of inebriation.

Tlachihualtepetl, the Manmade Mountain—The largest pyramid in the world, in terms of cubic volume.

Chapter 22
Colhuacan—This kingdom once held the Mexica (then called Mexihtin) captive for many years before they escaped and founded Tenochtitlan on the Isle of Mexico.

Four Hundred Brothers—"Centzonhuitznahuah," literally "Four Hundred Southern Ones," referring to the countless stars in the southern sky.

Chapter 23
"Orphan"—A translation and adaptation of song XIX of *Ballads of the Lords of New Spain*. Attributed to Nezahualcoyotl in that codex, which claims that he wrote the piece while in exile, fleeing from the soldiers of Emperor Tezozomoc.

Tezcatlipoca's avatars—Nezahualcoyotl seems to catch glimpses of Coyotlinahual (the Feathered Coyote) and Tepeyollotl (Mountainheart, the giant jaguar double of Tezcatlipoca).

Chapter 24
Quetzalmazatl—"Feathered Deer"

Hast thou heard?—In order to show the difference between the Acolhua and Chalca dialects of Nahuatl, I make some rural folks use antiquated language.

The dead man's helmet—One of the most famous images of Nezahual-coyotl depicts him wearing such a helmet.

Son of Nezahualpilli—This is a bit of an inside joke, as many years later, the son of Nezahualcoyotl (who succeeds him on the throne) will be named "Nezahualpilli" (Prince with a Fasting Collar).

Flower war—Ritual combat meant not for actual victory but for the capture of sacrificial victims.

Tomiccama—Literally "our beloved dead ones' hands."

Butterflies, hummingbirds, eagles—Nezahualcoyotl is suggesting that inferior warriors don't receive as much glory when accompanying the sun for four years after their deaths.

Eagle Knights—"Cuauhtin," an elite military order.

Nonohualca—An ethnic group from the former Toltec Empire that was *not* Nahua.

Chapter 25
Yes, Quetzalmazatzin—To address a noble—whether one's military superior or part of the ruling class—by their name is a dangerous breach of etiquette that could get one killed.

Beneath the shadow of our wings and tail feathers—Another metaphor that represents the responsibilities of a leader in Nahua thought is the shelter a mother bird gives her young.

Born on a shield with a sword in his hand—Huitzilopochtli was believed to have emerged from his mother's womb fully armored, dropping onto her shield and immediately launching into combat with his four hundred and one siblings.

Flood of fiery wrath—The Nahuas called war "tlahchinolli teoatl" or "fire and flood."

Chapter 26
Cuauhcalco—Literally "place of the wooden cages," a sort of jail for military prisoners

By the Thirteen Heavens—The heavens were thought of as having thirteen different layers or folds in which different gods or astral phenomena were located.

Eater of Sin—Tlazolteotl ("vice-goddess") was said not only to tempt humans to sin, but also devour it when they confessed to her, leaving them purer than before.

Xipe Totec—A god of agriculture and rebirth, depicted as wearing the flayed skin of a human being.

Chapter 27
Nexquimilli—Literally "ash-bundle," which in this case is the zombified, cremated remains of a person.

Centlapachton—"Little squashed one," a scary goblin.

Tzontecomatl—The word means "head" when separated from the body (literally "gourd with hair"). The monster version can hop around and pursue victims.

The Land of the Dead—Nahuas believed the sun went down into Mictlan, the Land of the Dead, each night so its flames could be replenished by the God of Fire.

Chapter 28
Copalxocotl—This fruit produces a nice-smelling lather one can use to clean oneself. Hygiene was very important to pre-Invasion Nahuas.

Chapter 29
Nine hells—Mictlan, the Underworld, was said to consist of nine deadly regions that souls had to cross in order to be purified and move beyond, into the Unknowable Realm.

Marry a princess?—This isn't a false promise. It will be several decades before Nezahualcoyotl finally marries a princess. He cannot marry Sekalli, as she is a commoner and such a ceremony would not be permitted.

Cuauhpilli—"Eagle noble," a commoner raised to knighthood.

Chapter 30
My precious jewel—Nahua parents often referred to their children as "jewel" or "quetzal feather," two of the most valuable items in Anahuac.

Chapter 31
House of Acamapichtli—Ironically, that first King of Mexico was only half Mexica. His mother was of Acolhua and Colhuahqueh nobility, and when the Mexica approached him to come rule in Tenochtitlan, Acamapichtli was living in . . . Tetzcoco.

Chapter 32
South to Tlaloc's water paradise—Called "Tlalocan," this afterlife was specially set up for those who were born disabled or who died via water or storms. It was a lush, perfect realm where they never suffered again.

I shall rewrite that tale—Nahua historians recorded that Tlacaellel carried out this historical revision, destroying all traces of the Mexica's less-than-glorious past. Other Nahua nations, however, preserved what they knew of the truth.

Self-Making—"Moyocoyatzin," an epithet that could also mean "Self-Governing."

His grandfather—Understand that Tlacaellel is *not* also Tezozomoc's grandson. The three principal rulers of Tenochtitlan have different mothers. Tezozomoc is Chimalpopoca's *maternal* grandfather. Tlacaellel's maternal grandfather is the king of Cuauhnahuac.

●◖◍◗●

Chapter 33

Flint, House, Rabbit, Reed—Years in the solar calendar get their name from last day of the last month of the year. Because of the alignment of the sacred calendar, only four signs can end the year. These are known as "bearers" of the year. The number that accompanies the name is raised by one every year, and then the numbers reset after thirteen.

A man of twenty-three—There are more tales of Nezahualcoyotl's deeds during these six years than could fit in one book. Suffice it to say that he garnered much of his enduring reputation while he awaited his chance to exact revenge.

Chapter 34

Temictli—"Dream." Ironically, it will be Temictli's daughter Azcalxo-chitl whom Nezahualcoyotl finally marries many years in the future when her first husband dies in battle. As he needs a fully royal heir at that point and she needs the protection of marriage, Nezahualcoyotl proposes.

Little sea monster—"Cipacton," a reference to the primordial levia-than that shares his name.

Chapter 35

Impossible for Quetzalayatzin—Had the deposed imperial heir refused to go, Maxtla would have rallied Tepaneca and Acolhua troops to invade the Isle of Mexico, which would have likely fallen.

Tlacopan—The importance of this rebel city can't be overstressed. The plans laid by Nezahualcoyotl, Itzcoatl, and Tlacaellel wouldn't have worked without Tepaneca defectors.

Bounced the ball off their hips—A sports metaphor, referring to the popular Mesoamerican ball game known today as Ollama.

Chapter 36
Essentially Tepanecapan—Chapoltepec is right on the verge of Tepaneca territory.

Mazatzintamalco—A small islet to the southwest of the Isle of Mexico.

Quite unlikely—Though sources claim this actually happened, Tlacaellel is too *smart* to walk into a lion's den like that. Tezozomoc would have had him seized immediately. And Emperor Maxtla *certainly* would not have sat still while Tlacaellel performed this ritual on his body.

Xiquipilli—Literally "sack of grain," this means a group of 8,000.

Zohuaehecah—"Women-winds," now most commonly known by the Spanish name for one of their kind: Llorona.

Chapter 37
Two thousand rods—A rod is a "tlalcuahuitl" and measures about 2.5 meters.

Ce Mazatl—As Nezahualcoyotl was actually born on 1 Deer, this is one of his names (though seldom if ever used).

Nothing but ants—Azcapotzalco means "Place of the Ant Hills."

Chapter 38
Three places of power—A version of the actual name of what we now call the Aztec Empire: In Excan Tlahtoloyan, "The Three Places of Decision-Making."

Their prejudices—The Mexica had stricter laws about same-sex relationships than other Nahua groups.

Chapter 39
Fire wyrm—"Xiuhcoatl," serving as both dragon-like beasts and weapons (as in the case of Huitzilopochtli, who wielded one like a cannon against his brothers and sister).

Chapter 40
Tetzcohtzinco—The ruins of this amazing garden are still one of the greatest wonders of the Americas.

The jeweled heart of Quetzalcoatl—At the end of his fifty-two years of life as Ce Acatl Topiltzin, the Feathered Serpent went to the seashore and set himself on fire. His heart rose into the heavens to become Venus, which in Mesoamerica is known as the smoking star.

The song of the mockingbird—These final lines are adapted from the poem ascribed to Nezahualcoyotl that appear on the hundred-peso bill in Mexico.

ABOUT THE AUTHOR AND
ILLUSTRATOR

David Bowles is a Mexican American author and translator from South Texas. Among his multiple award-winning titles are *The Sea-Ringed World: Sacred Stories of the Americas*; *Feathered Serpent, Dark Heart of Sky: Myths of Mexico*; *Flower, Song, Dance: Aztec and Maya Poetry*; and *Ancient Night*. David presently serves as the vice-president of the Texas Institute of Letters.

Amanda Mijangos was born in Mexico City, graduated from the Faculty of Architecture, and studied illustration in Mexico and Buenos Aires. She has illustrated literature and poetry in books and magazines for people of all ages and gives drawing and illustration workshops for all audiences. Her work has been recognized with awards from countries near and far. This her third book for Levine Querido, following *The Sea-Ringed World* and *Sheep Count Flowers*.

●◖○◗●

SOME NOTES ON THIS BOOK'S PRODUCTION

Art for the jacket, case, and interiors was drawn by Amanda Mijan-gos using a mix of graphite pencil drawings and digital illustration. The text and display were set by Westchester Publishing Services, in Danbury, CT, using LTC Kennerley Pro, a revival of Kennerley Old Style. The latter was designed by Frederic W. Goudy for publisher Mitchell Kennerley in 1911 and is considered an original American classic, as it is not based on historical type designs. The book was printed on x FSC™-certified paper and bound in China.

Production supervised by Freesia Blizard
Book jacket, case, and interiors designed by Sarah Lopez
Editor: Nick Thomas
Assistant Editor: Irene Vázquez

LQ
LEVINE QUERIDO